PENGUIN BOOKS

The Lost Throne

Chris Kuzneski is the international bestselling author of *Sword of God*, *Sign of the Cross*, and *The Plantation*. His thrillers have been translated into more than fifteen languages. Although he grew up in Indiana, Pennsylvania, he currently lives on the Gulf Coast of Florida. To learn more, please visit his website: www.chriskuzneski.com.

Praise for *The Lost Throne*

'A reader's delight from beginning to end. Tautly written, expertly told, smart and exhilarating' Steve Berry, *New York Times* bestselling author

'*The Lost Throne* reads like an AK-47 on laughing-gas, as Kuzneski runs a gauntlet of mystery and mayhem, wisecracking all the way' John Case, *New York Times* bestselling author

'Chris Kuzneski's *The Lost Throne* is a lightning-paced tale that seamlessly stitches threads from the past into the fabric of the present. Genre giants Steve Berry, James Rollins and Brad Thor may soon find themselves looking over their shoulders as Kuzneski stakes his claim as the Next Big Thing. A smoothly layered, serpentine and scintillating thriller' Jon Land, bestselling author of *The Seven Sins*

Part Tom Clancy, part Dan Brown, *The Lost Throne* is fast, fun, and exciting!' James O. Born, bestselling author of *Burn Zone*

Praise for *Sword of God*

'A non-stop locomotive of a thriller. Combines labyrinthine plot twists, global terrorism and the darkest depths of psychological warfare in a thriller that had me burning the midnight oil till breakfast . . . Kuzneski is a master in the making' Vince Flynn, author of *Consent to Kill*

'*Sword of God* is as convincing as it is terrifying. Riveting and relentlessly paced, here is a novel that will be consumed in one sitting. Chris Kuzneski proves again that he is a thriller writer for the new millennium' James Rollins, author of *The Judas Strain*

'Reading *Sword of God* is like jumping on a runaway freight train hurtling towards disaster, with the fate of the world in the balance . . . A fabulous premise, great characters, rich settings and Mach-five pacing. Explosive!' Douglas Preston, author of *The Codex*

'Action-packed and full of taut suspense, *Sword of God* crosses continents in a world-class adventure that will keep you guessing, chuckling, terrified and utterly riveted. Go into lock-down mode. You won't want to leave your favourite chair until you've finished this terrific tale' Gayle Lynds, author of *The Last Spymaster*

The Lost Throne

CHRIS KUZNESKI

PENGUIN BOOKS

PENGUIN BOOKS

Published by the Penguin Group
Penguin Books Ltd, 80 Strand, London WC2R 0RL, England
Penguin Group (USA) Inc., 375 Hudson Street, New York, New York 10014, USA
Penguin Group (Canada), 90 Eglinton Avenue East, Suite 700, Toronto, Ontario, Canada M4P 2Y3
(a division of Pearson Penguin Canada Inc.)
Penguin Ireland, 25 St Stephen's Green, Dublin 2, Ireland
(a division of Penguin Books Ltd)
Penguin Group (Australia), 250 Camberwell Road, Camberwell, Victoria 3124, Australia
(a division of Pearson Australia Group Pty Ltd)
Penguin Books India Pvt Ltd, 11 Community Centre, Panchsheel Park, New Delhi – 110 017, India
Penguin Group (NZ), 67 Apollo Drive, Rosedale, North Shore 0632, New Zealand
(a division of Pearson New Zealand Ltd)
Penguin Books (South Africa) (Pty) Ltd, 24 Sturdee Avenue,
Rosebank, Johannesburg 2196, South Africa

Penguin Books Ltd, Registered Offices: 80 Strand, London WC2R 0RL, England

www.penguin.com

Published in Penguin Books 2008
1

Set in 11.75/14 pt Monotype Garamond
Typeset by Rowland Phototypesetting Ltd, Bury St Edmunds, Suffolk
Printed in England by Clays Ltd, St Ives plc

ISBN: 978-0-141-03707-3
TRADE PAPERBACK ISBN: 978-0-718-15432-5

www.greenpenguin.co.uk

Acknowledgments

Publishing a book requires a collective effort, so I would like to thank a few of the people who helped *The Lost Throne* see the light of day.

As always, I'd like to start off by thanking my family. Without their love and support, I wouldn't be the writer (or the person) that I am today.

Professionally, I want to thank Scott Miller, my remarkable agent. Before we teamed up, I couldn't find a publisher. Now my books are available in several languages around the world. How he pulled off that miracle, I'll never know. While I'm at it, I want to thank Claire Roberts, my foreign agent at Trident Media, who landed my British deal and many others. To say that I am thrilled with Penguin UK would be an understatement. In particular, I'd like to single out my editor, Alex Clarke. Working with him has been wonderful.

Next up is my extraordinary friend Ian Harper. Through the magic of e-mail, he gets to read my work before anyone else, and his suggestions and advice are always invaluable. So if anyone's looking for a freelance editor, let me know. I'd be happy to put you in touch with him.

Last but not least, a big thanks to all the readers,

booksellers, critics, and librarians who have read my books and recommended them to others. At this stage of my career, I need all the help I can get, so I would appreciate your continued support.

Okay. Now that I'm done expressing my gratitude, it's time for the good stuff.

Just sit back, relax, and let me tell you a story . . .

Greece and the Aegean Sea

ALBANIA

MACEDONIA

BULGARIA

Istanbul

Thessaloniki

Mt Olympus

Mt Athos

LIMNOS

Aegean Sea

Metéora

Pindus Mts

NORTHERN
SPORADES

TURKEY

LESBOS

Gulf of
Corinth

GREECE

SKYROS

CHIOS

Izmir

Athens

Corinth

SÁMOS

Olympia

PELOPONNESE

CYCLADES

DODECANESE

Ionian
Sea

Spárti

RHODES

Sea of Crete

CRETE

N

W   E

S

0   50   100   150 miles

0   100   200 kms

Prologue

Christmas Day, 1890
Piazza della Santa Carità
Naples, Italy

The greatest secret of Ancient Greece was silenced by a death in Italy.

Not a shooting or a stabbing or a murder of any kind – although dozens of those would occur later – but a good old-fashioned death. One minute the man was strolling across the Piazza della Santa Carità, pondering the significance of his discovery; the next he was sprawled on his stomach in the middle of the cold square. People rushed to his side, hoping to help him to his feet, but one look at his gaunt face told them that he needed medical attention.

Two policemen on horseback were flagged down, and they rushed him to the closest hospital where he slipped in and out of consciousness for the next hour. They asked him his name, but he couldn't answer. His condition had stolen his ability to speak.

The man wore a fancy suit and overcoat, both of which revealed his status. His hair was thin and grey, suggesting a man in his sixties. A bushy moustache covered his upper lip.

Doctors probed his clothes, searching for identification, but found nothing of value. No papers. No wallet. No money. If they had only looked closer, they might have noticed the secret pocket sewn into the lining of his coat, and the mystery would have ended there. But as hospital policy dictated, no identification meant no treatment. Not even on Christmas morning.

With few options, the police took him to the local station house, an ancient building made of brick and stone that would shelter him from the bitter winds of the Tyrrhenian Sea. They fed him broth and let him rest on a cot in an open cell, hoping he would regain his voice.

In time, he regained several.

Starting with a whisper that barely rose above the level of his breath, the sound slowly increased, building to a crescendo that could be heard by the two officers in the next room. They hurried down the corridor, expecting to find the stranger fully awake and willing to answer their questions. Instead they saw a man in a semi-catatonic state who was babbling in his sleep.

His eyes were closed and his body was rigid, yet his lips were forming words.

One of the officers made the sign of the cross and said a short prayer while the other ran for a pencil and paper. When he returned, he pulled a chair up to the cot and tried to take notes in a small journal. Maybe they'd get an address. Or if they were really lucky, maybe even a name. But they got none of those things. In fact, all they got was more confused.

The first words spoken were German. Then French. Then Portuguese. Before long he was mixing several languages in the same sentence. Dutch followed by Spanish and Latin. English layered with Greek and Russian. Every once in a while he said something in Italian, but the words were so random and his accent so thick they made little sense. Still, the officer transcribed everything he could and before long he noticed some repetition. One word seemed to be repeated over and over. Not only in Italian but in other languages as well.

Il trono. Le trône. El trono.

The throne.

This went on for several minutes. Language after language from one man's mouth. Like the devil speaking in tongues. Then, just as quickly as it had started, it stopped.

No more words. No more clues.

The man would never speak again.

Two days later, after he had been identified, newspapers round the globe reported his death. Yet there was no mention of his strange behaviour. Nothing about his ramblings or the throne he kept describing. Instead, reporters focused on the colourful details of his life – his wealth, his accomplishments, his discoveries. All the things that made him famous.

Of course, if they had known the truth about his

final days, what he had finally found out after years of searching, they would have written a very different story.

One of fire, deception, and ancient gold.

One that wouldn't have an ending for two more centuries.

I

The monk felt the wind on his face as he plummeted to his death, a journey that started with a scream and ended with a thud.

Moments before, he had been standing near the railing of the Moni Agia Triada, the Monastery of the Holy Trinity. It was one of six monasteries perched on natural rock pillars near the Pindus Mountains in central Greece. Known for their breathtaking architecture, the monasteries had been built 2,000 feet in the air with one purpose in mind: protection.

But on this night, their sanctity had been breached.

The intruders had crossed the valley and climbed the hillside with silent precision. They carried no guns or artillery, preferring the weapons of their ancestors. Swords stored in scabbards were strapped to their backs. Daggers in leather sheaths hung from their hips. Bronze helmets covered their entire heads except for their eyes and mouths.

Centuries ago the final leg of their mission would have been far more treacherous, requiring chisels and ropes to scale the rock face. But that was no longer the case – not since 140 steps had been carved into the sandstone, leading to the entrance of Holy Trinity. Its front gate was ten feet high and made of thick wood, yet they breached it easily and slipped inside, spreading through the compound like a deadly plague.

The first to die was the lookout who, instead of doing his job, had been staring at the twinkling lights of Kalampáka, the small city that rested at the base of the plateau. Sadly, it was the last mistake he ever made. No questions were asked, no quarter was given. One minute he was pondering the meaning of life, the next his life was over.

No bullets. No blades. Just gravity and the rocks below.

One of the monks inside the church heard his scream and tried to warn the others, but before he could, the intruders had burst through both doors. Brandishing their swords, they forced all the monks into the centre of the room where the holy men were frisked and their hands were tied.

Seven monks in total. A mixture of young and old.

Just as the intruders had expected.

For the next few minutes, the monks sat in silence on the hard wooden pews. Some of them closed their eyes and prayed to God for divine intervention. Others seemed reconciled to their fate. They knew the risks when they accepted this duty, what their brotherhood had endured and protected for centuries.

They were the keepers of the book. The chosen ones.

And soon they would be forced to die.

With the coldness of an executioner, the leader of the soldiers strode into the church. At first glance he looked like a moving work of art. Muscle stacked upon muscle in statuesque perfection. A gleaming blade in his grasp. Unlike the others who had entered before him, his helmet was topped with a plume of red horsehair, a crest that signified his rank.

To the monks, he was the face of death.

Without saying a word, he nodded to his men. They sprang into action, grabbing one of the monks and dragging him towards the stone altar. Orthodox tradition prevented the brethren from trimming their facial hair after receiving tonsure – a symbolic shaving of their heads – so his beard was long and grey, draping the front of his black cassock like a hairy bib.

'What do you want from us?' cried the monk as he was shoved to his knees. 'We have done nothing wrong!'

The leader stepped forward. 'You know why I'm here. I want the book.'

'What book? I know nothing about a book!'

'Then you are no use to me.'

He punctuated his statement with a flick of his sword, separating the monk from his head. For a split second the monk's body didn't move, somehow remaining upright as if no violence had occurred.

Then suddenly it slumped forward, spilling its contents on to the floor.

Head on the left. Body on the right. Blood everywhere.

The monks gasped at the sight.

'Bring me another,' the leader ordered. 'One who wants to live.'

2

The phone rang in the middle of the night, sometime between last call and breakfast. The time of night reserved for two things: emergencies and wrong numbers.

Jonathon Payne hoped it was the latter.

He rolled over in the hotel bed and reached for the nightstand, knocking something to the floor in his dark room. He had no idea what it was and wasn't curious enough to find out. Still feeling the effects of his sleeping pill, he knew if he turned on a light he would be awake until dawn. Of that he was certain. He had always been a problem sleeper, an issue that had started long before his career in the military and had only got worse after.

Then again, years of combat can do that to a person.

And he had seen more than most.

Payne used to lead the MANIACs, an elite Special Forces unit comprised of the top soldiers from the **M**arines, **A**rmy, **N**avy, **A**ir Force, **I**ntelligence, and **C**oast Guard. Whether it was personnel recovery, unconventional warfare, or counter-guerrilla sabotage, the MANIACs were the best of the best. The bogeymen that no one talked about. The government's secret weapon.

Yet on this night, Payne wanted no part of his former life.

He just wanted to get some sleep.

'Hello?' he mumbled into the hotel phone, expecting the worst.

A dialling tone greeted him. It was soft and steady like radio static.

'Hello?' he repeated.

But the buzzing continued. As if no one had even called. As if he had imagined everything.

Payne grunted and hung up the phone, glad he could roll over and go back to sleep without anything to worry about. Thrilled it wasn't an emergency. He'd had too many of those when he was in the service. Hundreds of nights interrupted by news. Updates that were rarely positive.

So in his world, wrong numbers were a good thing. About the best thing possible.

Unfortunately, that wasn't the case here.

Several hours later Payne opened the hotel curtains and stepped on to his private veranda at the Renaissance Vinoy in downtown St Petersburg. Painted flamingo pink and recently restored to its former glory, the building was a stunning example of 1920s Mediterranean Revival architecture. The type of grand hotel that used to be found all over Florida yet was quickly becoming extinct in the age of Disney-fication.

The bright sunlight warmed his face, and the sea breeze filled his lungs as he stared at the tropical waters of Tampa Bay, less than ten miles from many of the best beaches in America. Where the sand was white and the water was turquoise. Where dolphins frolicked in the surf. Born and raised in Pittsburgh, Payne rarely got to see dolphins in his home town – only when he went to the aquarium or when the Miami Dolphins played the Steelers at Heinz Field.

In many ways, Payne looked like an NFL player. He was 6 feet 4 inches tall, weighed 240 pounds, and was in remarkable shape for a man in his late thirties. Light brown hair, hazel eyes, and a world-class smile. His only physical flaws were the bullet holes and scars that decorated his body. Although he didn't view them as flaws. More like medals of honour because each one stood for something.

Of course, he couldn't tell their stories to most people because the details were classified, but all of the scars meant something to him. Like secret tattoos that no one knew about.

The droning of a small aircraft caught Payne's attention, and he watched it glide across the azure sky and touch down at Albert Whitted Airport, a two-runway facility on the scenic waterfront, a few blocks away. It was the type of airfield that handled banner towing and sightseeing tours. Not large commuter jets. And certainly not the tactical fighters that he had observed during the last forty-eight hours. They required a lot more asphalt and much better pilots.

Every few months Payne visited US military installations around the world with his best friend and former MANIAC, David Jones. They were briefed on the latest equipment and offered their opinions to top brass on everything from training to tactics. Even though both soldiers were retired from active duty, they were still considered valuable assets by the Pentagon.

Part expert, part legend.

Their latest trip had brought them to Florida, where MacDill Air Force Base occupies a large peninsula in the middle of Tampa Bay – eight miles south of downtown Tampa and nine miles east of St Petersburg. All things considered, it wasn't a bad place to be stationed. Or to visit. Which is why Payne and Jones always looked forward to their next consulting trip.

They picked the destination and the military picked up the tab.

'Hey!' called a voice from below. 'You finally awake?'

Payne glanced down and saw David Jones standing on the sidewalk, staring up at him. Jones was 5 feet 9 inches tall and roughly forty pounds lighter than Payne. He had light brown skin, short black hair, and a thin nose that held his stylish sunglasses in place.

Sadly, the rest of his outfit wasn't nearly as fashionable: a green floral shirt, torn khaki cargo shorts, and a pair of flip-flops.

'I'm starving,' Jones said. 'You want to get some chow?'

'With you? Not if you're wearing *that*.'

'Why? What's wrong with it?'

'Honestly? It looks like Hawaiian camouflage.'

Jones frowned, trying to think of a retort. 'Yeah, well . . .'

'Well, what?'

'Maybe I'm looking to get *leid*.'

Payne laughed. It wasn't a bad comeback for a Sunday morning. 'I'll meet you in the lobby.'

Ten minutes later the duo was walking along Bayshore Drive. The temperature was in the mid-seventies with low humidity. Gentle waves lapped against the stone wall that lined the harbour while palm trees swayed in the breeze. Payne wore a golf shirt and shorts, an outfit considered dressy in Florida where many people wore T-shirts or no shirts at all.

As they turned onto Second Avenue NE towards the St Petersburg Pier, Payne and Jones spotted a parked trolley bus called the Looper. It was light blue and filled with tourists who were taking pictures of a tiny brick building with a red tiled roof. A senior-citizen tour guide, wearing a beige Panama hat and speaking with a southern drawl, explained the building's significance over the trolley's intercom system. They stopped to listen to his tale.

'You are looking at the fanciest public restroom in America, affectionately known as Little St Mary's. Built in 1927 by Henry Taylor, it is a scaled-down replica of St Mary Our Lady of Grace, the gorgeous church he built on Fourth Street that we'll be seeing soon. Both buildings are typical of the Romanesque Revival style, featuring several colours of brick, arched windows, and topped with a copper cupola. This one's approximately twenty feet high and fifty feet wide.'

Cameras clicked as the tour guide continued.

'As the legend goes, the local diocese offered Taylor a large sum of money to build the octagonal church that he finished in 1925. However, for reasons unknown, they chose not to pay him the full amount. Realizing that he couldn't win a fight with the Church, he opted to get revenge instead. At that time the city was taking bids to build a comfort station, a fancy term for bathroom, somewhere near the waterfront. Taylor made a ridiculously low bid, guaranteeing that he would get the project. From there, he used leftover materials from the church site and built the replica that you see before you, filling it with toilets instead of pews.'

The tour guide smiled. 'It was his way of saying that the Catholic Church was full of crap!'

Everyone laughed, including Payne and Jones, as the Looper pulled away from the kerb and turned towards the Vinoy. Meanwhile the duo remained, marvelling at the stone-carved columns and the elaborate tiled roof of Little St Mary's.

'Remind me to go in there later,' Jones said. 'And I mean that literally.'

3

The Colombia Restaurant is the world's largest Spanish restaurant. Opened in 1905 in Ybor City, a historic district of Tampa where hand-rolled cigars and Cuban mojitos are ubiquitous, the Colombia has fifteen dining rooms and enough seating for 1,700 people. Throw in the kitchens and the wine cellar, and the restaurant occupies 52,000 square feet, filling an entire city block.

Payne and Jones had eaten there on many occasions – it was practically a requirement any time they visited MacDill AFB – and had been tempted to drive there for brunch. That was before they learned the Colombia had opened a St Petersburg branch within walking distance of their hotel. Built on the fourth floor of the Pier, an inverted five-storey pyramid filled with shops at the end of a quarter of a mile turnaround, the restaurant had the same menu as the original while offering 360-degree waterfront views.

The duo took their seats next to a massive window overlooking the bay and the airfield. Within seconds, water was poured and freshly baked Cuban bread was placed on the table. Jones wasted no time, tearing the flaky crust with his hands and stuffing a chunk into his mouth.

Payne laughed at the sight. 'Hungry?'

'Famished. I've been up since dawn. Damn seagulls woke me up.'

'Seagulls? I've seen you sleep through enemy fire.'

Jones shrugged. 'Have you ever heard those relaxation tapes where they play new-age music over whales humping and birds singing? Those things freak me out. No way in hell I could fall asleep to that. I'd lie there all night, counting grunts and squeaks . . . But give me the rumble of a turbine or the gentle patter of gunfire, and I'm out like a light.'

Payne smiled. 'You're one messed-up dude.'

'Me? Look who's talking! What time did you fall asleep? Or haven't you yet?'

'Actually, last night wasn't too bad. It would've been perfect if it wasn't for the damn phone. Woke me up in the middle of the night.'

'Anything important?'

'Who knows? They hung up before I could answer.'

'No caller ID?'

Payne shook his head. 'It was the hotel phone. At least I think it was. I was groggy.'

'Did you check your cell?'

'I tried but I had a slight problem.' He reached into his pocket and pulled out his phone. Both pieces of it. 'I was hoping you could fix it.'

Jones put down his bread and studied the device. He had majored in computer science at the Air Force Academy and was a whiz with electronics. 'How'd you manage this?'

'I think I knocked it off the nightstand. But I'm not sure. I was sleeping.'

'No big deal. It's just the battery. Unfortunately, something is jamming the slot.'

'I know. That's why I brought it to the wizard. I figured you could work your magic.'

Jones grabbed a butter knife and went to work. Five minutes later it was fixed. He pushed the power button just to be sure, then put it on the table in front of Payne. 'Good as new.'

'Thanks! You just saved me a hundred bucks.'

'Not really,' he assured him. 'I'm gonna eat more than that, and you're paying.'

Jones flipped through his menu, searching for some of his favourite dishes: roasted pork loin à la Cubana, sliced eye round of beef stuffed with chorizo, and paella à la Valencia – a mixture of clams, chicken, pork, shrimp, scallops, and rice. Meanwhile Payne looked for lighter fare, settling on a pressed Cuban sandwich with a cup of Spanish bean soup.

The waiter came over to take their orders but before they could speak, Payne's phone started to buzz. All three of them stared as it vibrated wildly, bumping against an empty plate which made a loud pinging sound. It was so loud that other diners turned and stared.

'Sorry about that,' Payne apologized. Cell-phone manners were a pet peeve of his, and he had just violated one of his major commandments. *No cell phones in restaurants.*

Without looking at the screen, he turned off the power and put it in his pocket.

And that's where it stayed for the next few hours as precious time ticked away.

Payne gave it no thought until their return trip to the hotel. Hoping to kill time while Jones left a donation inside Little St Mary's, Payne turned on his phone and waited for it to warm up.

Several hungry pelicans sat on a nearby railing, begging for handouts from the dozen fishermen who fished off the pier. A young boy felt sorry for the birds and tossed them some bait. Within seconds, five more pelicans swooped out of the sky and landed by their friends. All of them squawking for attention.

Smiling at the scene, Payne glanced at his screen and was surprised by the summary.

Seventeen missed calls. Three voicemails. One text message.

Damn. Something was wrong.

All his friends knew he was a reluctant cell-phone user, only carrying it for emergencies. Therefore seventeen calls were a big deal. Especially in one day.

Worried, he clicked through his options until he reached the list of missed calls. He scrolled through the numbers, looking for the source, but the same message appeared over and over.

Restricted.

Seventeen calls, seventeen restricted numbers.

'Shit,' he mumbled to himself, realizing what that meant. It was probably the government.

They were the masters of the blocked call. Always trying to conceal their identity.

The only question was, who? Payne had done consulting work for the Pentagon and every branch of the armed service, not to mention the FBI, CIA, and NSA. Of course, if those agencies were trying to reach him, they wouldn't call seventeen times. They'd stalk him quietly and throw him into the back of a white van.

No, if he had to guess, he would have said the Air Force.

Not only was MacDill an air-force base, but it had paid for his trip to Florida. Maybe the generals wanted to get one more lecture out of him before he returned home.

'What's up?' Jones asked as he left the restroom. 'Did your phone break again?'

'I wish. I had seventeen missed calls. All of them blocked.'

'Fucking government.'

'What about you? Any calls?'

Jones checked his phone. 'Nope. *Nada.*'

'That's strange.'

'Tell me about it. I'm used to booty calls, day and night.'

He laughed. 'I was referring to MacDill, not McLovin.'

'What time did they start?'

Payne scrolled through his screen. 'Let's see. First call was 3.59 a.m. Damn. Maybe my cell phone woke me after all. I could've sworn it was the room phone.'

'Any messages?'

He nodded. 'Three voice, one text.'

'Start with the text. You can read it now.'

The device looked tiny in his massive hands, yet somehow Payne clicked the appropriate buttons, dancing from screen to screen. The text was tough to read in the Florida sun, forcing him to shield his phone from the glare. But in time, he was able to read the message.

It was straightforward and unsigned.

The type of message that no one wants to receive

This is not a prank. Life or death. Please call at once.

4

The stranger stood on the edge of the cliff and gasped at what he saw. Massive rock pillars sprang out of the earth like giant stone fingers, each of them rising several hundred feet from the valley below. Yet somehow the natural beauty of the scenery paled in comparison to the architectural wonder of Metéora, a site that hovered in the heavens like the throne of God.

He heard footsteps behind him but refused to shift his gaze from the Monastery of the Holy Trinity as the sun slipped behind the Pindus Mountains to the west.

Marcus Andropoulos, the man who approached, spoke with a local accent. 'The monks who built this place climbed the rock with their bare hands then refused to leave until construction was finished. They stayed on top for many months, lifting supplies by rope during the day and sleeping in a cave at night.'

The stranger said nothing, still admiring the view.

Andropoulos stepped closer, tentative. 'Eventually they built retractable wooden ladders that reached the crops they had planted in the fields below. Grapes, corn, potatoes. They even had sheep and cattle.'

The stranger tried to picture the ladders. They must have stretched for a quarter of a mile.

'I don't believe we've met,' said the Greek. 'My name is Marcus Andropoulos.'

'Nick Dial,' he said over his shoulder.

'You're an American, no? Are you a tourist?'

Dial shook his head. 'What does Metéora mean?'

'It is a local word. It means suspended in air. Originally there were twenty-four monasteries on the surrounding peaks. Many were destroyed during World War Two. Now only six remain.'

'How old is this one?'

'Fifteenth century,' he answered, still trying to figure out who Dial was and why he was there. 'Are you with the media?'

Dial laughed. 'Definitely not. I can't stand those guys.'

Andropoulos paused, thinking things through. If Dial wasn't a journalist, how did he get past all the officers on the main road? 'In that case, I think you need to leave.'

'Because I hate the media? That seems kind of harsh.'

'No, because this area is restricted. Didn't you see the signs?'

Dial turned and stared at the man who was trying to throw him out.

Andropoulos was young and lanky, dressed in a cheap suit that was two sizes too small. His hands and wrists hung three inches beyond his sleeves – as though he had recently grown and didn't have enough money to get a new wardrobe. Or visit a tailor. Or get a haircut. Because his head was covered with dark curly hair that went over his ears and the back of his neck. Like a Greek afro.

Dial said, 'You seem to know a lot about this place. Are you a tour guide or something?'

Andropoulos reached into his pocket and pulled out his badge. 'I am definitely *something*. I am the NCB agent assigned to this case. In fact, I am in charge of the investigation.'

Dial smirked, then refocused his attention on the monastery. In this light its beige walls appeared to be glowing. Almost like amber. It was truly a remarkable sight.

'Please, Nick. Don't make me tell you again. It's time to leave.'

But Dial wasn't ready. He picked up a pebble and tossed it over the edge. It fell for several seconds yet never made a sound, swallowed by the chasm below. He whistled, impressed.

In all his years, he had never worked in such a difficult location.

Simply put, this crime scene was going to be a bitch.

Dial picked up a second pebble, slightly larger than the first, and leaned back to throw it. He hoped to test a theory about the valley. But before he could, the young officer grabbed his arm.

'I wouldn't throw that if I were you.'

'Really? Why not?'

'Because I'm in charge, and I said so.'

Dial grinned. This was going to be fun. 'And if I were you, I'd let go of my arm.'

'Really? Why is that?'

He yanked his arm free and whipped out his identification. 'Because I'm your boss.'

Nick Dial ran the Homicide Division at Interpol, the largest international crime-fighting organization in the world, which meant he dealt with death all over the globe. His job was to coordinate the flow of information between police departments any time a murder investigation crossed national boundaries. All told he was in charge of 186 member countries, filled with billions of people and hundreds of languages.

One of the biggest misconceptions about Interpol was their role in stopping crime. They seldom sent agents to investigate a case. Instead they used local offices called National Central Bureaus in the member countries. The NCBs monitored their territory and reported pertinent information to Interpol's headquarters in Lyons, France. From there, facts were entered into a central database that could be accessed via Interpol's computer network.

Unfortunately, that wasn't always enough. Sometimes the head of a division (drugs, counterfeiting, terrorism, etc.) was forced to take control of a case. Possibly to cut through red tape. Or handle a border dispute. Or deal with international media. All the things that Nick Dial hated to do. In his line of work, the only thing that mattered to him was *justice*. Correcting a wrong in the fairest way possible. That was the creed he had lived by when he was an investigator.

If he did that, all the other bullshit would take care of itself.

Then again, in a brutal case like this, was justice even feasible?

'I apologize for my behaviour. I should have recognized your name,' Andropoulos said. His face was bright red from embarrassment. 'I didn't expect anyone from France so soon.'

'Well,' Dial said, 'I was on the continent, so I thought I'd drop by.'

Although he meant it as a joke, his comment was accurate. Dial had started the day on the other side of Europe where he had been awakened by news of the massacre. He had taken the first flight from France to Athens then had flown by helicopter to Metéora, which was in the northern district of Thessaly. In reality, he rarely took trips like that on a moment's notice, but how often were a bunch of monks slaughtered in the middle of the night?

'If you had called,' Andropoulos said, 'I would have been ready for you.'

Dial stopped. 'What are you saying? You only work hard when your boss is watching?'

His face got redder. 'No, I'm not saying that at all.'

'Then what are you saying?'

Andropoulos stammered, 'I . . . just, I would have been more ready for your visit.'

Dial tried not to smile. He was just busting the kid's balls and would continue to do so until he learned more about him. Until then, he would have some fun at the young agent's expense. 'Speaking of my visit, I need somewhere to stay. Somewhere nice. And close. But not *too* close. I don't want any dead monks falling on me.'

'Yes, of course. I'll find something for you in Kalampáka. It's the city over the hill.'

Dial nodded but didn't say a word.

Andropoulos stared at him, waiting, not sure what to do.

Finally, after several painful seconds, Dial shooed him away. 'Go!'

The kid sprinted up the hill like he was being chased by wolves. Only then did Dial start to laugh, remembering how he had been treated by senior officers when he was a rookie cop – how they used to call him Nikki and made him feel like a piece of shit but later admitted that they were just trying to toughen him up. Dial wasn't nearly as mean as they had been, but he still used some of their tactics. After all, their methods must have worked because a quarter of a century later Dial was the first American to run a division at Interpol.

It was an unbelievable honour from the European agency. But one he completely deserved.

Few investigators had the success that Dial had.

Anticipating the rugged terrain, he was wearing a short-sleeved shirt, blue jeans, and hiking boots. He reached into his pocket and pulled out his cell phone. It was equipped with a special antenna that allowed him to get a signal just about anywhere, which was necessary in his line of work. He needed to be reachable at all times from any country in the world. Not only to make decisions but to be briefed on the latest details of his case.

After punching in his office number, Dial lifted his phone and rested it on his chin. His massive, movie-star chin. Although he was in his mid-forties, he had a face that looked like it was chiselled out of granite. Clean lines, thick cheekbones, green eyes. Short black hair with just a hint of grey. Five o'clock shadow that arrived before noon. Not overly handsome, yet manly as hell. The type of guy who could star in an action movie or a Marlboro commercial.

A woman in one hand, a horse in the other, and a cigarette dangling from his mouth.

Except he didn't smoke, didn't have time to date, and liked his animals medium-rare.

Other than that, he sure as hell looked the part – thanks to his world-class chin.

'Hello,' said a French voice on the other end of Dial's phone, 'I'm not in right now because my boss is out of town. When he gets back, I'll get back. And not a moment before . . .'

Dial smiled at the greeting. Henri Toulon was the Assistant Director of the Homicide Division and a notorious slacker. A wine-loving Frenchman who practically lived at the office yet spent half of the day avoiding work, Toulon was still an invaluable member of his Interpol team, mostly because he was the smartest person Dial worked with. Toulon had the ability to speak at length on every subject under the sun – whether it was history, sports, politics, or popular culture. Unfortunately, sometimes he talked for hours just to avoid his other responsibilities.

'Hey, Henri, it's Nick. I'm still waiting for your background information on Metéora. So give me a call when you wake up from your nap. Oh, and if you're sleeping in my office, make sure you open a window. Last time I came back, the whole place smelled of booze.'

Dial laughed and hung up the phone.

If that didn't light a fire under Toulon's ass, nothing would.

5

Payne read the text message several times, not sure what to make of it. Normally he would've dismissed it as a joke – despite claims to the contrary – but for some reason it didn't feel like one. Seventeen calls that started in the middle of the night screamed of urgency, not hilarity.

Without saying a word, he handed the phone to Jones and waited for his opinion.

Jones read it once. Then again. Then aloud. 'This is not a prank. Life or death. Please call at once.' He paused for a moment, giving it some thought. 'What the hell?'

'My thoughts exactly.'

Jones clicked a few buttons, hoping to get additional information. 'It was sent from a restricted number. Unfortunately there's no way to tell if the message came from the same phone as all the calls. It probably did, but we can't tell for sure. At least not from your phone.'

'Meaning?'

'If I access the phone company's server, I can locate the number. Even if it's blocked.'

'Can you do that from Florida?'

Jones nodded. 'With a computer and an internet connection, I can do just about anything.'

'Well, that might not be necessary. I still haven't listened to my voicemail yet.'

'Hold on. Before you do I want to check something.' Jones scrolled to a different screen and studied the time of each missed call. He quickly noticed a pattern. 'Thirty minutes.'

'Excuse me?'

'Whoever it was called you every half hour. First call was 3.59 a.m. Next call was 4.30. Then 5.01. Then 5.29. And so on. All the way until 11.28.'

Payne grabbed the phone and looked at the times. The calls came approximately thirty minutes apart – except for an extra call at 9.14 a.m. 'Who would call that often?'

'Someone desperate.'

Payne glanced at the clock. It was nearly 1.00 p.m. Nothing for the last ninety minutes.

One phrase echoed in his brain.

Life or death.

He prayed that wasn't the reason the calls had stopped.

They spotted an empty bench near Little St Mary's where they could listen to the messages without any distractions. Jones had a pen in one hand and a windshield flyer he had grabbed off a parked car in the other, ready to write names, numbers, or anything he deemed important.

Payne turned on his speakerphone and hit play.

The first message was filled with static.

'Jon, my . . . ame is . . . I was . . . your number by . . . er. He told . . . you . . . help. I am call . . . you . . . phone. I don't know the . . . I'll have to . . . back. Please, it's urgent.'

Payne hit the save button so they could listen to it over and over. Unfortunately the quality of the sound didn't improve during multiple attempts. Still, they learned some basic facts. The caller was a male with no detectable accent. He mentioned Payne by name, which meant it wasn't a wrong number. And he stressed the urgency of the matter.

Not a lot to go on, but better than nothing.

The second message was recorded an hour later. And during that time, the static had worsened.

'Jon, I . . . early. I apologize . . . but . . . death. Someone is . . . us. Hello? Can . . . hear me?'

Payne frowned. 'Is that my static or his?'

'Definitely his. Since you never answered the call, the message was recorded by the phone company on its server. So all the hissing and the dropped words are from his end.'

'Does that help us pinpoint his location?'

'Probably not,' Jones answered. 'He could be calling from a rural area with poor coverage, or he could be in a major city with bad weather. Or he could be using a crappy cell phone. There are simply too many variables.'

Payne shrugged. He'd figured as much.

'Play it again,' Jones said, 'but concentrate on the second half.'

They listened to the message again. 'Someone is . . . us. Hello? Can . . . hear me?'

Jones smiled. 'Call me crazy, but I think he said, "Someone is after us."'

Payne nodded in agreement. 'I think you're right. Of course, that leads us to the next question. Who is he with?'

'No way of knowing. Not from what we've heard.'

'So it could be his friend or his wife.'

'Or kids.'

Payne frowned. 'Great. Now we have to save an entire family.'

'Or maybe, just maybe, he's alone. For all we know, this guy is delusional.'

Payne shrugged. 'Either way, here's the final message. It was left at 11.28, right after you fixed my phone. It's the call I ignored at lunch.'

He pushed the button and listened to the caller.

Static was no longer a problem, yet somehow the call sounded distant. Muffled.

'Sorry, I had to switch phones. I'm using a payphone now. Hopefully no one is listening. I will keep calling as long as I can, but I'm being watched . . . Damn! Where are you? Your friend assured me that I could trust you. Please. We need your help.'

They listened to it twice more before commenting.

Jones said, 'He used the word *we*, so we're definitely

dealing with more than one person. Unfortunately, I can't tell if your friend, whoever that is, is part of the we.'

'My guess is no. If my friend was there, he'd be calling me himself.'

'Unless he's hurt. Or being held captive.'

'Great.'

'Any idea which friend?'

Payne shook his head. 'Clueless. No idea at all.'

'Well, what time did—'

'Hold up,' Payne said, interrupting him. He clicked a few buttons on his phone until the first message was ready to play. 'I'm not sure, but he might've mentioned my friend in the first voicemail. It was garbled by static, but I think he did. Just listen.'

Payne hit play, focusing on the second sentence.

'Jon, my . . . ame is . . . I was . . . your number by . . . er. He told . . . you . . . help. I am call . . . you . . . phone. I don't know the . . . I'll have to . . . back. Please, it's urgent.'

Jones smiled, filling in the holes. 'I was *given* your number by *blank*. Something that ends with *er*. Like Miller. Or Harper. Know anyone like that who would give out your number?'

'Nothing rings a bell.'

'That's okay. No pressure. Give it some time. It'll come to you. It always does.'

Payne nodded half-heartedly. He appreciated Jones' confidence but realized time was of the essence. It had been ninety minutes since the last call, an eternity in a life or death situation.

For all he knew, he was already too late.

6

Nick Dial followed Andropoulos as he trudged down the dirt path from the main road. The hill was steep and the footing treacherous in the dying sunlight, yet Andropoulos navigated it with ease, never losing his balance despite his leather dress shoes.

'What are you?' Dial demanded as he stopped to catch his breath. 'Part mountain goat?'

Andropoulos smiled. 'I am all Greek. I was born in Kastraki, a small village to the east. I used to play in these hills as a boy. I know them quite well.'

'Is this the only path to Holy Trinity?'

'The only path, yes. The only way, no.'

Dial glanced round. He saw nothing but cliffs. 'How else can you get there?'

'The monks have a cable-car system, meant to handle supplies. It is strong enough to carry a man. However, it is controlled from inside the monastery.'

'So it would require an accomplice.'

Andropoulos nodded. 'That is why we are on this path. This is how the killers came.'

With that, he started walking again, weaving round boulders and bushes until he arrived at the bottom of the gorge where he was greeted by a large blue sign. At the top in white letters in both Greek and English, it said HOLY MONASTERY OF AGIA TRIAS. In gold letters underneath, it warned in four different languages that shorts and short-sleeved shirts were not permitted; neither were women in sleeveless dresses or pantaloons.

Dial read the warning and smiled. He hadn't seen the word pantaloons in years.

Andropoulos asked, 'Are you ready for the tough part? The footing gets worse from here.'

'Are you serious? How could it get worse?'

He turned on a flashlight and shone it forward. 'You shall see.'

A steep trail rose before them. It meandered up the hillside past a small grove of oriental plane trees, the most common tree in the valley, until it stopped at the bottom of a rocky crag where a series of steps had been carved into the stone. Although he wasn't afraid of heights, Dial dreaded the next part of their journey – especially at night. One misstep meant a nasty fall.

'Let me borrow your flashlight,' Dial said.

Andropoulos nodded, willing to do just about anything to impress his boss.

The Greek had been an officer for less than two years but hoped to move on to bigger and better things. Perhaps something in Athens. Or maybe Interpol headquarters in France. The truth was he would kill for a job in the Homicide Division, which was why he was wearing his father's suit instead of his everyday uniform. He wanted to make a good first impression.

'Do you see something?' Andropoulos wondered.

Dial shone the light against the surface of the cliff, surprised by what he saw. From a distance he figured the stone fingers were made of volcanic rock, cooled underground then exposed to sunlight after millions of years of soil erosion, but on closer inspection he realized that wasn't the case. The natural pillars were hardened sandstone, filled with tiny pebbles of many shapes and colours. The result was a geological mosaic that seemed to breathe and flow with the constant movement of the earth. A living sculpture that stretched towards the sky.

'Let me guess,' Dial said. 'This region was once under water.'

Andropoulos nodded. 'Scientists say that Thessaly was a giant lake that emptied into the Aegean Sea when an earthquake split the mountains. However, according to Greek mythology, the flood was caused by Zeus, who hoped to bring fertile farmland to the region.'

Dial smiled at the myth and gazed across the valley one last time, trying to enjoy the landscape for a few more seconds before it was permanently disfigured in his mind. From this point on, he knew Metéora would for ever be tarnished by the things he was about to see.

'Okay,' he said. 'I'm ready.'

Andropoulos turned and started the steep climb to the monastery. Dial stayed close behind, using the flashlight to find the footholds that had been carved into the rock several decades before. He also searched for any evidence that might have been missed by the local police.

'There are one hundred and forty steps. You can count them if you like.'

'One hundred and forty? Is that number significant?'

'Yes,' said the Greek. 'That is how many they needed to reach the top.'

'I meant—' Dial shook his head. There was no need to explain. 'Go! Keep walking.'

Andropoulos obliged, not saying another word until they reached the entrance which was cut into the side of the cliff like a natural fissure. The door was ten feet high and made out of solid wood that had not been damaged during the assault. Neither had the ancient lock, which still worked despite centuries of use. 'This is the only way in.'

Dial examined the hinges and frame. No scratches or holes. 'Is it locked at night?'

'Always.'

'Whose job is it?'

Andropoulos shrugged. 'I'm not sure.'

'Do me a favour and find out.'

'Of course.'

'One more thing,' Dial said. 'Once we're inside, I want to be left alone for a while. I always try to view the evidence and the crime scene with fresh eyes. It allows me to form my own conclusions before I hear anyone else's. Got it?'

'Yes, sir.'

Dial stared at him, sizing him up. 'You should try it some time. It's the best way to separate a good investigator from a bad one.'

Andropoulos nodded. 'I was the first one here. So my opinions are my own.'

Dial smiled. He liked the Greek's confidence. 'Glad to hear it, kid. Let's talk again in twenty minutes. I'll find out then if you have any brains or I need to get a new tour guide.'

7

If they'd had more time, Payne and Jones would have driven to MacDill AFB to do their dirty work, using one of the computers on the high-speed military network. The encryption level was so good and the speeds were so blazing fast that Jones could have floated round the internet like a ghost, grabbing whatever data he needed without worrying about being caught. But as things stood, they had to make do with Jones' laptop and the hotel's wireless network.

That and the help of a well-connected friend.

As a computer researcher at the Pentagon, Randy Raskin was privy to many of the government's biggest secrets, to a mountain of classified data that was there for the taking if someone knew how to access it. His job was to make sure the latest information got into the right hands at the right time. And he was great at it. Over the years, Payne and Jones had used his services on many occasions, and this had eventually led to a friendship.

Payne offered to give him a call while Jones turned on his computer.

'Leave me alone,' Raskin snapped from his desk in the Pentagon. 'I'm busy.'

'Well, hello to you, too.'

'Seriously, Jon. You shouldn't be calling me. Today is the Sabbath. A day of rest.'

Payne smiled. 'First of all, you're Jewish, so don't pull that crap with me.'

'What are you saying? Jews don't deserve a day off?'

'Secondly, I called you at the office. Therefore you're not actually resting.'

Raskin cursed, realizing he had lost the argument. 'Dammit! How come you always win? Tell me the truth. Were you on the debate team in high school?'

'No,' Payne joked, 'but I beat them up when they wouldn't do my homework.'

'I should've known. I'm going to make a note of that in your personnel file.'

'If you must. But before you do, I was wondering—'

Raskin interrupted him. 'If I could do you a favour.'

'Crap! Am I that predictable?'

'Both of you are. Let me guess, DJ is there, too.'

'You know it.'

'And you're calling from . . . Florida. Am I right?'

Payne nodded. 'How'd you know that?'

The ever-present clicking of Raskin's keyboard could be heard in the background. 'Because I'm tracking your call with Blackbird, our latest GPS satellite. Give me ten more seconds and I can shoot a missile up your ass. Seriously. Right up your *ass*.'

'Ouch! You're one scary geek.'

Raskin smiled. 'Don't you forget it.'

'Okay,' Jones said from across the hotel room. He sat in front of his laptop, which was logged onto an encrypted system at his office in Pittsburgh. 'I'm ready.'

Payne turned on his speakerphone. 'Randy, you're on with DJ.'

'So,' Raskin asked, 'what kind of trouble are you in this time?'

'It's not us,' Jones explained. 'It's a colleague of ours. And the clock is ticking.'

Raskin nodded in understanding. The joking stopped at once. 'What do you need?'

'We need access to restricted phone numbers. Seventeen calls in the last twelve hours. All of them placed to Jon's cell.'

'The line we're on now?'

'Affirmative,' Jones answered.

'No sweat. I started tracking it the moment he called. Give me a few seconds to get through his network's firewall, and I can retrieve everything you need.'

'Can you send it to my laptop?'

'If you'd like. Or I can just read it to you.'

Jones shook his head. 'No thanks. I want a hard copy.'

'Not a problem. I'll send it right now.' Raskin hit ENTER, sending the file. 'It might take a few minutes to arrive. My system is running slow today. I'm crunching some serious data.'

'In that case,' Payne said, 'would you mind answering one question about the calls?'

'Fire away.'

'Where did they come from?'

Raskin glanced at his middle screen. It was flanked by several others, all of them filled with data for other projects. 'As far as I can tell, the calls came from three different sources. But the majority of them were placed in one city: St Petersburg.'

'St Petersburg? We're *in* St Petersburg.'

Raskin shook his head. 'Sorry, dude. Wrong St Petersburg. I'm talking about Russia.'

Payne hung up, more confused than before. 'Someone's calling me from Russia? That makes no sense. I haven't been there in years.'

Jones said nothing as he waited for the file to appear on his screen. When it did, he hit a few keys and the document started to print on his portable printer that weighed less than three pounds and fitted inside his laptop bag.

'Here you go,' he said to Payne as he handed him a copy of the phone logs. Then he printed a second copy for himself, so he could make notes in the margin.

According to the list, fifteen calls had been made to Payne's phone from one number in St Petersburg, Russia. They had started at 3.59 a.m. and had ended at 11.01 a.m. That pattern changed at 11.28 a.m. when the caller switched to a payphone – a fact confirmed by his final message.

'Any thoughts?' Payne asked.

'A few. Take a look at the last column.'

The phone logs were divided into six columns, five of which were pretty straightforward. The first showed the date of the call. The second showed the time it was placed. The third showed the duration. The fourth showed the caller's number. And the fifth showed the location.

No problems reading any of those.

But the sixth was a different story. It was more complicated.

At the top of the column, there was a single word: TOW.

No description. No explanation. No help of any kind.

Payne and Jones tried to figure out what it meant by analysing the column itself, but the data was an enigmatic mix of numbers and letters, separated by a dash. 18-A. 22-F. 4-C. And so on. A few of the combinations appeared more than once, always on successive calls, yet there didn't seem to be a discernible pattern. At least not at first glance. And for all they knew, the letters might have been translated from the Cyrillic alphabet.

Payne asked, 'Is TOW an acronym?'

'Honestly, I don't know. Maybe time of something. Something that starts with a W.'

'Time of waking my ass up.'

'Somehow I doubt it. In fact, now that I think about it, time won't work at all. It doesn't correspond with the alphanumeric codes in the last column.'

'The what?'

'The things with the dashes.'

Payne smiled. 'Any thoughts on what could?'

Jones shrugged. 'It might be some kind of machine code – a basic set of instructions for the phone company's central processing unit. I'm not sure why it would be listed, though.'

'It wouldn't be. But I think you're on the right track. We're definitely dealing with a code. The only question is what kind. Why don't you fire up your computer and run a search? Who knows? Maybe Google can help us out.'

Normally Jones would have told Payne to wait, insisting that he could figure it out on his own. After all, solving mysteries was a passion of his, which was one of the main reasons that he had opened a private investigations firm in Pittsburgh when he left the MANIACs. But in this case, time was crucial, so he sat in front of his laptop and ran an internet search for TOW.

Hundreds of possibilities popped on his screen, none of which seemed likely.

But Jones kept trying, searching page after page until something clicked. And when it did, he shook his head in frustration, pissed off that he hadn't thought of it sooner.

It was a look that Payne had seen many times. 'Got something?'

Jones nodded. 'It's not an acronym. It's an abbreviation. It stands for tower.'

'As in phone tower?'

'As in cell-phone tower. Each letter and number combo refers to a specific area in the city. If we get a tower map, we can figure out where our mystery caller was each time he called.'

'And how will that help?'

'If necessary,' Jones said, 'I can access traffic cameras in each of those grids and look for familiar faces. Who knows? We might get lucky and get a picture of this guy.'

Payne frowned. It sounded like a lot of unnecessary work. 'I've got a better idea. Why don't we just call the number and talk to him?'

8

Dial crept anonymously round the monastery – never making eye contact, always blending in, never staying in one room for too long. He knew the moment he stopped was the moment someone would approach. And he wanted to avoid that at all cost.

In his mind, there was an appropriate time to discuss a case.

And that time was much later.

Built in 1475, Agia Triada had been remodelled on several occasions but remained true to its post-Byzantine roots. The interior of its church was architecturally ornate, both in design and material, while the artwork was colourful and vibrant. Dial did his best to ignore the religious frescoes that surrounded him, focusing instead on the crimson puddle on the main altar.

This was where the killings had occurred.

More than one person had died here – that much was certain. But he wouldn't know an actual number until he was briefed on the blood work. From the looks of things, he guessed somewhere between five and ten. They had been killed on the stone slab then immediately dragged towards the side door. He could tell that from the thickness of the blood trail. These victims, fresh from the slaughter, had continued to bleed as they were moved.

Following the path, he left the chapel and walked towards a four-foot restraining wall. It was made of stone and designed to keep people from falling over the edge. Only in this case, it hadn't done its job. Dial noticed a large patch of dried blood near its base. The red stain streaked up the side and continued to the top, as if the bodies had been picked up and dumped over the side.

Dial turned on his flashlight and leaned over the wall, careful not to touch anything. In the past few minutes a light fog had settled in the valley, obscuring the crime scene below. From this height all he could see were the surrounding peaks that rose above the mist like a lost city in the clouds. Yet somehow that seemed appropriate. The monks had chosen this place for its isolation, a way to avoid the dangers and distractions of the outside world. But in the end, they had neglected to consider a basic tenet of life.

Just because you ignore the world, doesn't mean the world will ignore you.

Since half the police force was in the church looking for evidence, Dial decided to roam the outer parts of the monastery, hoping to answer the one issue that plagued him the most.

Why were the monks killed?

Was this a hate crime against the Orthodox faith? A robbery gone bad? Or something more psychotic

– perhaps an ex-monk getting revenge against his former brethren?

The truth was he didn't know and probably wouldn't until he had a better grasp of the monastic way of life. In his mind, one of the biggest drawbacks of working for a worldwide organization like Interpol was how difficult it was to understand all the ideologies he encountered while travelling the globe. And since Dial had never visited this part of Greece, he knew he had a lot to learn about the local people and their customs.

For him, the quickest way to shed some light on Metéora was to find somebody to talk to. Not another cop, who would be inclined to discuss the case, but someone who could help him understand the culture of the local monasteries. Preferably someone who still lived in one.

With that in mind, Dial stopped looking for clues and started searching for a monk.

Halfway across the complex, he saw a bright light shining under an ancient door. It was made of the same wood as the front gate but was not nearly as tall. Dial knocked on it gently and waited for a response. A few seconds passed before an old man opened it. He had a long grey beard and piercing eyes that sat deep in their sockets. A coarse robe hung off his frail frame like loose skin, as if it was a part of him. It was tied at the waist by a white cord that dangled to his knees.

He stood there, silent, quietly studying Dial while Dial returned the favour.

Two men sizing each other up.

Finally, the old man spoke. His name was Nicolas. 'On most days you would be asked to leave.' He reached his pale hand forward and tugged on the cuff of Dial's short-sleeved shirt. 'This is not appropriate for a house of God.'

Dial lowered his eyes in shame. He had read the warning sign in the valley but had ignored it – mostly because he didn't think anyone was alive to enforce the rules. Now he felt like a total ass. He hadn't said a word, yet he had already offended the monk. 'I can leave if you'd like.'

'That won't be necessary. There are more important things to worry about.'

Dial introduced himself then said, 'Actually, I was kind of hoping that you could assist me with some of those things. As a foreigner, I don't know much about Greek monasteries – as you can tell from my clothes.'

Nicolas considered Dial's request for several seconds before he stepped outside and closed the door behind him. 'Let us walk. I'd like to show you something.'

Without saying another word, he started the long journey across the complex. His gait was hobbled, a combination of his advanced age and the uneven surface of the stone courtyard, but he was determined to reach his destination without any help. This was most apparent when they reached the spiral staircase to the bell tower. It stood three storeys high and was covered with a tiled roof. The monk grasped the handrail with one hand while lifting his robe with the other. Then he pulled himself to the top, one painful step at a time.

'Do you know the story of Agia Triada?' asked the monk as he struggled with the stairs. 'The hermits who built this place climbed to the top of the rock with their bare hands but weren't strong enough to carry supplies. So one might wonder how they accomplished their goal.'

Dial recalled what Andropoulos had said. 'Didn't they lift their equipment with ropes?'

'They did, but how did they get the ropes to the top?'

'On their backs?'

Nicolas stopped walking. 'Have you ever lifted two thousand feet of rope? Of course not. It would be far too heavy and cumbersome.'

'I hadn't thought of that.'

'So what did they do? How did they get the rope to the top?'

Dial was adept at solving mysteries, but even he was stumped by this one. 'I have no idea.'

'Not even a guess?'

'Nope. Not even a guess.'

Nicolas revelled in victory. 'My brethren used kites.'

'Kites? How did that work?'

'One monk stood at the bottom of the cliff and flew a kite high into the air. When the wind was right, he let it drift towards the top of the rock where another monk grabbed its tail. The long kite string was then tied to the end of a rope, allowing the monks to pull it up the cliff.'

'That's brilliant,' Dial admitted. 'How did they come up with that?'

Nicolas shrugged. 'Give a man enough time to think and he can accomplish anything.'

Dial smiled. He liked this guy. He had several more questions that he wanted to ask the monk, but he could see Nicolas was having trouble with the stairs. Out of respect, Dial stopped talking until they reached the top of the bell tower.

'I've spent many days up here,' said the monk as he fought to catch his breath. He stared at one of the nearby peaks, ignoring the darkness and the fog that surrounded them. 'This tower has the best view of the valley. And I should know. I've seen them all.'

'How long have you lived here?'

Nicolas shook his head. 'I haven't lived here for many years. Not since the decision.'

'The decision?'

'Holy Trinity was a working monastery for several centuries. Now it is a haven for tourists, and we are nothing but tour guides . . . Do you know how many monks live here?'

Dial guessed. 'Twenty.'

'One,' said the monk. 'And he is now dead.'

'Only one? What about the other victims?'

'What about them?'

'If they weren't residents, why were they here in the middle of the night?'

Nicolas shrugged. 'I have not been told.'

Dial paused for a moment, trying to think things through. He had been under the impression that the killers had broken into the monastery and slaughtered all the monks who lived here. Now he knew that wasn't the case. With the exception of one monk, all the other monks were late-night visitors. And the reason for their visit had been kept a secret. Suddenly, Dial realized, if he could figure out that reason, then he would be a whole lot closer to catching the killers.

'So,' Dial asked, 'who's in charge of all the monasteries at Metéora?'

'That would be the *hegumen*, the abbot.'

'Can I talk to him?'

'Unfortunately, that is not possible.'

'Why? Is it against the rules?'

Nicolas shook his head.

'In that case, where can I find him?'

'That depends. Where do you take the dead?'

Dial groaned, completely mortified. 'I am sorry. I didn't know.'

The monk remained silent as he stared into the distance.

'When will a replacement be named?'

'Once we have all the answers. There are still many questions that need to be asked.'

Dial knew the feeling. 'In the meantime, who's in charge of Holy Trinity?'

Nicolas turned towards Dial and pointed to himself. 'I am here, so I am in charge. I will tend to this place until a successor is named.'

'As luck should have it, I'm in charge, too.' Dial paused for a moment, thinking. 'If you're interested, maybe we can help each other out. I can answer some of your questions if you can answer some of mine.'

The monk smiled for the first time that night. 'Yes. I would like that very much.'

9

Jones had spent several minutes analysing the phone logs, focusing his attention on the coded sixth column while overlooking the simplest approach of all: dialling the number.

'You know,' Payne joked. 'For the smartest guy I know, you're pretty stupid.'

'Why didn't you say something sooner?'

'I did! I've been calling you stupid for years.'

Jones sneered. 'I meant about the phone.'

'Honestly? I got caught up in all your excitement.'

'In other words, you just thought of it yourself.'

Payne shrugged. 'Maybe.'

'When you call,' Jones said, trying to shift the focus from himself, 'remember to use the international code for Russia. It's zero, one, one, seven.'

Payne turned on the speakerphone and dialled the number that had placed fifteen of the seventeen calls. There was a slight delay before his call went through, followed by the unfamiliar sound of a foreign ring. Much different than the sound in America. More like a wind-up phone from yesteryear. It rang once. Then again. Then a third time. Yet no one picked up.

A fourth ring. Then a fifth. Then a sixth.

Finally, after the seventh ring, the ringing stopped and someone answered.

'*Da?*' said the voice in Russian.

Payne and Jones looked at each other, confused. Not only didn't they speak much Russian – although they knew that *da* meant yes – they realized this wasn't the same man who had left three messages for Payne. This voice was younger. More tentative.

'Hello,' Payne said, not sure what to say. 'Do you speak English?'

'*Nyet.*'

Payne grimaced. The guy claimed he couldn't speak English, yet he knew enough about the language to understand the question. 'Are you sure?'

'*Da!*'

Payne covered the mic on his phone. 'I think he's retarded.'

Jones tried not to laugh. 'Let me try.'

'Help yourself.'

He took a deep breath then spoke phonetically, mumbling one of the few phrases he knew, '*Govorite li vy po angliyski?*'

Payne stared at Jones, surprised. 'What the hell did you say?'

Jones signalled for him to shut up, hoping the Russian would respond. When he didn't, Jones repeated one word. '*Angliyski?*'

It meant English.

Several seconds passed before another word was spoken. This time it came from a female with a thick accent. 'Hello?'

'Hello,' said Jones, surprised by the development. 'Do you speak English?'

'Yes.'

'Great. That's great—'

'He find it,' she said, interrupting him.

'Excuse me?'

'He find it,' she repeated. 'He not steal it. He find it.'

'What are you talking about?'

'The phone. He find phone. My son not steal phone.'

Jones frowned at the news. Someone had ditched the phone. 'Where did he find it?'

'How you say . . . *garbage*? He find on garbage.'

'Did he see who threw it away?'

The woman talked to her son in Russian. A few seconds later she translated his response. 'He see no one. He find phone. Not steal.'

'Thank you,' Jones said, realizing this was a dead end. 'Tell him to enjoy the phone. We'll call back if we have more questions.'

She said nothing and hung up.

Payne asked, 'What do you think?'

'I think her kid found the phone.'

'That's not what I meant. Do you think our guy threw it away? Or did someone else?'

Jones shrugged. 'In his third message he mentioned that he had to switch phones, so maybe he threw it away. Maybe he was afraid it was being traced and decided to ditch it. I honestly don't know. As of now I don't know enough about this guy to make any assumptions.'

Payne nodded. It was a good point. 'Now what? Should we call the payphone?'

'It's worth a try. Who knows? Maybe he's standing next to it, waiting for our call.'

Somehow Payne doubted it. More than two hours had passed since the caller's last message and he had sounded way too spooked to stay in one place for long. But what other options did they have? They had no more leads and Russia was several thousand miles away.

'Here goes nothing,' Payne said as he dialled the number.

The same foreign ring emerged from the phone – more of a buzzing than an actual ringing. But unlike before, no one answered. It just rang and rang and rang.

'It was worth a shot,' he said as he hung up. 'I'll try again later.'

Jones nodded as he stared at the phone list. Something about it didn't seem right.

'What's wrong?' Payne asked.

'I don't know. I get the feeling we're missing something.'

'Like what?'

Jones ignored the question as he counted the phone

calls. 'Five ... ten ... fifteen ... wait! How many phone calls did you say you missed?'

'Seventeen.'

'That's what I thought. But there are only sixteen on this list.'

Payne picked up his copy of the printout and counted the calls. 'You're right. Sixteen.'

'Check your phone again. Count the missed calls.'

Payne did what he was told. 'Seventeen.'

'So we're missing a call.'

He nodded. 'And I know which one. The guy called every half hour except for one instance around nine this morning.' He scrolled through his phone. '9.14 to be exact.'

Jones double-checked his list. 'Bingo! That's the one.'

'Why wasn't it listed?'

'I have no idea. Let me check the original file again.' Jones hit a few buttons on his laptop and studied the document. Several seconds passed before he noticed the problem. 'For some reason my printer only printed the first page of the phone log. Hold on. Let me print page two. It looks like this call came in from a different country code so it was listed on a different sheet.'

Both men stared at the printer as it sprang to life.

A moment later it was spitting out a sheet of paper that was nearly blank. One line for the header. One line for the phone call. Then nothing but empty white.

Still, the missing page gave them their biggest break yet.

A phone number that they recognized.

I O

Andropoulos hustled from room to room, searching for his boss. He finally spotted Dial in the main courtyard where he and an elderly monk were leaving the bell tower. Andropoulos stopped in his tracks, not sure if he should approach, until Dial waved him over.

'Nicolas,' Dial said as an introduction, 'this is Marcus, my squire.'

The old man nodded but said nothing.

'Where have you been hiding?' Dial wondered.

'Sir,' Andropoulos whispered, 'we need to speak.'

'That's right. I promised you a chance to impress me. I guess now is as good a time as any.'

'No, sir. It's not that. It's something else.'

'Such as?'

Andropoulos shook his head. 'I'm sorry, sir. It's confidential.'

Dial glanced at Nicolas, half embarrassed. He had spent the past several minutes trying to convince the monk that he would be kept in the loop on everything, hoping to establish a level of trust that rarely existed between Church and state. Now the first thing out of Andropoulos' mouth was that he had a secret. Talk about shitty timing.

'Don't worry. I understand,' Nicolas said. 'Some things are not meant to be shared.'

'Talk tomorrow?' Dial asked.

The old monk nodded, then hobbled out of sight.

Dial waited until Nicolas was completely out of earshot before he turned his attention to Andropoulos. 'This better be good.'

'It is,' the young cop assured him. 'Potentially great.'

'How great are we talking?'

'I'm not sure,' he admitted. 'I'd like to show you something and get your opinion.'

'Oh goody. Show and tell!' Dial said sarcastically. 'Please, lead the way.'

The two of them walked across the monastery towards the small annexe that had been built behind the main chapel. It was an unremarkable building with several windows that hadn't been cleaned in weeks. Andropoulos opened the narrow door and ducked inside the stuffy room. Originally it had been used for meditation; now it served as a gift shop.

Dial stepped inside and stared at the cheap trinkets on the tables. Suddenly, snippets of his conversation with Nicolas sprang to mind.

The old monk was right. Agia Triada had become a haven for tourists.

'Don't tell me,' Dial said. 'You want me to buy you a T-shirt.'

Andropoulos ignored the comment. He was far too excited about his discovery. 'Earlier you said the difference between a good investigator and a bad one was the ability to examine a scene. Well, as far as I know, I'm the first one to notice this.'

Dial glanced round the room, confused. 'Notice what?'

Andropoulos pointed towards a chest of drawers that rested along the rear wall. The cabinet was carved out of local wood and stained a dark brown. On top sat a metal box where the monastery kept the money from gift purchases.

Dial walked over and examined it. He was less than impressed.

'You brought me here for this?'

The Greek shook his head. 'Look above you.'

Dial did as he was told. The ceiling was held up by ancient beams that were cracked and splintered. Most had been there for hundreds of years and looked like they might give way. Suddenly Dial didn't feel very safe. In fact, he was about to ask for a hardhat when he noticed something that was out of place. It was a flat piece of glass, roughly the size of a coin.

'Wait. What is that? Is that a camera?'

Andropoulos nodded as he approached the cabinet. 'The wire runs on top of the wood and drops down behind the stone. Then it comes out of the wall and goes into this.'

He opened the right-hand drawer, revealing a small video recorder.

Dial stared at the device. 'I'll be damned. The

monks have a nanny cam. Seems kind of strange in a place that teaches love and trust.'

'A nanny cam?'

'Sorry. It's an American term. It means a hidden video camera. Sometimes parents set it up when they aren't at home to spy on their babysitters.'

'Ah, yes! I have heard of this. We have something similar in Greece.'

'Really? What's it called?'

'A neighbour.'

Dial laughed. Sometimes old-fashioned methods worked just as well.

'So,' Andropoulos asked, 'did I do good?'

'Yes,' Dial admitted, 'this was good work on your part. Unfortunately, as far as I can tell, the viewing angle won't give us any video of the killers. Unless, of course, they came in here to pick out a souvenir.'

'Yes, I agree. That camera is no good for our needs. But it made me think. If they put a camera in here, maybe they put a camera out there.'

'Maybe.'

Andropoulos continued. 'Then I remembered that many local monasteries keep a tin box in the chapel so people can donate money. Do you have this in America?'

'Some churches do.'

'Well, do you know where the chapel is from here?'

Dial smiled in understanding. 'On the other side of this wall.'

'Yes,' said the Greek as he opened the left-hand

drawer. Inside was a second video system that was identical to the first. 'On the other side of that wall.'

Even though Dial used to be one of the top investigators in the world, his current job with Interpol was mostly administrative. He was allowed to make suggestions and give advice to NCB agents in the field, but when it came to gathering evidence, that was strictly the duty of local officers since they were responsible for the chain of custody in local courts.

In reality, Dial knew his involvement with this case was slightly premature. One of Interpol's bylaws prohibited him from working on any military or religious crimes, which was Interpol's way of staying politically and philosophically neutral. However, as a division chief, he was allowed to use discretion on any homicide with unknown motives, a grey area that he often took advantage of – including a famous case that had involved crucifixions on several continents. That was one of the reasons he had spent so much time talking to Nicolas about the monastic way of life. He needed to determine if this was a crime against the Orthodox faith or something else.

If it was a hate crime, Dial had no choice. He would be forced to step aside.

If not, there was still a major hurdle that he needed to clear if he wanted to stay involved. Dial needed to prove that this case affected multiple member states. Otherwise, it would be considered a domestic issue, and the Greeks could ask him to leave at once.

Strangely, Dial wasn't the least bit concerned. Experience had taught him to view everything as one piece of the puzzle. And he knew in his gut that something significant was going on, something that transcended religious crimes and crossed foreign borders.

He wasn't sure about specifics, but he didn't plan on leaving until he figured it out.

I I

Clinging to the southern slopes of the Lepontine Alps, Küsendorf is a village of nearly 2,000 people in Ticino, the southern-most canton (or state) in Switzerland. Known for its scenic views and local brand of Swiss cheese, Küsendorf is the home of the Ulster Archives, the finest private collection of documents and antiquities in the world.

Built as a temporary haven for Austrian philanthropist Conrad Ulster, the archives eventually became his permanent residence. During the early 1930s, Ulster, an avid collector of rare artefacts, sensed the political instability in his country and realized there was a good chance that his prized library would be seized by the Nazis. To protect himself and his books, he smuggled his collection across the Swiss border in railcars, under thin layers of brown coal, and hid them from public view until after World War Two. He died in 1964 but expressed his thanks to the people of Switzerland by donating his estate to his adopted home town – provided that they keep his collection intact and accessible to the world's best academic minds.

For the past decade, the archives had been run by his grandson Petr Ulster, who had been forced to rebuild several floors after religious zealots tried to burn the place to the ground. Their goal was to destroy ancient documents that threatened the foundation of the Catholic Church.

Thankfully the attack failed, thwarted by two men who Petr considered heroes.

Jonathon Payne and David Jones.

Ulster heard the ringing of his private line and lumbered across his office to answer it. He was a round man in his early forties with a thick brown beard that covered his multiple chins. Yet he came across as boy-like, due to the twinkle in his eye and his enthusiasm for life.

'Hello,' he said with a faint Swiss accent, 'this is Petr.'

'Hello, Petr. This is Jon.'

Ulster broke into a broad smile. 'Jonathon! How glorious it is to hear your voice. I've been thinking of you all day!'

'You have?'

'Indeed I have! Didn't you get my message?'

Payne furrowed his brow. 'What message?'

'The one I left at your home. Isn't that why you're calling?'

'Actually, I'm on the road right now. I'm calling because you called my cell phone.'

Ulster nodded. 'Don't be upset with me, Jonathon,

but I gave your number to a colleague of mine. He needs to chat with you right away and hasn't had much luck. That's why I called — to help you two connect.'

'Why didn't you leave a message?'

'Because I already left one at your house. You know how I hate redundancy.'

Payne paused, thinking things through.

Everything that Ulster said fit the facts. He was the one who called at 9.14. He had given Payne's number to the mystery caller. That meant the 'er' — the syllable that could be heard in the first message — referred to Ulst*er*. Or Pet*r*. Either way, that issue was solved.

However, one thing remained unclear. What did the caller want?

'Jonathon, is something wrong? You don't seem happy with me.' Ulster leaned back in his leather chair, which groaned under his weight. 'Did I overstep my bounds by giving out your number? If so, please forgive me.'

'Petr, it's fine. I'm not mad. Just worried.'

'Worried? About what?'

'Your colleague. What did he want from me?'

'Your advice.'

'My *advice*? On what?'

Ulster lowered his voice to a whisper. 'Smuggling.'

'Smuggling?' Payne asked, surprised. 'What do I know about smuggling?'

'Come now, Jonathon. I know all about your

former career, sneaking behind enemy lines and strangling men in their sleep. Remember, I saw you in action when you protected the archives.'

'*Protecting* is much different than *smuggling*.'

'Maybe so, but you were the first person I thought of when the topic was broached.'

Payne said nothing, not sure if that was a compliment or an insult.

'So,' Ulster asked, 'did Richard ever get a hold of you?'

'Richard who?'

'Richard Byrd. The colleague we're discussing.'

'That depends on your definition. Have I talked to him? No. But he's called me seventeen times in the last twelve hours.'

Ulster laughed. 'Stop exaggerating.'

'I wish I was, but I'm quite serious. Seventeen calls and three messages.'

'Good heavens! I had no idea he would be so intrusive.'

'I don't think *intrusive* is the right word. More like scared. Byrd is *scared* about something.'

'Scared? Why would he be scared?'

'You tell me. What was he trying to smuggle? Drugs? Weapons?'

'Weapons? Heavens no! I would *never* get involved in something like that.'

'Then what? What are we talking about?'

Ulster paused, detecting tension in Payne's voice. He sounded more serious now than two years ago when the archives were under attack. 'Jonathon, what aren't you telling me?'

'No, Petr, what aren't *you* telling *me*? If I'm going to keep your friend alive, I need to know everything – starting at the very beginning.'

'Alive? Who said anything about dead?'

Payne took a deep breath, trying to soften his tone. 'Your friend did. He sent me a text message that said: "This is not a prank. Life or death. Please call at once."'

'Are you serious?'

'Couple that with all his calls and you can see why I'm concerned.'

'Oh my Lord, I had no idea. I just thought he needed your advice.'

'Unfortunately,' Payne said, 'I think he needs more than that.'

'Jon,' Jones whispered, 'put him on speakerphone.'

Payne nodded. 'Petr, I'm going to put you on speakerphone so DJ can listen in.'

'Yes, of course. The more help, the better.'

Payne clicked the button and placed the phone on the desk between him and Jones.

'Hey, Petr,' Jones said, 'how are you?'

'I was much better five minutes ago. Now I'm worried for Richard.'

'Don't worry. We'll get to the bottom of this. But first we need some background info.'

'Whatever you need, just ask.'

'What do you know about him?'

'His name is Richard Byrd. He's an American collector from California. He's visited the archives a number of times during the past few years, spending most of his time with my Greek collection. In return, he loaned us several ancient coins to examine. Lovely items. Just lovely.'

The goal of the Ulster Archives was to foster the concept of sharing when it came to historical research, something of a rarity in academia where experts and collectors tend to hoard things for themselves. According to some estimates, only 15 per cent of the world's most valuable artefacts are displayed in public forums like museums or galleries. The other 85 per cent are kept in private collections or stored in crates for safekeeping. In order to gain access to the archives, a scholar had to bring something of value – either new research or an ancient relic – for his peers to study. Otherwise Ulster wouldn't let him enter the facility.

Jones frowned. 'Wait a second. Did you say Greek?'

'Yes, Greek.'

'Not Russian?'

'Russian? Why would I say Russian?'

Payne answered. 'Because that's where he was calling from.'

'From Russia? He was supposed to be in Greece!'

'Yet he was calling from St Petersburg. We have the phone records to prove it.'

Ulster grimaced, growing more confused by

the minute. 'That doesn't make any sense. The last time we spoke he said he had found a wonderful addition for my Greek collection and wanted to bring it here immediately. The only problem was getting it through customs since the Greek government is notorious for protecting its heritage. That's when he asked me for my advice and I gave him your phone number.'

'When was that?'

'Several days ago. However, earlier today he did leave a message. Thanks to static, it was virtually incomprehensible, but I recognized his voice and heard your name. I couldn't understand anything else. That's one of the reason I gave you a call. To see if you had spoken.'

'And you thought I would help him with smuggling?'

'Jonathon, please keep in mind I'm not talking about stealing or selling items on the black market. I would *never* support either of those activities. I'm talking about smuggling for academic purposes. Without it, we wouldn't know half the things we do about Egypt, Greece, or Rome. Without it, we would still view the Mayans, Incas, and Aztecs as savages, not the innovators that they were. Without it, the Ulster Archives never would have existed because the Nazis would have seized my grandfather's collection before he smuggled it out of Austria. And if that had happened, I would have been denied the greatest pleasure of my life!'

Ulster paused, trying to calm himself. 'I realize smuggling is an ugly word. But in the world of antiquities, it is often a necessary evil to unlock the mysteries of the past.'

I 2

Winter Palace
St Petersburg, Russia

The boat was named the *Meteor*. It was tied to the
quay on the Neva River behind the Winter Palace.
Stretching along the waterfront, the green and white
fortress had nearly 2,000 windows and looked as
though it had been built in France. In fact, much of
St Petersburg looked French. This was a Western
European city that happened to be in Russia.

On any other occasion, Allison Taylor would have
enjoyed the scenery. She would have stopped to take
pictures of the palace where Catherine the Great
once lived. She would have roamed the halls of the
Hermitage Museum, admiring the art of Michel-
angelo, Monet, Rembrandt, and Van Gogh. She
would have sat in the palace square, watching all the
other tourists as they gazed at the Alexander Column
in the centre of the plaza.

But today, none of those things were possible.

Not if she wanted to live.

Running to the ticket office at the end of the
platform, her blonde hair fluttered in the breeze. She

was an attractive woman in her mid-twenties with eyes the colour of sapphires. In a city where Nordic models roamed the streets, she definitely fit in. She was tall and lean and striking.

She was also trembling with fear.

She bought her ticket at the last possible moment to make sure no one was following. She scanned the crowd on the long wharf, searching for anyone who looked suspicious before making her way to the boat. She needed to reach her destination before dark, and this was her best option. No stops. No traffic. No distractions of any kind. She knew her intellect was the key to survival. She had to stay sharp or she'd be dead before dawn.

Taking a deep breath, Allison stepped on board and refused to sit down until the crew pushed away from the shore. She stood there, restless, nervously biting her lip, expecting someone to burst from the crowd and jump aboard the *Meteor* before she had a chance to jump off. But that didn't happen. The motor sprang to life, and within seconds she could see water churning behind them as they slowly picked up speed. Only then did she search for a seat.

She found an empty row in the back of the crowded hydrofoil. It gave her a great view of her fellow passengers as they glided down the Neva River through the south-west corner of the city. In forty minutes they would reach the Gulf of Finland, an important arm of the Baltic Sea.

It separated Russia from Scandinavia, and Allison from her freedom.

At least that's what she had been told.

Seventeen miles later, the *Meteor* arrived at the lower park of the Peterhof. Dozens of tourists stood near the water's edge, patiently waiting for their return trip to St Petersburg. Allison eyed them suspiciously before she left the boat and walked across the long pier towards the wooded shore. She was wearing blue jeans, a T-shirt, and a white blouse, a simple outfit that would help her blend in with all the people in the park. It would be closing shortly and, when it did, she hoped to disappear into the crowd.

Known as the Russian Versailles for its similarities to the château in France, the Peterhof was a series of palaces, fountains, and gardens that had been built as the summer residence of Peter the Great. Designed in 1714, the most remarkable feature of the sprawling grounds was the central role of water – whether it was the sea that bordered half the complex, or the massive canal that bisected it. Allison had seen pictures of the Peterhof when she was in junior high and had marvelled at its opulence, but nothing had prepared her for the things she was about to see.

Her first glimpse of the grounds came from the boat platform near the *Meteor*. She was walking across a concrete bridge when she noticed movement out of the corner of her eye. Paranoid, she glanced in that direction and saw a large pair of geysers spouting water on both sides of the channel that ran from the palace to the edge of the bay. Behind them was another pair of fountains. And another. And another. In fact, there were so many fountains blending in with each other that she was unable to count them from where she was standing.

Of course, none of that mattered when she spotted the grand palace. It was painted bright yellow and sat on top of a small hill that appeared to hover above the fountains. From where she was standing, the hill seemed to be moving, as if the ground itself was caving in under the weight of the building. Intrigued, she walked closer, taking the path on the right-hand side of the wide canal. A thick wall of pine trees blocked her view of the fountains, but she heard their constant trickling. The sound was soft and reassuring, somehow calming her nerves.

When Allison emerged from the grove, she was surprised by the sight. The section of hill that she thought was swaying was not a hill at all. Instead, it was the grand cascade, a series of seven water steps flanking both sides of a large grotto with water flowing from one level to the next. Each of the platforms was decorated by low-relief sculptures, gilded statues, and water spouts – all of them facing the Samson fountain that dominated the foreground. The gold statue in the centre depicted Samson ripping open the jaws of a lion, symbolizing Russia's victory over Sweden in the Great Northern War. A geyser from the lion's mouth shot water sixty-five feet into the air.

Remarkably, none of the Peterhof fountains were operated by mechanical pumps. Peter the Great chose this location for his palace because of several spring-fed reservoirs to the south. In 1721 a canal system was built so water could flow by gravity to large storage pools. When the pressure was released, water rushed through the pipes with so much force that it erupted through the spouts, feeding the dozens of fountains all over the grounds.

Allison watched the flight of the water as it left the lion's mouth. It sailed high above the balustrade and fell back to its circular basin. The resulting mist, carried by the light breeze that blew in from the bay, drifted towards the spacious patio at the rear of the palace.

And that's where she spotted him.

He was standing next to a decorative vase perched above the grotto. Just standing there, staring at her, waiting for her arrival. The instant she saw him she wanted to wave, but knew it was too dangerous. No need to attract attention – someone might be watching. Instead, she studied her surroundings, searching all the nearby faces for anyone who looked suspicious.

After several seconds, she breathed a sigh of relief.

As far as she could tell, the coast was clear.

The grounds extended in all directions, a labyrinth of sidewalks, gardens, and cul-de-sacs. Without a map, she didn't know which way to go, so she waited for him to decide.

It was a decision that would never happen.

Despite the distance, she saw the gun before the trigger was pulled. It emerged out of nowhere like a magic trick. One moment it wasn't there, and the next it was.

But the barrel wasn't pointed at her. It was aimed at the man she was there to meet.

Before Allison could react, his head exploded in a burst of pink mist. The roar of gunfire was muffled by a silencer. The first sound she heard was the loud splash as the man tumbled over the railing and landed in the upper fountain. He was dead before he hit the water.

It took a moment for things to sink in. But once they did, chaos erupted at the Peterhof.

Parents were screaming. Children were crying. Tourists were running everywhere.

And Allison wanted to join them. She wanted to sprint towards the exit and forget everything that had happened – like a bad dream that faded away when she woke up. Yet her legs refused to move. So she sank to her knees and tried to breathe as she stared at the waterfall.

Seconds later, the trickling water turned blood red from the corpse of Richard Byrd.

13

After Ulster's lecture on smuggling, Payne felt like a total hypocrite. He had always viewed smugglers as modern-day pirates, hardened criminals with rusty boats and no morals. Ruthless men who rarely shaved and reeked of sweat. The real scum of the earth.

Yet according to Ulster's definition, Payne was a smuggler himself.

Excluding his stint in the military – when he and Jones had frequently shipped men, weapons, and supplies across enemy lines – Payne had been involved in two recent smuggling operations, although he hadn't viewed himself as a smuggler at the time of the incidents.

The first had occurred shortly after he met Ulster. Payne and Jones had uncovered a plot to rewrite the history of Jesus Christ, and in the process they had recovered several religious artefacts that had no rightful owner. Since they didn't want the relics locked away in the Vatican basement, they had smuggled them out of Italy and delivered them to the Ulster Archives.

The second had been even more dramatic. Payne and Jones had snuck into the Muslim-only city of Mecca to thwart a terrorist attack and had ended up rescuing an American archaeologist who had discovered an Islamic treasure the Saudi government knew nothing about. Worried that the Arabs would claim it for themselves, Payne and Jones had smuggled it out of the Middle East and donated it to Ulster's facility where it could be examined by experts in that field.

Ultimately, that's one of the reasons why Payne never viewed himself as a smuggler.

He never stole anything. He never sold the treasures. And most importantly, he always donated them to academia instead of keeping them for himself.

'You know,' Jones said after their call to Ulster, 'we aren't exactly angels.'

'I never claimed to be.'

Jones smiled. 'Yet you want to be perceived that way.'

Payne shrugged. Deep down inside, he knew Jones was right. From the moment in the eighth grade when he lost his parents to a drunk driver, Payne had always craved the approval of others. It was his way of making up for the love and attention he had been denied. His paternal grandfather had done a wonderful job of raising him after the accident, yet due to his duties as the founder and CEO of Payne Industries, he simply wasn't round as often as Payne would have liked.

Instead of sulking or rebelling like teenagers are apt to do, Payne had poured his energy into every talent he had – academics, athletics, martial arts, and, eventually, the military – hoping his accomplishments would get him the positive attention he needed.

In the end, it made him a better person.

'So,' Jones wondered, 'how do you want to handle this?'

'Not much we can do from here. Not until Byrd calls back.'

'And then?'

'Then it depends on him. If he seems legitimate, I say we bail him out. I mean, a friend of Petr's is a friend of ours. On the other hand, if he seems shady in any way, I say we wish him well but tell him we're on vacation.'

Jones nodded. 'Agreed.'

'In the meantime, why don't you dig up some background on him?'

'I'm way ahead of you.' He turned his laptop towards Payne and pointed at the screen. 'As soon as Petr mentioned his name, I ran an internet search and came up with a few articles. It seems the two of you have something in common.'

'Oh yeah? What's that?'

'You both come from money.'

Payne sat at the hotel desk and studied the image on the screen.

Richard Byrd was a handsome man in his late forties. He had sandy brown hair that was grey at the temples and a deep Californian tan. In the picture he was standing on the deck of his yacht, *The Odyssey*, while Catalina Island loomed in the distance.

He looked cool, confident, and in total control – the exact opposite of how he had sounded on the phone.

Underneath there was a short biography, detailing his academic and professional careers. He had graduated from Stanford with a degree in history but never worked in that field. Instead, he had taken control of his family's fortune, which had been amassed during the gold rush of the 1800s, and multiplied it many times over in the banking business. According to this website, he had retired a few years ago to pursue outside interests, although none were listed.

'Let me guess,' Payne said, 'his hobbies include travelling, antiques, and Greece.'

'Is it just me, or does he look like a catalogue model?'

Payne smiled and handed the computer back to Jones. 'Enough with the fluff. Why don't you get some dirt on this guy? Anything that might suggest criminal activities. I want to know as much as possible before he calls again.'

As if on cue, Payne's phone started to ring on the nearby table.

'Speak of the devil.'

'Don't answer it,' Jones shouted as he scrambled for his laptop bag. He quickly unzipped a side pocket and pulled out a short black cord that he plugged into the back of his computer. 'Give me your phone.'

Payne did as he was told and watched Jones attach it to the cord. This would allow them to listen through the laptop's speakers while recording the call as a digital file.

Meanwhile, the phone kept ringing. Three rings, then four.

'Are we good?' Payne asked.

'Yeah, we're good.'

Payne took a deep breath and answered the call. 'Hello?'

A loud blast of static filled the room. Jones leaned forward and lowered the volume on his computer. It helped with the sound level but didn't help with the clarity. Static still filled the line.

'Hello?' Payne repeated.

There was a two-second pause before they heard a response.

'Hello,' said the voice. It was soft and meek and feminine.

Payne glanced at the number. It was restricted, just like before. 'Who is this?'

She ignored his question. After another pause, she said, 'Is this Jonathon?'

'Yes. This is Jon. Who is this?'

Static filled the line for a few seconds. Followed by a gasp and a sob.

'Are you all right?' Payne asked, keeping his tone as calm as possible.

'Is this Jonathon?' she repeated.

'Yes. This is Jonathon. Who is *this*?'

A slight delay then an answer: 'This is Allison.'

'Allison who?'

'Taylor.'

Payne looked at Jones, who shrugged. Neither of them knew who she was.

'Allison, where are you calling from?'

A few seconds of static. 'Russia. I'm calling from Russia.'

'Are you with Richard?'

She let out a soft wail. No talking, just crying.

'Allison, where's Richard?'

A slight pause, then a thunderbolt. 'Richard's dead.'

'What?' Payne said, stunned. 'What do you mean?'

'They killed him. They killed Richard.'

'Who is *they*?'

'I don't know. But they killed him.'

Payne paused, not sure what to ask. 'Allison, how did you know Richard?'

Static for a few seconds. 'I was helping him.'

'With what?'

'His trip.'

'And you're sure he's dead?'

'They shot him in the head. He fell in the fountain.'

'Allison, where are you in Russia?'

'St Petersburg.'

'Are you an American?'

'Yes.'

'Good. That's good. Then I want you to go to the consulate. There's an American Consulate in St Petersburg. If you go there, they'll protect you.'

She sobbed. 'I can't. Richard said we couldn't.'

'Why not?'

'I don't know . . . But he said we *couldn't* go there . . . He said if anything happened to him that I was supposed to call. He bought me a phone just so I could call you . . . He programmed your number into the phone . . . It's the only number I've got.'

Payne swore under his breath, not sure what to do. Byrd was dead. Allison was freaking out. And she refused to go to the only safe place he could think of. Back in the day, he used to know several places around the city where operatives could hide in an emergency, but he hadn't been to any of them in years. So there was no way of knowing if they were still in play.

'Jon,' Jones whispered, 'if they killed Byrd, Petr could be in trouble.'

Payne covered the phone. 'Explain.'

'Byrd went to the Ulster Archives on several occasions to do research. Who knows what he found there? If these people are thorough, they might go there next.'

Payne nodded in understanding. Suddenly they had little choice in the matter. They had to get involved to protect their friend.

'Allison,' he said with a firm voice, 'listen to me. Everything is going to be fine. Do you believe me when I say that?'

'They killed him,' she said meekly.

'I know that, Allison. It must be tough for you. But let me tell you a secret. Do you know *why* Richard

88

told you to call me? He knew if you needed my help, I would give it to you. And trust me when I say this, I'm a very helpful guy.'

Static filled the line. Several seconds' worth.

'Allison? Are you still there?'

Another lengthy pause. Finally, she asked, 'How can you help me?'

'It's pretty simple. I'm coming to get you out.'

14

While Andropoulos sealed the videotapes in evidence bags, Dial strolled into the main chapel and searched for the second camera. He spotted it in the rear of the church, right above the donation box.

Trying not to draw attention to himself, Dial casually leaned against the back wall and glanced upwards. The wire was attached to a wooden beam in the same fashion as in the gift shop. Except in this case, the viewing angle was slightly more favourable.

With a little luck, they might actually have footage of the killers.

Ideally, Dial would have viewed the videos right away, but considering their current location, that was an impossibility. Instead, they would have to wait until they drove to the station house in Kalampáka or got to a secondary location like Dial's hotel. The truth was Dial didn't care where he watched it, as long as he got to see the recordings as soon as possible.

A few minutes later, Andropoulos walked into the church and approached a uniformed officer who looked even younger than he did. The kid snapped to attention and listened intently as Andropoulos handed him the tapes and gave him a series of orders in Greek. When their conversation ended, the kid hustled out through the same door Andropoulos had entered.

Dial smiled, watching all of this from afar. 'Marcus!'

He spotted Dial near the back table and walked towards him. 'Yes, sir?'

'What was that all about?'

Andropoulos blushed. 'Did I do something wrong?'

'That depends. What in the hell did you just do?'

'I thought someone should view the tapes immediately. And since I can't leave here yet, I asked another officer to look at them.'

'That's what I thought you did.'

'Did I mess up?'

Dial shook his head. 'Not at all. In fact, that's the most impressive thing you've done all night. You just put justice ahead of your own ambition. That's pretty rare in a case like this.'

Andropoulos breathed a sigh of relief. 'So I didn't mess up?'

Dial laughed. 'Let's walk outside. I want to discuss the crime scene.'

Dial didn't speak again until they were outside, far away from the other officers. At this stage of the game, he still wasn't allowed to investigate the scene – since he lacked proof that multiple member states were involved – and would be forced to leave if he overstepped his bounds. Of course, it wouldn't be the first time that had happened. Turf wars were common in his business, one where egos were easily bruised and jurisdictions were guarded like jealous lovers.

For the time being, the local police were in charge of the monastery. Things would stay that way until the Greek government decided the locals couldn't handle it – or *shouldn't* handle it – and the Inspector General for Northern Greece showed up with a team of national experts from the Forensic Division and the Special Violent Crime Squad. After that, it was only a matter of time before Dial was thanked for his interest in the case then driven to the airport. Then again, Dial wouldn't blame the inspector. If Dial was in charge of the case, he wouldn't want an outsider lurking around, either. Especially someone who wanted to take control of things.

'So,' Dial asked Andropoulos, hoping to bond with his liaison, 'where did you learn English? Other than a slight accent, you speak it better than most Americans.'

The Greek beamed with pride. 'I learned English when I was very young. My parents owned a small café in Kastraki, and I worked there as a child. Half our customers were tourists who could not speak Greek. If I did not know English, I could not do my job.'

'And where did your parents learn it?'

'From James Bond.'

Dial grimaced. 'James Bond?'

'You know, 007.'

'Yeah,' Dial assured him, 'I know all about James Bond. I just don't understand your comment. How did he teach them English?'

'You do not know? They filmed *For Your Eyes Only* in Metéora. The cast and crew were in Kalampáka and Kastraki for weeks. This was in 1981, before I was born, but Roger Moore ate in my parents' café on many nights. My mother said he was a very nice man and so good-looking. I am told my father was very jealous, but he said nothing since Roger Moore has a licence to kill.'

Andropoulos laughed at his own joke. 'I think that is why I joined police. I wanted to carry a gun so I could impress my father.'

'Hold up,' Dial ordered. He was a James Bond fan but couldn't think of any scenes that took place in a monastery. 'Refresh my memory. What was the plot of that movie?'

'James Bond was searching for a weapon that was stolen by Greek villain. Holy Trinity was his secret lair, and Bond had to climb up the cliff to kill him.'

Dial nodded. 'Okay. *Now* I remember it. No wonder I had a sense of déjà vu when I first arrived. I had seen Metéora on the big screen.'

'I love American films. I watch them all the time. They help me with my English.'

'What about your French?'

Andropoulos shook his head. 'No. They do not help me with my French.'

Dial rolled his eyes. 'Yeah, Marcus, I know they don't help you with your French. I'm asking if you *know* any French.'

'Only a few words. Why do you ask?'

'Because Interpol is located in France. It might be helpful if you spoke the language.'

'What are you saying? You think I might be good for headquarters?'

'Not with that haircut, I don't. Or with that suit.' Dial tried not to smile or it would ruin his hazing. 'What happened? Did you grow a foot since this morning?'

Andropoulos was about to defend himself when Dial cut him off.

'On the other hand, I have been impressed with your work. If you keep this up, I might be willing to pass your name to someone in Lyons. No promises, though.'

'Yes,' he said excitedly, 'I understand.'

'Of course, you can help your cause even further if you do well on your assignment. Weren't you supposed to assess the crime scene?'

'Yes, sir. I studied the layout of the church and all the evidence. If we go back inside, I can explain my theories.'

Dial turned away from the young cop and leaned against the railing, staring at the fog below. Somewhere down there was a second crime scene – one he hadn't had a chance to visit because of the darkness and the treacherous terrain. 'Tell me about the bodies.'

'The bodies?'

'You know, the things that *used* to be people.'

Andropoulos frowned. 'But they weren't found inside the church.'

'What's your point?'

'You said you didn't like to hear about evidence until you've seen it for yourself.'

'Tell me, Marcus, are the bodies still down there?'

'Not any more. We recovered them this afternoon.'

'Then how in the hell am I supposed to see them at the scene?' The question was rhetorical, but Dial let it linger for several seconds, hoping to unnerve Andropoulos. 'Once again, if you don't mind, please tell me about the bodies.'

The young Greek took a deep breath, trying to calm himself. 'Villagers found eight bodies on the rocks below and called us in Kalampáka. Because of their clothes, we think all of them were monks. We are still trying to get names and backgrounds on seven of them. The eighth victim was the caretaker of Holy Trinity. He was the only one we found intact.'

'What do you mean by *intact*?'

'He was the only one who had a head.'

Dial glanced at Andropoulos to see if he was joking. 'As in they fell off when they landed?'

'As in they were cut off before they were dumped.'

'*Really?* I didn't know that.' Dial considered it for a moment. 'Did you find the heads?'

'Not yet. But we are looking for them.'

'And you're sure they were cut off while the monks were alive?'

'Yes, sir. That's why there was so much blood on the altar.'

'What about the rest of their bodies? Any missing appendages – besides their heads?'

'Some were mangled. But we doubt it was the killers.'

Dial glanced at him. 'Birds?'

'Wolves.'

'Great,' Dial muttered. Half the crime scenes in rural areas were ruined by wildlife. 'How badly were the bodies mauled?'

'Not too bad. We can still get fingerprints from all the victims.'

'What about their ages? Young, old, somewhere in-between?'

'A mixture of all three.'

'Any signs of torture? Burn marks, tape residue, water in their lungs?'

'Sir?' he asked, confused.

Dial paused. 'Tell me, why did they cut off their heads?'

'To kill them.'

'I doubt it. They could have done that by throwing their asses off the cliff. Or slicing their throats. Or a hundred different methods. Instead, they took the time to sever their heads. Why would someone do that?'

Andropoulos pondered the question. 'Intimidation?'

'For what reason?'

'To get answers.'

Dial nodded. 'That would be my guess. Which is why I asked about signs of torture. Different groups prefer different techniques. I was hoping I would recognize their signature.'

'Unfortunately, nothing stands out. Other than the head thing.'

'Which is a pretty good method if you ask me. I mean, if I saw my colleagues killed one by one, I'd be tempted to talk. The question is, about what?'

'Sorry. I don't know.'

'Don't worry. I don't know, either. But it's something to keep in mind as this case develops.'

Andropoulos pulled out a small tablet and jotted down a few notes in Greek. When he was done, he looked at Dial. 'Sir, may I ask you a question? Why would they take the heads with them?'

Dial shrugged. 'You tell me. Are there any customs or superstitions I should know about?'

He gave it some thought. 'Great Metéoron, the largest of the local monasteries, has a bone room where they display the heads of the monks who founded it several centuries ago.'

Dial stared at him like he was crazy. 'Are you serious?'

'Yes, sir. Dozens of skulls line their wooden shelves. But I don't remember why.'

'A room full of monk skulls? That's kind of warped, if you ask me. Then again, I've never been a big fan of religious symbolism. Most of that shit goes over my head. Pardon the pun.'

Andropoulos smiled. 'If you like, I can call the monastery and ask if there are any traditions that I am unaware of. Perhaps one of the older monks will know.'

Dial nodded. 'Speaking of old monks, I'd like to amend something you told me about the bodies. We know the identity of two victims, not one.'

'Sir?'

'One was the caretaker of Holy Trinity. Another was the abbot of Metéora.'

'The abbot is dead? Who told you so?'

'Nicolas, the monk I introduced you to.'

Andropoulos shook his head. 'Sorry, sir. That is incorrect. We have only identified *one* victim. We know nothing about the abbot.'

'As of when?'

'As of right now. I was briefed by the other officer when I gave him the videotapes.'

15

Leaving the monastery, Andropoulos led Dial through the dark terrain as they walked to the road in silence. Dial was tired from his trip and sore from all the climbing, but the main reason he kept to himself was his confusion.

How had Nicolas known about the death of the abbot before the police?

It was a question that Dial had wanted to ask before he left the monastery for the night. Unfortunately, by the time he got his facts straight, the light under Nicolas' door was no longer visible. Reluctant to wake the old man on such a traumatic day, Dial decided it would be best to wait until morning.

Besides, he had other things to worry about – like the evidence on the videotapes.

Dial slid into the passenger seat of the Citroën Xsara, the small hatchback that was used by the Greek police. White with blue stripes and a turbo-diesel engine, it wasn't a bad car, but it couldn't compete with the gas-guzzling Crown Victoria that Dial used to drive when he worked in the States. That thing roared when someone punched the gas. The Xsara barely purred. Then again, there was no way anyone could drive a Crown Vic on the mountainous roads of central Greece. Too many hairpin turns. Too many narrow streets. Both of which were on display during their drive to the station house.

Andropoulos sped through the curves at top speed, sometimes drifting on to the pavement in order to improve his angle for the turn ahead. Occasionally he drove on the wrong side of the road, which he felt was well within his rights since he was an officer of the law and knew the hills better than the goat herders who lived on them. And Dial was savvy enough not to complain, knowing full well that most Europeans felt traffic laws were for wimps. Still, Dial thought he was going to die so many times during the trip that he was tempted to update his will.

When they reached Kalampáka twenty minutes later, Dial got out of the police car and realized that he was no longer tired – thanks to the adrenaline that flowed through his body like ten cups of coffee and a case of Red Bull.

'Come,' Andropoulos said as he walked towards the back door, 'let's go inside.'

The station house was small but modern, much newer than Dial had thought it would be in such an ancient town. Most officers were off duty or examining the crime scene at Metéora, so the duo had the back conference room to themselves – except for the young officer who had been entrusted with the videotapes. His name was Costas, and they found him sitting in front of a television with a remote control in his hand and a grin on his face.

'Any luck?' Andropoulos asked.

'Yes,' Costas said with a thick accent. 'Very good!'

'You'll have to excuse his English. He's still learn-ing the language.'

Dial shrugged. 'He can use Greek if he likes as long as you translate for me.'

Andropoulos shook his head. 'No. He must learn to speak properly. It is the only way he'll get better.'

'Yes! I speak good!'

Dial smiled. 'Did you find anything on the tape?'

'Yes! You like. It is good!'

Costas hit rewind until the VCR display matched the first number he had written on his notepad. He double-checked the minutes, then hit PLAY. 'You watch! You like!'

The video was filmed from an elevated angle in the main church. It focused on the poor box and the wooden table that sat at the rear of the chapel. There was no sound. Dial stared at the screen, hoping to spot something of value, but saw nothing. Five seconds passed, then ten. Finally, after seventeen seconds, he saw a single shadow. It crept along the back wall then lingered in the centre of the frame, just long enough for Dial to study it.

'Freeze it!' he ordered.

Costas hit PAUSE and the shadow froze against the stone wall.

Dial and Andropoulos walked closer to the tele-vision. Both men stared at the image until it was seared into their brains. Dial said, 'Something looks wrong.'

Andropoulos agreed. He reached forward and touched the screen, tracing his finger along the top of the shadow. 'The shape of his head. It is too big.'

'Exactly. Like he's wearing a hood.'

'Me hit play,' Costas blurted. 'You see more! You like!'

Dial glanced at him and nodded. The young cop was excited about something, and Dial was anxious to see what it was.

Nearly a minute later, chaos erupted on the screen. Multiple shadows, one blending in with the next, rushed along the back wall like a bloodthirsty horde. Dial stared at the action, trying to count the shadows, trying to make sense of things, but they moved so quickly it was impossible.

'Freeze it,' he said.

But Costas ignored Dial's order. 'Wait! You like!'

Dial focused on the TV, not sure what he was waiting for. When the damn thing appeared, it happened so suddenly that he almost missed it.

Caught up in the excitement, Costas yelled, 'I freeze!'

Then he hit PAUSE by himself.

Andropoulos stood still, his mouth slightly agape, like he couldn't believe their luck.

Dial was just as thrilled, but didn't get lost in the moment. Instead, he calmly pulled out his camera phone and snapped a photo of the screen. He wanted a copy of the image just in case the tape was destroyed or he was removed from the investigation.

'So,' Dial asked, 'have you seen one of those before?'

Andropoulos nodded. 'In a museum. Not at a crime scene.'

'Anything you can tell me about it?'

'No, sir. History isn't my strength.'

'Mine, either. What about you, Costas?'

Costas smiled at Dial and said, 'I freeze!'

'Sorry. He's confused,' Andropoulos apologized. He rattled off several questions in Greek, which Costas answered while shaking his head. 'He knows nothing.'

Dial moved closer to the screen, focusing on the image. It was a silver sword, approximately three feet in length. The type of weapon that had been used in Ancient Greece. The handle was a different colour than the blade – maybe bronze or gold – though it was tough to tell for sure in the dim light of the church. The same thing applied to the man who held it. Only his hand and wrist were visible, but he looked Caucasian or Mediterranean. Definitely not black.

'Can you play it slow?' Dial asked.

'Slow,' Costas echoed as he clicked the remote control.

The image ticked by one frame at a time, yet nothing new revealed itself. Within seconds, the blade swung out of view as the warrior walked away from the camera.

'Is that all?' Dial wondered.

'No!' Costas assured him. 'Me hit play. You see more. You like!'

'Go ahead. I want to see why you're so excited.'

Two minutes later, Dial got his answer – one that was completely surreal.

From the left side of the screen, a muscular man walked into view and stood next to the rear table. On his head he wore a full-sized bronze helmet that covered his entire face except for his eyes and mouth. Guarding his nose was a long metal strip that started at his forehead and widened near his nostrils, hiding his eyes in shadows like two hollow sockets.

The effect was more than menacing.

A bronze breastplate hung from his shoulders, protecting his ribs and chest but not his brawny arms. This gave him freedom of movement, allowing him to swing his sword from side to side or reach the silver dagger he had tucked in his leather sheath. An empty scabbard clung to his back, waiting to be reunited with the weapon he held in front of him like a statue.

A blade that didn't move. A blade that didn't tremble.

Like he had been training for this mission his entire life and couldn't be stopped.

Somehow that was the scariest thing of all.

16

MacDill AFB
Tampa, Florida

Payne and Jones made the necessary arrangements as they drove to MacDill AFB. A cargo flight was leaving within the hour that would fly them to Ramstein Air Base in the German state of Rhineland-Palatinate where they could catch a plane to any country in Europe.

It was one of the perks of being special advisors to the Pentagon.

From there, they would travel to Kaiserslautern, approximately ten miles from the base. Known as 'K-Town' to American personnel, it was a city of 100,000 people and could provide them with anything they required: weapons, clothes, or a good German lager. They had been there several times over the years and knew the layout of the city. The only question was which of their contacts they wanted to involve in such a hastily planned trip to Russia.

That was one of the things they would discuss during their transatlantic flight.

Another was Allison Taylor.

She was the biggest unknown in a mission that

was full of them. They had gleaned some information during their initial conversation with her, but when it came right down to it, they knew very little about her background – other than her supposed connection to Richard Byrd.

Hoping to learn more, Payne called Petr Ulster and asked if Byrd had ever brought his assistant to the archives. Ulster could remember three different females during the last year. All of them were young. All of them were attractive. But none of them was named Allison.

'You know,' Jones said from the back of the cargo plane, 'there's no telling what we're getting into, other than it's dangerous and probably illegal.'

'I know. But I'm a sucker for a crying woman.'

'Yeah. Me, too. I just want to kiss their boo-boos and make them feel better.'

Payne laughed. 'Define boo-boo.'

'Not a chance,' Jones said with a smile. 'Anyway, the point I'm trying to make is this: I'm more concerned than normal.'

'Why's that?'

'Why? Because I can't get arrested in Russia. Maybe you can with your big muscles and your white skin, but I can't. I mean, there's a drink called a Black Russian but, as far as I know, that's the only black thing they've got. And I want to keep it that way.'

'No problem,' Payne assured him. 'If the cops are called, I'll shoot you myself.'

'I'm serious, Jon. I don't want to be the black Yuri Gagarin.'

'What in the hell does that mean? You don't want to be a cosmonaut?'

'No, I don't want to be a guinea pig. There's no telling what tests they'll run on my black ass if I get caught. Not to mention everything else that's done to a man's ass in prison.'

Payne laughed, knowing full well that Jones was joking about Russia. In fact, just about the only time race was mentioned by either of them was when they were joking round.

And it had been that way from the very beginning.

They had met a decade earlier when they were handpicked to run the MANIACs. After a rocky start – mostly because Payne attended Annapolis and Jones attended the Air Force Academy – they became good friends. That bond had strengthened over time, a common occurrence when two soldiers watched each other's backs in countries all over the world. Eventually it evolved into something stronger than friendship. They became brothers.

A few years ago, Payne's grandfather passed away, giving him the controlling interest in the family business. It had grown from a one-man shop near the Ohio River into a multinational corporation called Payne Industries. At the time, Payne hadn't been ready to leave the service, but out of love and respect for the man who raised him, he retired from the military and moved back home to fulfil his familial duties.

To help with his adjustment to civilian life, Payne convinced Jones to retire and move to Pittsburgh. He sweetened the deal by giving Jones office space in the Payne Industries complex and loaning him enough start-up capital to open his own business. It had always been Jones' dream to run a detective agency, and Payne had the means to help. So Payne figured, why not? After the death of Grandpa Payne, Jones was the only family that Payne had left.

Not surprisingly, the pace of their life had slowed significantly in recent years. Other than the rare occasions when Payne helped Jones with one of his cases, the only time they got to carry guns and have some fun was when they went out on their own.

And truth be told, even though they hated the circumstances of this particular adventure – i.e. the death of Richard Byrd – both of them loved the adrenaline rush of a freelance mission. Not only did it get their juices flowing, it helped them stay sharp in case the government ever needed their talents for a special operation.

Sitting in the belly of the cargo plane, Jones couldn't plug his computer into a phone line, which meant he wasn't able to do the research he required. Since they were cruising 30,000 feet above the Atlantic, the odds of getting a wireless connection were pretty damn slim.

One of the most important skills in the Special Forces was the ability to adapt. Whether it was hand-to-hand combat or the planning of a mission, a soldier had to make the best of a bad situation or he wouldn't survive very long. Knowing how much work needed to be done before they landed in Germany, Jones decided to contact one of the few people he could count on.

'Research,' said his friend as he answered his phone at the Pentagon.

'Hey, Randy. How's life?'

Raskin groaned. 'It would be much easier if you and Jon forgot my number.'

Jones smiled while adjusting his bulky headset. Without it, he couldn't hear anything in the back of the noisy plane. 'Truth be told, I didn't even dial your number. I simply asked the pilot to patch me through to the smartest guy at the Pentagon, and you answered the phone.'

'The smartest guy at the Pentagon, huh? Talk about faint praise.'

'At least it was a compliment. When Jon calls you, he insults you for ten minutes.'

'That's a very good point. I'm in counselling because of him.' Raskin laughed at his own joke. 'So what do you need from me now? Does your Russian friend need more help?'

'Actually,' Jones said in a serious tone, 'we think he's dead.'

'Oh, man. I'm sorry.'

'That's all right. We never met the guy. He was more of a friend of a friend.'

'Even so, I'm sorry for the loss. What can I do to help?'

'At this point we're looking for confirmation of his death. As you know, he was calling us from St Petersburg, but we never talked to him. According to one source, he was shot and killed in some kind of fountain. Can you check to see if anything matches that description?'

'Do you have a name?'

'Richard Byrd. Although he might have been using an alias.'

Raskin went to work on his keyboard, quickly searching the main criminal database in Russia. Insiders called it Kremlin.com because its real name was written in Cyrillic and impossible to pronounce. 'Bad news, I'm afraid.'

'No luck?'

'Just the opposite. I found something that matches your description. White male, mid- to late forties, discovered in one of the Peterhof fountains. Single shot to the head.'

'Damn,' Jones muttered. He glanced at Payne and made a slashing motion across his neck. Payne nodded in understanding. 'Was he identified?'

'Not according to this. Then again, that could mean a number of things. Maybe they're holding his identity until they notify his family. Or maybe the killer took his wallet. The truth is I have no way of knowing without calling them myself.'

'Which is something we don't want you to do. We need to keep a low profile on this.'

'I figured as much.'

'Next question. Can you check on Byrd's movement during the past few months?'

'Hold on. Different database.' Twenty seconds passed before Raskin spoke again. 'No visas listed for Russia, but he visited Greece, Italy, Germany, and several other countries in Europe. I can send you a list if you want.'

'Go ahead. But I won't have access until we land.'

'Where are you headed?'

'Ramstein.'

'Then what?'

'A rendezvous in Russia.'

'Sounds romantic.'

'I wish.'

'In that case, you should tell Jon how you really feel.'

Jones laughed. 'Damn, Randy! For you, that was pretty funny.'

'Thanks. Wait. What did you mean by that?'

'I'll tell you later. First, I have one more question. I need some background information on an American named Allison Taylor. Middle name and home town unknown. Current employer is believed to be Richard Byrd. At least until a few hours ago.'

'Hold on. That's *another* database.'

Jones figured it would be. 'Out of curiosity, how many databases do you have?'

'Let me put it to you this way. I have a database to keep track of my databases.'

Jones whistled, impressed. 'Seriously, Randy, I don't know how you do it.'

'Actually, it's pretty simple. I'm the smartest guy in the Pentagon, remember?'

'That's right. I forgot.'

Raskin smiled as he continued to type. A few seconds later, he found the information he was looking for. 'Okay, here you go. Allison Renee Taylor . . . Born in California . . . Graduated from Stanford . . . Single . . . Valid driver's licence . . . Hot as *hell*! Seriously, you should see her photo. She even looks great on her ID.'

'Send it to me. The highest resolution possible.'

'Done.'

'What about employment? Any connection to Byrd?'

'Duh! That's how I found her so fast. He filed a single document with the IRS. A personal services contract. Whatever that means.'

'Anything else?'

'Not that I can find. Then again, I can't stop staring at her picture. It's really strange. No matter where I move, it's like her eyes are following me.'

Jones laughed. 'Damn! How much caffeine have you had today?'

'Define *today*.'

He laughed again. 'Another all-nighter?'

'Another all-weeker. You know me, I never leave my desk.'

'That's one of the reasons we love you. Your dedication to your country.'

'That and the fact I do your dirty work for free.'

Jones nodded in agreement. 'Yep. That too.'

'Okay, chief, I gotta jet. But send me a postcard from Siberia.'

'Not funny,' Jones said. 'Not funny at all.'

17

Monday, 19 May
Kalampáka, Greece

The phone rang at the crack of dawn, roughly an hour before Nick Dial had planned to wake up. He rubbed his eyes, rolled over in the hotel bed, and checked his caller ID. It was Henri Toulon, the Assistant Director of the Homicide Division, calling from Interpol Headquarters in France.

If it had been anyone else, Dial would have let it go to voicemail. But since he had been trying to reach Toulon for the better part of a day, he decided to answer the call.

'Hello,' Dial said with sleep in his throat.

Toulon spoke with a French accent. '*Bonjour*, Mr Boss-Man. Did I wake you?'

'You know you did.'

'*Oui*, I know. That is why I called. Just to wake you. My entire day revolves round Nick. *Bonjour, bonjour, bonjour!*'

Dial grinned at the sarcasm. 'Let me guess. You're mad about yesterday's message.'

'Message? You left me a message?' Toulon put a cigarette in his mouth and desperately wanted to light it. 'Sorry, I heard no message from you. I was too busy taking a nap and drinking wine in your office. Then I ate some stinky cheese, just to improve the smell.'

'Wow. You're really pissy today. Do you want to talk later?'

'No,' Toulon said. 'I want to talk now. I want to get this over with.'

Dial grimaced, not sure if Toulon was mad at him or not. Then again, it was too early in the morning to actually care. 'Did you get my e-mail? I sent it from my phone.'

'One moment. Let me check.'

While Toulon checked his computer, Dial climbed out of bed and walked across the tiled floor of his spacious suite. Somehow Andropoulos had booked him a great room in the Divani Metéora, a luxury hotel in Kalampáka. It was so close to the monastery, he could stare at the towering cliffs from his private balcony.

'*Oui*. I found it. Give me a moment to read it.'

'Take your time,' Dial said as he wandered into the bathroom.

Toulon spoke again a few minutes later. He was staring at his computer screen, trying to make sense of the two images that Dial had sent to him. 'What am I looking at?'

'Pictures of the killers.'

'You are teasing, no? How did you get these?'

'The monks had a nanny cam.'

Toulon spat out his cigarette in disgust. 'I *hate* those damn things! I have been caught with too many nannies.'

Dial laughed, realizing that Toulon wasn't joking. 'Sorry to hear that, Henri. But in this case, we really lucked out. It's the biggest break we've had.'

'This is quite helpful. Do you know why?'

'Why?'

'Because I am an expert on Ancient Greece.'

'Don't sell yourself short. You're an expert on everything.'

'*Oui*, this is true. I am quite good.' Toulon ran his fingers over his grey hair, which was pulled back in his trademark ponytail. He certainly didn't look the part of an Interpol officer. But his brilliance more than made up for his attitude and attire. 'What do you want to know?'

Dial picked up hard copies of the two photos. 'Let's start with the sword.'

Toulon clicked on the first image then enlarged it until the sword filled the screen. He focused on the details, searching for the nuances that would define the weapon. It didn't take long for him to reach a conclusion. 'This is a *xiphos*. It was used by a hoplite.'

'A what?'

'A hoplite. An infantryman from Ancient Greece.'

'How can you tell?'

Toulon sneered. 'Do not insult me! I can tell with a single look because I am an expert. If a doctor said

to you, "Nick, you are dying of a brain tumour."
Would you say, "How can you tell?"'

'Definitely.'

Toulon paused. 'Yes, you are right. I would ask
him, too. That is a bad example.'

'Come on, Henri. Stop goofing round.'

'Fine! I will just tell you.' He mumbled a few curse
words in French before he continued his lecture.
'Look at the style of this sword. It is simple. It is
plain. No fancy hilts. No fancy pommels. This is the
blade of a soldier. Not an officer.'

Dial scribbled some key phrases on a piece of
paper. 'Go on.'

'Now look at its length. It is a short sword. Maybe
three feet long. It is perfect for close combat. Very
sharp. Very strong. The kind they used in the
phalanx.'

'The phalanx?'

'The wall of soldiers at the front of an attack. The
hoplites.'

Toulon leaned back and put the cigarette in his
mouth. He still needed his morning fix. With a cautious eye, he glanced round the office, searching for
anyone who outranked him. When he saw no one,
he decided to light up. Rules be damned.

Dial said, 'I know it's just a picture, but can you
give me a time period?'

'Maybe if I held the blade, but not from this photo.'

'Come on, Henri, take a wild guess. Are we talking

Russell Crowe in *Gladiator* or Harry Hamlin in *Clash of the Titans*?'

Toulon blew smoke into the air. 'We are talking Nick Dial in *Clueless*.'

'Be nice,' Dial warned him, 'or I'll fine you for smoking.'

Toulon coughed, practically swallowing his cigarette in the process. How did Dial know he was smoking? He looked round again. Maybe the sneaky bastard had a nanny cam.

'That is insulting,' Toulon said. 'I would do no such thing.'

'Of course you wouldn't. Now answer my question. How old are we talking?'

'The second one. Harry Hamlin.'

Dial smiled. He loved making Toulon think in American terms. It was one of the simple joys in his life. 'But this weapon is a replica, right?'

'Tell me, Nick. Do you know when Ancient Greece flourished?'

'Before Christ.'

'Several centuries before Christ. Now look at this picture. Does this sword look *that* old to you? Of course not. Therefore this sword is a replica.'

'Yet real enough to kill someone.'

'*Oui.* In that way, it is quite real.'

Dial nodded, thinking back to the blood at the crime scene. For a blade to pass through the bones and tendons of someone's neck, it had to be remarkably strong. Probably some type of high-grade steel, he figured. Just to be sure, he made a note to ask a local blacksmith.

'Okay. What about the other picture? Anything helpful?'

Still puffing away, Toulon switched images on his screen and zoomed in on the photograph of the warrior. He studied his uniform, focusing on the intricacies of his armour, the shape of his full-size helmet, the way he held his sword. All of it looked authentic.

'Well,' Toulon said, 'I've got good news and bad news.'

'Good news first.'

'If I had to guess, I would say this man is dressed as a Spartan.'

'Why do you think that?'

Toulon took a long drag on his cigarette, enjoying the flavour before he blew the smoke out of his nostrils like a cranky French dragon. 'Notice the design of his headgear. No patterns. No decorations. No fancy flourishes. This is a helmet, not a work of art. If it had been Corinthian or Trojan or even Athenian, it would have been far more ornate since those cultures supported the arts. The Spartan culture did not.'

He paused, taking another drag.

'Now look at the cuirass – the bronze armour that protects his chest and back. It is plain, too, except for the ridges of the ribcage and stomach. This is a design used by the Spartans. The muscular contours were meant to scare the enemy. And, trust me, they did.'

'Anything else?'

'That is all for now. I'll look some more once I drink my coffee.'

'Thanks. I'd appreciate that.' Dial finished his notes and was about to hang up when Toulon cleared his throat quite loudly. 'What now?'

'You are forgetting something, no?'

'I said, thanks.'

'No. It is not that. You still haven't heard my bad news.'

'Crap, that's right. What's the bad news?'

Toulon smiled, eager to show off his knowledge. 'The bad news is identical to the good news. If I had to guess, I would say this man is dressed as a Spartan.'

The comment puzzled Dial. 'What's your point?'

'Tell me, Nick, what do you know about the Spartans?'

'Not very much. They came from Sparta and they liked to fight.'

Toulon shook his head. 'That is the understatement of the year.'

'How so?'

'How so?' he echoed, as he leaned back in his chair. 'Since the dawn of man, there has *never* been a culture like the Spartans. From the moment of their birth until the time of their death, all Spartans were consumed by one thing: the art of war.'

'Can you give me an example?'

'I can give you thousands.'

'Great. But let's start with one.'

Toulon took another puff. 'Let's start at birth. When a baby was born, the child's father took it to a group of elders who decided, right then and there, whether the child was worthy of Sparta. If it was small or weak, it was immediately taken to Mount Taygetus, also known as the place of rejection, where it was thrown off the mountain.'

'They killed their own babies?'

'*Oui*. They killed their own babies.'

'That's disgusting.'

'That is simply the beginning. When a Spartan boy reached the age of seven, he was enrolled in the *agoge*. It was like a military boarding school except far more brutal. The boys were stripped, beaten, and underfed, all in the hope of toughening them up. This went on for ten years, until they were ready for the *crypteia*, a secret initiation where their most promising youths proved their worth. These teenage boys were abandoned in the countryside with simple instructions: kill any Helots they saw and steal anything they needed to survive.'

'What's a Helot?'

'The Helots were conquered subjects who worked the lands. This allowed the Spartans to focus all their time and energy on war, not farming.'

'And the boys killed them in cold blood?'

'*Oui*, but only Helots who were up to no good.

This, of course, accomplished two things. It taught the boys how to hunt human flesh, and it kept the Helots in line. Simply put, they were too scared to rebel or run away from Sparta.'

Dial grimaced at the brutality. 'And you think these guys are Spartans?'

'No, no, no! Do not misunderstand me. I think these men were *dressed* as Spartans. Whether they are or not, I do not know.'

'But could they be?'

Toulon laughed. 'Nick, you must realize that Sparta was conquered centuries ago. Today it is a series of crumbled ruins. Nothing more.'

'I know that, Henri. But look at the facts. Two days ago a group of men attacked a nearly impenetrable fortress and slaughtered everyone inside. Then, for good measure, they threw all the bodies off the mountain – just like the flying babies you mentioned. And even though they were wearing body armour and helmets and carrying swords, there were no witnesses to the crime. That means these guys moved with great stealth.'

Dial paused, trying to calm the emotion in his voice. 'I don't know about you, but doesn't that sound like the warriors you just described?'

'*Oui*,' he said. His tone was suddenly serious. 'It certainly does.'

'So, as crazy as it sounds, let me ask you again. Could these guys be Spartans?'

Toulon puffed on his cigarette one last time, then

mashed it into an empty cup until the embers were no more. 'If they are, I'd hate to be the man who's chasing them.'

18

Andropoulos pulled his car up to the front entrance of the hotel. Dial was waiting for him, staring at the rocky cliffs that faded into the morning mist. He was wearing jeans and the same boots as the day before but had opted for a long-sleeved shirt instead.

No sense breaking the dress code two days in a row.

Thanks to Dial's comment about his suit, Andropoulos had changed as well. He wanted to placate his boss from Interpol, so he had copied his wardrobe: jeans, dress shirt, and hiking boots.

'Good morning, sir,' Andropoulos said as Dial climbed into the front seat.

Dial nodded, then studied the Greek from head to toe. 'No time for a haircut?'

'Sorry, sir. I worked late last night.'

Dial grunted, trying his best not to smile. 'Anything to report?'

Andropoulos pulled into traffic. Despite the early hour, the narrow streets were filled with tourists who were hoping to see all the local sites in a single day. 'Three of the monks have been identified, including the abbot. The other two were foreigners. One was from Russia, the other from Turkey.'

'Turkey? I thought that was a Muslim country.'

'Ninety-nine per cent are Muslims. The other one per cent is mostly Orthodox.'

Dial considered the information and nodded. Victims from three different countries meant this was an Interpol case. Somehow he had always sensed it would be – otherwise he wouldn't have flown to Greece on such short notice – but now it was official. That meant he could turn up the intensity of his investigation. He could chase down leads. He could interview witnesses. He could do all the things that he wanted to do without needing permission from the Greek government. Suddenly his day was looking a whole lot brighter.

Unfortunately, his mood would change less than an hour later.

Andropoulos parked his car on the upper access road to Holy Trinity, right behind several other blue-and-white Citroëns. Dial counted the squad cars and shook his head. For some reason the entire police force was roaming round the cliffs, doing God knows what.

'If I was a criminal,' Dial said, 'I would head straight to Kalampáka and rob a bank. It would take thirty minutes for you guys to reach town.'

Andropoulos glanced at the city nestled in the valley. 'You are right. I am tempted to call my cousin and let him know.'

'Is he an officer?'

'No, sir. He's a pickpocket. But he has the potential to be so much more.'

Dial laughed as he followed Andropoulos down the steep hillside. They used the same path as the day before, though it didn't seem nearly as treacherous to Dial. Perhaps he was getting used to the footing. Or maybe it had to do with the sunlight, which was a drastic improvement over a single flashlight. Whatever the reason, he was able to pay closer attention to the terrain than he had on the previous night.

The first thing Dial noticed was the cable-car system that ran across the gorge to Holy Trinity. He slowed his pace when he saw its thin wires bouncing up and down like they were caught in a violent storm. Then he spotted the reason why. A single monk, wearing a black cassock and cap, was sitting in a rickety cart as it was being pulled towards the top, more than a thousand feet in the air. Dial stopped to stare at the spectacle, and when he did, he heard the distant squeaking of pulleys and wheels coming from somewhere inside the ancient monastery.

Dial said, 'You'd have to pay me a lot of money to ride in that thing.'

Andropoulos nodded in agreement. 'I once asked a monk when they replaced the cable. And he said, "When the old one breaks."'

'Strangely, I had a friend in college who had the same policy about condoms.'

'Sir, that's disgusting.'

Dial laughed at his juvenile joke as he continued down the hillside. He knew he couldn't make comments like that inside the monastery – at least not within earshot of any monks – so he tried to get them out of his system now. It was more difficult than it sounded. Working in a profession that was filled with so much violence and death, Dial relied on humour to keep him sane. Sometimes it was a racy comment. Other times it was a practical joke. Most of the time, it wasn't meant to be malicious – like teasing Andropoulos about his hair and clothes. He was just having some fun while trying to solve a case that would probably depress him. Otherwise, he figured, he'd have to drink himself to sleep like half the cops he'd met.

In his mind, humour was a pretty good alternative to alcoholism.

Fifteen minutes later, the two of them were inside Holy Trinity, re-examining the crime scene. To Dial, everything looked different during daylight hours. The colour of the stone was lighter. The construction of the monastery looked older, somehow more fragile. And the distance to the valley below was much further than he expected. He glanced over the wall and for the first time could actually see the ground. At least ten people were down there, searching for clues or cleaning the rocks or something. Dial couldn't tell for sure. Not from this far away.

'Hey, Marcus, do me a favour. Get me the names and backgrounds of all the monks they've identified. I'd like to have that asap.'

'Yes, sir. Where will you be?'

'I'll be speaking with Nicolas. I need to ask him a few questions.'

Dial strolled towards the bell tower, glancing down the stone corridors and peeking in windows, hoping to spot the old monk meditating or chanting or doing whatever it is that old monks do. Dial had enjoyed talking to him the night before and looked forward to chatting with him again. Perhaps he could shed some light on the different nationalities of the victims and how he knew about the dead abbot before the police did. That, in particular, still bothered him.

Halfway across the complex, Dial approached the door where he had met Nicolas the previous night. Only this time he was able to see the grain of the ancient wood in the bright sunlight. It had the same consistency as the front gate. Not nearly as tall, yet just as thick and strong. The type of door that would put up a good fight against a battering ram.

Dial was about to knock when he noticed a large stain between the handle and the antique keyhole. The smudge was six inches long and the colour of rust. If he had been sightseeing or entering an office building, Dial wouldn't have given it much thought. But in the context of a crime scene, he crouched down for a closer look.

Except in rare circumstances, Interpol never handled forensic evidence – that was the job of the local cops who would eventually prosecute the case – yet Dial had worked enough murders to recognize blood when he saw it. And this stain was blood. No doubt about it. From the look of it, someone had tried to open the door with bloody hands. Whether they had been successful or not was a different matter altogether. But they had definitely tried to get inside.

The question was, why?

It wasn't the only thing that popped into Dial's mind. The more he thought about it, the more he wondered if the stain had been there the night before when he talked to Nicolas. The only reason Dial had approached the door to begin with was because of the bright light shining under it – not because he had spotted the blood. Without the light, he would have kept on walking.

'Excuse me,' said a stern voice from behind. 'What are you doing?'

Dial, who was crouching near the keyhole, turned to face his inquisitor. He was expecting to find another cop. Instead, it was the monk in the black cassock and cap who had ridden across the gorge in the cable car. He was a man in his mid-thirties, with dark brown hair and a thicket of a beard that practically hid his lips. He was holding a box in his hands.

'I was looking for clues,' Dial said.

'Through the keyhole? Have you no dignity?'

Dial stood up. 'Not through it. Next to it. I found some blood by the lock.'

The monk stepped forward for a closer look. Once he saw the bloodstain, his tone changed immediately. 'I am sorry for my accusation. As you can probably imagine, I am still trying to grasp what happened here. It has been a shock to us all.'

Dial brushed it aside with a wave of his hand. 'No

apologies needed. I can only imagine what it looked like.'

The monk nodded in gratitude. 'My name is Theodore.'

'Nick Dial. I'm with Interpol.'

'It's nice to meet you, Mr Dial – despite the circumstances. If you have any questions about Metéora, I'd be happy to answer them. I'll be here for the duration.'

'Glad to hear it. I'm sure Nicolas will enjoy your company.'

'Nicolas? Who is Nicolas?'

Dial smiled. 'Old guy, grey beard. I met him here last night.'

'You met him where?'

'Here. Right here.' Dial tapped on the door for emphasis. 'He came out of this room.'

Confusion filled Theodore's face. The type of confusion that couldn't be faked.

'What? Is something wrong?' Dial asked.

Theodore tried to regain his composure. 'I'm sorry, Mr Dial. I don't mean to doubt you. If you say you met a man named Nicolas, I believe you. I truly do.' He paused momentarily. 'That being said, I can assure you of something else. Whoever you spoke to *wasn't* a monk, and he certainly *didn't* belong at Holy Trinity.'

19

St Martin's Square
Kaiserslautern, Germany

The Kaiserslautern Military Community (KMC) is
the largest US military community outside the conti-
nental United States, bringing in close to a billion
dollars annually to the local economy and housing
nearly 50,000 members of NATO personnel, mostly
from the US. This gave the German city, located
eighty miles south-west of Frankfurt, a uniquely
American flavour.

During their previous trips to Ramstein, Payne and
Jones had made several contacts, on and off the base,
who could have helped their cause. After discussing
it, they came to the conclusion that they should go
to their best source for this mission – even though
he wouldn't be cheap.

The man called himself Kaiser because he was the
King of K-Town.

At least when it came to getting supplies.

Payne and Jones reached him by phone shortly after
their arrival in Germany. He agreed to meet them for
breakfast at a small café right down the street from
the former Hotel Zum Donnersberg, where Napoleon

himself once dined. Neither of them had eaten a full meal since Florida, so they were starving by the time they reached the rendezvous point.

St Martin's Square (or the Martinsplatz) was the gateway to the old part of town, the section of the city that had survived the Allied bombings in World War Two. In the square was the old city hall, which now housed a school of music, and several large chestnut trees that shaded the square during the hot summer months. But at this time of year, the weather was perfect for eating outside. There was a light breeze and the temperature was in the upper sixties.

They spotted Kaiser at a sidewalk table, casually sipping coffee and reading a newspaper. He was wearing blue jeans and a brown leather jacket, the same clothes he always wore. Nothing about his appearance really stood out, which was advantageous in his line of work. He was in his mid-fifties with slicked-back grey hair and bushy eyebrows that dangled above his dark eyes. They knew he was American – an ex-supply sergeant who retired from the military when he realized he could make a lot more money on his own – but knew little else about him.

Just the way Kaiser liked it.

'Gentlemen,' he said getting up from his chair. He greeted them by name and shook their hands before offering them a seat. 'How long has it been?'

Payne and Jones sat across from each other. That way they could keep an eye on the traffic in both directions. 'A couple of years, I think.'

Jones agreed. 'Sounds about right.'

'I thought you guys got out of the game.'

Payne shrugged. 'Does anyone leave for good?'

Kaiser smiled. 'Not if they have a pulse.'

A waitress stopped by the table and handed them menus. She spoke fluent English with just a hint of a German accent. As soon as she left, Kaiser stared at them, dead serious.

'Since you are old acquaintances of mine, I'm going to help you guys out. Trust me when I tell you this: it's a *huge* favour.' He leaned forward as if he was going to share a national secret. Instinctively, Payne and Jones leaned in. 'Do not, I repeat, do *not* leave this café without ordering the sausage. I'm telling you, it's like heaven on a plate.'

Payne and Jones both laughed, glad that Kaiser was just messing round.

'Are you trying to give us a heart attack?' Jones asked.

'Trust me, if you eat enough of this sausage, you *will* have a heart attack. But man, oh, man, what a way to go!'

Payne patted him on the shoulder. 'Same old Kaiser. Still loving life.'

'Might as well. You only get one.'

They made small talk while glancing at the menus, which were written in English and filled with foods they were familiar with. Soft-boiled eggs, cereal, pancakes with a wide variety of fruit toppings, and a whole page dedicated to breakfast meats, some hot and some cold.

Kaiser said, 'Did you know that sausage is so ingrained in the German culture, instead of saying, "That's okay with me," they say, "*Es ist mir Wurst.*" That means, "It is sausage to me."'

Jones smiled. 'Wow, I didn't know that. But if I ever apply for a job at a slaughterhouse, I'll be sure to mention it. *Es ist mir Wurst!*'

Kaiser laughed. 'Okay, I can take a hint. No more sausage talk at the table. At least not until mine arrives. After that, no promises.'

'In that case,' Payne said, 'let's get our business stuff out of the way – just in case you want to debate the merits of links versus patties.'

'Dammit, Jon, don't get me started! That's a sensitive subject round here!'

'I kind of figured it would be.'

Kaiser laughed as he pushed his menu aside. He was ready to talk shop.

'So,' he said, 'what do you need on this little trip of yours?'

'Don't worry,' Jones assured him, 'nothing too crazy.'

When it came to missions, Jones was a brilliant strategist. He received the highest score in the history of the Air Force Academy's MSAE (Military Strategy Acumen Examination) and had organized hundreds of operations with the MANIACs. He had a way of seeing things several steps ahead, like a chess master. So Payne let him take control of the conversation.

For a trip like this, both of them realized that they

had to remain anonymous. Otherwise, the Russian government would follow them wherever they went. That is, if they even let them enter the country. Moscow commonly denied travel visas to foreign soldiers – even those who had retired long ago. And elite soldiers like Payne and Jones were automatically red-flagged.

'First things first, we need papers. Fake names, fake backgrounds. Preferably Canadian. Not only for us but a woman as well.'

'How soon?'

'Yesterday.'

Kaiser nodded. 'Get me some photos and I'll have them by lunch.'

'Next,' Jones said, 'we need weapons. Two guns each. Something clean and concealable. We aren't going through customs, but we'll be working in public.'

'My armoury is your armoury. I'll give you the pick of the litter.'

'We also need a ride.'

'From?'

'Helsinki.'

'To?'

'St Pete.'

'Night-time arrival?'

Jones smiled. 'Is there any other kind?'

'I'll see what I can do,' Kaiser said. 'This time of year, it shouldn't be a problem. In the winter, it's a much different story.'

'Why's that?' Payne wondered.

'Icebergs are a bitch.'

Jones laughed, then continued, 'We'll also need a return trip. One additional passenger. Maybe some cargo. Time and place to be determined.'

'Guesstimate?'

Jones did the math in his head. 'No more than twenty-four hours.'

'No problem. The boat can stay put for that long.'

Jones glanced at Payne. 'Anything else?'

Payne shook his head. 'Not that I can think of. Unless you have a travel advisory. Anything we need to know.'

'Maybe,' Kaiser said. 'Just maybe.'

'Meaning?'

There was an uncomfortable silence. 'How long since you've been to Russia?'

Payne answered. 'A few years.'

'What about you, DJ?'

'Never been there. Why?'

'Well, it's gotten worse for some people. A lot worse.'

'How so?' Jones wondered.

Kaiser grimaced. 'I have a black friend who just got back from Moscow. Nice guy, clean cut, about your age. He was invited by the Russian government to speak at an economic summit. Didn't matter, though. He got stopped by soldiers every ten feet. He was frisked. He was followed. He was called "monkey" to his face. He swore to me he'd never go back.'

'What about St Pete? Is it better than Moscow?' Payne asked.

'Things tend to be more liberal there, but I honestly don't know. I can't speak from experience.' Kaiser paused, not sure what else to say. 'I just thought I should mention it.'

Jones nodded, appreciative of the information. 'Don't worry, Kaiser. I can handle it. I get the same reaction when I go to a country and western bar.'

'And if things get too bad,' Payne assured him, 'we'll just shoot the bastards.'

20

The words hit Dial like a sucker punch. Their impact was so unexpected, he actually had a physical reaction. His cheeks flushed. His chest tightened. Acid gurgled in his gut.

'What do you mean he *wasn't* a monk? Who the hell was he?'

Theodore ignored the profanity. 'That is a question I cannot answer, for I do not know.'

Dial took a deep breath, trying to calm down. But the thought of being duped by an impostor got his blood boiling. 'You're *sure* you don't know him? Old guy. Walks with a limp.'

'I'm sorry, Mr Dial—'

'Nick. Call me Nick.'

Theodore nodded. 'I'm sorry, Nick. I have lived at Metéora for nearly a decade, but I don't know the man you describe.'

Dial grimaced as he replayed the previous night in his head. He remembered seeing the light under the door. He'd knocked. Nicolas had answered and closed the door behind him. Then they had walked to the bell tower where Nicolas had regaled him with stories of the monastic life. At no point had Dial found anything about their conversation suspicious.

In fact, he had been thrilled to talk to someone as knowledgeable as Nicolas. So much so, he had thought he was a godsend.

Now he didn't know what to think.

If Nicolas wasn't a monk, what was he? And what had he been doing at Metéora?

Could his presence have anything to do with the bloodstain on the door?

That possibility bothered Dial. It was something he needed to find out.

He said, 'Please forgive me. Where are my manners? There you are holding a box, and here I am standing in your way. Please let me help.'

Theodore nodded as Dial grabbed the box. It was crammed with books, toiletries, and a few personal items. Sitting on top was a large key ring, filled with the type of keys that a dungeon master might have used in the Middle Ages. They were old and long and made out of brass. Theodore picked up the ring and searched for the correct key. It took several seconds to find it.

Dial filled the silence with small talk. 'Sorry about your abbot. When did you hear?'

'This morning during breakfast. All of us were saddened by the news.'

'Us?'

'The brothers of Great Metéoron. It is the largest of the six monasteries. It sits in the hills above Kastraki. Perhaps you saw it on your drive to Holy Trinity.'

Dial shook his head. 'With the abbot gone, who selected you to come here?'

'Nobody. I volunteered.'

'That's awfully noble of you.'

Theodore said nothing, concentrating on the keys instead. He finally found the one he was looking for and put it in the old lock. It turned with a loud click. Pushing the door forward, he stepped inside then turned on the light. Dial followed him in, hoping to figure out why Nicolas had been in there the night before. Unfortunately, there wasn't much to examine.

The ceiling was supported by dozens of ancient beams, far more than necessary. There were so many planks up there, angled in so many different directions, it looked like a wooden spider's web. Fascinated by the haphazard design, Dial studied it with two things in mind. First, he hoped to spot another nanny cam somewhere in the rafters – just like they had found in the gift shop. But the only wires he saw were for the iron chandelier that lit the windowless room. Second, Dial wanted to figure out why the monks had killed half a forest to hold up such a small ceiling.

There had to be a rational explanation, hadn't there?

Theodore anticipated the question. 'No one knows why it was built in that manner.'

'Really? It's just seems so odd. Like an abstract painting.'

'We have a library at Great Metéoron. It is filled

with hundreds of manuscripts, including a history of our monasteries. Not only the six survivors, but the earlier ones as well. I have read these records myself, and no answers were given. It remains a mystery to this day.'

Dial searched the room for other anomalies but saw nothing out of the ordinary. The floor was made of large grey stones that were held together by some kind of mortar. Two small cots sat against the near wall, separated by a nightstand and a lamp. The only other furniture was a rickety table and four wooden chairs under the chandelier. Dial put Theodore's box on the table and instantly regretted it. A thick cloud of dust floated into the air, making him sneeze.

He nearly made a smart-ass comment about the previous tenant being lax in his cleaning duties, but he bit his tongue when he remembered that the previous monk was now dead.

Looking to change the subject, Dial focused on the only splash of colour in the dreary room. An enormous blue tapestry hung across the back wall. It was fringed with golden tassels round the edges and had a large gold cross in the centre. It looked like a Christian cross, except it had an extra bar above the horizontal beam and a slanted bar – that looked like a forward slash – underneath it. Dial had seen the same symbol inside the church.

'Is this your cross?' Dial asked. He had learned a lot about crosses when he worked his crucifixion case a few years back, so he was interested in the subject.

'Yes. The *crux orthodoxa*. The Eastern Orthodox cross. It is the cross of my faith.'

'What do the beams represent?'

Theodore pointed towards the tapestry. 'The top beam represents the sign that hung above Christ. It said, "Jesus of Nazareth, King of the Jews."'

'And the slanted beam at the bottom? Is that a footrest?'

'Some scholars believe so, but many of my faith disagree. To us, it represents the two thieves who were crucified next to Christ. The criminal on the left was repentant and accepted Christ as his Saviour, so his side points towards heaven. The thief on the right rejected Him, so his side points towards hell.'

'Really?' As someone who dealt with people of all religions and beliefs, Dial was surprised he didn't know that. 'I learn something new every day.'

'I'm glad I could enlighten you,' Theodore said. 'If you have any other questions, I'd be happy to answer them. Otherwise, I'd like to make myself available to the other officers.'

'Please, help them out. They need it more than I do.'

Dial glanced round the room again. But this time he had a strange feeling that he was overlooking something. He wasn't sure what it was, but he sensed it was something important. 'If it's okay with you, can I stay in here and look round some more? We already missed the blood on the door. I'd hate to think we missed something inside.'

Theodore frowned as he considered the request.

Hoping to charm him, Dial put his hand on one of the rickety chairs. 'Don't worry, I promise I won't steal the furniture.'

The monk cracked a smile then scurried out of the room.

Dial had been in the room for less than two minutes when Andropoulos knocked on the door.

'Sir?' he said. 'May I come in?'

'Of course you can come in. This isn't my apartment. It's a crime scene.'

Andropoulos blushed and stepped inside. He was carrying a folder filled with information about the victims. 'I have the background that you asked for.'

But Dial ignored him, focusing on the nightstand instead. It sat between two cots and was the only furniture in the monk's room where something could be stored. He opened the drawer, hoping to find something important, but it was empty. Just like the rest of the room.

'Speaking of crime scenes,' Dial said as he glanced back at the young cop, 'who's in charge of the perimeter?'

'The perimeter?'

'You know, the imaginary line that encircles a crime scene. Who's in charge of it?'

'We are, sir.'

'Who's *we*? Because I know *I'm* not in charge of it.'

'Us, sir. The local police department.'

Dial nodded. He had known the answer. He just

wanted Andropoulos to take ownership of the problem. 'And what's your policy for letting people into the crime scene?'

'Sir?'

'I mean, do you let *anyone* enter the crime scene?'

'Of course not, sir. Only authorized personnel.'

'Authorized personnel.' Dial practically spit when he said it. 'Does that include cops?'

'Yes, sir.'

'What about reporters?'

'No, sir.'

'What about monks?'

Andropoulos paused. 'I'm not sure about that one.'

Dial smirked. 'I don't blame you. That's a tough one. I mean, they're men of God, so we can trust them, right?'

'I guess.'

'You guess?' Dial shook his head in disappointment. 'Earlier today, we saw a monk entering the crime scene, didn't we? Up in the cable car?'

'Yes, sir.'

'And I'm guessing he didn't sneak in. Not while wearing a cassock and carrying a box.'

'No, sir.'

'So *someone* let him through.'

Andropoulos nodded. 'Did I do something wrong, sir?'

Dial softened the tone in his voice. He was angry at Nicolas' presence at the crime scene but didn't want to blame the young cop for something that wasn't his fault. 'Not you personally, but someone on your team screwed up big time. Remember the old monk I introduced to you last night? I just found out he didn't belong here. In fact, he might not be a monk at all.'

'What? Who told you that?'

'The monk from the cable car. Then again, maybe *he's* not a monk, either.'

'You mean, Theodore? He's *definitely* a monk. I've met him before.'

'But not Nicolas?'

Andropoulos shook his head. 'No, sir. He didn't look familiar to me.'

'Great,' Dial mumbled to himself. 'Next time speak up a little sooner.'

'I will, sir. In the meantime, what should I do to fix this?'

Dial stared at the kid. He had just lectured him over something he didn't do, yet Andropoulos had taken it like a man. He hadn't got defensive. He hadn't passed the buck. He simply wanted to know how he could make things right. It was the perfect reaction to the situation.

Dial said, 'Get word to the perimeter about Nicolas. Find out who let him in and why. Also find out what time he left and if anyone gave him a ride. I know when I came through last night, they recorded my name and ID badge into a log. Maybe they did the same thing with him. If so, get someone to verify the information asap.'

'I'll do it myself,' Andropoulos said.

'No. Get someone else. You have better things to do with your time.'

'Sir?'

'Do me a favour and look at the door.'

'Which door?'

Dial pointed. 'The one you just walked past.'

Andropoulos did what he was told. It didn't take him long to spot the stain near the handle. 'Is this blood?'

'It sure looks like it. And as far as I can tell, it hasn't been processed.'

'You're right, sir. It hasn't. I'll get forensics in here at once.'

Dial nodded and turned back to examine the interior of the room. Combine the bloodstain on the door with Nicolas' presence inside, and Dial knew he was missing something.

But what was it? What was being overlooked?

'Marcus, before you leave, I'd like your opinion.'

'On what, sir?'

'If you were a criminal, why would you come into this room?'

'Is this a test?'

'No, it's not a fucking test. I'm asking for your help. Is there something in here that would interest you?'

Andropoulos tried not to smile as he walked back into the room. Hoping to impress his boss, he scanned everything, focusing on the intricate wooden ceiling for several seconds before he moved on to the nightstand and the two cots that rested against the wall. Eventually he stopped near the table and chairs in the centre of the room. 'May I look in the box, sir?'

'Not the box. *Ignore* the box. I carried it in myself.'

Andropoulos considered Dial's statement then said, 'Did you carry anything out?'

'No, I didn't,' Dial said, 'but that's a pretty good question. When you talk to your people, find out if Nicolas was carrying anything when he left the grounds.'

'This is about Nicolas?'

Dial nodded. 'He was in here when I met him, but I can't figure out why. This place has nothing in it.'

'Maybe he was hiding in here, waiting for people to leave.'

'I considered that. But that doesn't explain why he chatted with me for twenty minutes. If you were hiding, would you answer a knock on the door? Or, at the very least, wouldn't you make up some kind of excuse so you didn't have to talk to me?' Dial shook his head as he continued to reflect on the previous night. 'Strangely, the more I think about it, the more I get the sense that he took me up to the bell tower because he wanted to get me away from here. There was something about the way he stepped outside and quickly closed the door behind him that bothers me.

It was – I don't know – like he didn't want me to see the interior of the room.'

Andropoulos glanced round the room again. 'Could someone else have been in here?'

'Maybe.'

'What about the blood? Was it here last night?'

Dial shrugged. 'I honestly don't know. It was too dark to see.'

'But you think it was, right?'

Dial furrowed his brow. 'When did *you* start asking the questions?'

Andropoulos stammered. 'Sorry, sir. I didn't mean to—'

Dial cut him off. 'Don't worry about it. Go on.'

He took a deep breath to calm himself. 'We're assuming the blood is from the killers, right? They opened the door to make sure there weren't any witnesses, and when they did, they left the bloodstain near the handle.'

'Or,' Dial suggested, 'they came in here looking for *something*. Not someone.'

'Like what?'

Dial growled softly. 'That's the same damn thing I asked you five minutes ago. I hope you realize the goal is to answer my question, not rephrase it.'

Andropoulos nodded. 'I don't know, sir. I don't see anything in here.'

'Me, neither,' said Dial as he moved to the back of the room. The two cots were old and rusty. The nightstand and lamp were second hand. So were the table and chairs. The only thing worth taking was the tapestry of the Orthodox cross. 'What do you think this is worth?'

The young Greek walked towards Dial. 'I don't know. It depends how old it is. I'd say several hundred euros. Maybe more.'

'That much, huh?' Dial moved closer to examine the golden tassels on the edges of the tapestry. 'Does Holy Trinity have any other artwork?'

'Some frescoes have been painted on the walls.'

'I mean *removable* artwork. Statues, pottery, precious metals.'

'No, sir. Not that I can remember.'

'Me, neither,' Dial said as he ran his fingers across the heavy fabric. It was much thicker than he had expected. Much more durable, too. The type of thing that could last for centuries. 'And the frescoes are in areas of worship, right? The chapel and so on.'

'Yes, sir.'

'So why is this in here? It's locked away in their private quarters for no one else to see.'

'I don't know, sir. Do you want me to find out? I could ask someone.'

Dial shook his head as he leaned closer to the tapestry.

It had taken a while, but he had finally found the answer he was searching for.

22

To create fake documents for Payne and Jones, Kaiser hired a world-class forger who lived in K-Town and specialized in visas and passports. Not only was he an expert on ink, paper, and handwriting, but he also had a unique perspective on the industry since he used to be a border guard at the Berlin Wall. So he understood the risks of a border crossing – what guards looked for, what they questioned, and so on – and guaranteed his creations would pass scrutiny.

For a trip to Russia, he recommended a single-entry tourist visa. Simple, straightforward, and rarely challenged. Especially if it was issued to a Canadian citizen. In the world of espionage, Canada was viewed as the Switzerland of the West. In other words, harmless. Payne and Jones knew this, which is why they had requested Canadian paperwork. Many countries round the world hated the United States. But few people – except jealous hockey fans – hated Canada.

When it came to border crossings, Payne and Jones were veterans. They had snuck into so many countries when they were in the MANIACs that they weren't the least bit stressed over their trip. Of course they realized their return trip would be a lot more difficult since they'd be escorting Allison Taylor, a wild card if there ever was one. From the sound of her voice on the phone, they were tempted to buy some horse tranquillizers, just to keep her calm.

To help with their cover, they stopped at a department store to buy some clothes. The designs and fabrics in Europe were much different to those of North America. That was one of the main reasons why Americans stood out when they were travelling overseas. Language was number one. Knowledge (manners, laws, decorum, etc.) was number two. Clothes were number three. Years of experience had taught Payne and Jones how to deal with the first two issues. They knew a shopping spree could rectify the third.

Payne was looking at shirts when his cell phone started to ring. The display screen read, *Restricted*. Thoughts of St Petersburg quickly entered his head.

'Allison?' Payne said.

'Sorry, pal. Guess again.'

The voice belonged to Randy Raskin, calling from the Pentagon.

'Wait a second! You're calling me? *That* might be a first.'

'It's been a whole day since you asked for a favour. I figured you were sick or something.'

Payne smiled. 'Nope. Just been travelling. Seeing some sights. Rescuing some damsels. You know, normal stuff.'

'I figured as much, which is the reason for my call. Do you have computer access?'

'We will for another hour. After that, no.'

'I'm sending a link to DJ. Tell him to follow panther protocols. He'll know what to do.'

'Okay,' said Payne as he grabbed the clothes he needed. 'Anything else?'

'That's all for now. If you have any trouble, let me know.'

Payne hung up and casually walked towards Jones, who was looking at trousers on the other side of the store. 'It's time to roll.'

'Why?'

'You've got mail.'

There was an internet café less than a block away. Jones grabbed a computer in the back corner while Payne paid for an hour. He always used cash when on a mission. Never credit cards.

To view Raskin's message, Jones followed the panther protocol, a simple procedure Raskin had designed for accessing data in a public place. Jones logged on to his office system in Pittsburgh, which was highly encrypted, and ran a program called panther that blocked all monitoring software on the public terminal. It was an effective way to erase all trails to the Pentagon, and it prevented any files from being saved in a temporary folder on a public network.

Once Jones was confident the computer was clean, he opened the e-mail:

hey guys,

i think you'll like this – or maybe not. he doesn't
seem like a nice person. make sure you cover
your tracks. i don't want him coming after me.
he's scary.

r.r.

A few minutes later, they understood what Raskin
was talking about when they viewed the file he
had attached to the message. Some time during the
night, he had hacked into a Russian surveillance company and downloaded the security video of Richard
Byrd's murder. Actually, it was more than a murder.
It was a cold-blooded execution, perpetrated by an
assassin in a highly public venue. The type of wet
work that was taught by the CIA, MI6, and other
security agencies round the globe – including the
old KGB.

At least that was the opinion of Payne and Jones.

The black-and-white footage was filmed from an
elevated angle on the back porch of the Peterhof. It
was a wide-angle shot, focusing on the banister above
the main grotto, right where Richard Byrd was standing. Although the video was grainy, Payne and Jones
were mesmerized by what they saw. The killer walked
with precision. Never wasting energy or stopping to
contemplate his next move. He approached Byrd,
raised his gun, and fired. No hesitation. Never breaking stride. Totally professional. Then he tossed his

weapon over the railing. It hit the water at the exact moment his victim tumbled into the fountain.

The timing was so perfect, the body and the gun made a single splash.

Payne and Jones replayed the video several times, looking for flaws in the killer's technique. There were none. He never looked at the camera. He never ran or panicked. He never did anything to give away his identity. Even during the chaos that followed.

Payne watched the execution one more time. 'What do you think? Ex-agency?'

'Maybe. Or Russian mob. No one we want to tangle with – if we can help it.'

'Famous last words.'

Jones smirked. 'I hope not.'

Payne tapped the computer screen. 'Do me a favour and keep it running for a bit. Allison said she witnessed the shooting. Maybe we can see her in the aftermath.'

'Good idea.'

They stared at the footage, focusing on the people in the background. Someone on the patio must have seen the body and screamed because all of a sudden everyone started running. Everyone, that is, except for one female with long blonde hair. As chaos erupted round her, she fell to her knees in front of the giant waterfall and wailed with grief. It was a sorrowful scene, one that tugged at their heartstrings and reaffirmed their decision to help her out.

She looked so lost and confused and scared.

No wonder she had been so emotional on the phone.

'Keep it going,' Payne said. 'I want to see what she's made of.'

Surprisingly, she cried for less than a minute. After that, she wiped her eyes, brushed the dirt off her knees, then walked away from the camera until she was no longer visible.

One minute she was a crying mess, the next she was calm enough to escape.

Jones stopped the video. 'Impressive. She's tougher than I thought.'

Payne nodded in agreement. 'Unfortunately, so is the shooter.'

23

The blue tapestry hung from the ceiling to the floor, covering most of the back wall in the monk's chamber. Dial had originally thought it was there to add a splash of colour to an otherwise dreary room. Then he noticed a colour that didn't belong. The colour was red. It was smeared on a few of the golden tassels near the bottom right-hand corner of the tapestry – as if someone with bloody hands had grabbed it and pulled it away from the wall.

Careful not to contaminate the evidence, Dial lifted the tapestry and peered behind it. He hoped to find a message scrawled on the stone or something attached to the back of the Orthodox cross. But what he found was better. And much more surprising.

'Holy shit,' he mumbled to himself.

'What is it?' asked Andropoulos as he tried to peek over Dial's shoulder.

'You'll see in a minute. Go close the door.'

Andropoulos hustled across the room, glanced outside to make sure no one was coming, then quietly closed and locked the door. By the time he returned, Dial was standing in front of the tapestry, wondering how they could move it without damaging it. Eventually he figured things out. The tapestry was hanging from two large hooks, one in each upper corner, that were drilled into the stone wall. All they had to do was remove the right corner from the right hook, fold the tapestry upon itself, and hang the right corner on top of the left corner. That way the tapestry would remain hanging, folded vertically, while dangling from the left-hand hook.

Working in unison, the two of them carefully lifted the tapestry so it wouldn't drag across the floor and hung it as Dial suggested. Then they stepped back and stared at their discovery.

In the centre of the stone wall, there was a door.

A secret door.

One that looked hundreds of years old.

Dial didn't know why it was there or where it might lead, but he knew they had stumbled onto something special. Not only because the monks had gone out of their way to conceal it, but because the door itself was more glorious than any door he had ever seen before. Intricately carved by a master crafts-man, it depicted dozens of Greek soldiers fighting a foreign horde on the battlefield. Some used spears. Others held swords. But all of them fought with honour.

Andropoulos moved closer to inspect the details, to appreciate the remarkable workmanship of his ancestors. He wanted to run his fingers across it, like a blind man reading Braille, just so he could touch a piece of history. That is, until he noticed the dried blood. It was just a small stain near the door's handle, yet it brought him back to reality.

He wasn't a tourist in a museum. He was a cop at a crime scene.

He said, 'I found more blood. Just like the other door, it's by the handle.'

Dial crouched down to study the stain. 'Strange. Very strange.'

'How so?'

'There's blood on both doors yet nothing in between. You don't see that very often. Normally you'd see a visible blood trail on the floor.'

Dial reached into his pocket and pulled out a clean tissue to open the door. He would have preferred latex gloves, but he was forced to improvise since he didn't have a pair.

'Any theories?' Dial asked.

'About what?'

'The source of the blood.'

Andropoulos shook his head. 'Not really. What about you?'

'I *always* have a theory. If I'm right, we'll know in three seconds.'

'What happens in three seconds?'

'You'll see,' he said cryptically. 'Are you ready? Three . . . two . . . one . . . breathe.'

Dial pushed the door forward and was instantly greeted by the stench of death. The smell, a mixture of blood and decaying flesh, caught Andropoulos completely off guard. So much so, he started to gag the moment it hit his nostrils. But not Dial. He was expecting it. With the tissue, he covered his nose and mouth then stepped inside the dark corridor.

'Mmmmm, death,' he said with a wry smile. 'Do you have a light?'

Still coughing, Andropoulos handed him a tiny penlight that he kept clipped to his belt. Dial turned it on and shone the beam ahead, revealing a tunnel about ten feet long with a stone floor followed by a spiral staircase that faded downwards from view. Creeping forward, Dial shone the light over the walls and the arched ceiling above him. Although it was made of stone, it was reinforced by several wooden planks – just like the one in the monk's room.

'How often does Greece have earthquakes?'

Andropoulos cleared his throat. 'Every year. They are small but very common.'

Dial nodded in understanding as he continued to explore. 'That might explain the wood. The monks who built this place were probably worried about cave ins. Miners used to do the same thing in the Old West. The boards kept their shafts from collapsing.'

'Where does it lead?'

Dial shrugged as he stopped at the edge of the steps. 'We'll find out shortly.'

He shone the light into the darkness below. The stairs curled to the right then disappeared into the depths. Dial turned back and looked at the Greek. 'Are you ready?'

Andropoulos coughed again. The sound echoed throughout the corridor. 'Yes, sir.'

'Good. Then stop your damn coughing and let's get moving.'

Dial eased down the staircase one step at a time, making sure each stair supported his weight before he moved on to the next one. Five steps. Then ten. Fifteen. Then twenty. Finally, after twenty-two steps, he reached the bottom. A few seconds later, he was joined by Andropoulos, who was no longer hacking – even though the stench was growing stronger.

'This is interesting,' Dial mumbled to himself.

The stone corridor opened into a rectangular chamber, approximately ten feet across and twenty feet long, with a slender archway in the back of the room. The left and right walls were lined with carved wooden shelves that were empty except for a pack of matches and a few cobwebs. The intricate craftsmanship of the shelves, which looked remarkably similar to the hidden door, suggested they had once been filled with something important. But neither of them knew what that might have been.

Hoping to find out, Dial walked deeper into the room.

Next to the shelves he spotted a decorative candle-holder that resembled a menorah but only held five candles. It was made of metal and bolted securely to the left-hand wall.

'Do me a favour,' Dial said, pointing towards the matches. 'Light those candles.'

Andropoulos did what he was told, and soon darkness was replaced with flickering light. On the opposite wall, he noticed a second candleholder, identical to the first, and lit those candles as well. Suddenly the room was bright enough for Dial to turn off the penlight.

'What is this place?' Andropoulos asked after blowing out the match.

Dial shrugged. 'It looks like a document archive. At least it was at one time.'

Andropoulos ran his finger along one of the shelves. It was coated with a thick layer of dust. 'Whatever used to be here was taken long before the massacre.'

Dial nodded in agreement. 'Speaking of the massacre . . .'

The phrase hung in the air as Dial crept through the archway at the back of the chamber. It led to a second room half the size of the archive but far more important. Not only because it contained a stone altar, but because it was the source of the horrible smell.

24

The candlelight from the first room barely penetrated the second, forcing Dial to turn on the penlight once again. He shone the narrow beam on the stone altar that stood against the rear wall. Seven sets of eyes stared back at him. All of them vacant. All of them human.

Dial recoiled at the sight, if only for an instant.

'Jesus,' he said to himself.

From the moment he had seen the blood on the hidden door, Dial had expected to find the monks' heads inside, a theory that was supported by the stench of rotting flesh. But he hadn't expected to find them like this. The heads were neatly stacked in a pyramid. Four in the bottom row, two in the middle, and one on top. Dried blood held it all together like papier mâché.

Andropoulos walked into the room. 'You called?'

Looking over Dial's shoulder, Andropoulos saw the gruesome scene and instantly gagged. All the colour rushed from his face, leaving his cheeks pale. Dry heaves were soon to follow.

Dial turned round to make sure the Greek was all right. Several seconds passed before he spoke. 'For the record, I said "Jesus" not "Marcus".'

Andropoulos kept coughing while trying to apologize. 'Sorry . . . I'm sorry.'

'No need to apologize. I gagged a little, too.'

The Greek leaned forward with his hands on his knees. 'Yes, but—'

'No buts. There's no reason to be embarrassed. Everyone has moments like this. And I mean *everyone*. Hell, I had several when I was a rookie. Trust me, I saw some things that could make a billy goat puke . . . Not to say you're going to puke. Because that would be bad.'

'No, sir, I won't puke.'

'Glad to hear it.' Dial patted him on his back. 'It smells bad enough already.'

Andropoulos smiled at the comment. Not a huge grin, but one that signalled he was going to be all right. Dial gave him a moment to regain his composure, then handed him a tissue.

'Wipe your eyes, blow your nose, or whatever you need to do. When you're done, I'll be back here, looking for more heads.'

'Thank you, sir.'

Dial nodded and returned to work, focusing on the altar room instead of his assistant. Deep down inside, he knew that's what Andropoulos needed. He didn't need attention. He needed space. And Dial gave him plenty. He figured the young cop would return when he was ready. And if he didn't return soon, he wasn't nearly as tough as Dial thought he was.

But Andropoulos didn't disappoint him. Less than

five minutes later he was standing in the back room, right next to Dial. And this time there were no signs of discomfort. No coughing. No hacking. No dry heaves. Even the colour had returned to his face. Somehow the kid had steadied himself without even stepping outside for a breath of fresh air. To Dial, that was more impressive than someone with an iron stomach who wouldn't have gagged in the first place.

It showed that Andropoulos had character. That he could overcome setbacks. That he wouldn't let his shortcomings keep him down.

And, strangely, Dial felt a hint of paternal pride.

'Look over there,' he said as he pointed to several garbage bags in the corner. The interior of the bags was covered in blood, as was the floor in front of the altar. 'I'm guessing they stuffed the heads inside the bags and carried them down here for their little display.'

'Why would they do that?'

'To send a message. You don't lug round a bag of heads if you aren't sending a message.'

'To us?' Andropoulos asked.

'Definitely not. If they wanted us to find it, they would've left a blood trail.'

To prove his point, Dial walked through the archway and shone the light on the floor in front of the empty shelves. As expected, there was no sign of blood outside the altar room.

'No,' he surmised, 'they used plastic bags to conceal this location. They wanted *someone* to find the heads – someone who knew about this place – but not us.'

'Someone like Nicolas?'

Dial shrugged. It was a fair question, but one he didn't have an answer for quite yet. Not this early in the investigation. To change the topic, he said, 'Any thoughts on the pyramid?'

'Actually, sir, I was going to ask you the exact same thing.'

'I told you, I *always* have a theory. But I'm more concerned with yours.' Dial handed him the penlight and told him to take a closer look. 'Let me know if you find anything.'

Andropoulos gulped and leaned closer to examine the heads. Although decomposition had started – which was the source of the horrible smell – they still had their hair and skin and looked remarkably lifelike. Expressions of horror were frozen on their faces like Halloween masks, as if they still felt the sting of the Spartan's sword. To Andropoulos, one head stood out among the others. It was someone he recognized the moment he set foot in the room.

'The man on top is the abbot,' he said.

'Really? What about the others?'

'Sorry. I don't know the others. Just the abbot.'

Dial nodded, wondering if the order of the heads or their configuration had any meaning. 'Refresh my memory. What's the name of the local monastery with the bone collection?'

'Great Metéoron.'

'Do they stack their skulls like this?'

Andropoulos closed his eyes, trying to get a mental picture of the bone room. It had been many years since he had visited the site. 'No, sir. They sit in six or seven rows, one row above another. But the skulls are not touching. They are separated by shelves.'

Dial pointed to the first chamber. 'Do their shelves look like that?'

'No, sir. The shelves at Metéoron are simple boards. Not fancy at all.'

'What about the altar? Does it look familiar to you?'

Until that moment, Andropoulos hadn't paid much attention to it. The sight and stench of the heads had been far too distracting. But now, under Dial's watchful gaze, he had no choice. He had to narrow his focus. He had to concentrate on the stone altar.

Made out of white marble, it stood in the centre of the rear wall and nearly came up to his waist. The heads rested on a rectangular slab that was smooth and ten inches thick. All four sides were adorned with carvings of Greek soldiers. Some of them marching, some of them fighting, all of them looking courageous. The slab itself was supported by four legs that resembled ancient swords. But unlike the blades used in the massacre, these were one-sided and topped with intricate handles that were designed for pageantry. The type of swords used by kings, not hoplites.

'Sorry, sir, I've never seen it before.'

'And you've been to all the local monasteries?'

Andropoulos nodded. 'All six of them.'

'Tell me about their artwork. Do they have any themes?'

'Themes, sir?'

'Does the art have anything in common? Like angels or whatever.'

'Most of the paintings are religious. Like scenes from the Bible.'

'In other words, typical church shit.'

'Yes, sir.'

'Nothing unusual?'

Andropoulos shook his head. 'Not that I can remember.'

'Nothing pre-dating Christ?'

'Sorry, sir, I don't know much about art.'

Dial nodded in empathy. History and art weren't his strengths, either. Still it seemed pretty strange that the public frescoes in the local monasteries showcased religion while the hidden artwork at Holy Trinity – the door, the shelves, the stone altar – featured war.

What did warfare have to do with Metéora?

Furthermore, what did it have to do with the murdered monks?

Obviously they were slaughtered for a reason. And in all likelihood their heads were severed to leave a message. But a message about what? About religion? About Greece?

Or, as he feared, something he knew nothing about?

Dial shook his head in frustration. How could he catch the killers if he couldn't put the murders in a proper context? Without context, he couldn't determine a motive. And without a motive, he couldn't come up with a list of suspects – unless, of course, trace evidence discovered something unexpected. But at this stage of the game, he wasn't counting on that.

No, if he wanted to solve this case, he realized he had to learn more about the hidden artwork. And why men of peace would worship war.

25

Kaiser sat on a bench underneath one of the chestnut trees in St Martin's Square. A newspaper lay next to him. His manner was calm, completely relaxed. Like someone enjoying the warm weather on his lunch break. As people strolled by, he occasionally smiled and nodded. Sometimes he even waved. Whatever helped him blend in with his surroundings.

Payne and Jones watched him from opposite ends of the square. They scanned all the faces round him, making sure nobody looked out of place. Not because they didn't trust Kaiser, but because they were about to break the law in a very public place.

And getting arrested was the last thing they needed.

Once Jones was sure the plaza was clear, he signalled to Payne by crouching down and tying his shoe. It meant Payne could approach the bench with caution. From that point on, if Jones repeated the action, it meant trouble was coming and he needed to leave. Just to be safe, Kaiser had a signal as well. If he noticed anything suspicious, he would simply stand up and walk away.

But so far, everything looked fine.

Payne approached from the front just to make sure he didn't startle Kaiser. For a large man Payne was incredibly light on his feet and had an innate ability to sneak up on people. His grandfather used to call it 'walkin' like an Indian'. Payne realized the expression was no longer politically correct, but 'walkin' like a Native American' didn't have the same ring to it.

'Take a seat,' Kaiser said.

Payne sat on the bench and glanced across the square. Jones was standing near a bus stop, casually looking for danger. He saw none. 'Any problems?'

'Nope. I got everything you needed. Passports and visas are inside the newspaper. They look wonderful. You'll be impressed.'

'Weapons?'

'In a shopping bag under the bench. Ammo, too.'

'Boat?'

'A fishing boat out of Finland. It looks shitty, but it'll do the job. Details are inside the newspaper. Word of warning, the captain is something of a character. He was paid for twenty-four hours of service. After that, he's out of there – whether you're aboard or not.'

Payne nodded. That's how most mercenaries worked. 'Money?'

'I checked my account. We're cool. Your transfer went through.'

'Good. The second half will arrive shortly.'

'I know it will.'

Payne smiled. It had taken many years to earn that level of trust through a combination of keeping his promises and keeping his mouth shut. Those two skills went a long way in this business.

'Anything else?'

Kaiser nodded. 'Now that you mention it, a couple of things are bothering me.'

Payne glanced at him but said nothing.

'I hope I didn't overstep my bounds when I told you guys about Russia. I know race is a sensitive subject to some people, but I would've felt like an asshole if I hadn't mentioned it.'

Payne shook his head. 'Not to worry. You didn't offend anyone. In fact, DJ appreciated your candour. You know us. We hate surprises – especially overseas.'

'Glad to hear it. I've been worried about that since breakfast.'

'Well, stop your damn worrying. Things are cool our end.'

'In that case, let's talk about the second thing. I wasn't going to bring this up if you guys were pissed at me about number one. But since you aren't, I figured I'd ask.'

'Go on.'

Kaiser leaned closer. 'I need your opinion on something. Your *honest* opinion. Lies will do me no good here. I need you to tell me the truth.'

Payne looked him and nodded. 'I promise. I'll tell you the truth.'

A few seconds passed before Kaiser broke into a

wide grin. 'Where *do* you stand on the links versus patties debate?'

Payne and Jones took a taxi back to Ramstein Air Base, arriving an hour before their flight to Finland. Unlike the first leg of their trip when they rode in the belly of a cargo plane, their second flight would be far more pleasant — thanks to good fortune and a few favours.

A brigadier-general by the name of Adamson was vacationing in Helsinki and needed to be picked up that evening for a military summit in Stockholm. The transport plane was a richly appointed private jet, equipped with leather seats, TV screens, and a wet bar, that was owned and operated by military lobbyists based in Kaiserslautern. The flight was scheduled to be empty on its journey north – except for four armed guards who were to accompany the general to Sweden. But all that changed when Payne called one of his contacts at the Pentagon.

Suddenly six passengers would be making the trip.

There were two main airports in Helsinki. Vantaa was the largest in Finland and the fourth largest in the Nordic countries. It handled most of the commercial flights into the capital city and served as the hub for Finnair, Finland's largest airline. The other airport, Malmi, was much smaller and handled most of the private traffic into Helsinki. So that is where they were headed. Located seven miles from the city, Malmi was much more relaxed than Vantaa in terms of rules, regulations, and inspections. Once they were on the ground, Payne and Jones knew they could slip into the terminal unseen. From there, they could take a taxi to Helsinki harbour where they would meet the boat captain that Kaiser had hired.

Reclining in a leather seat, Payne stared out of the window as the plane lifted off the runway. Within seconds, Germany disappeared from view, hidden by a bank of clouds that cast a shadow on the country-side below. Jones sat across from Payne, separated by a wooden table and a map of St Petersburg. Much like their earlier flight, they would do most of their planning while they were in the air.

'What's on your mind?' asked Jones as he tapped his pencil on the table. He'd known Payne long enough to recognize his moods. Especially his bad ones.

'Just thinking.'

'About what?'

Payne sighed. 'Sausage.'

Jones didn't smile or laugh. It would only encourage Payne to joke around as he was apt to do. 'Seriously, what's bothering you?'

Payne paused a few seconds before answering. 'When I was growing up, I used to goof round with the same group of kids from my neighbourhood. There were eight of us, all within two years of each other. A great bunch of guys. Every day after school we'd get together in this park near my house. Football, baseball, basketball, whatever. It didn't really matter. If the weather was nice, you knew where to find us.'

Jones listened, unsure where this was going.

'Not surprisingly,' Payne continued, 'I was the biggest kid on the block. Which, if you know anything about playground politics, meant I was the leader of the group. A real alpha dog.'

Payne laughed at the memory. It was a cherished part of his life.

'One day when I was nine, my best friend in the group – his name was Chad – couldn't play because he had to rake his yard. We lived in this wooded stretch of Pittsburgh where trees outnumbered the houses by about five hundred to one. I'm talking Sherwood Forest minus Robin Hood. Oak trees, maples, you name it. Everywhere you looked, nothing but falling leaves.'

Jones smiled in empathy. His town house was pretty close to where Payne grew up.

'Anyway, Chad was a clever kid. He tried to con vince me to get all the guys to help him rake his yard so we'd have the same number of players for our afternoon game. Obviously, I laughed in his face. No way in hell I was going to rake someone else's yard for free. I mean, I was nine years old. No one volunteers to do chores when they're nine. That's un-American.'

'Amen, brother.'

'So,' Payne said, 'the seven of us go to the park to play football. I'm quarterback for both teams, wearing my Steelers jersey, and we're playing three on three. The sun goes down, the lights kick on, and we keep on playing well past dinner time. This goes on for another hour or so. We're covered in mud, having the time of our lives, laughing like there's no tomorrow. Simply having a great day . . .'

Payne paused. 'Until we heard the siren.'

Jones felt his stomach drop.

'We're kids, right? And damn curious about life, so I grab the ball and run towards the noise. Soon another siren can be heard in the distance. And another. And another. We see the flashing lights and think it's the coolest thing in the world. Something exciting is happening on our block! I'm leading the pack because I'm the fastest runner. The whole time I've got the ball under my arm, pretending I'm being chased by the Dallas Cowboys. I'm dodging mailboxes, jumping over kerbs, acting like a total idiot. Without a care in the world. Until I saw Chad's bike in the middle of the street. The damn thing was completely mangled.'

Payne cleared his throat, fighting back his emotions. 'I skid to a stop and so do the other guys. There are seven of us, just standing there on the side of the road, growing up in the blink of an eye. None of us knew what to say or do. Finally, one of their parents – I can't remember whose – ran over to us and made us turn away so we wouldn't see the cops scrape Chad off the road. Sorry, too late. I had already seen more than I'd wanted to . . . Lucky me, huh?'

Jones asked, 'How did it happen?'

'My best guess is that he raked his yard until it was too dark to rake. After that, he knew we'd still be playing in the park under the lights, so he hopped on his bike and pedalled as fast as he could to join us. Some guy driving a truck didn't see him, and, well, that was that.'

Payne paused before continuing. 'That night, as you can probably imagine, I had trouble sleeping. My parents, who were still alive back then, came into my room in the middle of the night to make sure I was okay, but I wasn't in there. They looked all over the house, but I was nowhere to be found. So now they start panicking. One kid had already died that night, now they're worried about me. They call the cops. They call the neighbours. They call everyone they can think of. In less than an hour, a search party had formed and they're out looking for me. I mean, my parents were freaking out. Totally sick with worry. Finally, after an hour or two, somebody spots me and tells my parents where I am.'

'Where were you hiding?'

'That's the thing. I wasn't hiding. I was in Chad's yard, raking leaves.'

Jones smiled sadly. He had never heard this story before. 'Do you remember why?'

Payne nodded. 'I felt responsible for Chad's death. In some ways, I still do. I mean, if I had helped him out with his chores, he'd still be alive today.'

'Jon—'

'I know! It's *completely* irrational. But that's the way I feel. That's why I went to his yard in the middle of the night – to finish what he'd started. It's the same reason I went back the next day and the day after that. I raked until that yard was clean. Until it was spotless.'

Payne shook his head and laughed at himself. 'How messed up am I?'

Jones knew it was a rhetorical question. Instead of making an easy joke, he asked a question of his own. 'What made you think of this? You rarely talk about your childhood.'

'Honestly? This mission reminds me of Chad.'

'I don't follow.'

'Call me crazy, but if I had answered my damn phone Richard Byrd would be alive today.'

'Jon—'

'Don't even start with me,' Payne ordered. The tone of his voice suggested he wasn't in the mood to argue. 'I know it's nuts, but that's the way I feel. If I had answered my phone, if I had given him the help that he asked for, he'd still be alive today . . . Pretty ironic, huh?'

'Ironic?'

'The reason I can't sleep at night is because of Chad, and my parents, and all the bad shit we saw overseas. So what do I do? I take a sleeping pill to get some rest. Of course, in this case the sleeping pill is the reason I didn't answer my phone to begin with, so a lot of good it did.'

'Wow,' Jones said, trying to lighten the mood. 'You *are* fucked up.'

'For the record, I said *messed* up. But thanks for making me feel better about myself.'

'Hey! That's what friends are for.'

Payne smiled, hoping to change the subject. 'Anyway, enough about that crap. Let's talk about the mission.'

'I thought that's what we were doing.'

'No, we were talking about my demons.'

Jones shook his head. 'No, we were talking about your motivation. That's far more important than anything else.'

'How so?'

'Tell me, why are we going to Russia? Is it to rescue the girl, or is it to rake leaves?'

Payne grimaced. 'What in the hell are you talking about?'

'Don't play dumb, Jon. You know damn well what I'm talking about. Is saving Allison enough for you, or do you need more from this trip?'

'Like?'

'Finding out why Byrd was killed and completing his mission. If that's the case, I'm completely cool with it. I really am. I'm willing to do whatever I can to help you sleep at night. But you have to come clean and tell me now so I can adjust our itinerary.'

'And you won't be mad?'

'Mad? Not at all. In fact, I'm kind of curious.'

'About?'

'His death, the archives, his search, and so on. It's all very compelling.'

'Compelling, huh?' Payne thought about things for several seconds before he smiled. 'Fine! If you feel that strongly about it, I'll tag along with you. I mean, that's what friends are for.'

26

While Andropoulos searched for Theodore, Dial stood outside the monk's room, guarding the hidden door and the tunnel. Making sure it stayed his secret for as long as possible. To Dial, this was one of those times when the element of surprise was far more important than the collection of evidence. He couldn't wait to spring his discovery on Theodore and witness the monk's reaction. Would he stammer? Would he sweat? Would his pupils contract? In the long run, that information would be far more helpful to Dial's investigation than ten extra minutes of forensics.

It would help him decide if the monk could be trusted.

While Dial waited, his thoughts drifted back to the previous night when he had met Nicolas at that very spot. It was a conversation that Dial wished he could do over.

In the past, Dial had always considered himself a great judge of character — whether it was interviewing suspects or making new friends. Yet for some reason his instincts had failed him with Nicolas. Dial wasn't sure why, but he figured he must have let his guard down because Nicolas looked like a holy man, someone who could be trusted. If that was the case,

Dial knew he had to alter his mindset. Most of the people he'd be questioning in the coming days were monks, and if he didn't view them as fallible human beings – men who were fully capable of murder and deceit and all the other bad stuff that went on in the outside world – there was a damn good chance that Dial wouldn't get the information he needed to solve the homicides.

And that was completely unacceptable.

The first monk to be interviewed was Theodore. Dial wanted to look him in the eyes and see if he was telling the truth. If not, Dial was determined to make an example out of him – if for no other reason then to get full cooperation from every other monk at Metéora.

He had to seize control of the case, and he had to do it now.

When Theodore finally came into view, Dial didn't smile, or nod, or acknowledge the monk's approach in any way. He simply stared at him with unblinking eyes. Occasionally he clenched his jaw, causing his temples to pulse and his massive chin to jut forward.

His intensity was impossible to miss.

Theodore sensed the change in Dial from afar. This wasn't the same man who had joked with him about stealing furniture less than an hour before. 'You asked to see me?'

Andropoulos hovered behind the monk, hoping to unnerve him. It was a subtle technique that was usually quite effective.

Dial paused for a moment before answering. 'I did.'

'Is there a problem?'

He nodded slowly. 'There is.'

Now it was Theodore's turn to wait, and he did so for several seconds. He stood in his black cassock and cap, with his brown thicket of a beard, staring right back at Dial. Not the least bit intimidated by his badge or his glare. Not even tempted to speak.

If monks were good at one thing, it was silence.

A wry smile crossed Dial's lips. He wasn't backing down, either.

Finally, Andropoulos spoke. 'We found something we'd like you to explain.'

'Of course,' said Theodore, still staring at Dial. 'Do you have the item with you?'

'No,' Dial answered. 'I can't bring it out here. It's way too big for me to carry. We'll have to go inside to check it out.'

The monk extended his right arm. 'After you, Nick.'

Dial grinned, surprised the monk had remembered his name. 'Thanks, Ted.'

With that, Dial opened the door and walked inside. Everything was exactly as he had left it. The tapestry dangled from a single hook. The hidden door was open. The tunnel was fully exposed. Dial quickly turned round to watch Theodore's reaction as he entered the room.

A moment later, Dial was certain of one thing: the young monk knew nothing about the tunnel. That was obvious from his wide-eyed expression and the gasp that sprang from his lips.

'Go ahead,' Dial said. 'Start explaining.'

Theodore staggered towards the passageway. 'I can't explain *this*.'

'Why? Are you sworn to secrecy or something?'

'Because I know nothing about it.' Confusion filled the monk's face as he glanced back at Dial and Andropoulos. 'How did you find this?'

Dial shrugged, keeping the details to himself.

Theodore turned back towards the tunnel. 'Where does it go?'

'To the morgue,' Dial said bluntly. 'We found your brethren in the basement. I'd let you see it yourself, but I don't want you throwing up on your beard.'

The young monk blinked a few times as he absorbed the news. Then he mumbled a short prayer in Greek and made the sign of the cross, using only three digits – his thumb, index, and middle fingers – instead of the five digits used by Western Christians.

Dial said, 'Refresh my memory. How long have you been at Metéora?'

'Almost ten years.'

'And you've never heard rumours about a tunnel?'

Theodore shook his head. 'Never.'

'What about monuments of war?'

'War? I don't understand.'

Dial walked towards the hidden door, trailed closely by the monk. 'Look at the carvings. Tell me what you see.'

'Greek soldiers.'

'Downstairs it's the same thing. Soldiers and war, everywhere you look. That seems kind of strange for a monastery, don't you think?'

Theodore nodded.

'And you know nothing about this?'

'Nothing. This is a shock to me.'

Dial pressed the issue. 'Fine. Who *would* know about it?'

'The abbot might have known, but the abbot's dead.'

'Who else?'

Theodore paused, thinking it over. 'I don't know, I truly don't know.'

'See, I find that hard to believe. I mean, I know about the tunnel. And Marcus knows about the tunnel. Even the killers know about the tunnel. Yet you're telling me no one at Metéora knows about it? Pardon me for being so blunt, but I think that's bullshit.'

Theodore nodded in agreement, which surprised the hell out of Dial.

'Wait! What are you saying? Someone does know about the tunnel?'

But this time, Theodore was the one who didn't answer. Instead he stared down the stone corridor, trying to figure out where it went and why it had been built. Unfortunately he couldn't see much in the darkness. Not the stairs or the empty shelves.

Noticing the monk's curiosity, Dial was struck by

a simple idea. He could use the tunnel as a bargaining chip, one that would encourage Theodore to provide some inside information.

'Sorry,' Dial said as he pulled the door shut, nearly catching Theodore's beard in the process. 'That's a crime scene in there. I can't let you see it at this time.'

Disappointment filled the monk's eyes. Palpable disappointment.

'Earlier,' Dial said, 'when we were talking about the ceiling, didn't you say something about a library at Great Metéoron?'

'I did.'

'And it has a complete history of Metéora?'

'It does. It is filled with hundreds of manuscripts that document all of the monasteries, including those that have been destroyed.'.

'And you have access to this, right?'

The monk nodded in understanding. He knew where this was going long before Dial had asked the question. 'You would like me to research Holy Trinity and all of its artwork.'

'Indeed I would. It would be a huge help to our investigation.'

'And if I agree to your request?'

Dial smiled in victory. 'I'd be happy to bend the rules and allow you inside the tunnel.'

27

Kauppatori Market
Helsinki, Finland

Helsinki sits on the northern shore of the Gulf of Finland, the eastern arm of the Baltic Sea. Approximately 235 miles from St Petersburg, the capital city of Finland is flanked by thousands of small islands that protect its natural harbour. Sprawling for blocks along the scenic waterfront, the Kauppatori Market comes alive with tourists during the warmer months, attracting a wide variety of vendors who sell everything from fresh seafood to expensive jewellery.

Due to the chaos of the market and its proximity to the sea, it was the perfect spot for Payne and Jones to meet the boat captain who would be taking them to Russia. Details about him had been kept to a minimum – his name was Jarkko and he'd be waiting for them at a specific stall when the market closed. Other than that, they were told nothing. For his safety and theirs.

The cab dropped them off down the street from the Presidential Palace, which overlooked the market square from the northern side of the Esplanadi. Payne paid the driver as Jones walked towards a small sign on the edge of the marketplace. It was written in Finnish and English. The market opened at 6.30 a.m. and closed at 6.00 p.m. Jones glanced at his watch and nodded. They had an hour to kill before they met their contact.

'Where to?' Payne wondered as he caught up.

'Beats me. We'll have to ask somebody.'

The two of them entered the square from the west, unsure where they were headed but determined to find out. They strolled along the cobblestone road, marvelling at all the tents and stalls that seemed to go on for ever. This section of the market specialized in fruits, vegetables, and other home-grown produce. Tables were filled with tomatoes, potatoes, carrots, and more. Cartons overflowed with cloudberries, lingonberries, and several berries they didn't recognize – an edible rainbow of shapes and colours. The scent of fresh flowers filled the air.

Payne stopped at a tiny booth and got directions from a woman who spoke perfect English. She told him that he was at the wrong end of the market, but if he kept walking east, he would eventually find the stall he was looking for. Payne thanked her by buying a small bag of her strawberries. Remarkably, they were sweeter than any he had ever eaten.

Jones said, 'We better get more chow than that. I doubt our trip will be catered.'

Payne agreed. 'You pick the place. I'll buy the food.'

Five minutes later they came across several picnic tables that were nestled between a dozen food stalls. Most of the tables were filled with tourists. Some of them were eating. Others were watching the boats in the harbour. The view was like a moving postcard.

Jones led the hunt, walking from stall to stall, searching for something tasty to eat. He saw shrimp, crayfish, seafood paella, salmon and potatoes, grilled Arctic char, herring, perch, and octopus. The only non-seafood items he found were French fries and onion rings. A little farther down, Payne stumbled across a booth that featured exotic local cuisine – everything from bear-meat stew to moose salami. But one item in particular made him laugh: reindeer sausage.

He was half tempted to buy some for Kaiser.

Eventually, the duo decided to play it safe. They avoided anything fried or spicy before their long trip at sea and ordered grilled salmon, potatoes, and two loaves of Finnish bread.

After their meal, they casually strolled to the other end of the market. They passed stalls filled with jewellery, furs, artwork, toys, and everything in between. Finally at a few minutes to six, they hit the section of the market they were searching for. It was obvious in several ways. They heard seabirds screeching overhead, begging for scraps, and felt the temperature drop as they walked past huge blocks of ice. A variety of seafood was laid out in wooden crates; the stench of spoiled fish came from the garbage bins at the back.

'Damn!' Jones exclaimed. 'This place smells like Popeye.'

Payne laughed. 'I'm not even sure what that means, but it sounds about right.'

'I probably shouldn't mention that to Jarkko, huh?'

'Probably not.'

Jones looked round. Many fishermen were packing up their goods, preparing for the market to close at six. 'Where are we meeting him?'

Payne pointed to a stall across the way. The name above it was long and Finnish. It was identical to the name on Kaiser's paper. This was definitely the place they were looking for.

A burly man stood behind the counter. He did not look happy. He was wearing an oversized apron, the kind a butcher might wear to attack a cow. It was streaked with blood and guts and all kinds of filth. On his head, he wore a black knitted cap that covered half of his brow and the tops of his ears. His gnarled hands were hidden by thick rubber gloves that he tucked inside the sleeves of his waterproof jacket. A scowl was etched on his face.

Payne approached him with caution. 'We're looking for Jarkko.'

'Who are you?' said the man. He was in his mid-forties and spoke with a Finnish accent.

'We're friends of Kaiser.'

The man considered this response. 'Then I am Jarkko.'

He smiled and extended his right hand across the countertop. His glove was dripping with fish parts. Payne didn't want to offend him so early in their partnership, so he ignored the goo and shook his hand. Jarkko smiled even wider. 'You're American, no?'

Payne shook his head. 'We're Canadian.'

'Canadian, my *perse*! You are American. Do not lie to Jarkko.'

Payne wasn't sure what *perse* meant but assumed it was profane. 'For this particular trip, we *are* Canadian.'

Jarkko shrugged. 'As you wish.'

Jones stood a few feet behind Payne, listening to their conversation. He would have stepped closer, but he didn't feel like getting slimed. Instead, he simply nodded his head.

Jarkko nodded back. 'So, why are you here? You are day early.'

'No, we're not,' Payne assured him. 'Our trip is today.'

'Impossible! Russia is closed today. There is no getting through.'

'Closed? What do you mean it's closed?'

'Do you not understand Jarkko? My English is good. Russia is *closed*.'

Payne had visited enough places round the world and had dealt with enough shady characters to recognize a shakedown when he saw one. Sometimes the problem was solved with a few dollars. Other times it required a little finesse. But in his experience, there was always a workable solution. It was just a matter of figuring out what that was.

Jarkko picked up a hose from behind the counter and began spraying the ground in a slow, sweeping motion. A thin layer of grime floated towards the closest drain.

Payne spoke over the sound of gushing water. 'Obviously you're the expert here. If you say Russia is closed, then Russia is closed. Who am I to doubt you?'

Jarkko continued to work as he considered Payne's words. Finally, he turned off the hose. 'That is all? No bribes? No threats? No promises to Jarkko?'

Payne shook his head. 'Of course not. I wouldn't want to insult you.'

'But you *did* insult me. You lied to Jarkko, and Jarkko did not like. I am man of principle. A simple man. A fisherman. I work hard every day. I have no time for lies. Or men who tell them.'

'Really? So you expect me to believe that Russia is closed?'

'No! Russia is *not* closed. Do not be a *molopää!* How you close a country? Jarkko was lying to teach you lesson. You no lie to Jarkko, then Jarkko no lie to you!'

'Fine,' Payne said. 'No more lies.'

'Good! Start with name. Not name on fake passport. *Real* name. It is my secret.'

Payne realized he didn't have much of a choice. If he wanted a ride to St Petersburg, he had to get on Jarkko's good side. 'My name is Jon. That's DJ.'

Jarkko studied Payne's eyes. 'Yes, I believe you. Our trip is not cancelled.'

'Glad to hear it. We can't wait to leave.'

'Soon,' Jarkko said as he peeled off his gloves. He laid them on the counter top and pulled out a large thermos from behind it. 'First, we toast my new friends, Jon and DJ.'

Jones approached, no longer worried about being slimed. 'What are we drinking?'

'It is drink I invent. I call it Kafka. I name it after famous writer.'

Jones grimaced, unsure why a Finnish fisherman would name a drink after Franz Kafka, a German-speaking author. 'Are you a fan of his stories?'

Jarkko ignored the question, pouring the beverage into the top of his thermos. 'Drink!'

Jones eyed the cup suspiciously, then took a small sip. He immediately scrunched his face in disgust. 'Good Lord! My tongue went numb. What the hell is that stuff?'

'I already tell you. It is Kafka.'

'But what's in it?'

'You want recipe? It is coffee made with vodka. Cof-ka. Kafka!'

'No water?'

'Water? Why use water? I fish in water. I clean with water. I no drink water.' Jarkko pointed towards Payne. 'Give cup to Jon. He must drink before we go.'

'With pleasure,' Jones said as he handed the cup to Payne. 'Bottoms up!'

Not wanting to insult his host, Payne took a sip of the potent cocktail. It was more disgusting than he could have imagined. It was like drinking bile. Grimacing, he handed the cup back to the Finn. 'Now that we're done with that, it's your turn to tell me the truth.'

'Okay. What you want to know?'

'What's a *molopää*?'

Jarkko laughed as he gulped the rest of the Kafka. 'It is Finnish word for penis head.'

Jones grinned at the insult. 'Wait a second. You called him a penis head?'

'Never! I never insult my new friend. I say *don't* be a *molopää*.'

'Actually, that's good advice,' cracked Jones. 'I tell him that all the time.'

Jarkko laughed even louder. 'I like you, DJ! Come, give Jarkko hug!'

Before Jones could jump out of the way, he found himself wrapped in a massive bear hug. He tried not to breathe while his face was buried in Jarkko's bloody apron, but the Finn's grip was so tight that Jones wasn't able to push himself away before he was forced to inhale. In a flash, he knew what it smelled like inside the belly of a whale.

Jarkko released Jones, then said, 'Okay. Now we go to boat and visit Russia!'

28

The Greek police were ecstatic about the recovery of the monks' heads and the discovery of the secret tunnel at Holy Trinity. Dial realized it wouldn't benefit his career in any way, so he told everyone at the crime scene that Marcus Andropoulos had found it by himself. It was Dial's way of rewarding the young cop for his hard work during the past few days. It also freed Dial from the onslaught of questions that were sure to follow, time he could use on the investigation.

Before breaking the news, he photographed everything he could with a digital camera that he had borrowed from Andropoulos. The carved door. The stone walls. The wooden shelves. The stacked heads. The elaborate altar. And anything else that looked the least bit important. Experience had taught him the most significant clues often appeared in the smallest of details, so he took no chances. By the time he was done, he had taken more than a hundred photographs. Once Dial uploaded them to the Interpol server, Henri Toulon or anyone else with the proper clearance could examine them on their global network.

Awake since the crack of dawn, Dial knew he

needed to catch his second wind. A nap was a possibility. So was a cup of coffee. But before he did anything else, he wanted to wash the stench of death off his skin. Borrowing the car from Andropoulos, he drove to his hotel in Kalampáka where he was tempted to use the heated pool at the Divani Metéora. Unfortunately, he hadn't packed his swimming trunks, so he opted for a shower instead. A long, soothing shower.

It relaxed his muscles and allowed him to think.

In Dial's mind, the next twenty-four hours would be critical to his investigation – especially if Theodore lived up to his word and researched the history of Holy Trinity. If the monk found any information about the tunnel or the military artwork, Dial would finally have the historical context that he needed to extend his investigation. Without it, he knew he would keep spinning his wheels, unable to connect the secret of the passageway to the motive for the massacre.

As luck should have it, Great Metéoron was closed to the general public on Tuesdays, which meant Theodore could concentrate on his research for the next thirty-six hours without being disturbed by visitors. Except, of course, for Dial and Andropoulos, who would be stopping by on Tuesday morning for a private tour. Dial wanted to see the bone room and the manuscript library for himself, just in case there were some ancient clues or symbols that everyone was overlooking. He also wanted to interview some of the other monks about the murders, although he had been forewarned by Andropoulos that it would be an act of futility.

Most of the monks lived in silence, unwilling to mingle with the outside world.

At the very least, Dial figured his observations would give him a better understanding of the monastic way of life. He thought he had accomplished that goal the night before when he had the long conversation with Nicolas. Now he wasn't even sure if Nicolas was a monk. He looked like a monk and acted like a monk – except for his nasty habit of lying. Other than that, Dial would have bet big money that Nicolas was a monk somewhere.

The only question was, where?

While uploading the crime-scene photos through an internet connection in his hotel room, Dial got dressed in a nice shirt and slacks. He was scheduled to meet Andropoulos in town for an authentic Greek dinner. Whatever that meant. Dial had been to Athens on several occasions but had never visited central Greece. Based on the flocks of sheep he'd seen from his balcony, he was confident that lamb would be on the menu. In fact, he might have passed his entrée on his drive down the mountainside.

It was something he tried not to think about as he left his room.

A few minutes later, while walking towards the car,

Dial's cell phone started to vibrate. He checked the number on his screen. It was Henri Toulon.

Dial answered in French, '*Bonjour*, Henri.'

Toulon paused before speaking. 'Who is this?'

'It's Nick. Who do you think it is?'

'Oh,' Toulon teased, 'I did not know you spoke French. Please, do it no more. Your accent is crude. You sound like a tourist.'

Dial grumbled, 'You know, I was having a good hour until you called. Now it's ruined. I'm tempted to hang up on you, but you'd just use that as an excuse to stop working.'

'Nick, I am *always* working. Just, sometimes, I am working on *not* working.'

Dial smiled at the remark. Despite their bickering, they actually did get along.

'So, Henri, what's on your mind?'

'I promised you I would look at your Spartan photos again, *after* I had my coffee. Well, you know me, I really like coffee, so I am just calling now.'

'And?'

'I have nothing to add. I did a *great* job this morning.'

'Wonderful,' Dial said sarcastically. 'Thanks for the update. I'll talk to you tomorrow.'

'Wait! Don't hang up. I'm not finished.'

'Go on, I'm listening.'

'Next, I pondered what you said to me. You asked if these killers could be Spartans. I laughed at you and told you no because Sparta is no more. But the more you argued, the less sure I became. They sounded like real Spartans to me. So I called Spárti—'

'Spárti? What's Spárti?'

'It is city built on top of ancient Sparta. It is in the Peloponnese of southern Greece.'

'Never heard of it.'

'It is small, maybe twenty thousand people. It is located near the Eurotas River in Laconia.'

'If you say so. Currently I'm in a car park, nowhere near a map.'

'Well, trust me, Spárti is real. And the man I spoke with was quite helpful.'

'What man?'

'An NCB agent by the name of George Pappas. He has lived there for many years.'

'And?'

'You will not believe me, but he swore to me that Spartan soldiers still exist.'

'What are you talking about?'

Toulon laughed. 'See, I knew you wouldn't believe me. You *never* believe me.'

Dial ignored him. 'Give me details.'

'First, you must understand the geography. The Peloponnese is a large peninsula separated from the rest of Greece by the Gulf of Corinth. If not for a narrow land bridge in the north-east corner, it would actually be an island, not a peninsula. Spárti sits at the bottom on the southern end of the Laconian plain. It is guarded by mountains on three sides, isolated from the rest of Greece by distance and geology. Ancient Sparta was settled there for that very reason. These were men of war. They built their city in a location that would be difficult to attack.'

'Got it,' Dial said. 'I can picture it in my head. It's south of the city of Olympia, about halfway to the island of Crete.'

'Good job, Nick! Someone did his homework on his flight to Athens.'

'They didn't make me chief for nothing.'

'Well, we can talk about *that* some other time. For now, let's stick to my point: Spárti is very isolated. And since it is, it is very different to mainland Greece.'

'In what way?'

'For one, some of the people – particularly those who live in the mountain villages – don't speak Greek. They speak Tsakonian.'

'Tsakonian? I've never heard of it.'

'Let me make it simpler . . . They speak the language of Sparta.'

'Hold up! People still speak Spartan?'

'More or less. It comes from the language of Ancient Sparta, though it's been updated through the years. Some experts classify Tsakonian as a dialect, but that's incorrect. It is a separate Hellenic language, different from the branch of Ancient Athens, which eventually became modern Greek. Tsakonian is Doric Greek, not Attic Greek. So it is different.'

Dial grimaced at the information. 'Speaking of

foreign languages, I didn't understand half the shit you just said. But that's okay. I'm kind of used to it. You speak English like a tourist.'

'That was funny, Nick. Perhaps I will tell you the rest of this *en français*.'

'Sorry. I didn't understand that, either. We must have a bad connection.'

'*Oui*. Let us blame your ignorance on your cell phone.'

'And we'll blame your English on your drinking.'

Toulon smiled. '*Touché*.'

'Anyway,' Dial said, trying to get the conversation back on track, 'didn't you say something about Spartan soldiers?'

'*Oui*. I was just getting there.' Toulon opened his desk drawer and grabbed his pack of cigarettes. 'Some of these mountain towns, they are filled with people from a different era. They have no television. They have no electricity. They don't even speak Greek. All they have is each other and the culture they have always known. The culture of Sparta.'

'Continue.'

'This morning, I told you about their ancestors. Spartans boys were bred for war. They lived for it. They died for it. It's all they cared about. It was passed from fathers to sons for generations until it was so much a part of them that they could do nothing else. Some men are born farmers. Some men are born poets. And some men are born warriors. These are those men.'

Toulon pulled out a cigarette and held it under his nose like a glass of fine wine. 'You have these men in America, no? They live in Montana with their kids and their dogs and they follow their own rules. What is it you call them?'

'Militia.'

'*Oui!* Like the Unabomber, Ted Kuzneski.'

'Kaczynski.'

'Whatever! You know the men I mean. Every country has them. Some are called rebels. Some are called guerrillas. Some are freedom fighters. But they are one and the same. They choose a cause and fight for it because that is who they are.'

Dial was quite familiar with militant types and the damage they could do. He had been assigned to the south-western US in 1993 when a religious sect called the Branch Davidians, led by David Koresh, had faced off against the ATF and the FBI, nine miles outside of Waco, Texas. The resulting fifty-one-day siege had ended with the death of eighty-two church members including twenty-one children.

Exactly two years to the day, Timothy McVeigh parked a Ryder truck, filled with 5,000 pounds of explosives, outside the Alfred P. Murrah Federal Building in Oklahoma City and lit the fuse. The resulting blast killed 168 people and injured over 800 more. At the time, it was the deadliest terrorist attack on American soil – since surpassed by 9/11.

And in all these cases, Dial had been called in to help with the official investigation.

'So,' Dial asked, 'the hills round Spárti are filled with these men?'

'*Oui*, but they are different than militia.'

'In what way?'

'They use no guns. They use no bombs. They fight with their hands and their blades.'

'Just like their ancestors.'

'Just like the Spartans.'

Dial considered this while staring at the natural rock pillars that loomed behind the hotel. They stood at attention like ancient soldiers whose sole job was to guard the monasteries from any force that meant them harm. Over the centuries, they had performed their duty admirably during times that were far more turbulent than these: times of war and revolution in Greece.

That's why none of this made any sense.

What had brought on the sudden violence? And what did it have to do with Spartans? If, in fact, that's who the killers were. What connection could they possibly have with a bunch of monks who lived several hundred miles away from Spárti?

'Let me ask you a question,' Dial said, racking his brain for potential links between the two groups. 'Were the Spartans religious people?'

Toulon shrugged. 'That is a tough question. I do not know.'

'Really?' Dial teased. 'I thought you were an expert on Ancient Greece.'

'I am. But no one knows the answer to your question. As I've mentioned, the Spartans did *not* support the arts. This included the art of writing. According to Spartan law, historical records were not kept. Literature was not created. And laws were memorized, not recorded. That means everything we know about the Spartans comes from outside sources, written by men who never fully grasped the culture that they described.'

'Then how do we know they were great warriors?'

'Because *everyone*, even their most hated rivals, praised their skill as soldiers. That is the one thing that all of Greece agreed upon. Do not mess with the Spartans.'

'But all the other stuff – religion, politics, and so on – is just a guess by historians?'

'*Oui*. Just a wild guess. No one knows for sure.'

Dial nodded. 'Which ultimately worked to the Spartans' advantage.'

'In what way?'

'People fear what they don't understand.'

'This is true.' Toulon lit his cigarette and blew a large puff of smoke into the air. He enjoyed the flavour and his civil disobedience. 'That is why I fear nothing.'

Dial smiled at the comment as he pondered all the information he had been told. Unlike Toulon, who pretended to know everything, there were still several things that Dial didn't understand about the case. 'Do me a favour. Get a hold of that NCB agent from Spárti.'

'George Pappas.'

'Right. Get a hold of George and ask him to snoop round those mountain towns near Spárti. Who knows? Maybe we'll get lucky.'

29

Tuesday, 20 May
Gulf of Finland

The 235-mile boat trip from Helsinki to St Petersburg was uneventful, just as Payne, Jones, and Jarkko had hoped. The Gulf of Finland was calm. The weather was unseasonably warm. And due to the northern latitude, the sun didn't set until nearly 11.00 p.m. This allowed them to blend in with all the other fishermen who were taking advantage of the extra daylight. In Russia, the phenomenon is called *beliye nochi*, or white nights. During the summer months, the sun doesn't drop low enough behind the horizon for the sky to grow completely dark. At times, day and night are often indistinguishable. In fact, it is so pronounced in late June and early July that the city of St Petersburg saved money by not turning on its street lights.

Thankfully, the effect isn't quite as severe in May because Payne and Jones preferred darkness for border crossings. Fewer witnesses. Fewer guards. More freedom to improvise.

As they approached the Russian coast, all three watched for patrol boats. They rarely bothered local fishermen, spending most of their time searching for drug runners and warships but, occasionally, when the soldiers were bored, they stopped boats for the hell of it. Just to be safe, Payne and Jones wore waders and waterproof jackets over their normal clothes. That way if their boat was stopped, they would look like they belonged.

Jarkko asked, 'Where you want to dock? You tell Jarkko, we go there.'

Jones had never been to Russia, but he had spent enough time memorizing the layout of the city to know his best options. Located in the Neva River delta, St Petersburg is spread over 576 square miles, including forty-two river islands, sixty river branches, and twenty major canals. Known as the Venice of the North, the city of nearly five million people is connected by over 300 bridges, some of which have been standing for centuries.

The main dockyards sit to the west of the city, surrounded by factories and warehouses. Areas like those are patrolled round the clock, so Jones wanted no part of them. The same went for anything inside the city proper. Even though it was bisected by a twenty-mile stretch of the Neva River, a fishing boat would look somewhat out of place. Particularly at night. The last thing he wanted was to deal with the city police before they even set foot ashore.

'Maybe you can suggest a place round here,' Jones said as he pointed to a map of the coastline. 'I'm looking for a small marina, preferably something that isn't patrolled.'

'Yes! I know good dock. It is near bar that Jarkko go.'

'Why doesn't that surprise me?'

The Finn laughed as he changed his course. 'Jarkko work hard. Jarkko get thirsty.'

'I bet you do.'

Payne overheard the conversation. 'Have you always fished these waters?'

'When ice permits, I fish entire Baltic from Copenhagen to Oulu. I have since little boy. In winter, Jarkko try to stay warm. I visit Mediterranean near Spain. Ionian near Italy. Aegean near Greece. I like girls in Malta. They keep Jarkko warm.'

He unleashed a loud belly laugh, one that was contagious. Both Payne and Jones laughed as well, enjoying this portion of their trip much more than they could have imagined. If not for their mission, they would have been tempted to hire Jarkko for a week of fishing and drinking.

Payne said, 'I'm guessing you use a different boat down south.'

'Last time Jarkko check, Europe is big chunk of land. Tough to drive boat through. Or has that changed? I do not have TV.'

'Nope. It's still pretty big.'

Jarkko smiled as he guided his boat into the river channel that would take them to a private dock. 'Then, yes, Jarkko have two boats. This one is old. She is rusty and smells like fish, but she never lets me down. I will keep her till she sinks.'

'And the other?'

'The other is yacht. It has no rust and smells like champagne. Pretty girls love her.'

Jones grinned at the image. 'Are you serious? You *really* have a yacht?'

'Yes, Jarkko have yacht. She stays in Limnos. Why is this surprise?'

'Why? I didn't know fishing paid that well.'

Jarkko laughed. 'Fishing does not. But Americans do!'

As promised, Payne and Jones were put ashore on the outskirts of the city. The marina was deserted and had no surveillance. Jarkko would sleep aboard his boat until morning then head back to the shallow waters of the Gulf. He would, at all times, stay close enough to the coast to guarantee cell-phone reception. When Payne and Jones were ready to leave, they would phone him with a rendezvous point. If Jarkko didn't hear from them within twenty-four hours, he would assume that his services where no longer needed and would return to Helsinki.

However, they assured him that they would call. One way or another.

Due to the late hour of their arrival, they were unable to use most forms of public transportation, which was unfortunate because St Petersburg has an extensive network of buses, trains, and streetcars. Not only did it have more streetcars than any other city in the world, it also had the deepest subway –

designed to get under all the rivers and canals. But after 1.00 a.m., taxis were the only thing still running. So they walked to the nearest road and flagged down a yellow cab with a green light in the corner of its windshield. That meant it was available.

Jones opened the back door and asked, '*Govorite li vy po angliyski?*'

'Yes,' the driver answered. He spoke English.

'Good,' Jones said as he slid across the backseat. 'Nevskij Palace Hotel.'

'Yes.'

Payne climbed in, not saying a word, and closed the door behind him. Both he and Jones knew from experience not to talk in close quarters. There was no reason to draw any extra attention to themselves, whether it was giving away an accent, a personality trait, or an accidental nugget of information. Their objective was to remain as anonymous as possible.

Plus, truth be told, they were too exhausted to talk. Two days before, they had been lounging near the beach in St Petersburg, Florida. Now they were sneaking into St Petersburg, Russia. In between, they had lost eight hours on the clock and hadn't slept lying down. Back in the MANIACs, that sort of trip was normal. They constantly pushed their bodies and their brains to the limit, enduring what other people could not.

It's why they were considered the best of the best.

Although they were no longer on active duty, their years of training and experience were still a part of them. They knew what to do and when to do it – whether that was on the war-torn streets of Baghdad or in the jungles of Zaire. Their formula for success was simple. Pinpoint their objective. Accomplish their goal. Then get the hell out.

Everything else was meaningless.

But as things stood, they had a problem. A *major* problem. Their objective was ill-defined. What started out as a rescue mission had turned into something else along the way. Something messy. Payne used to call it a pot-luck mission because it had a little bit of everything. Part fact-finding, part rescue, part mystery, part death. The problem was that they wouldn't know what they were dealing with until they jumped into the fray. And that was dangerous.

Especially against an unknown opponent.

To make sure they didn't do anything reckless, they would get a good night's sleep in a nice hotel. They would shower, change, and eat a large breakfast. Maybe even go for a walk to clear their heads. After that, they would discuss everything they knew and make sure they were in total agreement on the mission's parameters. If they were, they would get started right away, doing whatever was required. If not, they would hash things out until their goal was clearly defined. Until both of them were comfortable with the stakes.

With their lives on the line, they figured it was better to be safe than sorry.

But first, before they slept – before they were able

to sleep – they had a promise to fulfil. One they had made to a scared stranger who was counting on them for survival.

Everything else could wait until morning. Everything except their pledge.

They had to rescue Allison Taylor.

30

Allison Taylor didn't need to be rescued. She wasn't the rescuing type.

She was a doctoral student at Stanford who had lived on her own since she was eighteen and knew how to fend for herself. She paid her own bills, had several jobs, and still found time to research her thesis – which she planned to finish if she got out of Russia alive.

But that was the problem. She was stuck in St Petersburg.

The murder of Richard Byrd had been a shock to her. It had shaken her to her very core, leaving her vulnerable for the first time in years. It was a feeling she despised. The tears, the grief, the displays of weakness. None of those things were a part of her life. Normally, she was the strong one. The rock in the raging storm. The one her friends clung to for support.

But this was different. Completely different.

What did she know about guns? Or assassins? Or sneaking through customs?

She was a student, not a spy. The rules of espionage were foreign to her.

A long time ago, when she was a little girl and her father was still alive, he used to say, 'A smart person knows when they *don't* know something.' For some reason, that expression had always resonated with her. It gave her the confidence to ask for help when she was confused or out of her element. It wasn't a sign of weakness. It was a sign of strength. It meant she was smart enough to recognize her limitations and secure enough to get assistance.

And this was one of those times.

She knew she needed help. And she hoped Jonathon could provide it.

In reality, she knew very little about him except his name. However, what she had learned during her frantic phone call was enough to soothe her. At least for the time being.

Jonathon was confident, not arrogant. He had listened to her problem then offered a sensible solution. Go to the American Consulate. Get its protection. It was a simple answer, but one that revealed a lot about his character. He hadn't suggested something dangerous or illegal. Instead, he had suggested the safest thing available: getting help from the American government.

Any other time, that would have been her first choice. But on this particular trip, she knew things weren't that simple. There were other issues to worry about. Byrd had made sure of that. Otherwise, she would have left the Peterhof and gone directly to the consulate.

On the phone, when she had baulked at Jonathon's idea and said she couldn't go, she had liked the way he had kept his composure. He hadn't yelled or tried to change her mind. He had simply offered another solution. He had calmed her down, reassured her of his expertise, and then said he was coming to help. Before she could reject his offer or question his abilities, he was telling her what she needed to do and where she needed to go. And she had followed his instructions like scripture.

She booked a suite at the Nevskij Palace Hotel, one of the most exclusive hotels in the city. She paid in cash, not by credit card. She registered under a false name. When the clerk asked to see her papers, she told him they had been stolen but replacements would be delivered within forty-eight hours. He was reluctant at first, until she asked for her money back and a cab ride to the Grand Hotel Europe, another five-star hotel in the area. Suddenly, he was willing to make an exception. She thanked him by giving him a large tip in American currency.

After that, she had been told to sit tight. When she got hungry, she ordered room service. When she got lonely, she was supposed to talk to herself. No one else. Not friends. Not family. Not even the maid. The lone exception was if Jonathon or his friend DJ called her cell phone. Other than that, she was to remain silent, in her room, until they showed up at her door.

And if anyone else came knocking, she should fight for her life.

* * *

The knocking started at 2.37 a.m. It was soft but forceful.

She was wide awake, staring at the ceiling above her bed, when she heard it. Her heart instantly leapt into her throat. She was wearing an extra-long T-shirt and panties, just like she would wear at home. Now she regretted her choice. She suddenly felt vulnerable.

A chair was wedged under the door handle. Both locks were set. The safety chain was attached as well. If someone tried to break in, it would take a lot of effort and a lot of noise. But not as much noise as her screaming. If necessary, she would wake the whole hotel.

Nervously, Allison stared through the peephole. Two men were standing in the hallway. One black, one white. Both of them looked muscular and lethal. 'Yes?'

Payne answered, 'I'm Jonathon. This is DJ. We're here to help.'

'Just a minute,' she lied, 'I'm getting my gun.'

'Great,' Jones mumbled, 'I feel safer already.'

Allison hurried away from the door and grabbed her cell phone, the one that Byrd had given to her. It was programmed with only one number. She hustled back to the peephole before she placed the call. A few seconds passed before she got the response she was hoping for. Payne looked at his phone and smiled. Then he held it up to the door. It was vibrating in his hand.

'Yes,' he said, 'it's really me.'

'Just checking,' she said through the door. 'Give me a minute. I have to get dressed.'

'Take your time.'

Jones leaned forward and whispered to Payne. 'She's smart, naked, and carrying a gun? She's my kind of girl.'

'Keep it in your pants, soldier.'

'Good point . . . She's scared enough already.'

A few minutes later, they saw the door rattle as she pulled the chair away. Then they heard the locks, one after another. Finally, she opened the door and peeked through the crack.

She was wearing a T-shirt and jeans. No shoes. No make-up. Yet she was stunning. Her hair was blonde and hung to her shoulders. Her eyes were the colour of sapphires. Payne offered his hand in greeting, and she grasped it firmly. Her skin was soft, but her grip was strong.

'I'm Jon.'

'Allison,' she said as she opened the door wider.

'Nice to meet you. How are you doing?'

'I'm fine . . . But I'm glad you're finally here.'

He smiled. The feeling was mutual. 'May I come in?'

'Of course,' she said, still holding the door.

'Thanks.' Payne brushed past her as he eased into the suite. He glanced round, making sure that she was alone. 'That's DJ. He's harmless.'

She smiled and shook his hand. 'Thanks for coming.'

'Thanks for the invitation.'

She laughed nervously. 'Aren't we a polite bunch?'

Payne gave Jones a nod, letting him know the place was clear. Only then did he come inside and lock the door. It was a simple precaution, but one that could have saved their lives.

'Nice suite,' Payne said as he roamed from the master bedroom to the sitting room. There was a couch, a few colourful chairs, and a glass coffee table. A plasma TV hung from the far wall. In the corner was a writing desk, right next to the entrance to the guest bedroom.

'It better be,' she said. 'I spent all my money on it.'

'Don't worry. I told you to come here, so it's my treat.'

She didn't argue. The room was expensive. 'I have to admit, I'm kind of surprised you chose this place. Aren't people supposed to hide out in seedy motels?'

'Dumb people do.'

'So do dead ones,' cracked Jones.

She grimaced. 'I don't follow.'

Payne sat on the couch and signalled for her to sit on one of the chairs. This way, he could study her as they spoke. He still had a lot to learn about her. Including her truthfulness.

'Let me ask you a question,' he said. 'Did you feel safe in the lobby?'

She nodded as she took her seat, folding her legs underneath her.

'Would you have in a seedy motel?'

'Probably not,' she admitted as she grabbed a

pillow. She clutched it against her chest like a security blanket.

'So right off the bat, there's a problem. Not only would you have to worry about the guy who's following you, but you'd have to worry about the crack dealer with the baseball bat.'

She smiled. 'Good point.'

'How about security? Does a roach motel have top-notch security?'

'No.'

'Of course not. No security guards, no video surveillance, no keycards or deadbolts. Even worse, seedy motels are reluctant to call the police for any reason because they don't want the cops snooping round. It's bad for their side businesses, like drugs and prostitution.' He shook his head. 'By comparison, this place is Fort Knox.'

'I have to admit, I never considered that.'

'That's okay. That's why you called us. For our expertise.'

'Speaking of which—'

'Uh-oh,' Jones teased as he sat on the couch. 'This is when she asks for our résumé.'

She blushed slightly. 'Not your résumé, but . . .'

'It's okay,' Payne assured her. 'You don't know us. We don't know you. All of us are tired and a little confused. What do you want to know?'

She gave it some thought. 'How did you know Richard?'

Payne shook his head. 'We didn't.'

Allison clutched her pillow tighter. 'Wait. I thought you were friends.'

'Nope, we never met the guy. Never heard his name until Sunday.'

'But he gave me your number. He said to call you if something happened.'

Payne nodded. 'I know, but we never talked to him.'

'Then . . .' Her voice trailed off.

'How did he get my number? A friend of ours named Petr Ulster. He runs a facility called—'

She interrupted him. 'The Ulster Archives.'

He looked at her inquisitively. 'Do you know Petr?'

'No, but I know the archives. They're legendary in my field.'

'Which is?'

'History. I'm a doctoral student at Stanford.'

She paused for a moment, waiting for the obligatory blonde joke that was sure to follow. Or a stupid question about her looks. How could someone so pretty be so smart? No matter where she went it was always the same. Especially with guys. For some reason, they were amazed that beauty and brains could exist in the same package. It was pathetic. And so predictable.

But Payne surprised her. 'How's your thesis going?'

The question made her smile.

'What?' he asked. 'Did I miss something?'

'No. It's just an interesting question. Slightly unexpected.' She bit her lower lip, trying to hide her reaction. 'My research was going well until Sunday . . . Now, not so good.'

'Wait,' Jones said. 'You were here for research? I thought Byrd was your boss.'

'Technically, he was. He hired me as a personal assistant for his trip to Russia. But since his project fell under my area of expertise, I've been working on my thesis as well.'

'Out of curiosity,' Payne asked, 'what is your area of expertise?'

Her smile grew wider. 'Ancient treasures.'

31

Payne and Jones were exhausted. Their bodies and brains craved a full night of sleep. But Allison's answer piqued their interest enough to keep them awake a little while longer.

'Did you say treasure?' Jones asked with a mischievous grin.

'Yes,' she answered, 'ancient treasure.'

'I like treasure.'

Allison smiled. 'Most people do.'

Payne leaned forward. 'What does that have to do with Byrd? What was his project?'

'Richard was fascinated with Ancient Greece. He spent half of his life looking for ancient relics. It was his obsession.'

'Was he successful?'

She shook her head. 'He spent millions to find thousands.'

Jones said, 'I'm pretty good with math, and, well, that sucks.'

Payne rolled his eyes. 'Ignore him. He's tired. It's been a long trip.'

'You know,' she admitted, 'when we spoke, I never asked where you were.'

'Actually, you didn't ask much.'

Her cheeks flushed. 'Sorry about that. I had just seen Richard . . . I think I was in shock.'

'There's no need to apologize. You weren't *that* bad. And you seem much better now.'

She shrugged. 'I think it's a different kind of shock. I'm no longer blubbering like I was on the phone, but I can't believe this is happening. Stuff like this doesn't happen to me.'

'Really?' Jones said through a yawn. 'Happens to us all the time.'

Payne shook his head at the comment. 'DJ, it's late. Why don't you go to bed?'

'I *can't*,' he whined. 'You're *on* my bed. Unless you're giving me the guest room.'

'Not a chance. I'm too tall for the couch.'

'Exactly. So get off my bed.'

Allison looked perplexed. 'Wait a minute. You're staying here?'

Payne nodded. 'That's why I told you to get a suite. So we can stand guard. You'll be safer this way. I promise.'

'I don't know,' she stammered. 'I wasn't really expecting . . .'

'Listen, if you're not comfortable with us, we can get a room down the hall. But I assure you, we didn't fly in from Florida to hurt you.'

'Wait. You were in Florida when I called?'

'Coincidentally, we were in St Petersburg. Talk about a small world.'

She gaped in amazement. 'You flew in from Florida to help me? Why would you do that?'

Payne shrugged at her surprise. 'I made a promise.'

'Who does that?' she asked. 'My friends promise me stuff all the time, and they never follow through. But you came here from Florida? They won't even meet me at the mall.'

He laughed. 'Maybe you need new friends.'

'Maybe I do.'

'On the other hand, maybe we're just special.'

She smiled. 'Maybe you are.'

'*Maybe* you need to get off my bed!' Jones growled.

Payne stood up. 'Maybe he's right.'

Allison laughed at their antics, which was a mini-miracle considering the violence she had seen at the Peterhof. She knew she should have been uncomfortable with two total strangers in her hotel suite, but for some reason, she wasn't. In fact, she felt the opposite. After two days of being scared for her life, she felt strangely confident – as though everything would be all right.

'Fine,' she said. 'You guys can stay the night, but I'm locking my door.'

Payne smiled and secretly pointed at Jones. 'That's fine. So am I.'

By five in the morning the suite was filled with sunlight, a by-product of the white nights. But it didn't bother Jones, who was curled up on the beige couch.

His guns sat next to him on the coffee table, and his shoes were on the floor. Other than that, he was fully dressed, ready to spring into action if someone breached the front door. Jones could nap on a mortar range and not even bat an eye, but a squeaking floorboard would pull him from the deepest REM sleep.

Thankfully, nothing woke him until nearly ten, when Allison wandered into the small kitchen. His left eye popped open and then his right. He glanced at her, looked at his watch, then decided he should wake up. They had a long day ahead of them, and a lot of decisions to make.

'Morning,' he said as he sat up. 'How'd you sleep?'

'Not too bad. How about yourself?'

'Better than Jon.'

'Really? Did you talk to him already?'

'No. But I always sleep better than Jon.'

He didn't explain his comment as he trudged into the guest bathroom, carrying both of his guns and a black travel bag. Allison shook her head at the sight. Weapons had always made her uneasy, but Jones handled his like they were a part of his morning routine. Some people carried coffee and a bagel. He carried two semi-automatics and a toothbrush.

Who in the hell were these guys?

Allison needed to find out before they left the suite.

She was wearing the same clothes as the night before with one addition: a casual white blouse covered her T-shirt. It was the same outfit she had worn to the Peterhof; the same clothes she had worn for two straight days. Everything else – her suitcase, her personal items, her research – was at a different hotel, waiting for her return. After the shooting, she had been forced to leave everything behind, afraid that someone was watching her room, afraid that she might be murdered. So for two days, she made do with the clothes on her back and a hotel robe.

Glancing through the mini fridge, she realized they needed food. Lots of food. Payne and Jones were big guys who looked like they could eat a lot. So she took it upon herself to call room service. Two days of dining had made her familiar with her options. She ordered half the menu and told them to hurry, hoping brunch would arrive before Payne and Jones emerged from the guest wing. Their timing couldn't have been more perfect. Jones heard the front door as he exited the bathroom. She assured him it was only room service, but he took no chances.

He ordered Allison into the main bedroom, then closed the door behind her. Meanwhile, Payne emerged from the guest room and checked the peephole. He saw a waiter in his mid-fifties. No one else was in the hallway. Payne opened the door while Jones covered him from the back of the room. Everything went smoothly, and within five minutes, they were helping themselves to a huge Russian breakfast – boiled eggs, cheese, black rye bread, cold cuts, oatmeal, fruit, and a pot of Nescafé. Their favourite item, by far, was the blini platter. Blinis were yeast-leavened buckwheat pancakes served with sour cream, smoked salmon, caviar, and an assortment of fruit spreads. Jones went the American route, stuffing his with eggs, cheese, and cold cuts, while Payne and Allison opted for the more traditional Russian toppings.

They ate their meal at the dining table, anxious to learn more about each other.

Payne said to Allison, 'I'm glad you're wearing the same clothes. That means you followed my advice and came straight here.'

She nodded. 'I did everything you told me. I wasn't taking any chances.'

'That's good to know. If you keep that up, you'll be fine.'

'About that,' she said, not quite sure how to word things. 'Don't be mad at me, but I need to go back to the other hotel. Just for a minute or two.'

Payne shook his head. 'No way. You can buy new clothes.'

'It's not my clothes. I couldn't care less about my clothes. It's my research. All of my research is at the other hotel.'

Jones put his hands in front of him, then moved them up and down like a giant scale. 'Your research . . . your life . . . Your research . . . your life . . . Sorry. I'm with Jon on this one. Your research isn't worth the risk.'

'It *is* my life that I'm worried about. My name and

personal information are all over my research. If someone finds it, they can find me.'

'Shit,' Payne mumbled. 'That changes things. We'll have to get it for you.'

Jones put his hands back out in front of him. 'Her life . . . our lives . . . Her life . . . our *lives*. That's *lives* with an *s* . . . This one's a little tougher for me.'

'Knock it off.'

'See, the *s* makes it *plural*.'

Payne ignored him. 'Where were you staying?'

'At the Astoria Hotel. It's across the street from the Hermitage Museum.'

'I know the place. One room? Two rooms? A suite?'

'*Definitely* two,' she stressed. 'I wasn't staying with Richard.'

'You weren't a couple?'

She scrunched her face and shook her head. 'Not a chance. That guy was a *player*. Good-looking, lots of money, and lots of girlfriends. I know he was hoping for something extra on this trip, but I was here to work. Nothing else.'

Payne nodded. 'That's a relief.'

'Why is that?'

'Why? Because if you were a couple, a good assassin would be able to figure out your name in a heartbeat. All it would take is a single call to California, and he'd know everything about you. But since you weren't together, I'm hoping you'll get lost in the shuffle.'

Allison turned pale as she set her fork down. 'You think an assassin is after me?'

'I didn't say that.'

'But . . .'

Payne believed in being upfront with people. 'From what we saw, a professional killed Byrd. Since we don't know why, we don't know if he's looking for a second target. If Byrd owed someone money or screwed someone over, then you'll be fine. This was a one and done, and you'll never be bothered again. On the other hand, if the two of you saw something or did something that you weren't supposed to, then that's a different story. Then I'd be worried.'

A moment passed before she spoke. 'What do you mean you saw him killed?'

'Good question,' Payne said. 'To help you understand, let me explain who we are.'

He gave her a brief rundown of their military careers. Nothing too in-depth. Nothing too personal. He didn't even tell her their last names. But he explained that they were ex-Special Forces, they were close friends of Petr Ulster, and they had a wide network of government contacts. And one of those contacts provided them with security footage from the Peterhof.

'You actually saw the killer?' she asked.

Payne nodded. 'Couldn't see his face, though. We were kind of hoping you did.'

She shook her head. 'I was too far away.'

'In that case,' Jones said, 'we need to figure out why Byrd was killed.'

'His name was Richard. Can you guys please call him Richard?'

Jones corrected himself. 'Sorry. Force of habit. Why *Richard* was killed.'

She took a deep breath and rubbed her eyes, afraid that she was going to get emotional again – which was something she didn't want to do in front of Payne and Jones. They had flown halfway round the world to rescue her and weren't looking for money or anything in return. The least she could do was keep it together when she was in their presence.

Allison said, 'For the past two days, I've thought about everything I've done in St Petersburg, and I don't have any answers. I simply don't know why Richard was killed.'

'That's unfortunate,' Payne stated, 'because you won't be safe until we know.'

32

Taygetos Mountain Range
(twenty-two miles west of Spárti, Greece)

The Taygetos Mountain range extends for sixty-five miles across the Peloponnese in southern Greece. Not far from the ruins of Ancient Sparta, the mountains are home to several small villages that have little contact with the outside world. No electricity. No telephones. And no public schooling. Instead, education is handled by the community in any way that it sees fit.

In some parts of the world, the Spartan way of life would be classified as barbaric.

Here, they viewed it as necessary.

Leon was only twelve years old, but he strode into the centre of the ring with the swagger of someone twice his age. Confidence filled his face despite the welts and scars that covered his back. His schooling had started at the age of seven, the same as every other boy in the region. But unlike them, this was his day to prove that he was ready for the next stage of training.

This was his chance to become a man.

He wore no shirt or shoes, for those were luxuries

that must be earned, much like food and water. He grasped a wooden sword in his right hand and a small metal shield in his left. Some day, if he survived his trials, he would carry real weapons like those used by his ancestors – warriors who were best known for their heroic stand in the Battle of Thermopylae. In 480 BC, 300 Spartans, led by his namesake King Leonidas, held off the invading Persian army. They killed more than 20,000 men before they were out-flanked, but only because the Persians were helped by a traitorous Greek.

People round the globe had been made aware of these events in the movie *300*. Yet he never saw it and never would. He had heard the true story from the time of his birth. It had been drilled into his head, over and over again, until he believed that the Spartan way was the only way to survive, that everyone else in the world was weak and corrupt, and someday when push came to shove, he would be ready to defend his family and his village with the tip of his blade.

It was a philosophy shared by both men and women in his culture.

In ancient times, before going to war, Spartan soldiers were presented their shields by their wives or mothers. They told the men to return home, 'With this, or upon this.'

That is, come home victorious or come home dead.

Nothing else was acceptable.

* * *

Rocks lined the perimeter of the circle. Dirt and stones filled the ground in between.

Leon stood in the middle of the harsh terrain, staring at all the boys who surrounded him. For the time being, he considered them the enemy, unsure who would attack him first. Their ages varied from seven to seventeen. The youngest were given whips; others were given wooden swords. It all depended on their stage of training. The oldest boys, who had proven their worth long ago, could use nothing but their fists; otherwise they would overwhelm Leon in a matter of seconds. Still, if given the chance, they would gladly beat Leon to death with their bare hands.

Leon's father, familiar with the same proceedings that he had endured as a child, loomed in the background, anxious to see if his son was worthy of living. The only other adults present were the instructors who worked for the *agoge* – the local equivalent of a martial arts *dojo* – which had been in existence in one form or another for more than 2,500 years.

Simply put, this was where boys learned to be Spartans.

Leon stood in a defensive position, waiting for the assault to begin. His left arm was tight against his chest, holding his small shield high. He slowly turned, always keeping his weight balanced on both feet. This allowed him to move and strike as soon as he sensed danger.

As expected, the first blow came from behind. He

heard the crunching of stones as someone lunged forward, followed by the snap of a whip. He tried to block it with his shield, but before he could, the leather nicked his thigh. Soon a rivulet of blood was running down his leg. A rush of adrenaline dulled the pain as he focused on the task at hand. He charged towards the nine-year-old boy, who had used the whip, and clubbed him across the forearm. The wooden sword didn't slice skin, but it shattered the boy's wrist.

Despite the fracture, he didn't scream or cry. He just stood there, whip at his feet, waiting for the exercise to end.

Meanwhile, all the instructors beamed with pride over the actions of both of the kids.

Leon inched backwards towards the centre of the ring, waiting for the next strike. This time it was someone his own age. He was armed with the same weapons as Leon: a small shield and a wooden sword. He crept forward quietly, hoping he wouldn't be heard until after his first blow had landed. But it wasn't a sound that gave him away, it was his shadow. Leon spotted it on the rocky ground and immediately turned towards his opponent.

Two boys, both aged twelve, each hoping to bludgeon his peer.

Their shields came together with a mighty clash, followed by the sweep of their swords. Leon blocked his opponent's strike with the corner of his shield and the reverberation forced the boy back on his heels. Using his body weight and momentum, Leon knocked the boy to the ground. Instinctively, the boy raised his shield to protect his face, so Leon aimed lower. He slammed the broad edge of his sword against the boy's chest.

The manoeuvre was a kill strike, one that guaranteed Leon's victory.

Disappointed, the defeated boy scrambled up from the ground and hustled to the edge of the ring where one of his instructors was waiting for him. The teacher grabbed a whip from one of the youngsters and used it on the twelve-year-old's back. Several lashes later, he pulled the boy aside and showed him what he had done wrong. It was a lesson he wouldn't soon forget.

Meanwhile, Leon had a final challenge to overcome, which would be the most difficult one of all. He would face off against an older boy. Someone unarmed but physically superior in every way. He would be quicker and stronger and outweigh Leon by several pounds.

This battle would determine Leon's fate.

Leon glanced over his shoulder and spotted his opponent the moment he stepped into the ring. He was the biggest boy in the *agoge*, a seventeen-year-old man-child with large muscles bulging under his scarred skin. There would be no stealth with this assault. The teenager would come right at him, crunching over the rock-strewn ground, forcing Leon to counterattack.

And Leon would be ready.

He adjusted his stance, just as he had been taught to do, and waited for his opening. The large youth waited until he was five feet away then lowered his shoulder and charged forward like an angry bull. Leon held firm for as long as possible, trying to remember the techniques that his father had showed him long before his formal training had begun.

At the last possible second, Leon dived to the ground, using his shield to help him spring back to his feet behind the older boy. Then, while his opponent whirled back around, Leon cocked his sword and thrust it forward with every ounce of strength he had. The sound of wood meeting skull was unlike any sound he had ever heard before. There was a loud crack, followed by an echo that he didn't think was possible from the human head. A heartbeat later, the teenager dropped to both of his knees with a solid thump, yet somehow remained upright. He swayed back and forth as though he was going to fall, as if a single gust of wind would knock him over.

And Leon just stood there, sword in hand, watching his opponent teeter.

It was an act of weakness that could not be tolerated.

Leon's enraged father pushed his way through the ring of kids. With a mighty wallop, he smacked his son across the face. The boy fell to the ground, spitting blood. He remained there for several seconds, which were a few seconds too long in the eyes of his father. Bubbling with rage, he grabbed Leon by the neck and yanked him to his feet. Then he shoved Leon towards the large teenager, who was still reeling from the earlier blow.

His father screamed, 'There is *no* mercy on the battlefield . . . Finish him *now*!'

Leon nodded, picked up his sword, and did what Spartans were expected to do.

He finished the job without mercy.

33

After breakfast they moved to the living room where they would be more comfortable. Each of them sat in the same spot as the night before. Payne and Jones were on the couch, and Allison was on a chair. Once again, she held a pillow in her lap.

Payne said, 'In my experience, it's much easier to solve a problem when you're emotionally detached from the situation. It allows you to consider options that would otherwise be difficult. Part of our training as soldiers was to acquire that skill. We learned how to compartmentalize our emotions in the harshest of environments. We learned how to analyse data calmly despite the threat of death. Without that ability, we wouldn't have been able to function.'

'Makes sense,' said Allison, as she tucked her feet underneath her.

'As you mentioned, you've spent the past two days racking your brain, trying to figure out why Richard was killed, yet you haven't made any progress. If I had to guess, I'd say that has more to do with your emotional state than your knowledge of the situation.'

'Maybe,' she conceded. 'I've been a little pre-occupied.'

Payne leaned forward and smiled, hoping to

connect with Allison. 'If it's okay with you, I'd like to ask you some questions about your time in Russia. We'll try to sort through all of your answers and come up with a logical explanation for Richard's death.'

Allison nodded. She wanted to solve the mystery as quickly as possible.

Payne began. 'You mentioned that Richard was fascinated with Ancient Greece. What does that have to do with St Petersburg?'

'How much do you know about archaeology?'

'I know a little,' Payne said, thinking back to their recent missions in Italy and Saudi Arabia. 'But not as much as DJ. He's something of a history buff.'

'No, I'm not,' Jones argued. 'I'm just naturally smart. I remember things that dumb people forget . . . Remember, Jon?'

Payne smirked but didn't dignify the insult with one of his own.

Allison glanced at Jones. 'What do you know about Heinrich Schliemann?'

Jones smiled at the mere mention of his name. 'That guy was a character and a half.'

She laughed at his remark like it was an inside joke – which, in this case, it was. Because Payne had no idea who Schliemann was or what he had to do with anything.

'Time out,' said Payne as he signalled for one. 'Who is Heinrich Schliemann?'

Jones answered. 'He was a German businessman who hated his day job and decided he would much rather be a famous archaeologist. The guy had no formal training, but he took all his money and went searching for Greek treasures. Amazingly, he hit the jackpot on more than one occasion, finding the lost cities of Troy and Mycenae and a number of other sites.'

'And?' Payne asked.

Allison jumped in. 'Rivals hated him for it. Since he lacked formal training, he didn't know how to preserve a site or catalogue the artefacts. He was more interested in finding treasure and being famous than anything else. For every piece of gold he discovered, he ruined ten pieces of historical evidence that would have helped scholars understand these ancient cities. Newspapers praised him for his frequent discoveries. The public adored him for his golden treasures. But historians hated him because they knew what he was destroying.'

'Not only that,' Jones added, 'he lied more often than a politician. People never knew what was real and what was bullshit.'

'True,' Allison admitted. 'But that was part of his charm. He lied about his methods. He lied about his treasures. He even lied in his own diary. He used to glue rewritten pages in his journals to change the facts of his life, so he would seem more important after he died. He talked about dining with presidents and surviving famous disasters, and none of it really happened. After a while, he started to believe his own stories, which made it even funnier. No one knew what he would do or say next. But people were captivated by his adventures.'

Jones laughed. 'Like I said, he was a character and a half.'

'That's one of the reasons I chose Schliemann as the focus of my thesis. I thought the modern world should learn more about him.'

'I'd love to read it when you're done. That guy was a classic.'

She smiled at Jones. 'I refer to him as the P. T. Barnum of archaeology. In my opinion, he brought fun and entertainment to a field that used to be bone dry. Pardon the pun.'

'Not a bad comparison,' Jones admitted. 'They lived about the same time, right?'

'They actually died four months apart. Schliemann in 1890. Barnum in 1891.'

Payne listened to the conversation, trying to sort through all the details. Some facts were relevant, others were not. But he would allow them to keep rambling on the topic. Not only to get as much background information as possible – since it was obvious that Schliemann factored into the equation in some way – but he also wanted to get a better sense of Allison's personality. What made her tick? What was her role in this? Could she be trusted in a tough situation?

All of those questions needed to be answered.

Then again, so did the question that got everything started.

'And,' Payne repeated, 'what does this have to do with St Petersburg?'

Allison's cheeks turned pink. 'Sorry. I tend to get excited when I talk about Schliemann. I've been researching him for the past few years. Right now, he's a major part of my life.'

'That's quite all right. Now I feel like I know him, too.'

She smiled at the sentiment. 'Schliemann was born in Germany. At the age of twenty-four he moved *here* to work for an import/export firm. He was very good at his job, and before long he was making a nice living. Four years later, he learned his brother Ludwig had died in California where he had been a speculator during the height of the Gold Rush. Considering Schliemann's lust for gold, he took it as his cue to move to Sacramento to settle his brother's affairs. Within a year, he had started his own bank that specialized in buying and selling gold dust. Before long, he had made millions and decided to move back to St Petersburg, which was a whole lot safer than the Wild West. Especially since he was accused of ripping off his business partner in California and taking advantage of his customers. They used to hang people for that.'

Payne asked, 'And that's why you came here? To research Schliemann's life?'

'Yes and no,' she answered cryptically. 'The first half of his life was important to my thesis because it revealed his character as a young man. He was someone who took big chances to accumulate his fortune, but when things got rough, he ran for the hills. Meanwhile, Richard's interest was completely different. He was fascinated with the second half of Schliemann's life, the decades when Heinrich searched for treasures.'

She looked at Jones. 'Earlier, you mentioned that Schliemann discovered the lost city of Troy. Do you know how he found it?'

Jones answered. 'By reading the works of Homer.'

She nodded, impressed. 'That's right. As late as the nineteenth century, people actually believed that Troy was a mythical city, much like the lost city of Atlantis. This belief was even shared by educated Greeks. When they read about the Trojan War in *The Iliad* and *The Odyssey*, they assumed Troy had been created by Homer, and was nothing more than a fictional landscape to base his riveting tales. But Schliemann was different. He used the epic poems as a treasure map, following their lyrics like a book of instructions to find the ruins in modern-day Turkey.'

She shook her head in amazement. 'Think about it. *The Iliad* is the oldest surviving example of European literature. It was written in the ninth century BC and is considered a vital part of the Western canon. It has been studied by students all over the world for nearly three thousand years, yet Schliemann saw something that no else did. He saw an *opportunity*. Despite his lies, despite his flaws, despite his harshest critics, Schliemann was a visionary. A genius of epic proportions. At the time of his death, do you know how many languages he could speak? Twenty-two. Twenty-two languages.'

Jones whistled. 'Now that's impressive. That's twenty-one more than Jon.'

She smiled. 'Do you know how Schliemann learned them? He used to memorize long passages of the same book, written in multiple languages. Then, if he couldn't sleep at night, he used to shout the passages at the top of his lungs. No one knows why it worked, but it did. In the meantime, he was kicked out of multiple apartments because his neighbours hated him.'

Jones laughed. 'I can understand why.'

Payne watched Allison as she spoke. The way her eyes danced with excitement. The way she used her hands to punctuate certain points. Her words were filled with such passion and enthusiasm, he barely had the heart to interrupt her. But he knew if he didn't, she would keep talking about Schliemann, and they wouldn't get any closer to solving Richard's death.

'And,' he said again, 'what does this have to do with St Petersburg?'

'Don't worry, I'm getting there,' she said. 'The treasure that Schliemann found on the site of Ancient Troy was nicknamed Priam's Treasure. He named it after Priam who was King of Troy in the story of *The Iliad*. This was a common theme with Schliemann. He named his treasures after characters in Homer even though he had no tangible evidence to support his claims.'

'Part of his showmanship,' Payne guessed.

'Exactly,' she said. 'When he made this particular discovery, he and his wife, Sophia, wanted to keep Priam's Treasure all to themselves. They lied to dozens of workers who were helping with their dig, telling them that it was Heinrich's birthday. In honour of it, everyone was given a paid day off. An hour later, once everyone had left the site, Heinrich and Sophia wrapped the gold in her shawl and smuggled it out of the country.'

Jones laughed at the tale. 'That's classic Schliemann. The guy was slippery.'

'Remember, fortune was only a small part of the equation with Schliemann. He also wanted to be the world's most famous antiquarian – that's what's archaeologists were called back then. So he photographed his wife wearing the fanciest items, which he dubbed the Jewels of Helen, and published her photograph next to a detailed description of his findings. He actually admitted in the media that he had smuggled everything out of the country. Well, let me tell you, it sparked a huge controversy. The Turkish government revoked his digging permits, they imprisoned some of his workers, and they sued him for their rightful share of the treasure. But Schliemann escaped to Greece before the Turks could arrest him.'

'And what happened to the treasure?' Payne wondered.

'The majority of it was acquired by the Imperial Museum of Berlin, which was Schliemann's way of endearing himself to his native Germany. But during World War Two, it was looted from a hidden bunker located underneath the Berlin zoo. For nearly fifty years, no one knew what happened to it. It was one of the greatest mysteries of the war. Then, one day in 1993, an exhibition opened at the Pushkin Museum in Moscow, displaying Priam's Treasure.'

'It surfaced in Russia?' Payne asked. 'How'd it get here?'

'The Russian Army's Trophy Brigade, as they were called back then, had seized it and lied about it for decades. Eventually, leaders in Moscow decided the treasure was too beautiful to hide, and they put it on display for the whole world to see. Which, of course, started another controversy. Despite multiple threats by Germany, the Russians refuse to give it back, claiming it was compensation for the destruction of Russian cities by the Nazis. Not to mention Nazi looting. If you know anything about World War Two, it wasn't a good time to own art.'

Payne and Jones nodded. They knew all about the spoils of war.

'Which brings us to St Petersburg,' she said as she glanced at Payne. 'Sorry it took so long to get here. I felt you needed to hear the whole story to understand.'

'No problem. I learned a lot.'

'Since Schliemann lived in St Petersburg for several

years, the Russian government decided that half of the treasure should be exhibited in the city. Since 1998, it has been on public display at the Hermitage.'

'And Richard wanted to study it?'

She shook her head. 'Richard didn't care about the treasures that Schliemann had found. He was more concerned with the treasures that had eluded him.'

34

Payne considered all the information he had been told and tried to figure out why Richard Byrd had been killed. But it was difficult. There were still pieces missing from the equation.

He knew Byrd was a treasure hunter who had an affinity for Heinrich Schliemann, an archaeologist who lived in St Petersburg during the nineteenth century. Allison was an expert on the subject, able to talk at length about every aspect of Schliemann's life, including his passion for Greek treasures. What Payne didn't know, though, was what role she served in Byrd's latest project. Or, for that matter, what the project was.

'When we spoke to Petr Ulster,' Payne said, hoping to shift the focus of the conversation back to Allison, 'he mentioned Richard's taste for young assistants. From what we were told, their talents were less than helpful in the archives.'

Allison agreed with the assessment. She was fully aware of Richard's former employees and their sexual reputations. 'Like I said, Richard was a player. He used his wealth and power to get what he wanted. And they, in return, travelled the globe.'

'Yet you were willing to work for him. How did that happen?'

'For two years I spent most of my free time in Stanford's library, trying to learn everything I could about Heinrich Schliemann. The more I learned, the more I realized that my thesis was lacking an important element: first-hand experience. Unlike most archaeologists of his day, Schliemann didn't live in a library. He lived in the field. He took his books and his shovels and started digging. How could I write a paper about him without experiencing the same things?'

Payne said nothing, waiting for her to continue.

'One day my thesis advisor told me that Richard was looking for a new assistant, preferably a doctoral student with an extensive knowledge of Greek treasures. Not only was it a paid position, but most of the fieldwork would be done in Europe. Obviously, it sounded perfect to me, so I submitted a letter of interest and my résumé. In the meantime, I researched Richard and discovered several interesting things. He came from old money. Ironically, it was made in the same manner as Schliemann – gold and banking. Later I found out their connection was even stronger than that. Richard's ancestors had actually worked with Schliemann during the Gold Rush. So Richard believed they were kindred spirits, destined to be linked for ever.'

Jones said, 'That explains his boat.'

She looked at him, confused. Not sure what he meant.

'We saw a picture of his boat. It was called *The Odyssey*.'

'Ah, yes. Richard's yacht. A tribute to Homer and the journeys he hoped to make.'

'Journeys that included you,' Payne said, trying to keep her focused.

She nodded. 'Richard called me a week later and asked me a number of questions about Schliemann and Greece. I must have passed his test because he hired me sight unseen.'

Payne smiled at the comment. It said a lot about her personality. She wanted them to know that she had been hired for her brains, not her looks. Then again, Payne had known that within five minutes of talking to her. 'When was that?'

'About a month ago.'

'A month? You've been here for a month?'

She shook her head. 'Not at all. I've been here less than a week.'

'But you worked with him for a month. What were your duties?'

'At first, not much. He flew me to Berlin where he spent most of his time at the local museums searching for information about Schliemann's treasures. He talked to curators and experts in various fields. Meanwhile, I waited back at the hotel.'

'Why was that?' Payne wondered.

'He didn't trust me. In fact, he didn't trust most people he met. In that way, he was just like Schliemann. He kept his plans to himself and only asked for help when he needed it.'

'What type of help?'

'He would summon me to his room where I was told to read a document or look at a picture. Then I was asked for my opinion. Did I think this? Did I think that? It was very strange.'

'In what way?'

'It was always something different. One minute it was about Schliemann. The next about Zeus. Or the geology of ancient Europe. There was never a consistent theme, like he was purposely trying to confuse me so I wouldn't know what he was looking for.'

Payne furrowed his brow. 'What *was* he looking for?'

'I have no idea. He never trusted me enough to tell me.'

'Come on. Don't give me that. A smart gal like you, you must have a theory.'

She smiled. 'I have a couple.'

'Such as?'

'As I mentioned, Richard didn't care about the treasures that Schliemann found. He was more concerned with the ones he didn't. So I focused my attention there, trying to figure out what Schliemann was hunting for in the latter stages of his life. Two days before he died, despite a horrible ear infection that had required several operations in the preceding weeks, Schliemann toured the ruins of Pompeii. As you probably know, the city was destroyed by the eruption of Mount Vesuvius in 79 AD and wasn't rediscovered until the mid-seventeen hundreds.'

'Pardon my ignorance,' Payne said, 'but isn't Pompeii in Italy?'

She nodded. 'Near Naples.'

'What does it have to do with Ancient Greece?'

'Nothing, as far as I know. But Richard had an interest in the place, probably because of Schliemann. One day he showed me ancient maps of Pompeii, along with some works of art that had survived the blast. Another time he asked me about Herculaneum, which was Pompeii's wealthier sister city that was also destroyed.'

Jones asked, 'And you're not sure why Schliemann was there?'

'I have absolutely no idea. Schliemann was consumed with Ancient Greece, not Ancient Rome. So it didn't make sense to me. However, a week before we came to Russia, Richard left me in Berlin for a few days. He wouldn't tell me where he was going or when he was coming back, but my room was paid for so I didn't complain. I used the time to work on my thesis. When he returned, he summoned me to his room where we did the same routine as before. I looked at pictures and offered my opinions. While this was going on, I noticed his suitcase sitting in the corner. It had an airport tag that read Aeroporto di Napoli. He had been to Naples.'

'Strange,' Jones admitted. 'Very strange.'

'So was this trip to St Petersburg. We weren't

supposed to come here. We were supposed to go to Greece. At least that's what I was told when I was hired. We'd be in Germany for a while, and then we were going to Greece. He changed our itinerary at the last minute.'

Payne nodded, realizing that Petr Ulster had mentioned the same thing on the phone. He had fully expected Byrd to be in Greece, not Russia. That meant either Byrd was playing a game, trying to deceive everyone who knew anything about his project, or something had altered his travel plans. If that was the case, it could be the reason he was killed.

'Out of curiosity,' Payne said, 'how'd you get into Russia?'

'By plane.'

He shook his head. 'Not *to* Russia, *into* Russia. This country requires a travel visa, which takes some time to acquire. Without it, you aren't getting in. So how'd you get in?'

Allison blushed and lowered her eyes. Payne noticed it immediately. It was the first time during their conversation that she had looked away. The first time he sensed something was off.

'What is it?' Payne demanded.

She took a moment to gather her senses, to recollect her cool. Then she looked at him. 'Sorry. I'm just embarrassed. I don't normally break the law.'

Payne stared at her, studying her every tick. Making sure that she was telling the truth.

She said, 'We snuck into the country. I'm not proud of it, but we did. There wasn't time to get a visa, so Richard got us fake ones in Berlin. Fake names. Fake visas. Fake everything. I don't know how he did it, but he did.'

Jones mumbled under his breath. 'Fucking Kaiser.'

Payne nodded in agreement. Byrd had the cash, and Kaiser ran the underground in Germany. It was a match made in smuggler heaven. 'That explains why you wouldn't go to the American Consulate.'

'How could I? I wasn't supposed to be here. Richard told me I'd be arrested on the spot.'

'Not arrested, detained. But you still should've gone. It's better than being shot.'

She conceded his point. 'You're right. You're definitely right. And if it wasn't for you, I would've gone to the consulate. I swear I would have.'

'Great,' Jones teased. 'Now she's blaming us.'

'What?' she said defensively. 'I'm not blaming you. I'm *thanking* you. Without you guys, I would be dead or in prison. There's no doubt in my mind. So thank you for coming here.'

'You're welcome,' Jones said. 'Glad we could help.'

Payne glanced at him. 'Don't go patting yourself on the back just yet. She's still in Russia. She's still in danger. And we still don't know why.'

'True,' he admitted. 'Very true. But I have a few theories on the topic – including a possible solution to her woe.'

'Did you just say "woe"?'

Jones smiled. 'I did, my good man, I did. Shall I define it for you?'

'That won't be necessary.'

'Good. Then I'll get straight to my point.' Jones looked at Allison. 'How long were you going to stay in Russia?'

She shrugged. 'I don't know. A couple of weeks.'

'So there's a good chance your rooms are still paid for, right?'

'Definitely. At least for a few more days. Richard always paid ahead.'

Jones continued. 'And since he was the private type, I'm sure he had a do not disturb sign hanging on his door the entire trip, right?'

She nodded.

'I'm also guessing that wasn't good enough for him, so he probably locked his documents in his room safe – even when he used the bathroom.'

'Like clockwork.'

'No problem,' bragged Jones, who had picked many locks in his day. Not only in the Special Forces, but also as a private detective. 'Hotel locks are easy. Give me five minutes and that safe is mine. Another two and I can collect your research. By the time I'm done, your room will be spotless. No one will even know you stayed there.'

'And then what?' Payne wondered.

'Then we come back here and look through

Richard's stuff. It's obvious the guy was hiding something. Once we know what it was, we'll be a whole
lot closer to solving his murder.'

35

From the moment Nick Dial entered the grounds of Great Metéoron, he felt like an outsider.

Unlike Holy Trinity, which was filled with talkative cops, bloodstained floors, and severed heads, Great Metéoron was a working monastery. Everywhere Dial looked, he saw silent monks, manicured gardens, and religious icons. It was enough to make his skin crawl. If he wanted to walk round in peaceful harmony, he would have moved to Tibet. Or smoked a lot of pot.

As it was, he was investigating a murder. He didn't have time to chant. Or inhale.

'I feel like I'm back in high school,' Dial said to Andropoulos as they made their way up the stone steps that led to the main courtyard. Potted flowers lined most of the walls and walkways.

'Why is that?' Andropoulos wondered.

Dial passed two monks who gave him the evil eye, as if they had just caught him pissing on a church altar. Other monks had acted the same way. He didn't know if it was due to his talking or because he was visiting the monastery on the one day it was supposed to be closed to the public. Whatever the reason, he felt the cold glares of the holy men everywhere he walked.

Dial said, 'My father was an assistant football coach, which is one of the least stable jobs in America. When he succeeded, he was hired by better colleges. When he failed, he was fired and we were forced to move. Either way, it meant I was always the new kid at school. And the new kid was always treated like this.'

Andropoulos smiled. It was the first time Dial had opened up to him. Even at dinner the night before, the two of them had mostly talked about the case, not their private lives. 'Don't take it personally, sir. These men have chosen a life of solitude. They view us as a link to the outside world. A world that recently claimed eight of their own.'

'Don't worry. I never take things personally. I didn't back then, and I don't now.'

Great Metéoron, also known as Megálo Metéoro, is the oldest and largest of the six local monasteries. Founded in 1340 by St Athanasios Meteorites, a scholar monk from Mount Athos, it had expanded several times over the years, housing as many as 300 monks in the mid-sixteenth century. What started as a single building carved into the rock had expanded to a small town on top of it – more than 2,000 feet above the valley below. There were four chapels, a cathedral, a tower, a refectory, a dormitory, a hospital, and several other structures.

Most of them made of stone. Most of them centuries old.

Dial soaked it all in as they followed the stone pathway between the buildings. Thankfully Andropoulos knew where they were going, or Dial would have been forced to ask directions from one of the monks. A conversation that would have been, undoubtedly, one-sided.

A few minutes later they met Joseph, a fair-haired monk and one of the youngest at Great Metéoron. Because of his low standing in the order, he had been assigned to be their tour guide while Theodore finished his research in the library. Joseph, who was so young he couldn't even grow a decent beard, was waiting for them outside the monastery's *katholikón*, an Eastern Orthodox term for cathedral. Dedicated to the Transfiguration of Christ, it was often called the Church of the Metamorphosis. Built in 1544 to replace a smaller *katholikón* that still served as its sanctuary, it was the most important building in the entire complex.

'Come,' Joseph said as he opened the door, 'I shall show you the interior.'

Dial stepped inside the *katholikón* and felt like he had been transported to another time, another place. While Holy Trinity was dusty and quaint, filled with simple relics and neutral tones, the Church of the Metamorphosis was just the opposite. It was bold and vibrant, bursting with a rainbow of colours that would have looked more at home in the Sistine Chapel.

Joseph pointed towards the centre of the church and recited a speech that sounded well-rehearsed. Like a bored tour guide. 'The nave is topped by a twelve-sided dome, which is eighty feet high and supported by four stone pillars. The frescoes were added eight years later. Most of them were painted by Theophanes the Cretan or one of his disciples. His fame as an artist grew in later years when he worked on the monasteries at Mount Athos. If you visit Russia, some of his work is displayed at the Hermitage Museum in St Petersburg.'

Dial stared at the nave and recognized several key scenes from Christian mythology – the raising of Lazarus, the Last Supper, Christ's entry into Jerusalem, the Assumption of the Virgin Mary, and the Transfiguration of Christ. All of them were well preserved or had been remarkably restored.

'Sir,' Andropoulos called from the narthex, the western entrance to the nave. His voice echoed through the entire cathedral. 'You need to see this.'

'Lower your voice,' Dial ordered as he walked between two pews that led to the other end of the church. 'What is it?'

Andropoulos whispered, 'When we were inside the tunnel, you asked me if there was any unusual artwork in the local monasteries, and I said I couldn't think of any . . . Well, I completely forgot about this place.'

'What are you talking about?'

Andropoulos pointed towards the ceiling to illustrate his comment.

Dial glanced up, expecting to see the same type of frescoes – images from the Bible that illustrated the glory of God – that filled the nave. Instead, he saw the exact opposite. It looked like Satan had been given a paintbrush and told to finish the ceiling.

'What the hell?' Dial mumbled as he stared at the grisly scenes.

Everywhere he looked he saw death and destruction, most of it more gruesome than a horror movie. Bodies pierced by ancient spears. Blood spurting everywhere. Headless bodies strewn on the ground like leaves from a dying tree. Christians persecuted by Roman soldiers. Chunks of flesh being ripped and torn. Saints slaughtered and martyred in multiple ways. Everything graphic and disturbing, like a manic painting by Hieronymus Bosch.

Dial stared at the brutality, trying to comprehend why any of it was in a church, when he spotted the most shocking image of all in the mural: a large pile of severed heads.

'Jesus,' Dial said as he angrily turned towards Andropoulos. 'How did you forget about this? There's a pile of fucking heads on the ceiling!'

Andropoulos was about to defend himself when he was saved by Joseph. The monk heard Dial's vulgarity and charged towards him like an angry rhino protecting her young.

'This is a house of God!' he snarled. 'You *must* show respect in here.'

'Sorry,' Dial apologized, quickly realizing his mistake. Embarrassed, he lowered his head to convey his shame. It was a technique he had learned while working in Japan. 'Please forgive me. I forgot where I was. I'm truly sorry for my behaviour.'

The young monk paused, as if he had been expecting a confrontation. Surprised by the development, his anger melted away replaced by mercy and forgiveness.

'This is our church,' Joseph said, his voice much kinder than a moment before. 'Treat it as you would your own.'

Dial nodded, apologetically. 'Speaking of churches,' he whispered in a reverential tone, 'I was wondering about these paintings. They seem out of place in a house of worship.'

'Not to us.'

'I don't follow.'

Joseph gazed at the ceiling, his eyes twinkling with awe and admiration. 'In the Orthodox faith, one must ask himself what he would do if his beliefs were ever challenged. Would he display the courage and stamina that is necessary to overcome the pains of the flesh? Does he have the devotion in his heart that would lead him to martyrdom? Most people would crumble like ancient ruins, unwilling to fight for what they believed in. But some, like those brave souls honoured above, were willing to die for their cause. And to them, we give our respect.'

Dial realized that Joseph was talking about Christianity. But given the circumstances of the massacre and all the connections that Dial had found to soldiers and war, he couldn't help but wonder if the monks had died for a cause as well – something that had nothing to do with their Orthodox faith. That would explain why seven elderly monks, from different parts of the world, were secretly meeting at Holy Trinity. The odds were pretty damn good they weren't debating religious doctrine. That type of conversation would be held during the day in a city like Athens, not in the middle of the night on top of a rocky plateau.

So, what had they been discussing? What was worth dying for?

Andropoulos pointed at the ceiling. 'What is the significance of the heads?'

The monk glanced upward. 'Those are the heads of saints, the men we admire most. They gave their lives for their faith . . . If you look closely, you will notice halos above them. It is our way of showing reverence to their sacrifice.'

In the dim church light, Dial strained to see the halos. On closer inspection, he noticed tiny gold loops above the severed heads. It was a strange twist to an already strange painting.

'Come,' Joseph said. 'If you are interested in heads, I have a special treat.'

A few minutes later, the three of them were standing in front of a wooden door. It was spotted with black knots and cracked down the middle from centuries of rot. Yet it still hung on its hinges, protecting its occupants from the outside world. The smell of incense leaked from a foot-high arch that was cut in the door. Dial moved closer and saw candlelight flickering inside the room. As the flames danced, he saw death.

'This is the ossuary,' Joseph explained as he opened the door. 'Some call it a bone room. Or a charnel house. This is where we keep our dead.'

Dial walked in first, not the least bit scared by what he saw. If anything, he was captivated by the morbidity. Seven rows of wooden shelves, all of them lined with skulls that stared back at him with empty eye sockets. He moved closer, marvelling at their shapes, the curve of their craniums, the hollowness of their nasal cavities. Even in death, after years of rot and decay, he could imagine their faces. He could picture the way they had looked when they were alive.

'These are our founders,' Joseph whispered. 'They remind us how short our life is on earth and how insignificant we truly are.'

Dial stared at the lowest shelf. Stacks of bones – femurs, tibias, ribs, and more – were wedged under and between the bottom row of skulls. Entire skeletons crammed into a tiny space like books in a library. None of it seemed respectful to Dial, who had seen burial traditions in many countries. But he realized different cultures believed in different things so he wasn't the least bit offended by the way they treated their dead. Just intrigued.

Turning to his right, he noticed a wooden cabinet standing next to the stone wall. He walked towards it, staring at the two framed photographs that sat on the top of the unit. Each one was a picture of a monk, dressed in their traditional black cassocks and caps, although the two men looked nothing alike. One was old and regal. His eyes filled with wisdom. His beard grey with age. Meanwhile, the other monk was younger than Dial. His cheeks were round and chubby. His smile full of life. Yet both of their pictures were displayed in the same manner. They were surrounded by several lit candles in metal trays and tiny gold lanterns filled with incense. The scent was piney and pungent, like a forest fire.

Dial asked, 'Who are they?'

Joseph answered, his voice vacant of any emotion. 'That is the abbot and the caretaker of Holy Trinity. We honour their sacrifice and mourn our loss.'

Dial glanced back at the monk, who showed no signs of sadness. Normally that would have raised a red flag with Dial, particularly in a community as small as Metéora where everyone knew everybody else. But considering the skulls and images he had seen in the last twenty minutes, Dial realized the monks had a much different view of death than most people.

Whether those views would help or hinder his investigation, he wasn't sure.

But he would keep it in mind when he talked to Theodore in the library.

36

Nevsky Prospekt, a bustling avenue that cuts through the heart of the city, is the most famous street in St Petersburg. Planned by the renowned French architect Jean-Baptiste Alexandre Le Blond, it honours Alexander Nevsky, a national hero who defeated the Swedish and German armies in the thirteenth century and was later canonized as St Alexander.

More importantly to David Jones, it gave him an easy route to Allison's hotel.

Glancing at his watch, Jones left the Palace Hotel and turned west on Nevsky. The sidewalks were filled with a lunchtime crowd, a mixture of tourists and locals. Jones had his fake passport in one pocket and his lock picks in another. His gun was covered by his untucked shirt.

Five minutes later, Payne and Allison left the hotel, using a different exit from Jones. They walked to the nearest intersection and waited for the light to change. Traffic whizzed by in both directions. Six lanes of cars, taxis, and buses. All of them rushing to get somewhere. When the traffic stopped, they crossed to the northern side of Nevsky and turned west.

They would shadow Jones from the opposite side of the street.

During the past week Allison had spent several hours in nearby museums and libraries doing research, while Richard Byrd roamed the city. By foot, the Astoria Hotel was only twenty minutes away. It was near the Winter Palace, St Isaac's Cathedral, and the Mariinsky Theatre. Tourists would be everywhere. Eating their lunches. Standing in lines. Enjoying the spring weather in the nearby square. It was a good spot to wait while Jones broke into Byrd's room.

Payne wanted to be close in case there was trouble.

In a perfect world, Payne wouldn't have brought Allison with him. He would have left her in their suite at the Palace Hotel until they returned a few hours later. But somehow she had talked him into it, convincing him it was worth the risk. She could take him to the dock for the *Meteor*, the boat she rode in to the Peterhof. She could point out the Hermitage Museum where Schliemann's treasure was kept.

Payne didn't know where clues existed, so he wanted to see everything.

On their side of the street, they passed a large trade house, which was adorned with multiple stained-glass windows and several patinated statues, the same colour as the Statue of Liberty. In sharp contrast, the building sat next to an Adidas clothing outlet and a discount record and video store. New and old sharing the same neighbourhood.

Back across Nevsky, Payne noticed an elaborate building that seemed to stretch for an entire block.

People of all ages streamed in and out of the front entrance.

'What's that?' he asked as they kept walking west.

'The Russian National Library. It's one of the largest in the world. It has over thirty million items. Since 1811, it has received one copy of every book published in Russia.'

Payne shook his head. 'You're as bad as DJ. He's always spouting facts like that.'

She smiled. 'Richard took me there when we first got into town. He wouldn't tell me what he was looking for, so I roamed the aisles on my own. I read that fact in a pamphlet.'

As they continued, his focus remained on the opposite side of the street. He noticed a pillared Greek temple called the Portik Rusca that used to be the entrance to a long arcade of shops. It sat next to an eight-storey clock tower, which was topped by a two-storey antenna that used to receive optical telegraphs in the 1800s. He had read about such devices – they were eventually made obsolete by the electric telegraph – but he had never seen one.

'So,' Payne said, shifting his attention back to Allison, 'what's your take on Richard?'

'What do you mean?'

'I mean, did you trust the guy?'

Her cheeks turned pink, her standard reaction any time she was embarrassed. In the world of poker, it would be a horrible tell. 'Please don't ask me that.'

'Why not?'

'Because he's dead. What good would it do to criticize him?'

'I'm not asking you to make fun of him. I want to know if you trusted him.'

'I don't know . . . I guess.'

Payne glanced to his right and saw St Catherine's Armenian Church. Its façade was painted turquoise, a colour that sparkled among the greys and beiges of the surrounding buildings.

'Was he a criminal?'

Her face registered surprise. 'What? Why would you ask me that?'

'Why? Because he was killed by a professional. It seems like a legitimate question.'

She remained silent while she sorted through all the thoughts that had plagued her during the past two days. And Payne didn't press her. He just kept walking, taking in the architecture, keeping an eye on all the people who filed past them on the busy side-walk. Every once in a while, he glanced over his shoulder, making sure they weren't being followed. He did this casually, using his peripheral vision or looking at the reflections in store windows.

Up ahead he saw the Grand Hotel Europe. Adorned with gold letters and stylish maroon awnings, it looked far more luxurious than where they were staying. At least from a distance. A black Mercedes limousine was parked in front while a chauffeur waited nearby. If they'd had more time, Payne would have glanced inside the lobby – just to see what it looked like. For some reason, he had always been fascinated by fancy hotels, especially in foreign countries.

'Yes,' Allison said out of the blue.

Payne glanced at her. 'Yes, what?'

'Yes, I think he might have been a criminal.'

Payne stopped on the busy sidewalk. Chagrin filled his face. He gently grabbed her elbow and guided her through the crowd until they were up against the wall of the closest building, out of the way of all the people who continued to surge past. 'What kind of criminal?'

'I don't know. A smuggler, a thief, I'm not really sure. It's just a gut feeling I've had.'

'Since when?'

'Since he was shot.' Her cheeks were redder than Payne had ever seen them, as if she had been running a marathon. 'For the last two days, I've been sitting in my hotel room thinking about all the cloak-and-dagger stuff: the secret meetings, the change in travel plans, the unexpected trips, the fake IDs. Either he was breaking the law, or he was onto something big. Something worth all the trouble.'

'Like what?'

She shrugged in frustration. 'I honestly don't know. If I did, I would tell you.'

Payne felt his cell phone start to vibrate. It was a brand new device he had purchased it in K-Town when he was shopping. One for him and one for Jones. They had left their other phones, Jones' computer, and their personal effects in a locker at Ramstein Air Base. One of the easiest ways to be compromised on a mission was to carry personal information of any kind – whether that was a credit card, a hard drive, or a Blackberry with an address book. Payne's new cell phone had no names or numbers. If he needed to make a call, he had to do it by memory. However, all of the calls placed to his old phone were forwarded to his new one, so he was able to stay in touch with the outside world without fear of being traced.

Payne answered it, expecting a call from Jones. 'Hello.'

'I'm at the Astoria. I'm pretty sure I'm clean. Am I clear to go?'

'Hold on.' He covered the mic and asked Allison, 'How far are we from the hotel?'

'Ten minutes or so.'

Payne returned his attention to Jones. 'We're ten minutes out. Can you hold?'

Jones glanced round the square. It was filled with dozens of people. All of them white. 'I don't know. I'm feeling slightly conspicuous here ... Jackie Robinson comes to mind.'

Payne smiled as he started walking again. 'It's your call.'

'In that case, I'm going in.'

Turning from the square, Jones strolled towards the entrance of the hotel. From his experience, people were less likely to stop someone who was talking on a cell phone. Sometimes, if necessary, he pretended to be on a call even when he wasn't. 'I have her room key, so I'll grab her research first. That will buy you some time before I hit Byrd's room. That's more likely to be hot.'

'Good idea. But if *anything* feels off, get the hell out of there.'

'Trust me, I will.'

'Then call me with an update.'

'Don't worry. You'll see me. I'll be the black guy running towards Finland.'

37

Located in St Isaac's Square, the Astoria Hotel first opened in 1912 and had been renovated in 1991. Complete with parquet floors, crystal chandeliers, and a world-class caviar bar, it was one of the fanciest hotels that Jones had ever broken into.

Smiling and nodding like he belonged, Jones cut across the lobby and took the stairs to the second floor where Allison's room faced the inner courtyard. Wasting no time, he put the key in the lock and slipped inside. Everything was as she'd described it. The room was small but tastefully decorated with Russian linens and fabrics. The bed sat on the right, facing a built-in wardrobe where she kept most of her clothes and all of her research. Just to be safe, he peeked into the bathroom and glanced under the bed, making sure he was alone.

As far as Jones could tell, nothing in the room had been disturbed.

It was a positive sign – one that meant Allison was probably in the clear.

If her research had been missing or her room had been tossed, the odds were pretty good that she had been linked to Byrd. It also meant Byrd had been killed for something other than a personal vendetta.

Possibly his secret mission – whatever the hell that was. But at first glance, Jones was fairly confident that the killer didn't know about her. Or didn't care.

According to Allison, Byrd had gotten spooked on Sunday when he had left the Hermitage Museum. He thought someone was following him, so instead of going back to the Astoria Hotel, he led the guy on a wild-goose chase for several hours. Ducking into churches and stores, changing cabs and trolleys, he did everything he could to lose his tail. But nothing worked. During his journey, he called Payne every half hour, hoping to get advice on how to get away. When that failed, he phoned Allison and told her to get to the Peterhof as fast as she could so they could leave St Petersburg together.

Unfortunately, he had been killed before they left the city.

Working quickly, Jones gathered her research and stuffed it into a book bag he found. He removed the identification tags from her suitcases and made sure no personal items – wallets, prescription drugs, mono-grammed jewellery – were left behind. He even went through her trash, looking for receipts and old airline tickets. When he thought the room was clean, he unplugged her computer and put everything by the door.

Then he searched her room again. Just in case.

Her clothes were too bulky to carry, so they would have to stay. The same thing with her shoes, toiletries,

and non-essential items. But he grabbed her iPod –
in case it was loaded with personal photos or contact
information – and slipped it into her computer bag.

Now he was positive the place was clean.

Payne and Allison stood in the middle of St Isaac's
Square, near the equestrian monument that honoured
Nicholas I, the former Emperor of Russia. The
twenty-foot-long bronze statue, which sat atop a
three-tiered ornamental pedestal across from the
Astoria Hotel, depicted Nicholas riding into battle
while wearing his grandest military outfit.

Allison stared at the statue while Payne glanced
round the square.

She said, 'See how the horse is rearing back on its
hind hooves? It's the first equestrian statue ever with
only two support points. It was hailed as an architectural marvel.'

Payne turned round and looked at the monument.
Until that instant it had never dawned on him that
this massive chunk of bronze was balancing on two
thin legs. 'That's pretty impressive.'

'Even the communists, who destroyed royal
statues all over Russia, left this one alone.'

'I can see why.'

'Strangely,' she continued, 'the person who had
the most trouble with it was Nicolas' daughter, the
Grand Duchess. It made her quite uncomfortable.'

Payne refocused on the square, searching for anyone who looked suspicious. 'Why's that?'

Allison pointed to the south side of St Isaac's Square. A large building made of reddish-brown sandstone stretched for more than a block. 'That's Mariinsky Palace, where the Grand Duchess used to live. If you look closely, you'll notice she has a unique view of the statue. Instead of gazing at her father's face, she was forced to stare at the horse's ass.'

Payne laughed at the remark. It was completely unexpected.

'So you were listening,' she teased. 'I wasn't so sure.'

'Don't worry. I can do several things at once.'

'That's good to know.'

He glanced at her, unsure what she meant by that. From the tone of her voice, it almost sounded like she was flirting was him. Which, considering the circumstances, would have been even more surprising than her remark about the horse. Not that Payne hadn't noticed Allison's beauty and intelligence. Those traits were obvious from the first time they'd met in the wee hours of the morning. But at the moment, he had more important things to worry about – like his best friend breaking into a dead man's hotel room and their getting out of the country alive.

If not for those things, Payne would've been tempted to flirt back.

'Do you get to travel a lot?' she asked.

Payne was about to respond when his phone started to vibrate.

'Hold that thought,' he said to Allison as he answered his phone. 'Hello?'

It was Jones. 'I'm ready to leave her room. Can you put her on the line?'

'Is everything all right?'

'It's fine. Just put her on the line.'

Payne handed the phone to Allison. 'DJ has a question for you.'

'For me?' she said, intrigued. 'Hello?'

'I forgot to ask you something before. Are any of your clothes personalized?'

'Personalized?'

'Initials on your jeans, tags on your shirt, names on your underwear. I don't want to dig through your panty drawer if I don't have to.'

She blushed. 'No, my panties are safe. But thanks for checking.'

Payne grimaced. He couldn't imagine what Jones had asked that had produced such a response, but he'd definitely question him later.

She handed the phone back to Payne. 'He wants to talk to you.'

'What is it?' Payne asked.

'I'm heading up to Byrd's room. Am I clear to go?'

'As far as I can tell.' Payne turned and glanced in all directions. 'Wait.'

'What?' Jones demanded.

'Jon,' Allison whispered. She noticed the problem, too.

Three Russian soldiers, dressed in full uniforms and carrying guns, were walking towards the monument of Nicholas I. Normally that wouldn't have concerned Payne, who was used to seeing soldiers and wasn't the least bit intimidated by them. But as these soldiers approached, they weren't focused on the statue. They were staring at Allison.

'Hang on,' Payne said to Jones. 'I might've spoken too soon.'

'What is it?'

'Some soldiers are coming straight towards us.'

'You'll be fine,' Jones assured him. 'You're white.'

Payne played it cool, casually glancing away. 'I don't know. They look determined.'

'Jon,' she said again. Her voice was filled with nervous energy.

Jones asked, 'What should I do?'

'You know. I gotta go.'

'I *know*? What the hell does that m—'

Payne hung up on him and slipped the phone into his pocket. As the soldiers approached, he casually put his left arm round Allison's shoulder. 'Play along,' he whispered.

'I'll try,' she whispered back.

'Don't worry. You'll be fine.' Extending his right arm upward, Payne pointed at the statue. Then in a much louder voice, he exclaimed, 'I'm telling you, it's made of *brass*!'

'Brass?' she said, quickly understanding his plan. 'It's made of *bronze*!'

The soldiers, all of them in their mid-twenties and looking rather serious, stood behind Payne and Allison, listening to their argument. The largest of the three, who was bigger than Payne and looked like a grizzly bear, tapped Payne on his shoulder, much harder than he needed to.

In a heavily accented voice, he said, 'Papers.'

Payne lifted his arm off Allison and slowly turned round, completely under control. No sudden movements of any kind. Then, with a smile on his face, he said, 'No problem.'

As he handed his papers to Grizzly, he prayed that Kaiser had hired the best damn counterfeiter in K-Town. Otherwise, things were going to get sticky in a hurry. Not only was Allison liable to turn the same shade of red as the patches on the Russian's jacket if she was forced to lie, but Payne knew if he was frisked, they would find a loaded gun. Or two.

All things considered, the *other* St Petersburg had been much more relaxing.

38

The library at Great Metéoron was rarely seen by anyone outside the monastic order. Its books and manuscripts, some of which were over 1,000 years old, were far too valuable to be touched by the general public. In fact, many of the earliest volumes were so delicate they were only accessible to a chosen few.

One of those monks was Theodore. He had been trained in archival science and knew the proper way to handle ancient documents. Although a lack of funding prevented the monastery from building a climate-controlled facility, they took pride in their preservation techniques, locking away their most valuable books in a hidden room that was properly ventilated.

Joseph, the fair-haired monk, was not permitted to enter the library. He knocked five times on its thick wooden door and waited for it to be opened from the inside. A few minutes passed before anyone responded. The inner locks clicked, then Theodore pulled the door towards him using his body weight and momentum. Inch by inch, the portal swung open. As it did, the metal hinges squealed, echoing through the stone corridor like a woman's scream.

'That will be all,' Theodore said.

Without saying a word, Joseph nodded. Then he turned and walked away.

'Please, come in.'

Dial went in first, followed by Andropoulos. Both of them glanced round the library, not sure what to expect. Neither of them was disappointed.

All the walls were lined with shelves, and all the shelves were lined with books. Hundreds of antique codices, manuscripts, and documents. All of them locked behind black metal bars. A carved wooden desk and three matching chairs sat in the middle of the floor. A simple chandelier hung above them, casting light in all directions.

'May I?' asked Dial as he gestured towards the shelves on the left.

'Of course.'

Theodore stepped aside. He was wearing the same cassock and cap as the day before, yet due to the bags under his eyes, he looked as though he had aged several years since Dial had seen him last. He had spent half the night doing research, hoping to learn more about the secret tunnel and the artwork at Holy Trinity.

'Our library is the finest in central Greece.'

Dial tilted his head to the side, trying to read some of the ancient titles. All of them were written in languages that he couldn't decipher. 'How did you acquire the books?'

'Great Metéoron was blessed by good fortune. A Serbian ruler named Simeon Uroš gave us a large endowment in the mid-fourteenth century. It allowed us to build the original *katholikón* and expand our cloisters. Eventually his son John Uroš joined our order. He took the name Iosaph and ran our monastery for many years. His wealth and guidance helped us persevere.'

'And the books?'

'Some were donated. Some were bought. Some were written here.'

'Really? What type of books did your brethren write?'

Slipping on a pair of gloves to protect the ancient relics, Theodore walked to the front corner of the room. With a set of brass keys, he unlocked the metal cage and removed a single book. It was nearly six inches thick and covered in tan-coloured goatskin. He carried it to the wooden desk and carefully laid it open. 'This is one of our recent volumes. It is less than a century old. Yet it reveals the quality of our bookmaking.'

Dial and Andropoulos leaned closer, both of them anxious to inspect it.

Even though it was written in Greek, Dial was overwhelmed by its beauty. The pages were filled with the most elegant calligraphy he had ever seen. Words flowed into each other like waves on the sea. The margins were illustrated in bold, bright colours – images that were so detailed, so transcendent, that Dial was able to understand the story without reading it.

'The birth of Christ,' he said. 'It's magnificent.'

Theodore nodded. 'Pride is discouraged by our order. Yet it is hard not to be proud.'

Dial gestured towards the shelves. 'How many of these books were made here?'

'Many,' he said cryptically. 'Centuries ago, every book of significance was either written in monasteries or protected by them. Our library has volumes on virtually every field: history, alchemy, philosophy, grammar, politics.'

'And religion. Don't forget religion.'

Theodore nodded. 'We *never* forget religion.'

Dial laughed as he walked to the right-hand side of the room. Andropoulos followed closely, browsing the bookcases for anything that looked out of place. As a native speaker, he was able to read most of the titles. Occasionally, for Dial's benefit, he translated their names aloud. But nothing stood out to either of them. No volumes on war or weaponry – other than some Grecian classics that were available in most libraries. Books like *The Odyssey* and *The Iliad*.

'So,' Dial said when he was tired of browsing, 'what did you learn about the tunnel?'

Theodore slid behind the desk and took a seat. He motioned for Dial and Andropoulos to sit in the two chairs across from him. 'Regrettably, not much.'

'Really? With all these books, I figured you'd find something of value. Didn't you say the entire history of Metéora was chronicled here?'

'Yes, I did.'

Dial shook his head and grimaced. 'I don't know about you, but I find it *odd* that something as elaborate as that tunnel is not mentioned in any of these volumes. In fact, I'd be tempted to go one step further. I might even use the word *unlikely*.'

Theodore said nothing. He simply folded his hands on the desk in front of him and returned Dial's stare. Unfortunately, because of the monk's beard, Dial found it difficult to read his facial expressions. Was he smirking? Or grinning? Or gritting his teeth? Dial couldn't tell. All he could do was study Theodore's eyes, hoping to find a clue as to what he was thinking.

'Marcus,' Dial said, as he started to stand, 'are you ready to go?'

Andropoulos glanced at him, temporarily confused. 'We're leaving?'

'The library, yes. The grounds, no. This monastery is filled with potential witnesses. Let's go pester some.'

Andropoulos nodded in understanding. He knew what Dial was doing and was anxious to play along. 'Should I call the station? I can get some reinforcements.'

'Let's start with five. Make sure they bring dinner. We might be here a while.'

'Yes, sir.'

'And coffee. Lots of coffee.'

In unison, the two of them headed towards the door. They made it halfway across the room before

Theodore cleared his throat. Dial tried not to grin as he stopped in his tracks.

'Yes?' Dial said over his shoulder.

'Sometimes, more can be learned by what is missing than what is found.'

He refused to turn round. 'Meaning?'

'Please have a seat,' the monk implored. 'There is something I must show you.'

Andropoulos glanced at Dial, who nodded his approval. The two of them returned to their chairs while Theodore fetched a book from the back corner of the room where some of the shelves were dotted with old black-and-white photographs of monks posing in the grounds. None of them smiling. Just standing there like it was torture. Dial knew that feeling. A similar photo used to hang on his parents' wall. It documented the day he graduated from college. It was a proud moment for his family, so he willingly stood there and let them take picture after picture to commemorate the occasion. But he sure as hell hadn't been happy about it.

'Who are they?' Dial asked, pointing at the photographs. As far as he could see, it was the only section of the room that had any personal items.

Theodore replied as he carried a single book back to the desk. 'They are monks who lived at Metéora . . . All have since moved on.'

'Moved on as in transferred, or moved on as in dead?'

'A little of both.'

'Why are the pictures kept in that corner section?'

'It's where our historical records are stored. The photographs are part of our history.'

Dial nodded. 'A picture is worth a thousand words.'

Theodore said nothing.

'So,' Dial continued, 'what did you want us to see? Or *not* see, as the case may be?'

'The history of Holy Trinity,' said the monk as he carefully opened the book.

Its cover was hard ornamental leather, dark brown in colour. An Orthodox cross had been embossed on the front. It stood a quarter of an inch higher than the rest of the leather. Tiny brass studs had been inserted into all four corners of the front and back, which lifted the book off flat surfaces, protecting it from dust or spills. The spine was etched with rustic gold, the same colour as the outer edge of the pages. They glistened under the light of the chandelier.

'Over the centuries,' he said as he turned the pages, 'my brethren have documented every significant moment at Holy Trinity. This includes all new construction. Whenever the monastery expanded, so did this book.'

'And you've done this for every monastery?'

Theodore nodded. 'We chronicle the past to enrich the future.'

'That's very noble of you. However, unless I'm missing something, your brethren weren't very thorough. If they had been, they would've noticed the tunnel that I found.'

'It isn't you who is missing something. It is this volume.' Theodore turned it towards Dial and Andropoulos so they could see it better. 'Pages have been taken.'

Dial stood up. 'How do you know?'

The monk ran his gloved finger down the centre crease of the book. A section had been removed, obvious from the torn fragments that still remained. 'I do not know who and I do not know when, but someone *butchered* this book as they butchered my brothers.'

Dial glanced at the monk and saw fire in his eyes. They were like two burning embers. Considering the lack of emotions that most of his brethren had shown, it was a surprising display of passion. Still, something about it seemed strange. Unless Dial was mistaken, the rage had surfaced over the mutilation of the book, not the execution of the monks. Which was eerily similar to Joseph's reaction earlier in the day. He had practically spit venom when Dial cursed inside the *katholikón*, plus he had been emotional over the artwork on the ceiling. However, he had barely blinked an eye over the death of the abbot or the caretaker of Holy Trinity – two men he knew.

Dial wasn't sure why, but something was seriously wrong with their priorities.

Andropoulos asked, 'Is this the only book that has been vandalized?'

The monk shrugged, visibly upset. 'It is too early to tell. I will know more later.'

Dial nodded as he walked over to the corner where the historical records were kept. He wasn't concerned about the books on the other shelves – the ones about grammar, alchemy, and religion. His main concern was the history of Metéora. If Holy Trinity had a secret tunnel, maybe the other monasteries did as well. Or something similar. 'Did you check any of these?'

'They were the first ones I inspected.'

'And?'

'I found nothing wrong.'

Dial looked through the iron bars that protected this section. The bars were solid and the locks were unharmed. There was an open slot on the third shelf from the top. It was where *Holy Trinity* had been pulled by Theodore. All the surrounding titles were written in Greek, which prevented Dial from reading them. But he noticed all of them had been bound in the same ornamental leather as *Holy Trinity*. He counted twenty-three volumes. Twenty-four, if he included the one on the desk. That was the original number of monasteries at Metéora.

That meant none of the other journals had been stolen.

Frustrated, Dial looked at the other shelves, hoping to find anything that might help his case. His eyes were immediately drawn to one black-and-white photograph. It featured seven monks standing on the balcony of Holy Trinity. The distant valley could be seen behind them, although much of it was blocked by the tall caps that they wore. Focusing on their faces, Dial tried to imagine what they looked like behind their beards. Remarkably, all of the monks looked *different*, a diverse mix of facial features that could best be explained by geography.

Dial had travelled enough in his lifetime to recognize ethnic features in certain people. Whether it was the shape of their eyes, the slant of their brow, or the curve of their mouth, he was often able to guess where people were from. And *these* men were not from the same country. They looked too dissimilar to be from the same regional gene pool.

'Theodore,' Dial said, pointing, 'may I see this photograph?'

The monk nodded and walked towards the corner shelf. He undid the latch and reached inside the case. The picture was displayed in a polished brass frame. He grabbed it and showed it to Dial. 'That was taken decades ago. I would guess forty years or so.'

Dial did the math in his head and came up with a date. 'Who were they?'

'I am not sure. That picture is older than I.'

Dial grunted. 'I wish I could say the same.'

'I know I can,' Andropoulos said from his chair.

Dial sneered at the young cop. 'I might be old but at least I'm on my feet and working.'

Andropoulos got the hint and decided to search the library for clues.

Dial returned his attention to the picture. The moment he did, his eyes locked on the young monk in the middle of the back row. A wave of recognition swept over him. It was so strong that a gasp emerged from his lips. 'Holy shit.'

Theodore frowned at the profanity.

'Sorry,' Dial said as he pointed at the picture. 'But I *know* that man.'

Andropoulos heard the comment from across the room. 'You know *who*?'

Dial tapped on the picture's glass. 'He's several years younger, but I'd recognize him anywhere. That's Nicolas, the old monk from Holy Trinity.'

'You're sure of this?' asked Theodore.

'I'm positive.'

Theodore considered this information as he walked towards the desk. With the picture in his gloved hands, he carefully removed the bottom of the brass frame and pulled out the photograph. He flipped it over and laid it flat on the desk. Dial and Andropoulos leaned forward as the monk silently translated the caption on the back. It was written in light pencil.

'You are right,' the monk said. 'His name is Nicolas. He once lived at Holy Trinity.'

'And the others? Who are they?'

'I can tell you their names, but they mean nothing to me . . . That is, except one.'

Dial raised an eyebrow. 'Which one?'

Theodore flipped the photograph over and pointed

to the tall man on the far left. Other than Nicolas, he was the youngest man in the picture. All the other monks ranged in age from thirty to seventy. 'This was our abbot. The one who was killed.'

Andropoulos nodded in agreement. He had met the abbot a few times.

'And neither of you recognize anyone else in the photo?' Dial asked.

Both men shook their heads. The other monks were from a different generation.

'Is there anyone – maybe an older monk in the monastery – who might know them?'

'Probably not,' Theodore admitted. 'Ours is a younger community. After a certain age, most of our older members move on to Mount Athos to continue their spiritual growth.'

'Mount Athos?' Dial asked, unfamiliar with the name.

Theodore nodded. 'Catholic priests have the Vatican. *We* have Mount Athos.'

39

While in the MANIACs, Jones had been forced to make life or death decisions on nearly every mission. Communication could rarely be counted on in the desolate outposts where they operated, so his men had relied on him to read Payne's mind any time their unit was separated.

It was a skill that had saved them from friendly fire on more than one occasion.

Their strange psychic ability continued in their everyday lives. Payne and Jones spent so much time together that they could read each other like identical twins – twins who happened to look nothing alike. Whether it was reaching for the phone just before the other called or finishing each other's sentences, they knew what the other was thinking most of the time. And in this situation, Jones had no doubt that Payne wanted him to search Byrd's room.

So that's what he set out to do. As quickly as possible.

Unlike Allison's single room facing the inner courtyard, Byrd was staying in a large suite on an upper floor that overlooked St Isaac's Square. Jones knew elevators were dangerous places, often equipped with video cameras and full of witnesses who had nothing better to do than stare at one another, so he opted to take the stairs instead. He climbed the steps two at a time, hoping to reach Byrd's window before anything bad happened between Payne and the soldiers.

In a worst-case scenario, Jones was willing to fire a few shots into the air just to make the Russians re-evaluate their priorities. What's more important: a man and woman sightseeing in the square or someone firing shots in a nearby hotel? Not only would the soldiers come running, but Payne and Allison could escape in the resulting chaos.

The hallway was deserted when Jones reached Byrd's suite. The do not disturb sign, written in Russian, still hung from the doorknob. Wasting no time, Jones pulled out his lock picks and went to work. Less than thirty seconds later he was slipping into the room.

'Hello,' he called softly. 'Is anyone in here? The door was wide open.'

He waited for a response. Hearing nothing, he closed and locked the door, put on the security chain, and then set Allison's book bag and computer on the parquet floor.

Allison had briefed him on the basic layout of the corner suite, so he had a pretty good idea where everything was. With gun in hand, he crept from room to room, making sure that he was alone, before he went to the bank of windows in the main sitting area. The white curtains were drawn, filling the suite with diffused light. He parted them and carefully peeked outside. He had a glorious view of St Isaac's Cathedral, its gilded dome glistening high above the city below, but was unable to see the monument to Nicolas I.

'Shit!' he swore as he hurried towards the next room. He passed through a set of French doors, hoping he would have a different angle from the bedroom, but quickly realized that it shared the same outer wall as the sitting room. 'Shit, shit, shit!'

His last hope was the bathroom. It was on the far side of the bedroom, away from the massive cathedral. He knew it had a small frosted window – he'd noticed it when he checked the bathroom for trouble – but wasn't sure what direction it faced. Heart pounding, he undid the lock and threw the window open. Glancing outside, he realized it was angled perfectly, overlooking the equestrian monument that towered above the square. And in front of it, he saw Payne, Allison, and three uniformed soldiers. None of whom looked happy.

Grizzly snatched Payne's papers then studied them intently, searching for anything that might be missing or incorrect. Meanwhile, the other two soldiers ogled Allison as though she was dancing on stage at a local strip club. They whispered obscene remarks to each other, describing what they would like to do with her if they ever got her alone. One even made a slurping sound. Neither Payne nor Allison could understand

Russian, but they had a pretty good idea what the soldiers were saying and who they were talking about.

And it sure as hell wasn't Payne.

Remarkably, he managed to keep his cool. If the same situation had presented itself in an anonymous tavern, Payne would have fought the soldiers and anyone who tried to intervene. And the odds were pretty good that Payne would have won. His fighting skills were that extraordinary. But as things stood, he had nothing to gain by being aggressive. The last thing he wanted to do was bring any attention to himself, so he casually put his arm round Allison's waist and pulled her close. It was his way of marking his territory.

'You no look Canada,' Grizzly declared without lifting his gaze from Payne's paperwork. His accent was thick and slurred. His face was scarred. 'You look Poland.'

Payne's paternal ancestors were actually from a small town outside Warsaw. When his great-grandfather came to America, the guards at Ellis Island had been unable to pronounce his surname, which was Paynewski. So they gave him two choices: either shorten his name to Payne or get back on the boat and return to Europe. His family name had been Payne ever since.

But he wasn't going to tell Grizzly that. The less the Russian knew, the better.

'Canadian, born and raised,' Payne claimed.

'What city?'

'Toronto.'

Grizzly glanced at Payne. He studied his face with the same intensity he had been studying Payne's paperwork. The two of them were roughly the same height, so Grizzly was able to look Payne directly in his eyes. Man to man. After an uncomfortable silence, he asked, 'You like the hockey?'

Payne nodded. 'I'm Canadian. I *love* hockey.'

'You know Evgeni Malkin?'

'Of course I do. He's a *great* NHL player. He's Russian, right?'

'*Da.*' He paused for a moment, still holding Payne's documents in his meaty grip. Then, with a hint of bravado, he claimed, 'I play Malkin in Magnitogorsk.'

'Really? You must be pretty good. How did you do?'

Grizzly sneered, crinkling his oversized brow. 'He win.'

'Sorry to hear that.'

He handed the papers back to Payne then turned his attention to Allison. 'Who is this?'

'That's my girlfriend,' he said, trying to talk for her as much as possible. 'She's a big fan of history so I wanted her to see St Petersburg. She loves the place.'

Grizzly stared at her with lust in his eyes. Starting with her legs, he slowly moved his gaze upwards, lingering in all the inappropriate places, until he finally stopped on her face. 'She does not look smart to me.'

Allison's cheeks turned a light shade of pink.

'But she is,' Payne claimed. 'At least *most* of the time. She thinks this horse monument is made of bronze.'

Grizzly looked at the horse and grinned. '*Da.*'

'Really?' Payne said. 'I guess I was wrong. I could've sworn it was made of brass.'

Allison managed a smile but said nothing in return. Not even a friendly retort.

And Grizzly found that unusual. Especially for a couple on vacation. 'Papers.'

The order frazzled Allison; she wasn't used to this type of deceit.

Payne encouraged her by patting her on her hip. 'Give him your papers, honey.'

She did as she was told but still said nothing. Too scared to speak.

Grizzly flipped through her passport and visa, studying all the signatures. Finally, after several anxious seconds, he said, 'You no look Canada. You look California.'

Allison's face turned bright red. In her mind, the Russian had figured out where she was from. Instantly, her heart started throbbing twice as hard. She could feel it pounding in her ribcage like someone playing a bass drum. And Payne felt it, too. His arm was draped round her back, but he felt the intense thumping in her chest. Panic was setting in.

In a flash, he knew he had to cover for her.

'Look!' he said as he pointed at her cheeks. 'You made her blush! She *always* gets that way when people compare her to a beach bunny. I tease her all the time. It's hilarious.'

'She no talk? Why she no talk?'

Payne shrugged. 'She's just a little shy. That's all.'

'I no like shy when I ask question.'

Grizzly stepped forward, invading her personal space. Standing close, he loomed over her like the monument loomed over the square, only the Russian seemed much more dangerous.

Threatened by the soldier's proximity, Allison reached her arm round Payne and clung to him for support. As she did, she felt the handgun tucked in the rear of his belt. Until that moment, she had completely forgotten about Payne's weapon and the threat of violence, but the cold touch of his gun made her flash back to the Peterhof. It made her remember the pink mist when Richard's brains were splattered into the fountain. It made her think of death.

Grizzly glared at her. 'He say you like history . . . Say something *smart*.'

'Smart?' she asked, meekly. It was her first word since he started questioning them.

'Tell me about city. Something I not know.'

Allison racked her brain, trying to remember one of the stories she had learned about St Petersburg since her arrival. For the past hour, she hadn't been able to keep her mouth shut, spouting random facts like a knowledgeable tour guide. But now that she needed one to save her life, she was drawing a complete blank. Which made her even more anxious.

Payne noticed the fear in her eyes and started to speak for her again. 'We went drinking last night, and she told me—'

Grizzly interrupted him. 'I no care what she say *then*. I care what she say *now*.'

'Tell him, honey.'

As luck should have it, Payne's comment about drinking actually helped her remember one of the best stories she had heard about the city's history. That wasn't his intent – she hadn't shared the story in their time together – but it triggered her memory.

'Did you know,' she said as her voice cracked, 'that Peter the Great opened the first museum in St Petersburg?' She took a deep breath, trying to maintain her composure as the soldiers continued staring at her. 'He wanted to bring culture to the city that he created and figured a museum would be a great way to start. Once it was built, though, he was worried that no one would use it, so he promised everyone a free shot of vodka when they reached the museum's exit. To this day, the residents of St Petersburg love their culture almost as much as free vodka.'

Grizzly's English wasn't great, but he knew enough to grasp the meaning of her words. Handing back her passport, he said, 'This is good story.'

'Thanks,' she said, relieved. 'I'm glad you liked it.'

He stepped back and patted Payne on his shoulder. 'You are correct. She is smart beach bunny. You are lucky man.'

Payne nodded. 'I know.'

'Keep eye on her. Other soldiers not friendly like me.'

With that, Grizzly walked away, followed closely by the other two soldiers. They cut across the busy square, conducting more random searches in the heart of the city.

Payne waited a few seconds as Allison trembled against him. Then he asked, 'Are you all right? I thought you were going to have a stroke.'

'I still might,' she mumbled, burying her face against his chest.

Payne smiled. He thought back to the video of her at the Peterhof. She had broken down for about a minute, and then found the courage to sneak away. 'I have to admit, you started out shitty, but you finished strong. You're tougher than you think.'

'Well, I *think* I'm going to vomit.'

Payne laughed. Early in his career, he had often felt the same way at the end of a mission. 'If you have to puke, do it on the statue. Not me.'

40

Alexei Kozlov used to work for the Federal Security Service of the Russian Federation (FSB), the organization that has handled domestic security in Russia since the KGB was disbanded in 1995. Over the years, several FSB officers have been removed from service due to criminal misconduct – mostly extortion, human rights violations, and payoffs from the Russian mafia.

Kozlov had been fired for all three. And more.

Nowadays, he used the skills he had learned and the connections he had made while in the FSB to become one of the best-paid assassins in Russia.

Not only was he highly trained, but he had a taste for blood.

His latest victim was a man named Richard Byrd. An American entrepreneur. Kozlov had put a bullet in his brain at the Peterhof, and then casually slipped away.

Normally, that would have been the end of things. The contract would have been complete, and Kozlov could have gone home. But in this case, he still had more work to do.

When Kozlov was hired, his employer didn't know where Byrd was headed but guessed he would surface in Moscow or St Petersburg. Most likely at one of the major museums. Other than that, Kozlov wasn't given much information. He was told to locate Byrd, determine what he was looking for, and then kill him before he had a chance to leave the country.

It sounded simple enough for a man like Kozlov.

Since he lived in Moscow, he had started his search there, staking out the Pushkin State Museum and the cultural facilities near Red Square. His employer wanted him to keep his manhunt highly confidential, which meant he wasn't able to show Byrd's picture round the city or hire additional personnel to locate the target. Instead, he used the FSB database to search hotel reservations, track credit-card purchases, and monitor phone logs.

For someone with little experience in counter surveillance, Byrd did a remarkable job of staying off the grid. He used cash and fake IDs, and he never called his family or friends in California. After wasting several days in Moscow – on foot and online – Kozlov switched his operations to St Petersburg, a place he rarely visited.

As in the capital city, many of the museums in St Petersburg had been built in a central location. Kozlov set up shop near one of the rivers. It allowed him to watch the Hermitage, the Academy of Fine Arts, the Marble Palace, and the smaller art collections scattered in cathedrals and buildings near Nevsky Prospekt. Occasionally he strayed to other parts of the sprawling city, yet he spent most of his time near the Winter Palace, scanning faces in the crowd.

His hard work paid off on 18 May. He was keeping watch on the Hermitage, like he had done several times before, when he bumped into Byrd in the main entrance. *Literally* bumped into him as he was leaving through the same door that Kozlov was entering. Kozlov tried to play it off as an accident – which, of course, it was – but the look of recognition in his eyes could not be concealed. He stared at Byrd like he was a winning lottery ticket.

And Byrd picked up on it.

Over the next several hours, they played an elaborate game of cat and mouse in a city that neither of them had mastered. A game that would have ended in less than a minute if Kozlov's mission was to assassinate Byrd. But that wasn't the task that he had been given. He was told to find Byrd, figure out what he was searching for, and *then* kill him. That required a lot more tact than going up to Byrd on a crowded street and slicing his throat.

Instead, Kozlov was forced to lay back, to track him from a distance, to make him feel safe. He needed Byrd to think he had somehow managed to escape. That he was too smart to be caught or cornered. It was the only way Byrd would feel secure enough to go back to his hotel or wherever he was staying. From there, Kozlov could follow him day after day, tracing his path through the city, trying to figure out what the American was looking for.

And then, when Byrd was finally ready to leave

the country, Kozlov would make sure it was in a coffin.

As the soldiers walked away from Payne and Allison, Jones closed the bathroom window and breathed a sigh of relief. He had watched their confrontation from his vantage point at the Astoria Hotel. Now that he knew they were all right, he could get back to the business at hand.

Allison had told him about Byrd's most important papers. They were kept in a room safe that was bolted to the floor inside his bedroom closet. But Jones wasn't concerned. She had described the safe to him in very specific terms, and he knew he could crack the lock. With lock picks in hand, he opened the closet door and studied his opponent. It was just as she had described. The safe was guarded by a simple warded lock, one of the easiest types to manipulate.

'Piece of cake,' he said to himself.

And Jones was correct. It took less than a minute to open the safe.

Inside he found a number of documents in an expandable binder. There was also a small pouch filled with fake IDs, foreign currency, and credit cards registered to several phoney names. It explained why no one had found his hotel room. Byrd must have paid a fortune to preserve his anonymity. That meant whatever Byrd's mission had been, he didn't want to be followed.

* * *

But Byrd had been followed. For several hours on Sunday, he ducked in and out of buildings, trying to lose Kozlov in the tourist-filled crowds. On more than one occasion, Byrd thought he had slipped away, only to spot the cagey Russian in the distance.

This forced Byrd in a direction he didn't want to go. He needed to leave St Petersburg at once.

While riding in a taxi, Byrd called Allison and told her to get to the Peterhof as quickly as possible. He said something was wrong and they needed to leave the country. Don't pack. Don't checkout. Just run. The fastest way to get there was on a boat called the *Meteor*. It was docked on the Neva River behind the Winter Palace. In the meantime, he would figure out how to cross the border. Just look for him on the rear patio of the Peterhof, and they would escape together.

Unfortunately, it was the last time they spoke to each other.

Kozlov didn't want to kill Byrd at the Peterhof. But he didn't have much choice.

There was no doubt in Kozlov's mind that Byrd was fleeing the country. The Summer Palace was on the Gulf of Finland, an extension of the Baltic Sea. If Byrd had a boat, there was no way that Kozlov could follow him. The bastard would get away and wouldn't come back.

That wasn't the sort of thing that Kozlov wanted on his résumé.

So Kozlov made a gutsy choice. Instead of doing things as ordered, he decided to shoot Byrd before he had a chance to get away. That meant, no matter what, Kozlov had fulfilled two requirements of his contract: he had found Byrd and killed him before he left Russia.

The last step, figuring out why Byrd was there, would have to be post mortem.

Jones gathered the documents from Byrd's safe and put them in a bag by the door. Then he returned to the bedroom to make sure he wasn't missing anything important.

He searched under the bed, in the nightstand, in the dresser, even in the air-conditioning vents. Then he continued with Byrd's belongings. He checked clothes and shoes, suitcases and toiletries, and a stack of books that sat in the corner of the room. From there, he moved his search to the other parts of the suite. There weren't a lot of hiding places, and considering Byrd's paranoia, Jones figured he wouldn't find anything of value sitting out in the open.

And he was right. After several minutes of searching, Jones was ready to pack up.

It took two days for Kozlov to pick up Byrd's scent. Two days of sitting on his ass in his hotel room, sifting through mountains of information in FSB's database. Two days of crunching numbers and making educated guesses before he noticed a pattern.

Of course, there is *always* a pattern. People are creatures of habit.

By studying old credit-card statements, Kozlov determined that Byrd, a man of great wealth, always went first class when he ventured round the globe. At least he did when he travelled as Richard Byrd. And since old habits were difficult to break, Kozlov predicted that Byrd would follow the same pattern when he was travelling under an alias.

The best hotels, the best restaurants, the best of everything.

In a city as large as St Petersburg, Kozlov knew he had to limit the scope of his search, so he decided to concentrate on one thing: luxury hotels. Particularly those close to Nevsky Prospekt. Not only was it the ritziest part of the city, but the avenue ran past several museums including the Hermitage, which was where he had bumped into his target to begin with.

So that's where Kozlov started – back at the Hermitage.

Armed with a gun, an old NCB badge, and a photograph of Byrd, Kozlov planned to visit every hotel on Nevsky Prospekt. He was going to flash his badge at every front desk and ask about the man in the picture. Now that Byrd was dead, he wasn't nearly as worried about keeping things quiet. He was more concerned about finding information as quickly as possible.

And he would start at the hotel that was next to the museum.

The same hotel that David Jones was leaving.

41

Spárti, Greece
(location of Ancient Sparta)

George Pappas was looking forward to this day. Even though he had been an NCB agent for twenty-one years, this was the first time he had ever been given an assignment from Interpol Headquarters. Not only that, but his orders came straight from the top. Nick Dial, the head of the Homicide Division, needed help with a multiple homicide at Metéora. He believed the killers might be from the mountain towns near Spárti, because of video evidence at the scene.

Normally Pappas, a small-town cop, spent most of his time dealing with the tourists who flooded Greece during the summer months. He worked full-time for the local municipality, which was the administrative capital of Laconia, but also received a stipend for his NCB duties that were usually limited to entering crime statistics into Interpol's criminal database.

But today was a different story. After all this time, he was being asked to do *real* police work for Interpol as opposed to really boring police work.

And he couldn't wait to get started.

Accompanying Pappas on the drive into the

mountains were two younger officers, Stefan Manos and Thomas Constantinou. Manos was a ten-year veteran of the Spárti police force and was quite familiar with the people of the region. Meanwhile, Constantinou was the exact opposite. He had finished his police training in Athens less than a month ago and had never visited Laconia before being hired by Spárti. This was Constantinou's first trip into the Taygetos Mountains, which made him an easy target for some teasing.

'Thomas,' Pappas said as he drove the four-wheel-drive truck up the winding road. 'Make sure you stay close to us once we get into the village.'

'Why is that?' Constantinou asked from the cramped back seat.

Pappas looked at Manos in the passenger seat. 'You didn't tell him?'

Manos shook his head. 'You invited the kid. I figured you would tell him.'

'Tell me what?'

Pappas glanced at him in his rear-view mirror. 'About your haircut.'

Constantinou rubbed his scalp, which he kept closely shaved. 'What about it?'

'Everyone in the village has hair like yours. Men, women, kids. Even their goats.'

Manos laughed at the comment. He knew all about the Spartans and their haircuts.

'I don't get it,' Constantinou said. 'What's so funny?'

'You mean you *really* don't know?' Pappas asked. 'I can't believe no one told you. How are you going to succeed in Spárti if you don't know anything about the locals and their customs? They should have told you this for your personal safety before they shipped you here.'

'Told me what?' he demanded.

Pappas tried not to smile, milking this for all it was worth. 'Back in ancient times, Spartan men were required to get married at the age of twenty. This was after living with nothing but boys and the older men who mentored them for thirteen lonely years. The boys spent their days wrestling and training and bathing until they knew each other's bodies like their own. In fact, they knew each other so well that the only people they were truly comfortable with were the other men in their squad . . . If you get what I'm saying.'

Constantinou nodded. 'What does that have to do with my hair?'

'Relax. I'm getting to that.'

Manos clenched his tongue between his teeth, trying to keep from laughing.

'Spartans were never into fancy ceremonies, so their weddings consisted of a man choosing his wife and abducting her, sometimes quite violently. Now don't get me wrong. This wasn't rape. This was just the way it was done in their culture. Spartans were bred to be aggressive and that trait revealed itself on the battlefield and in the bedroom.'

Constantinou shifted uncomfortably in his seat, not sure where this story was going.

'After the wife was abducted, it was time for their wedding night. The man would drag his bride into a private section of the barracks where he would take out his knife. Then in a ritual that some locals still perform today, the man would shave her head like he was shearing a sheep. I mean, he'd get right down to her skin and just carve away until she was completely bald.'

'He cut off all her hair? What for?'

'Be patient,' Pappas ordered. 'You'll find out shortly.'

Manos kept fighting his laughter. He had heard this story, which was completely true, several times before. But there was something about the way that Pappas told it that kept it funny – especially when his audience was a wide-eyed rookie who wasn't familiar with the Spartans.

'Anyway, here was the problem. Spartan men lived with nothing but males for the majority of their lives. They were told to love each other and protect each other because some day on the battlefield they would have to count on each other. Unfortunately, that ideology was so deeply embedded into their brains that they weren't able to get physically aroused unless the person they were screwing actually looked like a man. Hence, the shaving of the wife's head.'

'Are you serious?' Constantinou asked.

'Completely serious. When we get back to town, look it up if you don't believe me.'

Manos nodded in agreement. 'He's serious. These guys are scary.'

'But it didn't end there,' Pappas assured the rookie. 'For the Spartans, the goal of sex wasn't enjoyment; it was procreation. That meant no foreplay or romance of any kind. Late at night, a Spartan male would wait until all the other men were sleeping – because he didn't want to disturb their rest – and sneak out of his barracks. His wife, realizing that her husband had little time to get aroused before he had to return, made sure her head was shaven at all times. In addition, to help set the mood she slept in men's clothes, which we like to call Spartan lingerie. The combination of the darkness, the shaved head, and the men's clothing made her husband feel like he was back with the boys, cuddling for warmth along the Eurotas River.'

'That's disgusting,' Constantinou complained. 'Why would you tell me that?'

Pappas glanced at him in the mirror. 'How old are you, Thomas?'

'I'm twenty-two. Why?'

Manos shook his head with concern. 'You're twenty-two *and* you have a shaved head. Where we're going, that's a mighty attractive combination.'

Pappas nodded in agreement. 'Like I said, make sure you stay close to us in the village. Otherwise, you might get dragged into the woods for your honeymoon.'

* * *

The first village they visited had no name. That was uncommon in Greece where most people took pride in their communities and bragged about it every chance that they got. But these villagers were different. Like their Spartan ancestors who refused to mint coins because it would only encourage interaction with outsiders, the citizens of this town wanted to be left alone.

Which, of course, was the reason that Pappas stopped here first. He was familiar with these people and their violent ways. In fact, from the moment he fielded the call from Interpol, Pappas had this place in mind. He figured, if there were killers lurking in the Taygetos Mountains, the odds were pretty good that they were going to be in the village that he called Little Sparta.

'I've been here before, so let me do all the talking,' said Pappas as he climbed out of the truck. 'Stay close and keep your eyes open. These people do not like strangers.'

Manos and Constantinou nodded in silence.

The village was relatively small, no more than sixty homes spread against the rocky face of the mountain. But what it lacked in numbers, it more than made up for in intensity.

The first time Pappas had visited the village, more than fifteen years earlier, he had stopped by the school and had caught a quick glimpse of their training methods. He had been amazed by the children's level of discipline. The boys, even the youngest ones, didn't fidget or goof around. They stood board straight, like they were in the military, and did whatever they were told. Pappas figured that type of control was only achieved through severe physical punishment, but since he was there on a different matter and no complaints had been filed, he wasn't allowed to investigate the school further.

Still, the sight of those pre-teen warriors disturbed him to the core.

He always wondered what type of men they would grow up to be.

Unfortunately, he and his partners were about to find out.

42

Allison's book bag hung from Jones' left shoulder. Her computer dangled from his right. And he carried a large gym bag stuffed with Byrd's most important belongings. Thankfully, he wouldn't have to haul them very far. He was scheduled to meet Payne and Allison in St Isaac's Square.

Jones eyed the hallway in both directions before he stepped outside the suite. One of the advantages of staying on the top floor of a luxury hotel was a scarcity of neighbours. Wealthy people loved their peace and quiet. Then again, so did burglars. Obviously Jones didn't view himself as a thief — he was simply collecting things for Byrd's assistant — yet he knew the authorities wouldn't see his actions in the same light. So when Jones heard the elevator doors open at the opposite end of the corridor, he wasn't the least bit happy about it.

Keeping his cool, he turned towards the stairs and refused to look back even though he could hear footsteps. His goal was to reach the street while being noticed by the fewest number of people possible, and turning round would only increase his chances of being identified.

With his free hand, he opened the door to the stairwell and started his journey down.

For the first few floors, things were going well. He was alone on the stairs and making good time. He assumed his next trouble spot would be when he hit the lobby. Desk clerks tended to be nosy. A team of doormen and bellhops would be posted by the entrance, offering to help him with his bags. And hotel guests would be milling round, waiting for friends and family.

Once he survived that gauntlet, he figured he'd be home free.

But it wasn't to be.

Jones realized there was trouble when he heard the door above him open. It was the exact same door he had passed through a moment before on a floor that had few visitors. Either someone had exited a suite a split second after Jones had left the hallway *and* had also decided to walk down several flights of steps, or the person from the elevator was still behind him.

In his gut, Jones knew it was the latter.

Payne detected a problem the instant he saw Jones leave the hotel. Instead of turning towards the square like he was supposed to, Jones headed towards Nevsky Prospekt in the opposite direction.

'Shit,' Payne mumbled to himself, never taking his eyes off the exit.

'What's wrong?' Allison asked.

'Time to go.'

Fifteen minutes earlier, Payne would have sent her to safety in the Hermitage Museum or one of the nearby buildings, but considering Grizzly's warning about unfriendly soldiers in the area and the fact that Jones had altered their plans based on something he had seen inside the hotel, Payne couldn't abandon her. He couldn't take the chance that she would be accosted, arrested, or spotted by a hidden foe. That forced him to take her along while he figured out what to do.

Meanwhile Jones kept moving forward, never running or doing anything that would call attention to himself. That told Payne a lot about the situation. Jones' life wasn't in immediate danger. If it had been, he would have signalled Payne to enter the fray, or dropped the bags he was carrying and started shooting. But due to Jones' methodical pace and calm demeanour, it meant he was being followed. Or at least he thought he was.

It was up to Payne to figure out if that was true.

And if so, by whom?

Allison walked beside him as Payne crossed the street towards the hotel. The entire time he studied the exit, watching everyone who left the building. An elderly couple appeared first, then a woman in a dress, then a bellhop. None of them turned towards Jones so they weren't the shadow that Payne was searching for.

The fourth person to exit was a man in his late

forties. He had a buzz cut, a grey suit, and a board-stiff posture that was common in the military. The instant he hit the sidewalk he stopped, casually scanning Nevsky Prospekt in both directions before he found his mark. Turning east, the man continued his pursuit of Jones, tracking him from a healthy distance.

Payne smiled at the scene. Now he could track his target as well.

Kozlov had reached Byrd's floor at the perfect moment, just in time to see the black man leaving the room. If Kozlov had arrived a minute sooner, he would have bumped into him inside Byrd's suite, but what good would that have done? Kozlov would have been forced to kill the intruder on the spot, gather whatever was being taken from the suite, and then slip away before the police arrived.

On the other hand, if he had shown up a minute later, the black man would have been long gone, Kozlov would have found nothing inside, and his employer would have been pissed.

No, Kozlov was thrilled with the way things had worked out. He could shadow the intruder wherever he went, hoping to generate more leads to follow. With a little luck, Kozlov could recover Byrd's things, figure out why Byrd had come to St Petersburg to begin with, and catch the morning train to Moscow so he could start working on his next contract.

Two days earlier, bumping into Byrd had been the result of horrible timing.

But this was just the opposite. This couldn't have worked out better.

At least that's what Kozlov believed.

Payne eyed the Russian like a cheetah eyes a gazelle. He wasn't ready to spring on him just yet. That would come later. For now Payne was more interested in studying his opponent, deciding if he was alone or part of a dangerous herd.

'What's going on?' Allison demanded.

'DJ is being followed.'

'How do you know?'

Payne didn't have time to hold her hand or explain things. He could always fill her in later when they were safe. For now, he had to concentrate on his surroundings. He couldn't miss anything or it could cost them their lives. 'Just trust me, okay? I know what I'm doing.'

'I know you do, but—'

'Listen,' he ordered. 'If I tell you to do something, you do it. No questions. No delay.'

'Okay,' she said, nodding her head.

Payne kept looking straight ahead. 'If something happens to me or I tell you to run, go to the American Consulate. Don't go to the hotel. Go directly to the consulate. Understood?'

'Yes.'

'I doubt it will come to that, but I need to know you'll be safe.'

'I promise. I'll go to the consulate.'

Payne continued to watch Kozlov. He was a block behind Jones but was definitely following him. 'The man I'm tailing is in a grey suit. I mention that for one reason. Not because I want you to stare at him, but because I want you to know he's trouble.'

Allison spotted Kozlov a block ahead and nodded. 'Is that the man who killed Richard?'

'I can't tell. I didn't get a good look at him.'

'Come on,' he said as he grabbed her elbow. 'We're crossing the street.'

'Why?'

'What did I tell you about questions?'

Allison blushed but didn't say a word. Filled with adrenaline, she had forgotten her agreement from a moment before. All this was so new to her. It was one of the reasons that she had kept spouting random facts about the city: she didn't know how to handle the excitement. So she burned her nervous energy by babbling.

At the intersection, several pedestrians waited for the lights to change. Payne and Allison stood among them, hoping to blend in with the crowd. A few seconds passed before the entire group made their way across Nevsky Prospekt. Cars and buses filled every lane. It was mid-afternoon, but traffic was starting to build. Once they reached the far side, they turned right. They were now walking on the northern side of the street, the same side they had used on their journey from the Palace Hotel. The side they were most familiar with.

'Keep watching,' Payne said as they passed a small war monument that he had seen before. 'DJ will cross the street soon. It will help me spot other shadows.'

Sure enough, Jones did as Payne predicted. He walked across Nevsky Prospekt in the middle of a block, dodging cars as he did. This simple act, crossing the street with no one else round, forced Kozlov to react. He didn't have time to wait or think. He had to cross immediately or risk losing Jones in an alley, a building, or a taxi heading in the opposite direction.

Payne studied the avenue, checking to see if Kozlov was the only one who followed.

And as far as Payne could tell, Kozlov was acting alone.

While crossing the busy avenue, Jones spotted the man in the grey suit. He didn't have a chance to look for Payne and Allison, but he knew they were back there, too.

Probably a block behind.

In situations like this, that was a safe distance. Close enough to keep an eye on his shadow but far enough to be inconspicuous. Normally a man of Payne's size would have a tough time blending in. Yet that wasn't the case with Allison on his arm. She was the perfect cover. The two of them would look like a happy couple, strolling through the high-rent district.

And that gave Jones an edge that he planned on using.

Knowing virtually nothing about his opponent – who he was, who he worked for, what he wanted – left Jones with few options. Especially if this was the same man who had killed Byrd. Jones had seen video of him in action and realized he was highly trained. That meant there was little chance that Jones was going to lose him, not while carrying three bags that he couldn't afford to drop. Not in a city that he wasn't familiar with. Not without the help of a friend.

A friend with the skills of Jonathon Payne.

43

The Church on Spilled Blood, a breathtaking Russian cathedral built on the spot where Tsar Alexander II was mortally wounded by revolutionaries in 1881, sits off of Nevsky Prospekt beside the Griboyedov Canal. The church's onion domes and ornate façade looked beautifully out of place in St Petersburg. Contrary to the European look of the city's architecture, it resembled St Basil's Cathedral, the famous church that overlooked Red Square in Moscow.

As a tourist boat chugged up the waterway towards the colourful landmark, Jones crossed the canal on foot, hoping his blood wouldn't be spilled next to the tsar's.

For the time being, he felt optimistic that his shadow was working alone. Back at the Astoria Hotel, Jones had heard a single set of footsteps in the stairwell, and only one man had followed him across Nevsky Prospekt. Still, in this age of technology, Jones knew reinforcements were just a phone call away.

And phone calls were something Jones wanted to prevent.

While prepping for this mission, he had studied a map of the local terrain. He had memorized street names, bridges, and multiple escape routes. He had learned as much as he could as fast as he could, just in case something bad happened along the way. Something like this. Thankfully, his knowledge of the city gave him several choices. Instead of being trapped like a rat in a maze, he knew exactly where he wanted to go and what he hoped to accomplish when he got there.

In this situation, there was one obvious solution: the St Petersburg Metro.

A white sign with a blue letter 'M' marked the entrance to the Nevsky Prospekt/Gostiny Dvor stations. Jones had never been inside, but he understood the basic layout of the system. Four lines, all assigned different colours, extended throughout the sprawling city and its suburbs. The blue Moskovsko-Petrogradskaya Line ran north and south. The green Nevsko-Vasileostrovskaya Line ran east and west. Both lines could be accessed from this central location, which happened to be the busiest terminal in the city.

To Jones, the large crowds were a bonus. If he timed things right, he might be able to slip away in the chaos underground. He was also thrilled that he could leave the city in any direction. That made it tougher for his opponent to anticipate where he was headed next.

However, in his mind, the best asset of the Metro system was the natural geology of the city. Due to potential flooding from all the rivers and canals in St Petersburg, the Metro is the deepest subway system

327

in the world, buried under a thick layer of bedrock that prevented cell-phone reception of any kind.

And no phone calls meant no reinforcements.

Kozlov smiled at the development. He had used the Metro several times in the past week, so he was familiar with all four lines, where they went, and which stations would be crowded.

His immediate goal was to follow the black man wherever he went, hoping to generate as many leads as possible. But at some point, Kozlov knew he would be forced to grab the bags that the black man carried – just in case they were filled with information about Byrd.

And when Kozlov made his move, the black man would have to die.

Jones slipped inside the station and studied the flow of people in front of him. A row of turnstiles prevented passengers from entering the subway without a card or token. In the corner of the lobby, he saw three small booths manned by women cashiers. Jones hopped into the shortest line while digging through his pockets for local currency. A moment later, he placed a fifty-rouble note on the counter and signalled for one subway token.

She mumbled something in Russian, then gave him a bronze token and a handful of change.

His ticket to freedom cost him less than an American quarter.

Jones hustled towards the turnstile, put the token in the slot, and pushed through the revolving bar. An arched hallway funnelled all the passengers towards a long bank of escalators. Jones thought nothing of it until he reached the top step and had a chance to look down. The escalator was so long he couldn't see the bottom, as though it was going all the way to hell.

The person behind him pushed him gently, urging him in Russian to keep moving.

Jones nodded, stepped forward, and started his descent to the tunnels below.

Suddenly, he found himself trapped for the next several hundred feet. He couldn't run or hide or change directions. His options were blocked by a waterfall of people, all of them inching forward at the same pace. Frustrated, Jones looked at his watch, wondering how long this journey was going to take. When the woman in front of him pulled out a novel, he groaned.

'You've got to be shitting me,' he said to himself.

But there was nothing he could do about it.

He was stuck until he reached the bottom.

Earlier in the week, Kozlov had purchased a Metro card worth several subway trips. So there were no lines or delays for him. He walked through the turnstiles, barely breaking his stride.

This helped him close the gap.

Up ahead, he spotted the black man carrying the

three bags. At no point did his target turn round and look for someone behind him.

The guy was either crafty or clueless; Kozlov didn't know which.

But he would find out when they reached the labyrinth below.

The trip took for ever. At least it seemed that way to Jones.

Finally, the people in front of him gathered their things and stepped off the escalator. One by one, they scattered in both directions towards the different tracks.

The vaulted ceiling arched above him, lit by recessed lighting. The floor was made of polished stone. No trash or graffiti stained the terminal. The place was spotless. Jones stared at the sign on the wall in front of him. It was written in Russian. No translations of any kind.

'Damn,' he muttered.

This was going to be tougher than he thought.

Glancing to his left, he saw a neon sign with green Cyrillic text. To his right, one was written in blue. He couldn't read any of the words, but he knew the blue trains went north and south. He remembered that fact by thinking of the map he had studied earlier in the day. In his mind, the north arrow pointed up towards the blue sky above.

And north was the direction that he was supposed to go.

Wasting no time, he hustled to his right and looked for another sign. The vaulted corridor stretched for a hundred feet before it branched again. This time both of his choices were written in blue. One was going north; the other was going south. He stood there in the intersection, calculating his options, as people streamed past him in both directions. The sound of screeching brakes echoed in his ears, followed by a whoosh of air and the heat of a surging train.

Or maybe that was Kozlov breathing down his neck.

44

The leader of the Spartans was named Apollo. His name was derived from the ancient Laconian word *apollymi*, which meant to destroy. And that was how he viewed himself, as a destroyer. His entire life had been dedicated to the art of war. How to attack. How to defend. How to conquer. The lifestyle had been beaten into him when he was a boy, and now that he was in charge, he returned the favour to the next generation – just like his mentor had done for him.

That was how his village had survived. They followed the code of their ancestors.

When the police officers arrived, Apollo was waiting for them. He had watched their slow approach up the treacherous mountain road. It gave him more than enough time to tell the village to be on full alert. In this part of Greece, the local authorities rarely stopped by, and when they did, it was usually for a very specific reason. The last time was a month ago. The cops had been looking for two missing tourists who had gone camping in the Taygetos Mountains and didn't return when they were supposed to. A couple of questions were asked, a flyer with their pictures was shown round, and the police had departed soon after.

The whole process had taken less than fifteen minutes.

Apollo hoped for the same efficiency on their current visit.

'Hello,' George Pappas said in Greek. He knew the villagers preferred Laconian, their native tongue, but he wasn't able to speak it. Neither could Manos or Constantinou.

Apollo wore sandals on his feet and a simple white tunic that hung to mid-thigh. He nodded at them but said nothing. He let his muscular physique and the coldness of his glare do his talking. One look from him stopped most men in their tracks.

'Sorry to disturb you,' Pappas said as he flashed his badge. 'We were hoping you could help us with one of our cases.'

Apollo shrugged, refusing to say a word. Instead, he stared with unblinking eyes.

Somehow Pappas found the courage to return his stare. Not only did he have the backing of two armed officers, he was here on official Interpol business. That gave him the confidence he needed to stand up to this guy – even though he scared the hell out of Pappas.

'Stefan,' he said to Manos, 'hand me the picture.'

Manos took a step forward, gave Pappas the sur-veillance photo from Metéora, and then took a quick step back. Meanwhile, Constantinou kept his hand on his gun and his head on a swivel.

Pappas studied the helmeted man in the photo and

compared him to Apollo. No way were they the same person. Apollo was at least fifty pounds heavier with a much larger physique. Hell, his arms were nearly as thick as Pappas' legs.

Side by side, Pappas and Apollo looked as if they belonged to two different species.

'We're looking for the man in this picture. I'd appreciate if you could take a look.'

Apollo grabbed the photo, expecting it to be another missing tourist. Instead, the suspect in the photo was one of the soldiers that had accompanied him to Metéora.

This was not good. And very unexpected.

Apollo didn't show surprise – he was too disciplined for that – but his mind started racing. How did the police have a photo from the monastery? What other evidence did they possess? Normally he didn't give much thought to the outside world, but on the eve of such an important mission, he knew he couldn't afford any type of police interference.

He had to stop their inquiry before the cops had a chance to return to Spárti.

'Yes,' he said in fluent Greek. 'I know the man. He is a troublemaker in our village. What has he done now?'

The response shocked Pappas. He was expecting to be stonewalled at every turn.

'I'm afraid I can't say. Our investigation is still pending.'

Apollo nodded in understanding. 'How can I help you?'

'Can you show us where he lives?'

'I can do better than that. I can bring him to you.'

Before Pappas could argue, Apollo called out to a few of his men who were lingering in the background, watching the proceedings unfold. When he spoke, his orders were in rapid Laconian. The language sounded similar to Greek, but there were enough differences that Pappas and the other officers weren't sure what was being said which made them uneasy.

Pappas immediately asked, 'What did you say to them?'

'I said go and get the troublemaker and bring him here.'

Pappas frowned. He knew more had been said. 'Does the troublemaker have a name?'

'Of course. But you will need to ask him yourself. The code of my village prevents me from revealing his name. We have a code of silence.'

'What about *your* name? Are you allowed to tell me that?'

He nodded. 'My name is Apollo. And yours?'

'George.'

'George,' he said with a smirk. 'Such a simple name. One without significance.'

Pappas shrugged off the insult. 'We can't all be named after gods.'

Apollo nodded. Most people didn't deserve to be named after gods. Not like he had been.

'Tell me, George, what's the worst pain you have ever felt in your life?'

'Excuse me?'

'Before you arrived, my friends and I were discussing the worst pain we have ever felt. I was wondering what your answer might be.'

Pappas glanced back at Manos and Constantinou, who were keeping a close eye on the perimeter. Due to the rocky terrain and the nearby trees, it was impossible to tell if anyone was out there. Just to be safe, the two officers unsnapped the straps that held their guns in their holsters. But not Pappas. He was being closely watched by Apollo, and he didn't want to do anything that might be interpreted as aggressive behaviour.

'That's an awfully strange question. One that might be misconstrued as a threat.'

'A threat? That was not a threat,' he said with a laugh. 'But *this* is a threat.' He moved one step closer. 'We have you severely outnumbered. Lay down your weapons or you will have a new answer to my question about pain.'

The colour instantly drained from Pappas' face. There was no way he was going to surrender his weapon – especially since the odds were currently three against one. Still, there was something about Apollo's words that resonated with truth. Pappas knew it wasn't a bluff. He realized the man standing across from him was fully capable of making good on his threat.

Pappas said, 'If I pull my gun, you'll be the first to die.'

Apollo glared at him and gave him a one-word retort. '*If.*'

Before Pappas could react, Apollo slipped a small knife from the folds of his tunic and lunged forward. With a wicked slash, he sliced through the veins and tendons of Pappas' right forearm, rendering his gun hand obsolete. Blood gushed from the open wound, spurting high into the air and splashing onto the dusty ground.

It reminded Apollo of the eight monks he had killed at Metéora.

Manos and Constantinou were stunned by the quick attack. They reached for their guns a second too late, as two Spartans crept up from behind. Each soldier carried a sword, and each sword hit its mark. The blade that struck Manos was raked across his back. The resulting wound started at his left scapula and ended at his right hip. Every muscle in between was severed, as were some of his ribs. He slumped to the dirt, gurgling, while his lungs filled with fluid.

Death was imminent.

But Constantinou wasn't as lucky. The Spartan's sword struck him flush above the elbow. A moment later, most of his arm fell to the ground beside him while he screamed out in agony. His fingers twitched for a few extra seconds like a spider that had been poisoned and was slowly waiting to die. He stared at it, disbelieving, unwilling to accept that his hand was no longer a part of him. As he stared, blood poured from the chunk of meat that hung below his shoulder.

'Bind his wound,' Apollo ordered. Then he pointed to Pappas. 'Same with his.'

The Spartans disarmed the policemen and tended to their wounds, making sure they didn't die. At least not yet. Opportunities like this were rare, and Apollo wanted to take full advantage – just as he had done with the missing tourists who he had found camping near the village.

The best way to teach the boys was to give them a taste of blood.

They would butcher the cops, piece by piece, until everyone had a turn.

Like a lion teaching his young.

45

Jones lingered near the train platform, purposely standing still while he pretended to be confused. He turned round, pondered the blue sign above him, and then grimaced in frustration.

It was a beautiful job of acting, one that accomplished several things.

First of all, it stopped Kozlov in his tracks. There was no way the Russian was going to walk towards the blue line if Jones was still pondering the green. There was too great a risk of being spotted in the narrow hallway that connected the two platforms, or of being recognized later if Kozlov was forced to turn round and follow Jones back towards the other trains.

Secondly, it allowed Jones to glance down the corridor to see if Kozlov was still there. And he was. But the Russian played it smoothly, strolling over to a vending machine where he bought a copy of the local newspaper. Then he leaned against the wall and pretended to read the headlines while dozens of people poured off the escalators in front of him.

Finally, and most importantly, Jones' acting bought him the extra time that he needed. The truth was that Jones did *not* want to take the train that had just pulled into the station. It had arrived too soon. For his plan to work, he needed to miss this train and catch the next one, which would be arriving in roughly five minutes.

That was the only way that everything would be in place.

So Jones kept acting like a tourist. He scratched his head in confusion, asked a few people if they spoke English, and listened to the train as it pulled out behind him. Once it was gone, he slipped into the blue station where he waited to spring his trap.

As far as Kozlov was concerned, there was no reason to hurry. He knew Jones couldn't go very far. This wasn't like the subway system in New York City where vagrants were able to sneak into the tunnels for warmth or drugs. The local Metro had been built during the Cold War, and had been designed to double as a bomb shelter capable of saving thousands of lives.

With that in mind, St Petersburg took its security very seriously. Heavy blast doors protected the exits. Tunnels were monitored via closed-circuit television. Photography was banned throughout the subway in order to prevent advanced surveillance for terrorist attacks. And uniformed officers roamed the corridors, searching for trouble.

So he wasn't the least bit worried about Jones slipping away.

Furthermore, Kozlov guessed that every camera

in the tunnel was currently focused on Jones. Not because he was black, but because he was carrying three bags and fidgeting like a criminal. In fact, Kozlov was surprised that Jones hadn't been stopped or questioned already.

Because in Moscow, he probably would have been arrested.

This wasn't the first time that Jones had used this manoeuvre in a subway. From experience, he knew the key was in the execution. If he timed things perfectly, he would walk away free. No doubt about it. Plus, his shadow wouldn't even know what hit him.

He glanced at his watch as he strolled along the concrete platform, passing several thick pillars that supported the roof above him. While waiting for the train, Jones made sure that he could be seen at all times. This wasn't about hiding. This was about timing.

Kozlov strolled into the terminal as the train roared into the station. The loud squeal of brakes reminded him of the tortured screams of some of his previous victims.

Men, women, children – he didn't care as long as the money was right.

Several commuters stood behind a black line on the floor, waiting for the train to come to a complete stop. Kozlov eyed them suspiciously, searching for the man he was tracking. Then he saw him. Jones was waiting near the back of the pack, about halfway down the platform. A look of confusion filled his face, as if he was still unsure if this was the train that he wanted.

This made Kozlov leery. Maybe Jones wasn't going to board the blue line after all.

The mechanical doors sprang open, and a few passengers stepped out. All of them walked in an orderly fashion along the edge of the platform, staying clear of the waiting commuters. It was Russian discipline at its finest, remnants of the Soviet days when citizens had been forced to stand in lines for just about everything. Once the passengers had cleared the area, all the commuters entered the train en masse.

Everyone except two people.

Jones and Kozlov.

Both of them stood there, trying to decide what to do.

Suddenly, Kozlov had no choice. He had to enter the train. That didn't mean he had to stay on it, but he had to leave the platform or else Jones would spot him – if he hadn't already.

Cursing to himself, Kozlov stepped aboard. He didn't sit down like all the other passengers. Instead, he lingered inside the doorway, watching Jones out of the corner of his eye, trying to see what he was going to do before the train pulled away. If Jones entered the train, Kozlov would take a seat and try to blend in with all the other commuters who filled the car; if not, Kozlov would have to jump off the train – even if it blew his cover.

Of course, Jones knew this. He knew he was forcing Kozlov's hand, which is exactly what he wanted to do. He had lured Kozlov on to the train. Now he had to keep him there.

And the way he would do it was ingenious.

Jones stepped across the black line on the floor and tentatively approached the train, as if he was still making a decision. The bags he carried were starting to get heavy, which weighed him down and limited his mobility. The doors were about to close, so he climbed aboard.

One car ahead, Kozlov grinned with satisfaction. He had been watching Jones through the window and felt a huge sense of relief when he got on the train. If Jones had remained on the platform, there was no doubt in Kozlov's mind that he would have been spotted. Now, he didn't have to worry about that until he was ready to make his move. He could follow Jones to the northern suburbs, steal his three bags, and silence him for ever.

But Jones wasn't about to let that happen. He waited inside the doors until a recorded voice blared over the train's speaker system. The announcement was in Russian, but Jones knew what it meant: the train was getting ready to leave the station. He had heard the exact same announcement five minutes earlier while he was waiting for the previous train to depart.

The message came first, followed by the closing doors, and then the train pulled away.

The announcement was the sign he had been waiting for.

Jones took a giant step backwards onto the platform. His stride was long enough that he left the train in one quick motion. At the exact same moment, a loud voice could be heard from the corridor that led back to the escalators. Someone was yelling in English.

'Wait! Hold the train!' the voice demanded.

Suddenly, Kozlov didn't know what to do. He had watched Jones slip off the train, but the shouting made him think, if only for a second, that the police were coming after the man he was following. And that momentary delay cost him. Once it dawned on him that it wasn't the cops, he tried stepping off the train. But before he could set one foot on the platform, he spotted a giant blur heading straight for him. A tall, muscular man sprinted full-speed towards the door that Kozlov was exiting.

'Watch out!' the man screamed as he dipped his shoulder and barrelled into Kozlov, knocking him backwards with the force of a small car. Kozlov slammed into the back wall, clanging his head against a metal support before he slumped to the floor.

Payne towered above him, trying not to smile. Leaning forward, he looked into Kozlov's dazed eyes. 'Man, I am *so* sorry! I was trying to catch the train. Didn't you hear me yelling?'

The doors closed behind him with a clang, followed by the roar of the engine as they pulled away from the station. Payne glanced over his shoulder and spotted his best friend on the platform. Allison was back there, too, waiting for Jones to escort her to safety.

'Seriously,' Payne continued, 'I feel like *such* an idiot. First I went over to the green line, then I ran back to the blue—'

Kozlov blinked a few times, trying to shake out the cobwebs.

'Sorry. I'm sure you don't want to hear any of this.' Payne grabbed the Russian by his suit and tried to help him up. 'Here. Let me give you a hand.'

Kozlov cursed loudly at Payne and tried to push him away, but he wasn't strong enough to budge him very far. It was like trying to shove an oak tree.

The surrounding passengers stared with bemusement.

Stuff like this rarely happened on the Metro.

Payne shook his head in mock disgust. He had no idea what the Russian had said to him but knew it wasn't pleasant. 'Fine! I can take a hint. You don't want my help. But you didn't have to be rude about it . . . What did I ever do to you?'

46

Despite being free of his shadow, Jones knew there was more work to be done. He and Allison were still several blocks away from their suite at the Palace Hotel, and there was always a chance that Kozlov wasn't working alone. Jones also realized they had to steer clear of all the cops and soldiers who might want to chat with the black man and the gorgeous blonde.

Other than that, they were home free.

'Take this,' Jones whispered as he handed Allison her computer. 'It will look better if we're both carrying bags.'

She slung the thick strap over her shoulder. 'Where to now?'

'Back to the hotel. You need to look through Byrd's things.'

'What about Jon?' she asked, concerned.

'Don't worry about Jon. He can take care of himself. My job is to worry about you.'

They turned down the central corridor, which was getting more and more crowded. Rush hour would be starting soon, and when it did, the Metro would be packed with people.

Moving through the crowds, Jones kept his

head on a swivel, watching everyone round him. He searched for faces that looked the least bit familiar and stares that lasted a little too long. As they walked, he noticed several security cameras along the ceiling. He had seen the same thing in the lobby and near the train platform. But so far, no one had pestered him about his race. It was a pleasant surprise. He was expecting to be hassled everywhere he went.

Maybe Russia wasn't so racist after all.

When they reached the escalators, Allison stepped on first, followed by Jones. For the next few minutes, he would have a chance to question her.

'When we were outside, did Jon point out my shadow?'

She nodded. 'Back near the square.'

'Did the guy make any phone calls or talk to anyone on the street?'

'Not that I could see. He never stopped moving.'

'Good.'

Jones glanced over his shoulder, checking for eavesdroppers. The person behind him was listening to loud music through headphones. Further back there was an older couple who didn't look like they could hear each other, let alone Jones.

'What did the soldiers want?'

She blushed slightly. 'I think they wanted me.'

'You? What did they want with you?'

Her face turned even brighter.

'Ohhhhh!' he said in understanding. 'They *wanted*

you. I know exactly how you feel. Women constantly treat me like a piece of meat. It's disgusting.'

She smiled at his claim. 'It must get pretty hard for you.'

'See! That's *exactly* what I mean. Raunchy comments like that.'

'Wait!' she blurted, realizing her double entendre. 'I meant *tough* for you. Not hard.'

Jones laughed at her discomfort. 'Relax, I'm just teasing. I knew what you meant. I just wanted to see how red I could make your face. It's kind of fun. Like colouring without a crayon.'

She shrugged in resignation. 'Don't ask me why, but I've always been that way. Even as a little girl they used to tease me. I have fair skin so the red comes shining through.'

Jones pointed to his face. 'I have the exact same problem.'

She smiled, amazed that Jones was so relaxed despite his narrow escape.

His confidence gave her confidence.

'Back to my shadow for a moment. Did he look familiar to you?'

'Jon asked me the same thing.'

'And?'

'I honestly don't know. He was too far away to see.'

'Not to worry. If he killed Richard, we'll find out shortly.'

'We will?'

Jones nodded. 'Of course we will. Jon is very good at his job.'

'What do you mean? Jon is *talking* to him?'

'Talking? I guess you could call it that.'

A look of discomfort crossed her face. One that Jones instantly recognized. He had seen it many times before when civilians listened to stories about life in the military. They freaked out over tales of brutality, not able to understand that violence was often done to ensure peace.

'Listen,' he said, 'if we had simply wanted to lose my shadow, we would have handled things differently. But the truth is that we have to question him. The sooner, the better.'

'I don't get it. Why do you have to talk to him?'

Jones groaned. 'Do you want the truth, or do you want to stay calm?'

'To hell with calm. I want the truth.'

'Simply put, we're doing it for your safety.'

'My safety?'

'Think about it. The guy knew where Richard was staying. How long would it take him to figure out that Richard paid for two rooms, not one? Hell, he probably knows already.'

'But I thought you cleaned my room?'

'I did. But I didn't have a chance to delete video surveillance from the lobby. For all we know, he bribed a security guard and has your picture in his pocket right now.'

She gulped at the thought.

'Hey, you wanted the truth.'

'I know I did, but . . .'

'Listen,' Jones said, trying to reassure her. 'I swear to you, Jon is great at what he does. He'll have a pleasant conversation with the guy and find out what he knows. After that, you won't have to worry about him any more.'

Concrete whizzed by as the train roared through the tunnels underneath St Petersburg. Every few minutes a recorded voice would make an announcement in Russian, and the train would slow to a stop. People would get on and people would get off, but Payne never moved. He kept staring out of the window at the concrete, refusing to make eye contact with any of his fellow passengers – including the assassin at the other end of the car.

The initial plan was for Payne to block Kozlov's path, trapping him on the train while Jones slipped away. That was how they had done the manoeuvre in the past, and it had always worked. But the more Payne thought about it on the long ride down the escalator, the more he realized that his current objective was different to the previous times. This wasn't about escape. This was about levelling the playing field with an experienced professional.

That's when Payne decided to run the bastard over.

Not only did it leave Kozlov dazed, it also left him defenceless.

When Payne was five years old, his grandfather

bought him a deck of cards and showed him some simple tricks. Payne was so amazed that he became hooked for life. Over the years his grandfather encouraged him to read books about famous magicians. By the time Payne was a teenager, he had mastered the art of prestidigitation. He could pull coins out of thin air, make small objects disappear, and dazzle his toughest critics – including Jones.

One of his best skills was his ability to pick pockets. He was smoother than a hungry gypsy.

If he bumped into someone, he could steal just about anything he wanted. A watch. A ring. Or a set of keys. And the victim would be none the wiser.

That's why Payne decided to get rough with Kozlov. He had to distract him for as long as possible while he took everything he could. His wallet, his badge, even his gun.

And the best part of all?

Kozlov didn't realize that anything was missing.

The Chernaya Rechka River flows through the northwest corner of St Petersburg. It is a minor tributary of the Bolshaya Neva, which is the largest armlet of the historic Neva.

In the grand scheme of things, the Chernaya Rechka isn't much of a river. It is three miles long and less than eighty feet across at its widest point. The water is cold and murky and only a few feet deep. Some Russians consider it a stream. Others view it as a nuisance. Nothing more than a barrier that they have to cross when driving into the city. A watery pain in the ass.

To alleviate bridge traffic and to encourage northern expansion, the city built the Chernaya Rechka station near the banks of the waterway. The goal was to lure industry to the area by providing an efficient mass transit system for potential employees. Unfortunately, while the city waited for companies to build new factories, the Metro station was less popular than the river it was named after. After all, it was in the middle of nowhere.

That's why it was perfect for Kozlov's home base. He wanted to be seen as little as possible, yet he needed quick and easy access to the city. So when he first came into town, he booked a room at a cheap hotel near the station and had used the Metro ever since.

And it had worked out fine until the incident at Nevsky Prospekt.

His ears were still ringing from the collision.

The doors sprang open at Chernaya Rechka, and Kozlov stepped off the train. The last ten minutes had been filled with major disappointment. The black man had slipped out of his grasp, and so had the things he had taken from Byrd's room. Kozlov hated to think what might have been lost. For all he knew, it might have solved the mystery behind Byrd's trip to St Petersburg and allowed him to head back to Moscow to collect his hefty pay check.

Instead, he was stuck here for a few more days. If not longer.

The thought did not make him happy.

For the time being, all he wanted to do was go to his room and pour himself a tall glass of vodka. Perhaps that would dull the throbbing in his head. Then, once his senses returned, he would go back to the Astoria Hotel and check both of Byrd's rooms for any scraps that might have been left behind. He would also slip some roubles to the hotel staff and find out all he could about the black man who had eluded him on the train.

Maybe he was working for Byrd.

Maybe he could provide some answers, if he could only be found.

Kozlov pondered these things as he walked across the deserted platform, temporarily unaware that Payne was lurking behind him, waiting for his opportunity to strike.

But the Russian would find out soon enough.

47

When Dial and Andropoulos left the library at Great Metéoron, they decided to explore the grounds. Neither man said much as they strolled among the pink and white flowers and the manicured shrubs that lined the walkways. For them, it was a time of reflection, not discovery – a chance to ponder all the information they had learned before they returned to Kalampáka.

Many things stood out from their meeting with Theodore, including the missing pages in the history of Holy Trinity and the way the monk had fumed about it. But nothing mattered more than the black-and-white photograph of Nicolas. His connection to the abbot, which had lasted more than forty years, struck a chord with Dial.

Somehow he knew their relationship was vital to his case.

Finding a picturesque spot, Dial sat on a wooden bench that faced the valley below. His view was unobstructed except for a thin railing made out of crisscrossing logs. Andropoulos sat next to him, unwilling to speak until spoken to. He hadn't known Dial for very long, yet he understood the dynamics of their relationship. Sometimes Dial just wanted to think.

A few minutes passed before Dial asked, 'Have you ever been to Mount Athos?'

Andropoulos shook his head. 'No, sir. Not many outsiders have. Visitors must have special permission from the Orthodox Church.'

'Why is that?'

'The Church likes its privacy.'

Ironically, Theodore was the one who had brought up Mount Athos, saying it was where older monks went to continue their spiritual growth. Then he had instantly regretted mentioning it. When Dial had tried to get more information about the place, Theodore had been reluctant to answer, claiming he had never been there so he didn't want to speak out of turn. Dial hadn't pressed the issue, not wanting to sour their relationship after a very helpful conversation. Yet Theodore's reluctance piqued Dial's curiosity, as did the possibility that Nicolas might be recognized there.

'Is Mount Athos far from here?' Dial wondered.

'A couple of hundred miles. It sits to the east, surrounded by the Aegean.'

'It's an island?'

Andropoulos shook his head. 'It is a mountain on the tip of a peninsula. Greeks call it the Holy Mountain. It stretches from the water to the sky above.'

Dial tried to visualize it. Other than Hawaii and a few other islands that were formed by volcanic explosions, he had never seen a mountain surrounded by water. 'It sounds scenic.'

Andropoulos nodded. 'It is quite beautiful. I have seen many pictures.'

'Would you like to take some yourself?'

'Sir?' he asked, confused.

Dial glanced at the young officer. 'I get the feeling that we've learned all that we're going to learn round here. That leaves us with two choices. We can go back inside and help Theodore look through his old books, or we can go to Mount Athos and interview some old monks.'

'Just so you know, the drive would take all day.'

'No, it won't. I have access to a helicopter. If we left now, we could reach Mount Athos by mid-afternoon. That is, if you're interested in going.'

'Yes, sir! I would like that very much.'

Dial grimaced at his enthusiasm. 'Don't get *too* excited. This isn't a date. I need an interpreter just in case the monks don't speak English.'

'And some won't,' Andropoulos assured him. 'But . . .'

'What?'

'As I mentioned, visitors aren't admitted without clearance. How will we get in?'

'Please!' Dial sneered. He was insulted by the question. 'I'm in charge of the Homicide Division at Interpol. My credentials can get us *anywhere*.'

Henri Toulon burst out laughing when he heard Dial's request. 'You must be joking! I can't get you access to Mount Athos.'

'Why not?' Dial growled into his cell phone. He stood up from the bench and walked away from Andropoulos so the young cop couldn't hear. 'This is for my investigation.'

'They will not care. They do not recognize our authority.'

'Why the hell not? Greece is one of our member states!'

Toulon nodded, sitting at his desk. 'True, but Mount Athos is *not* a part of Greece.'

Dial paused, confused. 'What are you talking about?'

'Its official name is the Holy Community of the Holy Mountain. It is a self-governed state and has been for more than a thousand years . . . As my boss, you should know this.'

Dial wasn't in the mood for insults. He wanted clarification. 'What are you saying? It's a separate country, like Vatican City?'

'Technically, no. Mount Athos *is* a part of Greece, but Greece doesn't govern it. It is controlled by the Ecumenical Patriarchate of Constantinople.'

'Which is what?'

'A Church council located in Istanbul.'

Dial shook his head, trying to absorb the information. 'Mount Athos is run from *Turkey*? That doesn't make any sense. That's like Mecca being run from Rome.'

Toulon smiled at the metaphor. 'That is a good line. May I use it?'

'Use whatever you want. But first, tell me what you're talking about!'

Dial was fully aware of the political tension between Greece and Turkey. It had existed long before Greece declared its independence from the Ottoman Empire in 1821 and had been fuelled over the years by several wars. There were many reasons for their disagreements, but Dial knew the fundamental difference between the two countries was religion. In simple terms, most Greeks were Christians and most Turks were Muslims. Which is why Dial found it so hard to believe that Mount Athos was run from Istanbul, a city with more than 2,000 mosques.

Toulon asked, 'Are you familiar with Constantine the Great?'

'Of course I am. He was Emperor of Rome.'

'Constantine was more than just an emperor. He was *the* emperor when it comes to Christianity. In the fourth century, he made the controversial decision to shift the capital city of the Christian world from Rome to Byzantium, a small city that was unstained by Roman politics and much closer to the lands of the east. Over a period of ten years, he expanded his city in hopes of expanding his empire. He built streets, sewers, aqueducts, and more. Then he decorated it with the finest treasures from Greece and Rome. In some cases, he actually disassembled temples, column by column, and reassembled them in Byzantium. Nothing was too good for Nova Roma, or New Rome, which officially became the capital in 330 AD.'

'Great,' Dial said sarcastically. 'You only have seventeen hundred more years to go.'

Toulon smiled. 'Eventually the city became known as Constantinople, in honour of the emperor. It stayed that way until last century when the Turks officially named it Istanbul.'

'And that helps me how?'

'It explains why Mount Athos is run from Turkey. At one time, the entire Christian world was ruled from Constantinople. So it makes sense that the Ecumenical Patriarchate, an organization that is several hundred years old and provides spiritual leadership to the Greek Orthodox Church, would exist in that city – despite the presence of Islam.'

Dial nodded in understanding. Sometimes Toulon took longer to make a point than Dial would have liked, but the Frenchman always got there eventually.

'Okay,' Dial said, as he thought things through. 'Turkey is a member country, too. So pick up the phone, call the Patriarchate, and ask *them* for a permit. I need to get to Mount Athos.'

Toulon shook his head. 'It's not that simple, Nick. The Patriarchate provides spiritual guidance to Mount Athos, helping them with religious decisions. Meanwhile, the Holy Mountain is governed on a day-to-day basis by a different body, known as Holy Administration. It is made up of representatives of the twenty ruling monasteries and an elected governor.'

Dial growled in frustration. He didn't care about

the details. He just wanted an answer. 'Let me make this simple. Who is in charge of permits?'

'It is a joint decision. Every application is reviewed and thoroughly debated. This isn't a rubber stamp procedure. The committee evaluates a candidate's worth and grants access only to those who qualify. From what I hear, they are very strict.'

'So what are you saying? I don't qualify?'

'I am not sure. I will have to review their entry requirements. However, even if you qualify, these decisions are made weeks in advance. Permits must be granted. Sponsors must be found. It is all very complicated. There is no way I can accomplish this in an hour.'

'Fine! I'll give you *two* hours. But I'll need twice as many permits. One for me and one for my translator. His name is Marcus Andropoulos.'

Toulon cursed in French. He had worked with Dial long enough to know that he was serious. 'You are asking for a miracle.'

'Come on, Henri. You're always bragging about how intelligent you are. I'm sure if you put your mind to it, you'll come up with something.'

'*Oui*, it is true. I am very smart.'

'I know you are. So do me a favour and use all that brainpower to help me out. Get me access to Mount Athos and I'll give you a long weekend off.'

Toulon paused. 'In that case, I will see what I can do.'

48

The blow to his head had left Kozlov dazed. It dulled his ability to think. To focus. To perceive the world round him. And that left him in a dangerous place, one where he was no longer the hunter. Suddenly he was the target, trapped in the middle of nowhere, with no way out.

Ironically, he had made his living in places like this, luring his victims to the nether regions of Moscow where he killed them in isolation. Sometimes, when the situation called for it, he would finish a job in public, but he preferred the solitude of the woods where his victims could beg and plead as loudly as they wanted before he silenced them for ever. He loved that feeling of absolute power, the ability to turn someone off like a light switch.

The rush was better than sex or drugs or anything he had ever felt.

It made him feel like God.

Kozlov walked across the Metro car park and turned down a wooded path that led to his hotel. It was the same route he had taken several times during the past week, a scenic trail that ran along the banks of the Chernaya Rechka. Strolling along the water's edge, he rubbed the back of his skull and felt the large lump that had started to form. It was tender to the touch, yet the pain was welcome. It was like a whiff of smelling salts, helping him regain his faculties.

It helped him sense trouble before it struck.

The first time he heard the sound he assumed it was an animal. Maybe a rabbit or a fox looking for a meal. He turned slowly round and glanced along the path behind him, but saw nothing. So he kept moving forward, anxious to get to his room and his bottle of vodka.

The next time he heard the noise, it was much closer. Maybe thirty feet to his right. He stopped abruptly and scanned the tree line, searching for the source of the sound. A quiet snap could have been dismissed as a furry creature scampering through the underbrush. But this noise was louder, heavier. Like a bear. Or a wolf prowling for meat.

Instinctively, Kozlov reached for his shoulder holster.

To his surprise, it was empty.

'Looking for this?' Payne asked from the middle of the path.

Kozlov whipped his head round and spotted the man from the train. Somehow he was standing in front of him, holding the gun that should have been in Kozlov's holster.

Payne smiled. 'I found it on the Metro. I think it belongs to you.'

Kozlov studied the weapon but said nothing. It was definitely his.

Next, Payne pulled out Kozlov's wallet and his badge. 'When you fall down, you need to be more careful with your stuff. Otherwise it could end up in the wrong hands.'

A surge of adrenaline cleared the remaining haze from Kozlov's brain. Suddenly the events at Nevsky Prospekt started to make sense. The man with his gun was working with the black man. They had worked together to guarantee his escape from the train. Kozlov had no idea who they were or how they were connected to Byrd, but it was obvious they were professionals.

Their level of precision required years of fieldwork.

'By the way,' Payne said as he tossed Kozlov's pistol into the river. He was much more comfortable with his own gun, so he pulled it from his belt and aimed it at the Russian. 'I know you can understand me. I glanced through your wallet and saw some business cards that were written in English. No way you would have kept those if you didn't speak my language.'

Kozlov remained silent. Not willing to confirm or deny anything. At least not yet.

Payne continued as he walked forward. 'How's that bump on your head? I'm guessing it's a mild concussion. Probably the reason you didn't notice that your gun was missing. A healthy hit man would've noticed that sort of thing.'

'What is hit man? I am businessman.'

'A businessman who killed Richard Byrd.' Payne

had no idea if Kozlov was actually the killer, but he hoped to trick him into admitting his guilt. 'I saw surveillance footage of you from the Peterhof. I have to admit, I was impressed by your skills. That was a textbook shooting – except for the getting filmed part. You really should have smiled more.'

'I know nothing about shooting. I am businessman.'

Payne added more details to strengthen his claim. 'I particularly liked the way you tossed your gun into the fountain at the exact same moment the body hit the water. It takes a lot of balls to shoot someone in the head and then drop your weapon. Huge fucking balls.'

Kozlov beamed with pride. 'You have killed before, yes?'

Payne shrugged as he moved closer. 'What do you think?'

'I think you are like me. A man with taste for blood.'

'I am *nothing* like you. For one, I'm not dumb enough to say I'm a businessman when I'm carrying a gun and a fake shield.' Payne recognized the FSB emblem on the badge but assumed it was fake. No way this guy was on active duty. Not without a partner or a radio. 'Where I'm from, we call your organization KGB Lite. It's the KGB minus all that Soviet bullshit.'

Kozlov smiled. It made him look like a rat. 'Who is *we*? CIA?'

'Not a chance. I'm just a tourist.'

'And I am businessman.'

Payne narrowed their distance to ten feet, hoping to read the Russian's eyes. 'In some ways, you *are* a businessman. Because there's no doubt in my mind that you got paid a lot of money to kill Byrd. My only regret is that you killed him before I had a chance to chat with him.'

Kozlov considered Payne's statement. 'He was known to you.'

'Of course I knew him. That asshole robbed me blind.' Payne was lying, trying to get extra information from Kozlov. 'Same thing with the other investors. He stole millions of dollars from us and hid the money somewhere in Russia. Now, thanks to you, it's probably lost for ever.'

'You say millions?'

'Damn! How hard did I crack your head? Yes, Boris, or whatever your name is. I said *millions*. Many, many millions. And we don't know if it's here, in Moscow, or Siberia.'

Payne glanced over his shoulder, making sure that they were still alone. As far as he could see, the only things moving were the swaying trees and the flowing river.

'Is that why Byrd was killed? Revenge for money?'

'Why are you asking me? *You* killed the asshole.'

Deep down inside, Kozlov knew only one of them was going to survive this conversation. He knew he had to do something to lure Payne closer. It was the only way he stood a chance, the only way he could use the weapon that Payne hadn't stolen. In the meantime, if he had to tell Payne the truth about a few things so he would drop his guard, then so be it.

One of them would soon be dead. So what did it really matter?

Kozlov said, 'I was told nothing. Find Byrd, kill Byrd. I not know why.'

Payne nodded. 'You were paid to kill him and nothing else.'

'Yes, nothing else.'

'If that's the case,' Payne said as he aimed his weapon, 'why did you follow my friend? If your job was to kill Byrd, why are you still hanging round?'

Kozlov grimaced. He preferred being on the other side of the gun. 'I was paid to follow Byrd. To learn why he was here. I went to room to learn.'

'Two days *after* you killed him? No way you waited that long to search his room. You should have jumped on it at once – before the *real* cops arrived.'

'He use fake name. I find room only today. That is why I follow friend. I see him leave. I see him carry bags. I follow him to learn of Byrd.'

Payne nodded. Everything the Russian said fit the facts of the case. Byrd *had been* using a fake name. Kozlov did spot Jones when he was leaving Byrd's suite. And he had followed Jones to see where he was going. All of that made perfect sense.

Unfortunately, there were still some facts that Payne didn't know like who had hired the Russian and what was the real reason that Byrd had been killed. But Payne figured those answers would be tougher to acquire. They would require a little more finesse.

'So,' Payne said as he stepped closer, 'how much were you paid?'

'Nothing. I have not been paid.'

'Not even a deposit? That sounds like bad business to me. I mean, you've already killed Byrd, yet you haven't made a cent? That's pretty damn foolish.'

'You no worry about me. Money will be paid when job is done.'

'Tell me, what happens to your money if you never finish the job?'

Kozlov sneered at him. 'Are you threatening me?'

'Threatening you?' Payne laughed as he lowered his gun to his side. 'I was thinking about *hiring* you. A man of your skills might come in handy during my search.'

'What you mean?'

'I mean, I've got millions of dollars missing – money I won't be able to find without some help. I know Byrd stashed it somewhere, but I need a Russian to help me track a few leads. Someone who's not afraid to get his hands dirty, if you know what I mean.'

Kozlov stared at Payne, considering his words. 'How much you pay me?'

'I was thinking a flat percentage. Let's say, one per cent.'

'One per cent? I no work for one.'

'I'm talking millions of dollars here. If we find ten, you'd make a hundred grand. I know damn well you didn't make that much to kill Byrd.'

'And if we find one million, I make ten thousand. I worth more than that.'

'Touché. Maybe you are a businessman after all.'

Kozlov nodded. He doubted that Payne was telling the truth about any of this, but on the off chance that he was serious, Kozlov wanted to hear as many details as possible – if for no other reason than to lure his opponent even closer.

Right now they were seven feet apart. A few more feet and Kozlov could strike.

Payne continued. 'I'll tell you what I'm willing to do. One per cent with a guaranteed minimum of twenty-five thousand. That way, no matter what, you'll be paid for your time.'

'Minimum of twenty-five? For helping you with search? This is tempting.'

'I thought it would be. Of course for that kind of cash, I need some upfront information. Right here, right now. No bullshit.'

'What information you need?'

'Who hired you to kill Byrd?'

Kozlov smirked. 'This is big question.'

'This is big money.'

He nodded. 'This is true . . . How I know you will pay me?'

'The same way I'll know if you're telling the truth. Just trust your instincts.'

Kozlov considered this. 'In Russia, there is better way. Look man in eye as shake his hand. This is more valuable than promise. This is contract.'

'Fine,' Payne said, only happy to oblige. He moved his gun into his left hand while staring at the Russian. 'Let's shake on it.'

Kozlov nodded and took a tentative step forward. Payne followed his lead and did the same.

The two of them were four feet apart, just out of each other's grasp.

As Kozlov stretched his right hand forward, he inched his left hand towards his belt. Made out of black leather, it was held in place by an elaborate silver buckle. Though it looked decorative, it was actually the handle of a sharp dagger. The blade itself was tucked into the leather like a sheath. One simple flick of his wrist, and the weapon would be free of its constraints.

Payne kept his finger on the trigger even though his gun was pointed towards the ground. He reached his right arm towards Kozlov and grabbed his hand with a firm grip. The two men shook, while staring into each other's eyes. Neither trusted the other.

Kozlov moved first, extracting his blade with speed and precision. One moment it was in his belt, the next he was thrusting it under Payne's arm towards his gut.

But Payne had anticipated the manoeuvre. Using all his strength, he pulled Kozlov's right hand down and outside, which turned the Russian at a forty-five-degree angle and prevented his knife from striking. Suddenly Kozlov found himself off balance and facing away from his opponent. Thinking quickly, he swung his blade behind him, hoping to catch Payne in the ribs or his exposed left shoulder. Instead, the Russian felt his right knee explode as Payne used all his weight to drive his knee into the side of Kozlov's leg.

The popping sound was so loud that both men could hear it.

Kozlov dropped his knife and fell to the ground in a writhing wave of agony. The pain was more intense than anything he had ever experienced, including the time he was shot.

Cartilage, tendons, and kneecap – all destroyed with a pinpoint strike.

Kozlov wanted to scream, but before a sound could leave his lips, it was stifled by the taste of metal in his mouth. His eyes opened wide with surprise as he choked on the gun that would soon end his life. It rested in the hands of the man he had just tried to stab.

Suddenly, Payne was in complete control.

And he would milk it for everything that it was worth.

'You know,' he said as he knelt on Kozlov's chest, making it tough for the Russian to breathe. 'Back when I was in the Special Forces, I developed a nasty reputation. Among all the other officers, I was known as a *closer* . . . Does that translate into Russian?'

Kozlov tried to nod his head. The gun in his mouth made it difficult.

Payne glared at him. 'I don't want to bore you with the details, but I have the ability to read people. It doesn't sound like much, but it's a gift that I can use in so many ways. In situations like this, I love looking into the enemy's eyes and figuring out what scares him more than anything else in the world. Then I take that information and I use it against him.'

While Payne was training for the MANIACs, he had learned that one of the most effective ways to get information from a prisoner wasn't through torture but rather the *insinuation* of torture – the act of planting a psychological seed in someone's head and then waiting for panic to set in. If done correctly, some people would literally piss their pants long before they were touched.

'So far, I've disarmed you, given you a concussion, and shattered your knee *without* using any weapons. Imagine what I can do to you when I start getting serious.'

Payne leaned to his left and grabbed Kozlov's dagger off the ground. It was razor sharp. 'Wow. This is a really nice knife. And I should know. I'm great with a blade. Hell, you should see me in the kitchen. I'm like one of those gourmet chefs. Chop, chop, chop, chop, chop! I'm particularly good with cuts of meat. Give me a chicken and I can debone that cock in two seconds.' Payne tapped the knife on Kozlov's groin. 'Does *cock* translate into Russian?'

Kozlov's eyes got even wider – so wide his eyebrows looked like they might pop off.

'Anyway, enough about me. Let's talk about you. A few minutes ago, I asked you a simple question that you promised you would answer. Instead, you tried to stab me. That made me pretty mad. That's why my gun is in your mouth and your knife is in my hand.'

Payne glanced round. They were still alone. He could take as long as he wanted.

'Since I'm such a nice guy, I'm going to give you another chance. I'm going to ask you the same question again. If you lie to me, I'm going to get really angry. And if that happens, you'll find out why my platoon mates were scared of me.'

Payne inched the gun from Kozlov's mouth. Before he pulled it the whole way out, he rattled it back and forth against the Russian's teeth. It sounded like he was shaking dice.

'Okay, Boris. Answer my fucking question. Who hired you to kill Richard Byrd?'

49

Most operatives would have been spooked by the events on Nevsky Prospekt. They would have assumed that their cover was blown and a new hideout needed to be found. But not David Jones. Even though he had been followed from the Astoria Hotel, he was confident that they were now clean. He kept a watchful eye on the street as he and Allison made their way back to their suite. They took a circuitous route, one that allowed Jones to search for shadows. They walked a few blocks, took a cab, and then walked some more. After thirty minutes, they entered the Palace Hotel through a back entrance, staying clear of the lobby and the main bank of elevators.

The back stairs led them to their room. Jones went in first and looked round. Everything was how they had left it. He waved Allison inside and brought the bags in from the hallway. After carrying them for more than an hour, he never wanted to see them again. Yet Jones knew if they had any hope of solving the mystery of Byrd's murder, the answers would be found in his belongings.

'Where do you want these?' Jones asked.

'By the table,' she replied from across the room.

Jones dropped the bags and noticed her standing near the kitchen. 'What's wrong?'

'Nothing . . . It's nothing.'

'Don't give me that. What is it?'

'Sorry,' she said as she stared at Richard's bag. 'I feel kind of strange going through his papers. He was so protective of his stuff. It makes me feel like a vulture.'

Jones leaned against the edge of the table. 'Allison, come over here and sit down. We need to discuss a few things.'

'That doesn't sound good.'

'Just come and sit down.'

She nodded and did what she was told.

'Listen,' he said in a soft voice, 'I've known you less than a day, so I won't even pretend to know what you're thinking or feeling. Everyone handles death and fear in different ways. Your way is different to my way and so on. Agreed?'

'Agreed.'

'That being said, you need to get something through your head. And the sooner you do, the better it will be for all of us.'

'Okay,' she said tentatively. 'What is it?'

'Richard Byrd was a selfish prick.'

'Excuse me?'

'He was an *asshole*.'

'Why are you saying that?'

'Why? Because you're showing the guy way too much respect. He treated you like shit. He refused to tell you what he was searching for, and he put your life in danger. That sounds like an asshole to me.'

'He wasn't that bad.'

Jones unzipped Byrd's bag and pulled out the stack of fake IDs and credit cards that he recovered from Byrd's safe. He scattered them on the table for effect. 'Go ahead. Take a look. What did he have? Five fake names? Ten? And those are just the ones I found. Who knows how many he has back in California. I'm telling you, the guy was bad news.'

As she glanced through the items, disappointment filled her face. She was aware of one fake identity – the one he had used to enter Russia. All the others were a surprise. 'Why did he have so many?'

Jones shrugged. 'Who knows? He might have been running from someone, or he might have been planning a crime. Whatever the case, he was up to no good. And it started long before he came to Russia.'

She nodded slowly, almost imperceptibly. Then it became more pronounced as she reflected on the last month of her life: the time she had spent with Byrd. Earlier in the day, she had told Payne that she thought her boss might have been a criminal. Now she was sure of it.

Jones continued. 'I'm not saying that he deserved to die. Still, as you look through his things, I want you to keep something in mind: this situation is all his fault. *He* dragged you into this mess. *He* put your life in danger. All you're trying to do is claw your way out.'

* * *

Allison appreciated the pep talk. It helped her erase any feelings of loyalty that still lingered. In her mind, she was no longer violating her boss's privacy. No longer going through a dead man's things. Instead, she was doing the job that she had been hired to do. She was a researcher. A damn good one. This was the one part of her life where she felt totally at ease. Whereas Payne and Jones excelled in the field, this was her comfort zone. She felt at home.

'Please hand me that book,' she said, pointing towards the far end of the table. 'That's where Richard wrote his appointments. Maybe we can figure out what he's been up to.'

'Good idea,' said Jones as he passed her the journal.

It was bound in black leather. Byrd's initials were embossed in fancy script on the front cover. A gold ribbon, glued to the binding of the book, marked the current week. Allison flipped to that page and studied the schedule for Sunday, 18 May – the day that Byrd was killed.

'One entry,' she said. 'There's a man's name and a phone number. Nothing else.'

'What's the name?'

She tried to read Byrd's handwriting. It was barely legible. 'Ivan Borodin.'

'Ring any bells?'

'Nope. Never heard of him.'

'Local number?'

She nodded. 'Should we call it?'

'Not yet. First, look back a day or two. See if anything else stands out.'

Allison flipped back a page. 'That's strange. The same name and number. Only it's been scratched out.'

Jones walked behind her for a better view. 'Go back one more page.'

The same name appeared, also crossed off. 'Ivan Borodin.'

'You're sure you've never heard of him?'

'Positive. Richard never told me anything.'

'Flip back some more. Find the first time Ivan is mentioned.'

Allison turned the pages slowly, trying to decipher Byrd's scribbles. Some of his entries made sense, particularly the appointments that involved her in some way – a lunch meeting, a trip to the library, etc. But most of his notes were nonsense. They were either written in code or simply illegible. 'As far as I can tell, Ivan's name first appeared on the eighth. There's even a star written next to it.'

'The eighth? I thought you were in Germany on the eighth?'

She nodded. 'We were. We flew to Russia on the tenth.'

Jones considered this information. 'Okay. Now we're getting somewhere. See if this makes sense. He calls Ivan on the eighth. They talk about *whatever* and set up a meeting in St Petersburg. The only problem is that Richard can't get into Russia without a fake visa. So he takes a day or two to get the phoney paperwork and arrange a flight. Bing, bang, boom. Next thing you know, your plans to Greece get cancelled because he needs to meet with Ivan.'

She smiled. 'Bing, bang, boom?'

'What? You've never heard that expression?'

'Of course I have. I simply prefer, "yada yada yada". It's classier.'

'Oh my goodness! You made a joke. I can't wait to tell Jon.'

Allison blushed slightly. 'Just so you know, I *do* have a personality'

'I know you do. I'm just glad to see you finally using it.'

'Ouch.'

'Anyway,' Jones said, feeling guilty about teasing her, 'if my theory is correct, that means Ivan has something that Richard needed. Any ideas on what it was?'

She shook her head. 'No clue. But the answer might be among his papers.'

'I was thinking the same thing.' He wrote Ivan's number down on a piece of hotel stationery. 'Why don't you start looking through this stuff? Meanwhile I'll make a few calls and see what I can come up with.'

Jones walked into the guest bedroom and partially closed the door. He didn't want to disturb her or leave her unattended. For the time being, she was his responsibility. Using the cell phone that Payne had bought for him, Jones dialled a number that he knew by heart. A few seconds passed before the phone started ringing at the Pentagon.

Randy Raskin answered. 'Research.'

Jones glanced at his watch. It was still early in America. 'Damn! Do you *ever* sleep?'

'There's no need. That's why God invented caffeine.'

'Good point.'

'By the way, I have to commend you on your trickiness.'

'My trickiness? What are you talking about?'

'You called me from a different number. You're lucky, too. If I had known it was you, I probably wouldn't have answered.'

Jones smiled. He peered into the other room, just to make sure Allison wasn't listening. 'And if you hadn't picked up, I wouldn't have been able to tell you about your future girlfriend.'

'My future girlfriend?' It took a moment for the comment to register, but when it finally did, Raskin's voice went up an octave. 'Hold up! You mean that hot blonde from California? You actually found her?'

'Not only that, she wants you to do her a favour.'

Drool practically dripped from Raskin's mouth. He and his computer lived a lonely life in the Pentagon basement. 'Anything she wants. And I mean *anything*. With a touch of a button, I can name a battleship after her.'

'Ahhh! How romantic! What a sweet and totally inappropriate gesture.'

'Hey, it's the thought that counts.'

'Thankfully, her idea of a favour is a little smaller than that. She needs information on a man named Ivan Borodin. I have a phone number, if that will help.'

'Of course it will help.'

Jones read it to him. 'I'm pretty sure it's in St Petersburg.'

Raskin waited for the details to flash on his screen. 'You are correct. Ivan Sergei Borodin lives in St Petersburg on some street I can't pronounce. I can spell it for you, though.'

Jones wrote down the address. 'Anything else?'

'From what I can tell, the dude is pretty old. He's eighty-eight.'

'Eighty-eight? That *can't* be right. Does he have a son or something?'

'Hold on. Different database.' The sound of typing filled the line until Raskin spoke again. 'Nope. No kids listed. His wife is deceased. His brother is deceased. His sisters are deceased. Surprisingly, his parents are still alive.'

'What?!'

'Just kidding. Wanted to make sure you were listening.'

Jones smiled. 'What about employment history?'

'I'm going to go out on a limb and say he's retired.'

'From where?'

'Hold on . . .'

'I know. Different database.'

'Okay,' Raskin said. 'Last known employer was the State Hermitage Museum. I can get you the address if you need it.'

'No thanks. I'm familiar with the place. Do you know what position he held?'

'I sure do. Until eight years ago, Ivan Borodin was the director of the museum.'

50

While Dial made the arrangements for their trip to Mount Athos, Andropoulos drove him to his hotel in Kalampáka. It took nearly thirty minutes from Great Metéoron.

'We have some time to kill before the helicopter arrives,' Dial said when they reached the hotel car park. 'I'd like to show you something.'

'Of course, sir. Whatever you want.'

Dial led the way to his hotel room. A do not disturb sign hung from the knob. He unlocked the door and walked inside. A large bulletin board was sitting on a table, leaning against the far wall. The board was covered with handwritten notes on index cards and several photographs from the crime scene.

Andropoulos stared at it with a mixture of confusion and wonder. 'Sir, what is all of this?'

'It's my way of organizing a case.' Dial had assembled it the night before while trying to digest his authentic Greek dinner. His project was finished long before his indigestion had disappeared. 'Some people prefer computers. But not me. I'm old school when it comes to investigations. I like seeing everything in front of me all at once. I like having the freedom to shift things round as the pieces fall into place. It helps me see the big picture.'

Andropoulos pointed at the board. 'Is this what you wanted me to see?'

Dial nodded. 'If you're going to be my translator at Mount Athos, I need to make sure we're on the same page.'

'In that case, you better walk me through everything.'

Dial started with the index card at the top of the board. On it he had written the numbers one through seven, followed by the names of the monks that had been identified by the police. 'So far we know about four monks, not including the one who kept his head. Each of them is from a different country, right?'

'That is correct. Russia, Turkey, Bulgaria, and Greece.'

'Seems kind of strange, doesn't it? That monks from four different countries were having a secret meeting in the middle of the night in a place as isolated as Metéora.'

'Very strange.'

'I have a feeling it's going to get even stranger. In fact, I'd be willing to bet you that the remaining three monks are from different countries as well.'

'Countries with ties to the Orthodox Church.'

Dial smiled. 'Exactly.'

'Yet you don't think this meeting was about religion.'

'My gut tells me no. And after talking to my

colleague at Interpol, I'm even more confident than before.'

'Why is that, sir?'

Dial pointed to a small map that was thumb tacked to the bottom of his board. It showed the geography of Greece and several surrounding countries. 'Originally I had assumed that the seat of the Greek Orthodox Church would be in Greece. Nope, stupid me. It turns out the Ecumenical Patriarchate is located in Istanbul.'

'The Patriarchate is in Turkey? I thought it was in Athens.'

'That's what I assumed, too. But it's not.'

Andropoulos stared at the map. 'And why is that important?'

'If this diverse group of monks was having an official meeting about Church doctrine, where would it be held?'

'In Istanbul.'

'And if they were having an unofficial meeting, where would they go?'

'Probably Athens.'

Dial nodded. 'Makes sense to me. Major airport. Centrally located. A very solid choice.'

'But they chose here instead.'

'Exactly. Which makes no sense at all. Why arrange a meeting in the middle of the night on top of a mountain unless you had a specific reason to do it?'

'Such as?'

Dial tapped Andropoulos on his chest. 'See, that's

a question right there that needs to be answered. Once we figure that out, all of this other stuff will start to fall into place.'

Andropoulos nodded as he returned his attention to the bulletin board. Underneath the index card with the names of the dead monks, Dial had tacked two additional cards. One said 'Nicolas', the other said 'Spartans'. 'What do those mean?'

'Tell me, Marcus, what does Nicolas have in common with the Spartans?'

He gave it some thought. 'Both of them are Greek.'

Dial grimaced. 'And so are you, but what does that have to do with anything?'

'I don't know. I just—'

'Come on, Marcus, use your head. Don't waste your time on superficial bullshit. Focus on what's important . . . Why would I place those two cards right next to each other?'

'Because they're connected.'

'Right. And how are they connected?'

Andropoulos stared at the cards, struggling to find the link.

'Look at the card above. How do the dead monks connect to Nicolas and the Spartans?'

'Well,' he said, trying to talk his way through the process, 'we don't think that Nicolas is a Spartan, so we can rule that out.'

'Go on.'

'Actually, we aren't quite sure who Nicolas is. Or why he was there.'

'But . . .'

'But . . . somehow he knew.'

Dial smiled. 'Knew what?'

'Nicolas *knew* about the meeting. Somehow he knew when and where the meeting was being held. Just like the Spartans. They knew about the meeting, too.'

'Not only that,' Dial added, 'Nicolas knew about the abbot's death before we did. That means he knew the time, the place, and the guest list. That's an awfully large chunk of information for someone to possess.'

'Which is why we're going to Mount Athos. To look for Nicolas.'

Dial nodded. 'Admittedly, the odds are pretty slim that we'll find the guy. Mount Athos is large, and Nicolas probably looks like half the monks there. Still, I think it's worth our time and effort. Especially after I saw that old photo of him at Holy Trinity. That clinched the trip for me.'

'Why, sir? Why is that picture so important?'

'Let me show you,' Dial said as he removed the photograph from a plastic sleeve designed to protect it. Theodore, the monk from the library, had been kind enough to lend it to them for their investigation. 'Look at the people in this picture. What do they have in common?'

'Most of them are dead.'

'And how do you know that?'

'The picture was taken four decades ago, and the monks were already old back then.'

'Define old,' Dial ordered. 'And you better watch your word choice.'

'Sorry, sir. I didn't mean to imply—'

Dial pointed to the oldest monk in the photo. 'How old do you think he was?'

'I don't know. Maybe seventy.'

'And what about this guy here?'

'Early sixties.'

'And this one?'

'Fifties.'

'Noticing a pattern?'

Andropoulos nodded. 'Their ages are staggered.'

'Exactly. Seven monks, each of them born several years apart. Kind of interesting, huh?'

'In what way, sir?'

Dial sighed. He thought his point was rather obvious. 'Take a look at the bulletin board.'

'Okay.'

He pointed to a single photo. Seven heads were stacked in a pyramid in the secret passageway underneath Holy Trinity. 'Ignore the blood and the brutality. Focus on the faces. What can you tell me about these monks?'

Andropoulos stared at the image, trying to figure out the answer that Dial was looking for. Several seconds passed before it came to him. 'The monks were different ages.'

'Exactly! Seven monks with staggered ages. Where have we seen that before?'

'In the other picture.'

'Not only that, but the abbot was in each one. He was a young monk in the old photo and the old monk in the new photo. Somehow I doubt that's a coincidence.'

'I don't get it, sir. Why would they stagger the ages?'

'Only one reason I can think of: succession.'

'Succession?'

Dial nodded. 'The monks were trying to keep something alive, whether it was a secret or a tradition or whatever. The way I figure it is this. When one of the monks died, they brought a new one into the fold. That guaranteed a new generation to keep things going. Hell, they might have gone so far as to choose seven monks from different countries just to make sure that a natural disaster didn't wipe them all out at once. That would explain the wide variety of faces in the photos. A new monk from a different place to keep something alive.'

'I'm confused, sir. What kind of *something* are you talking about?'

He tapped Andropoulos on his chest again. 'That goes back to my earlier question. What were these monks discussing in an isolated monastery in the middle of the night?'

'Do you have any theories?'

'Of course, I do. I *always* have theories. How many times do I have to tell you that?'

'But you're keeping them to yourself.'

'For the time being, yes. I don't want to taint your opinions until I'm a little more certain.'

'Fair enough.'

'What about you? Do *you* have any theories?'

Andropoulos smiled. 'Actually, sir, I might.'

'Let me guess, you're going to keep them to yourself so you don't taint me.'

'No, sir. I'd be happy to share it with you if you're willing to listen.'

'I'm all ears. What's your theory about?'

'I think I just figured out why they were meeting at Holy Trinity, not Athens or Istanbul.'

'Go on.'

'It never dawned on me until you said the word, but maybe the reason they were meeting locally was *tradition*. After all, the photograph from forty years ago was also taken here. Maybe they met here every year. Maybe it was a part of their ritual.'

Dial stroked his chin in thought. 'You know what, Marcus? That's a pretty good theory. It makes more sense than anything I've come up with.'

'Thank you, sir. I'm glad you like it.'

Dial walked closer to the bulletin board, staring at all the pictures and index cards. As he did, he ran different scenarios through his mind, trying to decide if he needed to shift anything round. Sometimes that was how it worked with Dial. One thing fell into place, followed by another and another until all of his questions were suddenly answered.

'What are you thinking about, sir?'

'The reason. What was the reason they started meeting at Holy Trinity?'

'That, I don't know.'

'I'm glad,' Dial teased. 'It will give me a chance to earn my big pay check.'

Andropoulos smiled and was about to say something else until he noticed the faraway look in Dial's eye. He was no longer paying attention to the young cop. Instead, he was focused on the bulletin board, crunching all the data in his head, trying to figure out the answer to the question that he had just asked. Why were they meeting at Holy Trinity?

A few minutes passed before Dial spoke again. 'The tunnel. This whole thing is about the goddamn tunnel.'

'The tunnel?'

'More specifically, what used to be *in* the tunnel.'

To make his point, Dial tapped on a photo of the stone altar that they had found underneath Holy Trinity. 'Look at the craftsmanship of that thing. That altar used to hold something important. I'm not sure what, but it was important. Same with all those empty shelves we found. Something important used to be down there.'

Andropoulos nodded in agreement. 'You're probably right.'

'I'm assuming that's why the Spartans took the time to leave the heads on the altar. They wanted somebody to know that they had found their secret tunnel and weren't going to stop killing people until they found what they were looking for.'

'Wanted *who* to know?'

'Maybe Nicolas. Maybe they wanted *him* to know for some reason. Maybe that's why he showed up, to see the message for himself.'

Andropoulos glanced at the bulletin board, focusing on the card that said *Nicolas*. As he did, a question popped into his head. 'Sir, if your theory is correct about succession, why wasn't Nicolas killed? I mean, shouldn't he have been here for the meeting? He was in that picture from forty years ago, the one with the abbot.'

'I was wondering when you were going to mention that. That question has been plaguing me, too. Maybe death wasn't the end of a monk's term. Maybe there was an age limit. Maybe that's the reason he wasn't there when the rest of the monks were killed. Being old might have saved his life.'

'Maybe. Or maybe Nicolas did something to get thrown out of the group.'

Dial nodded. 'Trust me. That thought had crossed my mind, too.'

51

Jones was excited by the news. He walked into the other room to share it with Allison, who was going through Byrd's papers. 'I found Ivan Borodin. He lives here in St Petersburg.'

'That's great. Now all we have to do is figure out who he is.'

'I found that out, too. He used to be the director of the Hermitage Museum.'

'Wow,' she said as she considered what that meant. 'I guess I shouldn't be surprised. Richard never liked wasting time with peons. He always went straight to the top.'

'Maybe so, but Borodin retired eight years ago. Why talk to him now?'

'Remember what I told you last night? The Hermitage launched its Schliemann exhibit in 1998. That means Borodin was the man who brought it here. Imagine what information he has? He would know, better than anyone, what items aren't on display.'

Jones nodded. 'Petr Ulster once told me that eighty-five per cent of all artefacts are never shown to the general public. That's a lot of stuff that Richard might have been interested in.'

'I'll keep looking through his notes. Maybe I can figure out what he wanted to see.'

'Meanwhile, if you don't mind, I'd like to use your computer. I want to get some background information on Borodin. The more we know about him, the better.'

'Help yourself. It's fully charged.'

Jones grabbed the laptop bag and carried it to the writing desk near the guest bedroom. He was about to turn on the computer when he felt his cell phone vibrate. 'Hello?'

It was Payne, calling from the back entrance to the hotel. 'I'm on my way up.'

'Already?'

'Do me a favour. Run interference for me. I need to take a shower.'

'No problem.'

Jones knew not to ask any questions. Payne would talk about his confrontation with Kozlov when he was ready. Depending on what had happened, it might be five minutes or an hour. In the meantime he didn't want to be bothered. Not by Jones or anyone else.

This was standard protocol for Payne. He needed time to decompress.

'Hey Allison,' Jones said as he hung up his phone. 'I need to let Jon in. Just to be safe, hang out in the bedroom for a few minutes.'

'Is everything all right?'

'Of course it is. I'm just being cautious.'

She nodded, too preoccupied with Byrd's journal to challenge Jones' request. Taking the book with her, she went into the bedroom and closed the door.

A short time later, Payne entered the suite. His clothes were dirty and slightly damp as though he had been working all day in the hot sun. His eyes were intense and focused. He patted Jones on the shoulder as he walked towards the guest wing. His gesture was a simple one, but it let Jones know that everything had been taken care of and he was all right.

Then, without saying a single word, Payne closed and locked the guest room door.

The sound of running water soon filled the hallway.

Forty minutes later, Payne emerged a new man. He had showered and changed his clothes. A smile was on his face, and his stomach was growling. He strolled into the kitchen looking for something to eat, finding nothing but a bowl of fruit left over from breakfast. He grabbed an apple and walked towards the dining-room table where Jones and Allison were working.

'What have we learned?' Payne wondered.

Jones answered. 'We went through Byrd's planner and one name stood out: Ivan Borodin, the former director of the Hermitage Museum. We don't know what they were discussing, but we assume it was Schliemann. Ivan was in charge of the Schliemann exhibit before he retired.'

Payne pondered the information. 'Is that why Byrd came to town, to meet Ivan?'

'That would be my guess, but we don't know for sure. It fits the timeline, though.'

'What do we know about him?'

'We have his home phone and address. Oh, and the guy is eighty-eight years old.'

'Damn. How long ago did he retire?'

'Only eight years.'

'He retired at eighty? That explains why Byrd wanted to talk to him. He must know the location of the fountain of youth.'

Jones smiled. 'You might be on to something. I searched the internet and came up with several articles about his career. Ivan devoted most of his life to the Hermitage. He worked there for over sixty years, starting out as a tour guide and working his way up through the ranks. You rarely see that type of dedication any more.'

'Sixty years in one place? That's plenty of time to learn a lot of secrets.'

'We were thinking the same thing.'

'How many times did they meet?'

Allison entered the conversation. 'We don't know. Ivan's name and number appeared several times in Richard's planner, but he never mentioned his name to me.'

'We have his number, right? Why don't we give him a call?'

Jones nodded. 'We planned on it. I was just waiting to get your approval.'

On the surface, it seemed like a straightforward

comment. But Payne knew otherwise. He had worked with Jones long enough to know he wasn't requesting permission to make a phone call. He was asking Payne if he wanted to continue their investigation. As things stood, Byrd's killer had been taken care of and Allison was temporarily safe. One quick call to Jarkko and the thirsty Finn would have them drinking Kafka in international waters in less than an hour.

For the time being, that option didn't interest Payne. Not until they solved the mystery of Byrd's death. What was Byrd looking for that was so important?

Payne needed to know before he was willing to leave Russia.

'Make the call,' Payne said, 'but have Allison do the talking.'

'What?' she stammered. 'Why me?'

'Because you were Byrd's assistant. Maybe he didn't tell you about Ivan, but he might have told Ivan about you. Besides, your voice is slightly less threatening than ours.'

'Yeah, but—'

'Allison,' he said, not in the mood to argue, 'you're making the call.'

Before she did, Payne and Jones coached her on what to say, anticipating the questions about Richard that were sure to come. If possible, they wanted to meet Ivan immediately. With the Russian's advanced age, they figured he probably wouldn't have a hectic social calendar. In fact, he might even welcome some company. The goal, though, was to meet with him face to face, whether that was at his home or the museum. And the sooner, the better.

Allison turned on the speakerphone so Payne and Jones could listen in. Ringing filled their suite until Ivan answered.

'*Da?*' he said.

'Hello? Is this Ivan Borodin?'

'Yes. Who is this?'

'My name is Allison. I'm Richard's assistant.'

'Richard Byrd?'

Allison exhaled. She was glad that Byrd had used his real name, not one of his fake identities. That would make things so much easier. 'Yes, sir. I'm his assistant.'

'I was expecting him on Sunday. He never showed up.'

'I'm sorry, sir. He was called away on business. He asked me to apologize.'

'I see.' Ivan's voice was weak, as one might expect from an eighty-eight year old. It was also tinged with a Russian accent, which made it difficult to read his emotions over the phone. 'I assumed he was no longer interested in the coat.'

Allison whispered to Payne and Jones. 'The coat?'

They shrugged. They had no idea what Ivan was talking about.

Jones whispered back. 'Say you're interested.'

'No, sir. We're still interested. Could I stop by today?'

Ivan paused, longer than he should have to answer such a simple question. Eventually, he cleared his throat and replied. 'Tomorrow would be better. Is ten o'clock too early?'

Allison grinned. 'Ten o'clock is *perfect*. Should I come to you?'

'Yes. That would be best. I don't move about like I used to.'

Jones took the phone from Allison and shook her hand. 'Well played, my lady.'

'Wow,' she remarked. 'That was kind of fun. Who can I call now?'

Payne glanced at his watch. It was late afternoon. No way would they be ready to leave before their deadline. He needed to call Jarkko to make new arrangements.

'Nice job,' he said to Allison. 'But now comes the hard part. You have to figure out what Ivan was talking about. What is "the coat" that he referred to?'

'Honestly, I have no idea. And I knew more about Schliemann than Richard ever did.'

'Maybe it has nothing to do with Schliemann,' Jones suggested.

She shrugged. 'Maybe so. But now that I know what to look for, I should be able to find something in Richard's notes. At least I hope I can.'

'I'll help you search. Four eyes are better than two.'

Payne nodded at Jones. 'I have to make some calls. As soon as I'm done, I'll help as well. In the meantime, why don't you guys order some dinner? It's going to be a long night.'

52

Jarkko was more than happy to stay an extra night in St Petersburg. He was getting paid to drink on his boat, an activity that he normally did for free.

Once the arrangements had been made, Payne asked Jones to join him in the guest room. They still needed to discuss the information learned from Kozlov. It was a conversation they didn't want to have in front of Allison. For the time being, she was focused on Byrd's documents, consumed with Ivan Borodin and his mysterious coat.

Distracting her with death and violence would be counterproductive.

Jones entered and closed the door behind him. Two chairs and a small table filled the right corner of the room. He grabbed one of the chairs and turned it backwards, allowing him to prop his arms in front of him. Meanwhile, Payne sat on the foot of the bed.

'Who was he?' Jones asked.

'His name was Alexei Kozlov. He was ex-FSB.' Payne handed him Kozlov's badge. It was gold with Cyrillic lettering. 'He assured me it was fake.'

Jones recognized the emblem. 'It damn well better be or we need to leave now. We don't want to tangle with the FSB.'

'Don't worry. I'm confident he was telling the truth.'

Jones nodded. He trusted Payne's judgment. 'What else did you learn?'

'He killed Byrd. Never got paid, though. Kozlov worked through an intermediary with the Russian mafia. They gave him a phone number to call. He talked to the man who hired him but never knew his name. He was told to find Byrd, figure out what he was doing, and then kill him before he left town.'

'Anything else?'

'His boss spoke with a Mediterranean accent. Couldn't tell if it was Greek, Turkish, or Italian. But definitely Mediterranean.'

Jones fiddled with the badge. 'This sure looks real to me.'

'At one time it probably was. But killing pays better than government work.'

'It always does.' He handed it back to Payne. 'Should we be worried about the mafia?'

Payne shook his head. 'He wasn't in the mafia. This was a contract job, plain and simple.'

'Which means Allison is safe.'

'She is from Kozlov. I can guarantee that.'

No explanation was necessary. He knew what Payne meant.

'Changing subjects,' Jones said. 'Any theories on Byrd?'

'Not yet. I've been kind of busy. What about you?'

'I found a stack of phoney passports and foreign

currency. Either Byrd was on the run, or he was expecting to be.'

'Then why come to Russia? And why bring Allison with him?'

'Those are two good questions, especially since he didn't take her to Italy.'

'Hell,' Payne said, 'he didn't even tell her he went to Italy. If she hadn't seen the airport tags on his suitcase, she wouldn't have known.'

'Exactly. So why bring her to St Petersburg and not take her to Naples?'

'Only one reason to do that. He *needed* her here for something.'

Jones nodded. He was thinking the exact same thing. 'If I had to guess, this has to do with Schliemann. According to her, she knew a lot more about Schliemann than Byrd ever did. That has to be the reason he brought her here. To help him with Schliemann.'

'Guys!' Allison called from the dining room. 'I might have found something important!'

Payne and Jones left the guest room and joined her at the table. A small journal, yellowed with age, was open in front of her. Next to it sat a modern-day legal tablet. It was filled with crisp white pages and several columns of information. The words were written in blue ink.

Jones studied the top page. 'Someone's been busy.'

'Not me,' she assured him. 'This is Richard's notebook. I found it in his files.'

'And what is that?' Payne asked, pointing at the journal.

'*That* is the reason I'm so excited. I think I know why Richard went to Italy.'

Payne and Jones glanced at each other, amused. They had just been discussing that topic in the other room. Intrigued, Jones slid out of his chair and moved behind her. He wanted a better view of the book, which looked more than a century old.

Allison continued, 'Remember what I told you last night? When Richard returned from Naples, he asked me all kinds of questions about Pompeii and Herculaneum, the two cities that were destroyed by the eruption from Mount Vesuvius. Schliemann had toured that area prior to his death, and I assumed that Richard went there to figure out what he had been looking for.'

'A fair assumption,' Jones remarked.

'Well, I was wrong. That might have been a smokescreen. I'm pretty sure Richard went to Naples to buy *this*.' She tapped the journal for emphasis. 'Do you know what *this* is?'

'If we did,' Payne said, 'we wouldn't be staring at you.'

'It's a transcript of Heinrich Schliemann's final words, recorded by one of the police officers who found him unconscious on the street. I think Richard bought it in Naples.'

Jones leaned closer to inspect the journal. 'How could it be a transcript? If he was unconscious, how did he talk?'

'According to this journal, Schliemann was taken to the police station while they tried to establish his identity. At one point, despite being incoherent, he started talking in his sleep.'

'Were you aware of that?'

'Not at all. But rumours have circulated for years about Schliemann's final days, including his quest to find the largest treasure of all time. Most academics assumed it was part of the hype that he had created during his lifetime. I mean, this was a man who funded the construction of his own mausoleum and paid for the inscription to read, "To the Hero Schliemann".'

Jones laughed. 'The guy wasn't modest.'

'No, he wasn't. That much is certain. But little else is. When it comes to Schliemann's life, there was always a fuzzy line between fact and fiction.'

'Tell us more about the journal,' Payne said.

'At first glance, I thought it was written by an idiot. Every other word is badly misspelled or abbreviated. I could tell that right away, and I don't even speak Italian.' She picked up the legal tablet and showed it to Payne. The top page was divided into several different categories. 'Then I found this. Richard had gone through the journal and translated everything into English.'

'What's with the columns?' Payne asked.

'Each column represents a different language.'

'What do you mean?'

'Remember, Schliemann wasn't an Italian. He was a German who had lived all over the world and could speak twenty-two languages. From what I can tell, he used several of those languages on his deathbed. The officer did the best he could to write the words phonetically. It was the only way he could keep track of what was being said.'

She ran her finger down the first column. The word ENGLISH was written at the top. Next were columns for GERMAN, GREEK, RUSSIAN, ITALIAN, and FRENCH. Then she flipped the page. Six more columns appeared. They were labelled SPANISH, PORTUGUESE, DUTCH, and so on. Some of the columns were filled with words; others were nearly empty.

'Richard went through the journal and placed words in corresponding columns. Then he translated each of those words and tried to figure out what Schliemann was saying.'

'And?' Jones asked, excited by the possibilities.

'Unfortunately, Richard came up with gibberish.'

'Damn!'

She glanced back at Jones, who was looking over her shoulder. She was thrilled that he cared enough to curse. 'Don't worry. There's still hope. I have plenty of information to work with. Give me some time and I might be able to figure it out.'

'Or maybe not. I've seen a few people die. They

didn't always make sense at the end. In fact, some of them were pretty damn delusional.'

'Well,' she said, trying not to think about it, 'I'll do my best.'

Payne asked, 'At first glance, does anything stand out?'

She nodded. 'One word is repeated over and over in many different languages. *Il trono. Le trône. El trono.* And so forth.'

'I'm hoping *el trono* means the coat.'

She smiled. 'Actually, it means the throne. But Richard does mention the coat on the final page of his translation.'

She pointed to the words that filled the bottom of the last page. They had been written in capital letters, and then the message had been circled. A giant star was drawn to the left of the note, stressing how important it was. It read:

THE COAT = THE KEY

53

As the black helicopter touched down in an open field on the outskirts of Kalampáka, dirt and dust swirled into the air like a cyclone. Andropoulos, who had never ridden in a chopper before, watched with childlike wonder from inside his car. His vehicle rattled from the whooshing of the powerful blades until the pilot flipped a switch and stopped the turbines.

'This is going to be awesome!' Andropoulos gushed. 'Thanks for bringing me along.'

Dial rolled his eyes at the enthusiasm. For him, air travel had lost its lustre a long time ago. 'You aren't on board yet. Keep it up, and I'll hire the pilot to be my translator.'

'Sorry, sir.'

'Don't apologize. Make yourself useful. Grab our bags from the trunk.'

Andropoulos scurried off to complete his task while Dial cracked a smile. No matter how helpful the young Greek was – and so far he had exceeded Dial's expectations – Dial planned on busting the kid's balls every chance he got. As a veteran member of the law enforcement community, it was his God-given right and duty to toughen the youngster up.

Plus, it was a hell of a lot of fun.

Dial was about to step out of the car when his phone started to vibrate. He glanced at the screen. It was Henri Toulon from Interpol. '*Hola*, Henri.'

'Spanish?' he growled. 'I tell you not to speak French, so you speak Spanish?'

'What can I say? I'm an equal-opportunity linguist.'

'*Oui*. You mangle all languages the same amount.'

Dial smirked. 'From the insolent tone of your voice, I'm assuming you have good news about my permits to Mount Athos. Otherwise, you wouldn't be so rude.'

'I have good news. I also have bad news. Which would you like first?'

'Not this shit again,' he muttered, remembering that Toulon had played the same game when telling him about the Spartans. 'Just tell me *all* the news, Henri.'

'Now who is rude? People say we French are rude, but no one ever talks about Americans. And you know why we don't mention you? Because your country has the most bombs. If that was not so, people would say Americans are ruder than the French!'

Toulon was obviously frustrated about something, so Dial responded in a calm voice.

'What's wrong, Henri? What's the bad news?'

'I have let you down.'

'How so?'

'I try and I try but you cannot visit Mount Athos today.'

Dial groaned. They were ready to take off. 'Why not?'

'Because the monks are very strict. And you are arriving late.'

He glanced at his watch. It was mid-afternoon in Greece. 'Late? I'll be there by dinner.'

'Which is too late for them. The monks live regimented lives. They work together. They pray together. They eat together. Your arrival will interrupt that schedule. After a certain time each day, the guards will not allow anyone to enter Mount Athos – even those with permits. As I say, they are *very* strict.'

'Fine. What's the good news?'

'I have arranged two meetings for you. One is with the Governor of Mount Athos. He was appointed by the Greek Ministry of Foreign Affairs and is in charge of the civil administration of the Holy Mountain. For requests like yours, he is the man who must sign off on your visit. He has the authority to grant you emergency admission, if he feels it is warranted. So when you speak to him, you must be convincing.'

'Don't worry, I will be.' Dial jotted down a few notes. 'Where will I meet him?'

'In Ouranoúpoli, a small village just across the border from Mount Athos.'

'Great. What about the second meeting?'

'There are twenty monasteries on the mountain. Each of them has a guest-master, a monk who is in charge of guided tours, showing relics, and more. He is the main contact person at each site. Visitors must check in with him before they enter his monastery.'

'But I don't know which monasteries I need to visit.'

'This is why you will meet with the supervisor of all guest-masters – if the Governor grants you access to their community. The supervisor has an office at Karyes. It is the largest settlement on Mount Athos. It is where all administrative matters are handled.'

Toulon gave him further details, including times and directions.

'Thanks, Henri. I appreciate it.'

'So, you are not mad at me?'

Dial shook his head. 'Why should I be mad?'

'Because you asked me to get you access today, and I have failed.'

'Hey, it was a tough task – especially considering their rigid schedules.'

Toulon paused. 'Does this mean you will give me a long weekend off like you promised?'

Dial laughed. 'I don't know about *that*. The big prize was incentive for a miracle. And you didn't produce a miracle. You produced a couple of meetings.'

'*Oui*. This is true. I have been to your meetings. They are not miraculous.'

'Speaking of miracles, what's the latest on that officer from Spárti?'

'George Pappas.'

'Right. Did he have any luck on his search for Spartans?'

410

Toulon fiddled with his ponytail. 'I do not know. I have spent all my time talking to the officials at Mount Athos. I have not had time to talk to George.'

'Well, now that you're done with the monks, I'd appreciate it if you could give him a call. The more information I have before I meet with the Governor, the better.'

'I will call him now. Would you like him to call you directly?'

'Only if he has something major to report. Otherwise, just call me back and leave a voicemail. I doubt I'll hear my phone in the chopper.'

'You are leaving now?'

Dial nodded. 'I don't have much of a choice. I commandeered the chopper from the Greek police, and they need it back as soon as possible. I'll just have the pilot drop us off at Ouranoúpoli. That way I'll be ready for my morning meeting. The last thing I want to do is be late for the Governor.'

'*Oui*, that would be bad.'

'Besides, this will give me a chance to see the Holy Mountain today. I'll have the pilot do a few flyovers, just so I can get a feel for the place.'

54

Payne read the words aloud. 'The coat equals the key. What does that mean?'

Allison shrugged. 'I have no idea since I don't know what the coat is. I could have asked Ivan on the phone, but I figured that would've appeared suspicious.'

Jones nodded in agreement as he returned to his chair. 'Any theories?'

'It might be referring to a coat of arms. Many cities in Europe, both new and ancient, use decorative shields as a symbol. Perhaps the coat is pointing towards a specific location.'

'Look in the French column on the tablet,' Jones suggested. 'Coat of arms is the translation of a French term, *cote d'armes*. It might be listed there.'

Payne stared at him like he was speaking French. Which, in fact, he had been. 'How in the hell do you know that?'

Jones shrugged. 'Doesn't everybody?'

Payne wanted to tease him, but Allison interrupted him before he could.

'Sorry. There's no coat mentioned in French.'

'What about Schliemann's family?'

'What about them?' she asked.

Jones explained. 'Many important families in Europe have their own coat of arms. That sounds like something Schliemann might've had done to boost his status.'

'Hmmm, I never thought of that. I don't remember seeing one during my research, but I can look through my notes. I have some pictures of Iliou Melathron. Maybe I'll spot one there.'

Payne grimaced in confusion. 'What is Iliou Mel . . . ?'

'Melathron. It is Schliemann's former residence in Athens. The term translates to the Palace of Ilium, which was the name of the Roman city built on top of the site of Troy. Schliemann's mansion was so extravagant it was purchased by the Hellenic Ministry of Culture for the Athens Numismatic Museum. It now houses over six hundred thousand coins.'

'That's a lot of change,' Jones said.

Allison smiled. 'We were going to visit it when we went to Greece. It's near the Acropolis.'

Payne recognized the look in her eyes. She was about to go off on a wild tangent, probably talking about the Parthenon or some other site that she hoped to see. Payne knew if they were going to get out of Russia before he died of old age, he had to keep her rambling to a minimum.

'Let me ask you a question,' he said to Allison. 'Even if Schliemann had a coat of arms, what does it really matter? I mean, I doubt it was a family secret. That would have gone against his motivation to get a coat of arms to begin with. So what good would it do us?'

Allison sighed. 'You make a good point.'

'For the time being, I think it would be best if you kept working on the journal. See if you can figure out why Richard rushed to Naples to buy it and then spent so much time translating it. Obviously he thought it was important.'

She nodded in agreement. 'You're right. Richard didn't like wasting time. He must have been looking for something in particular. I'm not sure what, but something.'

'What about a throne?' Jones suggested. 'Schliemann mentioned it several times in several different languages. He must have done that for a reason – even if he was delusional at the time. According to Richard's notes, the coat is supposed to be the key. But Schliemann didn't mention a coat. He mentioned a throne, over and over again.'

She corrected him. 'Not *a* throne. *The* throne. Like a very *specific* throne. Unfortunately, it doesn't sound familiar to me. I've been studying Schliemann for two years, and I don't remember him searching for any thrones.'

Jones glanced at Payne. He was sitting quietly, listening to their discussion like an outsider. 'Hey, Jon, while we're looking through Richard's stuff, why don't you run an internet search for ancient thrones? Maybe you can find something related to Schliemann.'

Payne stood up from the table. 'I can do that. Where's her computer?'

'On the writing desk in the corner.'

Normally computer searches would have fallen into Jones' area of expertise. He wasn't as skilled as Randy Raskin – then again, nobody was – but Jones had majored in computer science at the Air Force Academy and spent half of his free time designing and building computers in his garage. He simply loved tinkering with electronics. Making things faster and more powerful.

Payne, on the other hand, used his computer for simple tasks, like checking e-mail and sports scores. Other than that, his knowledge was pretty limited. In some ways that embarrassed him – especially since his company, Payne Industries, had its own hi-tech division – but when it came right down to it, Payne didn't like being stuck behind a desk, typing on a keyboard.

In fact, he hated it.

However, in the context of this particular mission, Payne knew that his computer skills were far more advanced than his knowledge of ancient history. And Jones realized it, too, which was the reason he asked Payne to use the internet to get some background material.

Payne couldn't read multiple languages, interpret historical data, or discuss the most important moments in Heinrich Schliemann's life.

But he was fully capable of running a search for ancient thrones.

He could handle that like a champ.

Payne took his job seriously, even though it didn't seem quite as important as the work going on behind him. But in missions like this, he knew a breakthrough could occur at any time.

He remembered a similar situation at the Ulster Archives when he and Jones had been asked to help some colleagues look for information about the crucifixion of Christ. Payne had been relegated to menial tasks while Jones dug through a series of ancient texts. Yet it was Payne who had made the most important observation, one that led to a major archaeological discovery.

To this day, he still teased Jones about it every chance that he had.

Viewing this opportunity in the same light, Payne went to his favourite search engine and typed ANCIENT THRONES. A split second later, he had several hundred thousand links to choose from. He scrolled through the most popular choices and ignored anything that seemed unlikely – relics from Asia, Africa, and Western Europe. Instead, he focused on the areas that could be linked to Heinrich Schliemann, particularly Italy, Russia, and Greece.

Payne changed his search query to ANCIENT THRONES ITALY and scanned the results. One article stood out. A Roman throne had been recently discovered in Herculaneum, one of the cities destroyed by Mount Vesuvius. These were the ruins near Naples that Schliemann had toured shortly before his death. Payne clicked on the link and read the entire story.

'How big of a discovery am I looking for?'

'Why?' Jones asked from the table.

'Back in December, experts found a wood and ivory throne in Herculaneum. It was discovered in the house of Julius Caesar's father-in-law. According to this, it's the first original throne from the Roman era ever to be recovered.'

Allison spoke up. 'I remember reading about that. Academically speaking, it was a wonderful discovery. But that's not the type of item that Richard would have been interested in. Think *much* bigger. Something that would've put him on the cover of *Time*.'

'Like a huge treasure?'

'Exactly.'

'Also,' Jones cracked, 'you probably shouldn't look for things that have already been discovered.'

'That is a very good point.'

Payne tweaked his search criteria for Italy a few different ways and found nothing of interest. So he decided to move on to the next region on his list.

He typed ANCIENT THRONES RUSSIA and scanned the results.

At first glance, St Petersburg seemed to have more thrones per square mile than any place on earth. The Winter Palace, which was part of the Hermitage

Museum that Ivan Borodin once worked for, had multiple thrones including the great throne room where the emperor and empress used to receive their guests. There was also a different throne at the Peterhof and a few more in locations near Nevsky Prospekt that Payne had seen during the past day.

However, they weren't looking for thrones that were on display.

They were searching for thrones that hadn't been found.

55

Payne moved the computer into the kitchen so he could eat dinner and search for ancient thrones at the same time. Halfway through a three-course meal that consisted of cabbage salad, meat soup, and broiled fish, Payne shifted his focus to Greece.

Despite his limited knowledge of Heinrich Schliemann, Payne knew the German spent most of his time looking for Greek treasures. This was reinforced by a simple internet search. Whether Payne was reading about a new exhibit in Athens or an ancient site in the Peloponnese, Schliemann's name always seemed to get mentioned. Some of the articles praised him; others despised him. Yet there was no denying he'd had a major impact on modern-day archaeology.

With too many articles to choose from, Payne changed the parameters of his search. Instead of looking through long sections of text, he clicked the image-only option on his search program. A few seconds later, his screen was flooded with pictures of Ancient Greece.

'Much better,' he said to himself.

He carefully scrolled through the images, looking for anything that resembled a throne. He paid more attention to paintings and sketches than he did to photographs. His rationale was simple. If an artefact had been photographed, it had already been discovered. Unfortunately, most of the artwork he saw depicted scenes from Greek mythology and the gods of Mount Olympus. He recognized many of their names in the captions – Apollo, Poseidon, Athena, Hermes, Aphrodite, and Zeus – but assumed these ancient deities would play no role in his current search.

His opinion changed a few minutes later.

Ironically, it wasn't a colourful painting that caught his eye, rather a photograph of an antique coin that made him think of America. Minted at Elis, an ancient district on the western coast of Greece, it depicted the profile of a bearded man who looked strangely similar to the image of Abraham Lincoln on the American penny. Payne admired the precise details of the face – the swirls of his beard, the curve of his cheekbone, and the shadows near his nose – and wondered if the US Treasury had based their design on this 2,000-year-old coin.

His curiosity piqued, Payne clicked on the link and was redirected to another website. The moment the page opened, his eyes widened in surprise. Two images filled the screen. The same picture as before, plus a different one showing the back of the coin. In it, the bearded man was now seated on an elaborate throne. He clutched a sceptre in his left hand and held a winged female in his right. She was roughly one-sixth of his size.

Underneath the photograph, the caption read:

Payne moved his cursor over the text and realized there was another link, one that would take him to a detailed description of the statue. Suddenly the coin didn't matter. Only the statue did.

With the click of a button, details filled the screen.

The Statue of Zeus was made by Phidias, a famous Greek sculptor whose art adorned the Parthenon, in 432 BC. The chryselephantine statue – it was made of wood and overlaid with gold and ivory – had been housed in a massive stone temple at Olympia, the site of the original Olympic games. Though Zeus was seated, the statue stood forty feet tall and filled the width of the great hall in which it was placed. His robe, sandals, and sceptre were made of gold. An olive-leaf crown was sculpted on his head. The throne itself was made of cedar wood and ornamented with ivory, gold, and precious stones. To put its original value into perspective, a first-century historian compared its worth to 300 warships.

As a graduate of the Naval Academy, Payne was staggered by that amount. He knew how important warships had been to ancient cultures and realized if a single statue cost that much to build, then its modern-day value would be immeasurable. Simply put, it was the type of discovery that would have put Heinrich Schliemann or Richard Byrd on the front page of every newspaper round the globe. After all, it was one of the Seven Wonders of the Ancient World.

Unfortunately, Payne had no idea what had become of it. Had it been lost or destroyed? Or was it still standing in Greece?

As far as he knew, the Great Pyramid in Egypt was the only ancient wonder that still existed, but Payne wasn't 100 per cent sure about that. To find out, he skipped ahead in the article. He spotted a section labelled 'The Fate of Zeus' and began reading the report. A minute later, there was no doubt in his mind that he needed to tell Jones and Allison, who were still sorting through Byrd's notes, about the throne.

Payne carried the laptop towards them. 'Are you familiar with the Statue of Zeus?'

'The one at Olympia?' Allison asked. 'What about it?'

'Zeus is sitting on a large throne made out of gold, ivory, and precious jewels. From top to bottom, the whole statue was forty feet tall.'

'Unfortunately,' she said, 'it was destroyed fifteen hundred years ago when the Temple of Zeus collapsed.'

Payne shook his head. 'Not according to this. Some scholars believe it was carried off to Constantinople where it was housed in a new temple. Supposedly it was part of the Roman Emperor's plan to beautify his new city with the finest relics of Greece and Rome.'

Jones crinkled his forehead. 'Really?'

'But it doesn't end there. Some experts believe the statue was moved once again, prior to the great fires that engulfed the city in the sixth century AD. In fact, many of the most valuable relics were thought to have been removed before the fires were set by rioters.'

Jones pointed at the computer. 'Let me see that.'

He quickly scanned the article, which was featured on a reputable website, then leaned back in thought. Allison took the opportunity to grab the computer and read the story as well. When she was done, she had the same reaction as Jones. She sat back and said nothing.

Silence filled the suite. For an entire minute, nobody spoke.

Payne stared at them and grinned. He knew what they were thinking.

Heinrich Schliemann had found the Statue of Zeus, and he died before he could recover it.

Jones was the first one to speak. He glanced at Allison and said, 'Let the record show that I told Jon to search the internet. I expect to be given full credit in your thesis.'

She laughed. 'Screw my thesis. If we find this statue, I can buy a college and give myself a doctorate.'

Payne smiled at both comments. 'So what do you think? Could this have been the throne that Schliemann was talking about?'

'Yes,' she said, turning serious. 'I mean, if anyone had inside information about a treasure in Turkey, it would have been Heinrich Schliemann. After all, he discovered the city of Troy on Turkish soil, so he would have heard rumours about any artefacts near Constantinople. In fact, he and his wife spent a lot of time in that city.'

'But if he knew about the statue, why didn't he get it?'

'Why? Because there's a big difference between knowing about a treasure and actually acquiring it. According to his journals, Schliemann took nearly a decade to locate Troy even though he used Homer's epic poems like a road map. Now imagine trying to find something that was moved from place to place over fifteen hundred years ago. That search would take a very long time. Especially with the interference he was bound to face.'

Jones asked, 'What type of interference?'

'Even though the citizens of Turkey loved him, the Turkish government did not. As I mentioned last night, he smuggled Priam's Treasure out of their country, which upset all the officials who had given him permission to dig. Over time, he eventually smoothed things over, and they let him back into Turkey to do further excavations at Troy. Only this time, they assigned a guard to follow him. In fact, every time he went to Turkey from that point forward, he was followed round the clock.'

Jones nodded in understanding. 'Which would

have prevented him from searching for the throne. He might have known where it was located, but he wasn't able to recover it.'

'Exactly. And Schliemann wasn't the trusting type, so there's no way he would have asked someone to do it for him. He had screwed over too many people in his life to trust *anyone*.'

'Speaking of trust,' Payne said, 'can we believe anything that Schliemann said? So far, you've painted a pretty negative picture of the guy. Despite his genius, he was a known charlatan, a con man of the highest degree. Isn't it possible that he was making all of this up? Perhaps this was a big joke to him. A final cry for attention before he passed away.'

Allison considered his comment. The thought had crossed her mind, too.

'Normally, I'd agree with you. I'd say this had the makings of a wild-goose chase. But the more I read Richard's notebook, the more confident I became that Schliemann wasn't conscious when he talked about the throne. At least that's what the police officer claimed in his journal. And if that's the case, the odds of Schliemann lying were pretty slim. He was an amazing man and all, but I don't think he was capable of making stuff up while he was in a coma.'

Payne smiled. 'You're probably right.'

Allison smiled as well. Then slowly but surely her expression turned into a frown, as if the weight of the world was suddenly on her shoulders.

'What is it?' Payne wondered.

She took a moment to answer. 'We aren't the only ones who think Schliemann found the throne. Obviously Richard believed it as well.'

Payne corrected her. 'Make that two people. Richard and the person who had him killed.'

56

Wednesday, 21 May
St Petersburg, Russia

The process took a lot longer than they had hoped. In fact, it chewed up half the night.

Allison read the police officer's journal aloud, sounding out the words phonetically, while Jones used a translation program from the internet to determine what language was being spoken. Then, after a healthy debate, the two of them decided what Schliemann had said.

It wasn't an exact science, and it was made even tougher by the evolution of language that had occurred during the past century. But by the time they reached the end of the journal, they were satisfied with the results. Although the translated passages couldn't be read smoothly – the officer had skipped far too many words for them to reconstruct complete sentences – enough clues had been uncovered to assure them that they were on the right track.

While this was going on, Payne left the Palace Hotel to work on another project. He realized he wouldn't be much help during the translation process. If anything, another voice would have slowed them down. Besides, his skills were much more useful on the streets of St Petersburg. Their meeting with Ivan Borodin was scheduled for ten o'clock, and he wanted to survey the residence to make sure they weren't walking into a trap.

At first glance, everything appeared fine, but he would check again in the morning.

When Payne returned to the suite, he felt a palpable buzz in the air as if Jones and Allison had important news and they couldn't wait to share it. For some reason it made him think of his dad – the moment when his father would come home from work and a five-year-old Payne would run into his arms and tell him about all the things that had happened that day. Now the roles were reversed. Payne walked through the door and was greeted by a burst of enthusiasm.

'Get over here,' Jones said excitedly. 'We just finished the translations.'

They were still sitting in the same chairs as before. Most of Byrd's documents were now on the floor. The only things that remained on the table were the officer's journal, Byrd's legal tablet, the computer, and the notebook filled with their work. The top page was divided into three columns, and those columns were filled with words in different coloured ink. Payne wasn't sure where they had found the coloured pens from, but he assumed they belonged to Allison. She seemed like the type of person who would carry office supplies in her purse.

Jones handed him their notebook. 'We translated the entire journal.'

'The entire thing?'

He nodded. 'Tell me what jumps out at you.'

'The dumb-ass grin on your face. I'm guessing you're pleased with the results.'

'Just look at the damn notebook.'

Payne smiled. 'Okay, I'll look at the damn notebook.'

He scanned the blue list first, and many terms stood out. THRONE appeared several times, as did STATUE, ZEUS, OLYMPIA, and GOLD. All of them seemed to support their theory: Schliemann had been talking about the lost throne right before his death.

Next, Payne moved on to the middle column. It was written in red ink. The words weren't used as frequently as those in the first list, yet CONSTAN-TINOPLE, FIRE, TREASURES, BOOK, and CAVE were repeated. How they were connected, he wasn't sure.

The third list, written in green, was much shorter than the others. But it was the list that caught his eye. COAT was written at the top. Then LOCATION. Then KEY.

'Tell me more about the green,' Payne said as he took a seat.

Allison obliged. 'Richard said the coat equals the key. Now we have linguistic proof of that. Schliemann mentioned coat and key on two different occasions.'

'In what context?'

'Unfortunately, context is rather difficult. The policeman did his best to record what Schliemann was saying, but he struggled a bit. Sometimes we couldn't read his shorthand. Other times he mangled the words. Occasionally he drew long blank lines in his journal to indicate that something was being said that he couldn't comprehend at all.'

'And the different colours?'

Jones answered. 'That was our attempt to give the words some kind of framework. After a while, we noticed that Schliemann clustered the same words together over and over again. We weren't able to reconstruct long passages – there were too many missing words – but we lumped certain words together. By doing so, we felt it added meaning.'

'And what did Schliemann mean by coat and key?'

'Both times he said coat and key he also mentioned location. So we know those words are connected. Our best guess is still a coat of arms. We're hoping it will point to a city or a specific family, thus revealing the location of the treasure. Or, at the very least, another clue.'

Payne studied the lists some more. 'I only see two cities mentioned. And no names.'

'Actually, we had some problems with proper nouns. Most translation programs have a limited number of words in their vocabularies. Common words like key and coat were easy to translate because they are words that tourists might use. But names and locations were much harder for us. We lucked out on Olympia and Constantinople. The cop must have been familiar with them because he actually wrote them in his journal.'

'Speaking of Constantinople, how do the red words connect together?'

He handed the notebook to Allison to refresh her memory. But she didn't need to look at it. She had spent so much time with the words she knew them all by heart.

'Three words – Constantinople, treasures, and fire – support the original story. Treasures were supposedly removed from the city before fires were set by rioters.'

'What about the other red words?'

'Schliemann mentioned them with the others, occasionally changing his word order. As for what he meant, we're still unsure. At this point, any theory would be conjecture.'

'Actually,' Jones admitted, 'most of this is conjecture. I mean, we translated a century-old conversation, which had been spoken in more than a dozen languages and was then transcribed in Italian. The odds are pretty good we messed some stuff up.'

Allison agreed. 'He's right. Errors are a distinct possibility. But that being said, if we were unsure about a word, we didn't put it in one of our columns.' She slowly turned the pages and showed Payne everything that they had attempted to translate. There were far more words in their scrap heap than in their actual lists. 'We're pretty confident in what we showed you.'

Payne nodded his approval. He considered it a minor miracle that they had been able to do all this work in a single night. It would have taken him a month, if he could have done it at all. 'One question, though. Why didn't Richard have coat or key in any of his columns?'

'You know,' Jones said, 'that bothered us, too. He wrote the coat equals the key at the bottom of a page, but we couldn't find those two words anywhere in his translations.'

'Any theories on why not?'

Jones nodded. 'One. And you're not going to like it.'

Payne leaned back in his chair. 'Go on.'

'We think maybe, just maybe, that Richard used his legal pad as his scratch pad. You know, to work things out before he transferred them to a different page. Kind of like we did.'

'Sounds practical to me. So where's his main page?'

'We think there's a chance that he had it on him when he was killed.'

Payne groaned. 'Why do you say that?'

Jones glanced at Allison. 'Go on. Tell him.'

'Because Richard often carried a folded piece of paper in his shirt pocket. Depending on the colour of his shirt, you could see it in there.'

'But you never read it?'

She shook her head. 'Nope. I never read it, so it could have been anything.'

'Still,' Payne said, 'we have to assume the worst.'

'Which is?'

Jones answered the question. 'All the work we just did is currently in the hands of the Russian police, and they're trying to figure out what it all means.'

'But that's not all,' Payne stressed. 'On the day that Richard was killed, he was scheduled to meet with Ivan Borodin. If Ivan's phone number was on that paper, there's a good chance the cops have called him and asked him about Richard's death. And if that happened, there's a damn good chance that Ivan called the cops and told them about us.'

57

Nick Dial's eyes sprang open in the darkness. He blinked a few times, trying to regain his bearings, before he realized where he was and what was happening. His cell phone was ringing on the nearby nightstand. Outside his window, the sun had not made an appearance. The only light in the hotel room was coming from the phone's tiny screen.

Dial tried to read the name on his caller ID, but drowsiness prevented it.

'Hello?' he answered groggily.

'Nick, it's Henri.'

There was no teasing or joking. Toulon's voice was solemn.

Dial sat up and rubbed his eyes. It was early in Greece but even earlier at Interpol Headquarters in France. 'What's wrong?'

'The Spárti police just called. George Pappas and two other officers never returned from their fact-finding trip in the Taygetos Mountains. No one's heard from them since they left yesterday afternoon.'

A few seconds passed before the information sank in. 'What do we know?'

'Pappas is well respected in Spárti. He's not a drinker or a hothead. He has a wife and family. He's not the type of guy who would go on a bender and disappear for a few days. Plus, there were two other officers with him. One's a ten-year vet, the other a rookie. What are the odds that they all ran off together?'

Dial considered other variables, not ready to jump to any conclusions. 'Any theories?'

'Car problems are a possibility. Many of the villages are remote, and cell-phone coverage is shaky at best. There is always a chance that they are stranded.'

'But you don't think so.'

'A few hours I could understand. Twelve hours seems unlikely. Three officers should have been able to flag someone down in that time.'

'What about a car wreck? Some of the roads near Metéora were pretty treacherous.'

'That's another possibility. But not a pleasant one.'

Dial nodded as he pictured three cops bleeding at the bottom of a ravine. 'Yet somehow I sense that's better than foul play.'

'*Oui*. This is true.'

'What do the cops in Spárti think?'

'They are hoping for stranded. They are preparing for something worse.'

'Meaning?'

Toulon explained. 'The reason Pappas took two officers with him is because of the reputation of some of the local villagers. A few of them are known for their brutality, which is why Pappas suspected them in the first place.'

'What are the cops planning?'

'They are forming a search party, a mixture of police and soldiers from a nearby army base. At first light, they are going into the mountains. I am told they will be fully armed.'

'Are you serious?'

'They want to be prepared, just in case.'

Dial swung his feet off the bed and on to the stone floor. It was cold and unforgiving, like the regret surging through his head. He was the one who had ordered Pappas to investigate the Spartans. If something had happened to him, the feelings of guilt would stick with Dial for a very long time.

'Keep me posted, Henri. I want to know as soon as you know something.'

'Not a problem, Nick.'

'One more thing. Please stress to the cops that Pappas was looking for the men responsible for the Metéora massacre. If they locate any suspects, it would be helpful if they brought them in alive.'

Unfortunately, the police would find nothing of value in Little Sparta.

Shortly after the young Spartans had finished killing

Pappas and Constantinou, Apollo ordered them to dispose of all the bodies on the other side of the valley, far away from any roads or trails. He knew the wolves that roamed the hills at night would feast on the dead cops long before a search party was assembled in Spárti.

Meanwhile, Apollo and his men handled the evidence in the village. The blood puddles were covered with dirt and rocks. The murder weapons – more than fifteen in total – were cleaned and sharpened. And Pappas' vehicle was used to transport several Spartans to Leonidi, a small town on the Aegean Sea, where they would launch the final phase of their mission.

If everything went as planned, the Spartans would return home in a few days and continue living the way that they had lived for more than two millennia.

If not, they would die protecting their most treasured possession.

The legacy of their ancestors.

The Spartans' mission had started several weeks earlier when a foreigner arrived at their village. Unlike the police who only caused problems, this man wanted to solve one.

Apollo wasn't the trusting type, especially when it came to outsiders. After all, it was a traitorous Greek who had helped Xerxes and the invading Persian army to defeat the Spartans at the Battle of Thermopylae. But this foreigner seemed different.

Although he spoke with a funny accent, he knew more about the history of the Spartans than any of the village elders. Plus he had in his possession the type of historical evidence that was tough for Apollo to ignore – an ancient document that was written long before any of the villagers were born.

If his parchment was correct, a Greek holy man by the name of Cydonius had spent his life compiling the true history of Ancient Greece. Written in the second century BC, the book used information from some of the best known Athenian historians and orators – Herodotus, Thucydides, Xenophon, Plato, and Aristotle – and combined it with data from lesser-known historians from the other city-states. This helped to eliminate the pro-Athenian bias that has always slanted the modern view of Ancient Greece. By utilizing writers with different backgrounds, Cydonius was able to paint a more accurate picture of the events of that time.

And according to the foreigner, the Spartans were portrayed in a negative light.

They weren't described as heroes. They were depicted as dim-witted barbarians.

Even their legendary stand at the Battle of Thermopylae was called into question.

Obviously the existence of such a book infuriated Apollo. His life and that of the village were based on a core of Spartan values in the same way some cultures are based on religion. Therefore, in his mind, anything that threatened his beliefs needed to be found and destroyed before it could do irreparable damage to the memory of his ancestors and his way of life.

Thankfully, the foreigner had inside knowledge about the men who protected the book and several other relics from Ancient Greece. They were called the Brotherhood, and they met once a year at a secret location. Desperate to find these men, Apollo was willing to cut a deal. He would help the foreigner and, in return, he would be allowed to burn the book before it was made public.

It was a win-win situation for both parties involved.

As promised, the foreigner pointed the Spartans in the right direction. They stormed the gates of Holy Trinity and killed the members of the Brotherhood, one by one, until one of the monks finally cracked. Not only did the monk reveal the location of the secret tunnel that used to house the book, but he also described where it had been moved several years before. It was now kept in the same place as all the other treasures that the Brotherhood had sworn to protect.

To thank the monk for his helpful information, he was beheaded like all the others. Then their heads were stacked on the stone altar that used to hold the book. It was Apollo's way of taunting his opponents, just as his ancestors had done in ancient times.

Now that the Spartans knew where the book was kept, they were coming for it.

And they dared anyone to get in their way.

58

Payne barely slept that night. His mind was far too busy to get any rest. By the time morning came, he had made a decision that affected them all. They would keep their meeting with Ivan Borodin, but they would push it forward one hour. That way, if Ivan had tipped off the police, they could slip away before the cops showed up.

Payne had already surveyed Ivan's house. He was familiar with the surrounding streets. He knew the dead ends and the blind spots. He knew where the police would lie in wait, if they were waiting at all. It was a quiet neighbourhood on the southern side of the city. The houses were small but well kept. Yards were virtually non-existent. If the cavalry came charging in, they would know about it – especially if someone stayed outside and kept watch.

That someone would be David Jones. He would remain in their car, which Payne had rented at the crack of dawn using his fake passport, and monitor things from down the street. At the first sign of trouble, Jones would call Payne's cell phone. He, in turn, would grab Allison, and they would slip out of the back of the house while Jones pulled round the corner to pick them up.

It wasn't a perfect plan. There were many variables that they couldn't control. Yet Payne decided it was worth the risk. They had come this far. One more meeting wouldn't kill them.

At least, he hoped not.

Payne and Allison got out of the car and walked half a block to Ivan's house. Payne had a gun tucked in the back of his belt and carried a book bag filled with the cash from Richard's safe. He had no idea what price had been negotiated by Richard, and Allison had failed to ask during her phone call with Ivan. If the item cost more than Payne was carrying, they were shit out of luck because Payne wasn't willing to have a second meeting. This would be a one-shot deal.

'If it's okay with you,' Payne said, 'I'd like to do most of the talking.'

Allison nodded her approval. 'I think that would be best.'

'We want to leave as soon as possible, so no long stories. Promise me: no long stories.'

'I promise.'

The nineteenth-century house was one storey tall and made out of wood – not aluminium siding like they were used to seeing in America, but actual strips of wood. No paint covered the surface. Only a light sealant protected the planks, letting the natural colour shine through.

A stone path led them to the decorative front door. The top half was made of stained glass. Payne put his face against it and tried to see inside. The interior was spacious yet plain. As far as he could tell, the front room was devoid of people except for an old man who was sitting in a green chair. Payne watched him for a moment then knocked on the door.

Several seconds passed before the old man answered it.

'*Da?*' he said with a confused look on his face.

'Mr Borodin?'

'Yes.'

'My name is Jon. And this is Allison. We phoned you about Richard Byrd.'

Ivan nodded and shifted his focus to Allison. He stared at her for a moment and then offered her a smile. 'You are more beautiful than Richard said. Please, come in.'

The comment caught her off guard. So much so that her cheeks turned pink as she entered the house. She wasn't used to compliments from Byrd. And she certainly hadn't expected to hear any from an eighty-eight-year-old Russian. But it was a nice surprise, one that put her at ease in an otherwise tense situation.

'You are early,' Ivan said to Payne. 'One hour early.'

'We're sorry about that. Our schedule got pushed forward because of an unforeseen event. We hope we're not disturbing you.'

'Disturbing me? What could you disturb?' He trudged back towards his living room. It was sparsely decorated with a couch, a coffee table, and a small bookcase. An oxygen tank and a plastic mask sat next to his favourite green chair. 'I am a sick old man who rarely leaves his home. There is nothing for you to disturb but death.'

He laughed loudly and immediately started coughing: deep, phlegm-filled coughs. As he sank into his chair, he grabbed the mask and placed it over his nose and mouth. After a few deep breaths, he signalled for Payne and Allison to sit on the couch across from him.

'Are you all right?' she asked, concerned.

Ivan shrugged as he lowered the mask. 'Life is no fun when a man cannot laugh.'

Neither Payne nor Allison said a word. They just waited for him to continue.

'So,' Ivan said as he stared at them. 'This event that changed your schedule, does it involve shooting at Peterhof?'

Payne instinctively tensed in his seat. Standing quickly, he reached behind him and put his hand on his gun while he scanned the room for danger.

'Let's go,' he said to Allison.

'Relax,' Ivan said in a soothing tone. 'You have nothing to fear. I am only one who knows you are here. Please, sit down.'

Payne stared at Ivan, trying to gauge his honesty. Ivan returned his stare. Never blinking or looking away, he wanted to assure Payne that he was telling the truth.

'You must remember,' Ivan explained, 'I grew up in a Russia where we feared police. KGB would knock on door in middle of night and people would not return. Entire families would disappear in blink of eye. Events like these are not forgotten. Or forgiven.'

Payne remained standing, still not satisfied. 'When did the police call?'

'Yesterday morning. Questions were asked but I did not answer.'

'What type of questions?'

'If you sit, I will tell you, and not a moment before.'

Admiring the old man's spunk, Payne did as requested. But he sat on the edge of the couch, ready to spring at the first sign of trouble.

'Is he always this tense?' Ivan asked Allison.

She smiled at Payne. 'From the moment we met.'

'Perhaps,' Ivan said with a mischievous twinkle in his eye, 'you should help him relax.'

Allison blushed at the innuendo while Ivan laughed and coughed. After a few short puffs from his oxygen mask, his breathing was back to normal and the smile had returned to his face. He rarely had visitors and planned on enjoying this conversation for as long as possible.

'Where was I?' Ivan asked.

Payne answered. 'The police.'

'Ah, yes. They asked me about Ellis Cooper, a name I did not know. They said he was killed at Peterhof, and my number was found in pocket. They wanted to know why.'

'And what did you say?'

'What could I say? I did not know Ellis Cooper.'

Payne realized Ellis Cooper was probably the name on the fake passport that Byrd had been carrying at the time of his death. Payne wondered what else Byrd might have been carrying.

'When did you realize it was Richard?'

'When police ask about Henry Shoemann . . . Do you know name?'

Payne grimaced. 'No, I don't. Who is he?'

'Man whose name was written on same paper as my number.'

'Henry Shoemann?' Payne said to Allison. 'Do you know a Henry Shoemann?'

She shook her head. 'Unless . . .'

'Unless what?'

'Could they have meant Heinrich Schliemann?'

Payne glanced at Ivan and noticed a smile on his lips. A big, broad smile.

Suddenly everything made sense to Payne. Byrd fell into the fountain at the Peterhof. By the time the cops had fished him out, the piece of paper in his pocket was waterlogged and the ink had run. The police had tried to decipher the words on the list and came up with Henry Shoemann instead of Heinrich Schliemann. In addition, they had probably had trouble reading the digits of the phone number, which explained why it had taken them two days to call Ivan.

Payne asked, 'How many people did they call before you?'

Ivan smiled some more. 'I am guessing fifty.'

The answer pleased Payne. He simply wasn't in the mood to deal with the police. He wanted to complete their transaction and get to Jarkko's boat as soon as possible.

'So,' Payne said, 'I was wondering—'

Ivan interrupted him. 'If you do not mind, now I would like to speak to Allison.'

Payne glanced at her. The look in his eye said make this quick. 'Of course.'

The Russian swung his gaze to her pretty face. He stared at her for a moment before he spoke. 'I was told you are fan of Heinrich Schliemann.'

She smiled and nodded. 'Yes, I am.'

'I am as well. I am one of few people old enough to have met his wife, Sophia.'

Her eyes widened in awe. 'You *met* his wife?'

'Yes. My father was professor who believed in showing me as much of world as possible when I was little boy. That included long trip to Athens before air travel was popular. He showed me ruins and explained their importance. I am not sure if he planned it or it simply happened, but Sophia was speaking at one of the museums. She shook my hand and pinched my cheeks and I was smitten for life. I knew then and there that I wanted to work in museum.'

'Wow,' she said, virtually speechless. 'That is *amazing.*'

'Over the years, I had chance to speak to his children as well.'

'Andromache and Agamemnon.'

Ivan smiled at the mere mention of their names. Schliemann was so fascinated with Homer that he had named his children after characters in *The Iliad*. 'It is true. You *are* fan.'

She nodded again. 'Schliemann's the topic of my dissertation.'

'So I was told.'

Allison paused, unable to let the moment pass. She knew Payne didn't want her to prolong the conversation, but she had to find out what Ivan meant. 'Richard talked about me?'

'You seem surprised.'

'Stunned. Richard barely talked *to* me. I find it hard to believe that he talked *about* me.'

Ivan smiled. 'Sometimes a man does not know how to handle the unfamiliar.'

'Meaning?'

'You were first woman he viewed as colleague and not conquest.'

Allison blinked a few times, trying to hold back her emotions. It was one of the nicest things that anyone had ever said about her. Strangely, it made her view Byrd in a whole different light.

'Had you known him long?' she wondered.

'Sadly, I never met Richard.'

'You never met him?'

Ivan shook his head. 'All our conversations were by phone.'

'But in his planner, he had several appointments scheduled with you.'

'And I broke them all. Some days my health will not allow visitors.'

Payne re-entered the conversation. 'Every appointment but Sunday's.'

Ivan nodded. 'That is correct. When he not show, I thought he was tired of me and no longer interested in coat.'

'No,' Allison assured him. 'I'm still interested in the coat. *We're* still interested.'

'I'm glad you are. I held on to it for as long as I could, but medical bills are mounting and money is needed. At some point, sentimentality needs to be pushed aside for reality.'

Ivan rocked forward in his chair until he had enough momentum to stand up. He trudged slowly towards the front door where a wooden rack had been mounted to the wall. A hat hung from the left hook and an umbrella from the right. In the middle was a black garment bag that looked nearly as old as Ivan. He lifted it by the hanger that protruded through the top and carried it towards the couch. As he did, he brushed off every speck of dust that he saw.

'Do you know story behind coat?' Ivan asked.

Payne and Allison shook their heads, stunned that the coat was *actually* a coat.

'Heinrich Schliemann was man with quirks that could not be explained. They helped define nature of his genius. Normal men who do normal things lead normal lives. But not Heinrich. He liked things in certain way and did not care what people thought.'

Ivan handed the garment bag to Allison and then inched back towards his chair.

'In final months of Heinrich's life, he wore coat everywhere he went. It did not matter if weather was hot or cold, that coat never left him. His friends and family asked him why, and he told them it was lucky coat. They were familiar with his ways, so they thought nothing of it. He kept his coat and they kept quiet. This way both parties were happy.'

Ivan sat in his seat and sighed. He thought about things for a moment before he spoke again. 'That coat stayed with him until end. He was wrapped in it on day he died in Naples.'

'He died in this coat?' she asked, amazed. 'How did you get it?'

'It was given to me by Heinrich's family. It was token of appreciation for all hard work I did at Hermitage Museum. I fought Russian government for many years to display Priam's Treasure. That coat was their way of saying thank you. I have cherished it ever since.'

'And I'll cherish it as well,' she assured him, feeling guilty for taking it.

'I know you will, Allison. Like me, you are true Schliemann fan.'

'About the money,' Payne said as he walked forward with the book bag. He unzipped it and showed its contents to Ivan. It was stuffed with all the cash from Byrd's safe. 'Is this enough?'

Ivan's eyes grew wide. 'More than enough.'

'I'm glad,' Payne said. 'Take it all. Richard would have wanted you to have it.'

59

While Payne called Jones to make sure the street was clear, Allison said goodbye to Ivan. She promised to be in touch in the near future, hoping to hear as many stories about Schliemann as Ivan was willing to tell. He assured her that it was a conversation worth living for.

Payne walked outside first, followed by Allison. She carried the garment bag with both hands, clutching it against her chest like it was the most valuable treasure in the world.

'You know,' she said, 'that was a really nice thing to do.'

'What are you talking about?'

'The money. You gave him all the money.'

'It wasn't my money. It was Richard's money.'

'Still,' she assured him, 'it was very sweet.'

He shrugged and said nothing. The old guy had reminded Payne of his grandfather. Full of wit and wisdom until his body finally gave out. Maybe the money would help Ivan live a little bit longer. Or, at the very least, a little more comfortably.

When they reached the car, Payne sat in the front seat and Allison climbed into the back. She hung the garment bag from a hook above the window, trying not to wrinkle its contents.

'What's that?' Jones asked as they pulled away from the curb.

'The coat,' Payne answered.

'The coat? You mean the coat was a *coat*?'

'Trust me, I had the same reaction.'

Payne turned round and looked at Allison. 'I thought you said that Richard wasn't the sentimental type, that he only cared about the treasures.'

'He did,' she assured him.

'Then why did he risk his life to buy a coat?'

'I don't know. I'm just as dumbfounded as you.'

Payne turned back round and stared out the front windshield. Buildings were blurred as Jones navigated through the traffic like a lifelong resident. It was amazing how quickly he could adapt.

'Where to now?' she wondered.

'To the hotel,' Payne replied.

'And then what?'

'Then we go to the boat. It's time to leave Russia.'

Jarkko was waiting when they arrived at the dock. He waved to them from the boat until he saw Payne and Jones weren't alone. One look at Allison and he came running.

'I am Jarkko,' he said proudly. 'I am captain of ship. Come, we must drink!'

He grabbed her by the hand and half dragged her to the boat. Meanwhile Payne and Jones were left carrying the luggage, which they didn't mind at all. It was worth the laugh.

'Maybe we should have warned her about Jarkko,' Jones said.

'Why? This is much more fun.'

Their trip got underway without incident. No police interference or trouble of any kind. Before they got too far from shore, Payne called the car rental office and told them the location of their car, claiming it wouldn't start. Jones had made sure of that by disconnecting the battery which also made it tougher to steal since he had to leave the keys on the front seat.

Once they were in international waters, they turned their attention to Allison. She was sitting in the back of the boat, staring at the Gulf of Finland. Jones sat next to her on a hard metal bench and asked her how she was doing. She shrugged and didn't say much.

'What's wrong?' Payne asked as he leaned against the rail of the boat.

'I was just thinking.'

'About?'

She paused before answering. 'Richard.'

'What about him?'

'Ivan said some things that makes me wonder if I misjudged him. I mean, on the day that he was killed, he was waiting for me at the Peterhof. He didn't have to do that. He knew someone was following him, yet he chose to stick around for me. If he had just hopped on a boat and left St Petersburg, he probably would have survived.'

'Maybe,' Payne admitted. 'But the odds are pretty

good that they would have found him eventually – whether it was in Russia or somewhere else.'

She shrugged again, not quite ready to accept reality. 'Well, what about the coat?'

'What about it?'

'This whole time I thought Richard only cared about a treasure. Now I find out he had a soft spot for Schliemann, too.'

Jones spoke up. 'Actually, I'm not quite sure about that. Jon told me about your conversation with Ivan, and I think something else might be going on here.'

She looked at him, confused. 'Like what?'

'Richard wrote, the coat equals the key. But when we did our translations, three words – coat, key, and location – were always linked together. We assumed it was a coat of arms that would reveal the location, or something like that, right?'

'Right.'

'What if the key was *actually* a key? Just like the coat was a coat.'

She scrunched her face. 'I don't follow.'

Payne explained. 'Ivan said that Schliemann never took off his coat. He kept it with him at all times. What if there was a reason for that? What if he kept something in his coat that he never wanted to leave his possession?'

Her eyes widened. 'Like a key!'

Jones smiled. 'That's what I was thinking.'

Payne said, 'We know it's a long shot, but we've got some time to kill.'

'I'll get the coat,' she said excitedly. She went and got the garment bag from the waterproof bin where Jarkko kept his valuables and brought it back to Payne and Jones. 'I haven't even opened it yet. I didn't want to expose it to the sea air.'

'If you'd rather not,' Payne teased.

'No, that's quite all right. The coat's lasted this long. A little moisture won't hurt it.'

She unzipped the bag and carefully removed the overcoat, which was black and single-breasted. The material was soft and solidly stitched, like a rich man's coat should be. She reached into the side pockets and found nothing. The same with the interior pockets. Either Schliemann was carrying nothing at the time of his death, or the items were removed long ago.

'It was worth a shot,' she said, frustrated.

'That's it? You're giving up?' Jones grabbed the coat from her. 'Please do me a favour and never take a job with airport security. That was the worst search I've ever seen in my life.'

He removed the coat's hanger and handed it to her. 'Hold this while I look.'

Right away he noticed that Schliemann was a small man. He figured that out when he placed his hand inside one of the sleeves and nearly got stuck. He repeated his search on the other side and then patted down the sleeves just to make sure he wasn't missing anything. After that, he looked underneath the collar. It was a great place to hide items because it was rarely searched.

Next he turned his attention to the lining of the coat. It was black with faint grey pinstripes. He ran his fingers along the seams, searching for any bulges. This process continued for several seconds until he felt something. It wasn't solid like a key; it was flat. He moved it back and forth and felt it crinkle.

'Allison,' he said glumly, 'I'm afraid I've got some bad news for you.'

'Let me guess. The coat's empty?'

'Actually, I think I found something. And if I did, I'm *never* going to let you forget it.'

60

Nick Dial glanced at his watch. It was 11.30 a.m. in Ouranoúpoli, Greece. He had been standing in front of the rendezvous point – a fourteenth-century Byzantine tower that was built as a sentry post next to the Aegean Sea – for more than thirty minutes, but the Governor of Mount Athos hadn't shown up for their appointment.

On most occasions, Dial would have left a long time ago. He didn't have a lot of patience when it came to tardiness. But in this situation he realized that the Governor held all the cards. If he wanted immediate access to Mount Athos, he needed special permission from the Governor, so Dial had little choice in the matter. He had to wait as long as necessary.

'Marcus,' Dial said for the third time in the last half hour, 'please check again.'

Andropoulos nodded and started his circular journey round the enclosed courtyard, just in case the Governor was waiting on the other side. The building was made out of tan-coloured stones and topped with a red-tile roof. The windows on the lower floors were nothing more than tiny slits, far too narrow for pirates or thieves to have slipped through. Nowadays the lone watchman was the skull of a former resident, which peered at the sea from its perch on a wooden balcony.

Dial followed the skull's lead and stared at the gentle waves as they kissed the sandy beach. The weather was in the low seventies with hardly a cloud in the sky. If not for the urgency of his meeting, he would have felt like he was on vacation. Other than the occasional fishing boat that dotted the horizon, there wasn't a lot of activity in this sleepy village.

Except for the man who was strolling along the shore.

Dial spotted him walking barefoot in the surf. He was older than Dial, but possessed the casual stride of someone who had nowhere to go and all the time in the world to get there. His skin was tanned, his silver hair was unkempt, and his light blue shirt was unbuttoned and flapping in the breeze. A pair of sandals dangled from his left hand. Occasionally they brushed against his cream-coloured shorts, but he didn't seem to mind.

'Hello,' he called, while waving at Dial.

'Hello to you, too.'

The man smiled and walked closer. 'American?'

Dial nodded. 'What about yourself?'

'Me, too. My name is Clive.'

'Hi, Clive. I'm Nick.'

The two of them shook hands.

'So, what brings you to Ouranoúpoli? We don't get many American tourists.'

'We?' Dial asked. 'You live here?'

'I live all over the world. But this time of year, I like Greece.'

'Must be nice. Going wherever the wind takes you.'

'I'm not going to lie, it's pretty great.' Clive grinned. 'How about you?'

'I'm here on business.'

Clive glanced round the empty shore. '*Business?* Are you sure you're in the right place?'

'I've been asking myself that same question for the last thirty minutes.'

'Why's that?'

'I was supposed to meet someone here at eleven o'clock. But I'm still waiting.'

'Is he a local? Maybe I know him.'

'Not *too* local. He's from Mount Athos.'

Clive smiled. 'Ahh, that explains it.'

'Explains what?'

'Why he isn't here. You missed him by several hours.'

Dial arched an eyebrow. 'Several hours? What are you talking about?'

'Mount Athos doesn't use Greek time. They use Byzantine time.'

'They use *what*?'

Clive laughed. Dial wasn't the first tourist to ask him that question in a similar tone.

'The monks on Mount Athos set their clocks according to the position of the sun. Midnight is at sunset, and so on. This time of year, they're roughly three hours ahead of us. Every few days they readjust their clocks to compensate for the setting sun.'

'You've got to be shitting me.'

He laughed again. 'It's not so bad when you're inside. You get used to it pretty quick.'

'You've been inside?' Dial asked, surprised.

'That's how I discovered Ouranoúpoli. I visited Mount Athos and liked it so much that I swing by every few years.'

'They let you do that?'

Clive nodded. 'If your paperwork is in order.'

'Really? You don't have to be a monk?'

'Not at all. In fact, you'd be surprised how many celebrities visit Mount Athos.'

'Such as?'

'Prince Charles from England. He spends a lot of time at Vatopedi, a monastery that resembles an Italian Renaissance village on the north-eastern part of the peninsula. It has many famous relics, including remnants of the True Cross.'

Dial rubbed his chin in thought. 'You seem to know a lot about the place.'

'Not as much as the guest-masters, but more than most. Sometimes when I'm lonely, I give boat tours. It's a great way to meet people. Especially women.'

Dial laughed. 'Somehow I doubt that.'

'I don't mean picking them up. I mean *meeting* them. They aren't permitted on shore, so I take

462

them round the peninsula and show them all the monasteries.'

'Hold up. Women *aren't* allowed on Mount Athos?'

Clive shook his head. 'No women at all. Not even female animals.'

'Damn. That's kind of strict.'

'Considering who owns the place, it's also pretty ironic.'

'What do you mean? Who owns the place?'

'According to legend, the Virgin Mary was sailing to Cyprus to visit Lazarus when her ship was blown off course. They dropped anchor close to the present-day monastery of Iviron, and Mary was instantly taken by the beauty of the mountain and asked her Son to make it her own. A voice from above said, "This is your garden, a haven for those who wished to be saved." Or words to that effect. From that day forward, no women have been allowed on Mount Athos.'

Dial smiled. 'This is the Virgin Mary's garden, and women aren't allowed to visit. That's priceless.'

'Like I said, it's pretty ironic.'

Dial was about to ask Clive another question when Andropoulos came into view. He had circled the tower and was now walking towards them from the opposite direction.

'Sorry, sir. No sign of the Governor.'

Clive glanced at Dial. 'Your meeting was with the Governor of Mount Athos?'

'It was. But apparently I missed him – by several hours.'

'Either that, or you're thirteen days early.'

Dial looked confused. 'What do you mean?'

'The monks also use the old Julian calendar instead of the Gregorian calendar. So they're thirteen days behind the rest of us.'

Dial shook his head. 'Someone in town said a trip to Mount Athos was like going back in time. I guess they meant that literally.'

'Literally and figuratively,' Clive assured him. 'Although in recent years there have been improvements to many of the monasteries. Some of them even have electricity.'

Andropoulos laughed. Metéora had recently gone through similar renovations, moving them out of the nineteenth and into the early twentieth century. Still a century behind, but much better than it used to be.

Clive extended his hand. 'Hi, my name is Clive.'

'Sorry,' Dial said as Andropoulos shook Clive's hand. 'This is my assistant, Marcus.'

'Your assistant? What kind of business are you in?'

Dial answered. 'I work for Interpol. He works for me.'

'Interpol? How fascinating! And you're here to meet with the Governor? Is there something dangerous going on that I should know about?'

'No, nothing like that. I'm just trying to get access to Mount Athos for a routine investigation.'

Clive groaned. 'Well, you're in trouble now. I've met the Governor on a few occasions, and he isn't exactly a cordial fellow. My guess is that you've made an enemy for life.'

'Great. Just great.'

'Of course, there are other ways to get to the peninsula.'

'Such as?'

'Me.'

'You?' Dial asked.

Clive nodded. 'I have no influence with the guards, but if I pull up to the main dock and you flash your badge, you might be able to talk your way on to the property.' He paused. 'You do have a badge, don't you?'

Both Dial and Andropoulos flashed their credentials.

He smiled and continued, 'At the very least, the guards have a special phone that connects with the administrative offices in Karyes. Any time there's a problem with a visitor's permit, the guards contact their bosses for clarification. So, even if they don't let you through, perhaps you can speak to someone who can help you with your investigation.'

61

Both Payne and Allison stared at Jones, trying to determine if he was serious. They realized he was when he made them feel the object for themselves.

Allison went first. She noticed the same crinkling as Jones. 'It feels like paper.'

'That's what I thought,' he said with a grin.

Payne rolled his eyes as he took his turn. 'I'm kind of hoping you're wrong. Otherwise you're going to be a bigger pain in the ass than normal.'

'I don't know about bigger. But I'll definitely be *richer*.'

Payne smiled. 'Don't buy a mansion just yet. We have to see what it is first.'

'And how are we going to do that?' Allison wondered.

Jones made a cutting motion with his two fingers. 'Snip, snip.'

'Wait. You're going to cut the coat?'

He nodded. 'You're damn right I'm going to cut the coat. But just the lining. It's not like I'm going to take off a whole sleeve.'

'Come on, guys. There has to be a better way.'

Jones turned towards Jarkko, who was steering the boat at the front. 'Hey, Jarkko! Do you have any X-ray gear on here?'

Jarkko stared at him. 'You mean X-rated movies?'

'Not X-rated,' he shouted. 'X-ray.'

'X-ray? What is that? Is that more sexy than X-rated?'

'Forget it. Don't worry about it.'

Jarkko threw his arms up in frustration. 'How will Jarkko learn if you not explain?!'

'Sorry,' Jones apologized to Allison. 'No X-rays on board. We're gonna have to cut it.'

She sighed. 'Fine! Cut the lining. But promise me you'll be careful.'

'Of course I'll be careful. I don't want to cut the paper.'

'I meant with the coat!'

Jones glanced at Payne and grinned. 'Man, I love revving her up. It's so easy.'

Payne smiled as he patted Jones on the arm. 'Before you start, let me tell Jarkko to stop the engine. The smoother the ride, the better.'

'Good idea.'

Jarkko cut the motor and the boat slowed to an easy crawl. Due to a lack of storms in the area, the winds were calmer than normal and so were the waves. Allison spread the garment bag across the bench, and Jones laid the coat on top. Their goal was to do as little damage as possible, whether that was from grime or the tip of his knife.

The first cut was along the edge of the seam. A tiny ripping sound was heard, followed by a loud groan from Allison. Jones made her turn round before he continued. The process was easier than he had expected. After getting through the layer of lining, he noticed a small compartment had been stitched into the coat.

Jones stuck his fingers inside and felt an object. 'There's something in here.'

'What is it?' she wondered.

'I don't know. I can't get it out. My hands are too big.'

'Here,' she said. 'Let me try. Or you might rip it.'

After switching spots, she stuck her slender fingers inside the secret pocket. With more wiggle room than Jones, she was able to finesse the object out, carefully sliding it through the gap in the lining until she held it in her hands.

It was an old piece of paper, folded and yellowed with age.

'What does it say?' Jones asked.

'I don't know,' she said excitedly. 'Someone move the coat.'

At this point Payne was tempted to chuck it overboard; he was much more concerned with the paper than the coat. Instead, he carefully hung it on its original hanger while Allison laid the document on top of the garment bag. Then, using the tip of her fingernail, she carefully unfolded it, trying not to smudge the writing.

'It feels so brittle. I don't want to turn it too quickly or it might tear.'

Jones glanced over her shoulder. 'I swear to God,

if Ivan dry-cleaned this coat, I'm going to kill the bastard.'

'It's not that,' she assured him as she kept unfolding the paper. 'It's in pretty good shape for its age. I just don't want to take any chances.'

Finally, after several seconds, the document was fully revealed. She held it flat with the tips of her fingers, making sure that a gust of wind didn't blow it overboard. Despite its age, the document was still legible, penned by a steady hand. It was written in Greek, a language that none of them could speak, yet all of them knew what they were staring at.

'Holy shit,' Jones mumbled. 'It's a fucking map.'

The comment made Allison grin. 'The correct term is *treasure* map, but—'

'Jon,' Jones blurted, 'it's a fucking *treasure* map.'

Payne laughed at his friend's joy. 'I see that, but what does it say?'

'I don't know! I can't read Greek, but I recognize the most important letter of all.'

Payne glanced down at the map. A mountain was drawn in the middle of a large land mass that was surrounded by water. Bays and inlets were labelled with Greek words, as were various trails up the mountain. Payne stared at the words, trying to figure out what letter Jones had been referring to, but he had no idea. 'Which letter is most important?'

Jones plopped his finger on the map about halfway up the mountain.

A single location had been labelled with the Greek letter, chi.

A letter that looks exactly like a capital X.

'Chi marks the spot!'

After their initial burst of enthusiasm, they realized they had no idea where this mountain was located – or if it still existed. Just because it was labelled in Greek didn't mean that it was *in* Greece. Schliemann had travelled all over the globe, so it could've been anywhere. And since they were floating in the middle of the Gulf of Finland, they weren't able to access the internet on Allison's computer. Research would have to wait until they reached the mainland.

They debated a variety of things for the next ten minutes. Allison and Jones did most of the talking since they were most familiar with Greek history. Payne was ready to make a point when he felt a large hand on his shoulder. It was Jarkko. He was curious about their argument.

'Sorry to disturb. But can you not fight while boat is moving?'

Payne nodded. 'You're absolutely right. We're wasting valuable time.'

'What is that?' he asked as he pointed to the map in Allison's hand. 'You are going to Greece and not invite Jarkko?'

Jones glanced at him, surprised. 'Wait. You know this place?'

'Of course! Remember, Jarkko keeps yacht in Greece. Jarkko knows entire Aegean.'

'Hold up. You *actually* know where this is?'

'What, you no understand Jarkko? Jarkko knows this place. Jarkko *hates* this place.'

Jones asked, 'You hate it?'

'Of course Jarkko hates. No women. No drink. No fun. Just monks and guns.'

'What in the hell are you talking about?'

Jarkko looked at Payne. 'Is Jarkko slurring? It is too early to slur. Maybe Jon should drive?'

Payne signalled Jones to shut up. Then he asked a question of his own. 'What's the name of the mountain?'

'That is Mount Athos. It is home to Orthodox monks. Holy land to Greeks.'

'Have you been there?'

'One day Jarkko run out of supplies. Jarkko tried to dock near mountain but guards with guns would not allow. Land is holy. Permission must be granted by fat monk in charge.'

Payne turned his attention to Allison. 'Have you ever heard of this place?'

She nodded. 'I've heard of it. But I don't know much about it. It's in northern Greece, far away from Athens. As far as I know, it's filled with monasteries and nothing else.'

'How far from Constantinople?'

She gave it some thought. 'Not far at all. Why?'

'Close enough to move a statue to?'

'It's *much* closer than Olympia. So the answer is definitely yes.'

Payne looked at Jones. 'What do you think?'

'What do I think? I think there has to be a reason that armed guards are protecting a bunch of monks in the middle of nowhere.'

'I was thinking the same thing.'

Jarkko raised his hand. 'May Jarkko ask question?'

'Go on,' Payne answered.

'Will you need guide to Mount Athos?'

Payne smiled. 'Why? Are you offering?'

'Yes, if you are paying . . . Are you paying?'

He nodded. 'Yes, I'd be paying.'

'Then Jarkko is offering! When you want to leave?'

'As soon as possible.'

Jarkko grinned. 'We can leave soon . . . But first, we must drink!'

62

Before boarding Clive's boat, Dial called Henri Toulon at Interpol for an update on the Spartan situation and also to let him know about his missed meeting with the Governor.

'Nick,' Toulon said, 'I was just about to call you. We have some news on George Pappas. His truck was found in Leonidi, approximately thirty miles away from Spárti.'

'His truck was *found*? Was he inside?'

'No. It was abandoned next to a wooden pier.'

Dial grimaced. 'What's a pier doing in the middle of the mountains?'

'No, no, no. Leonidi is not in the mountains. It is a small fishing village. His truck was found next to the sea.'

Dial pictured a map of Greece in his head. The Taygetos Mountains were west of Spárti, located in the middle of the Peloponnese. Meanwhile, the Aegean Sea was to the east, completely in the opposite direction. 'Why in the world was he over there?'

Toulon answered. 'We do not know that he was.'

'Wait. You think his truck was stolen?'

'*Oui*. It is a possibility.'

'If that's the case, where are Pappas and his men?'

'We are not sure. Right now, the police in Leonidi are searching for witnesses. They found his truck, so they might be able to find someone who saw the driver.'

Dial nodded. 'That's a start. What else is being done to find him?'

'The Spárti police went to the village that Pappas was planning to visit first. And they found something strange.'

'What do you mean by *strange*?'

'No adults. No kids. No clues of any kind. The entire village was empty.'

'Empty? How can the village be empty?'

'I do not know. But no one was there.'

'Shit,' Dial cursed. 'The villagers cleared out because they didn't want to be questioned. Something bad happened up there, and they knew the police would be stopping by.'

Toulon nodded. '*Oui*. That makes sense.'

'Does Spárti have access to hounds?'

'I do not know.'

'If they do, have them start there. Maybe they'll pick up a scent. At the very least, maybe they'll find the villagers hiding in the mountains. That might be just as helpful.'

Toulon made a note. 'I will suggest it at once.'

'Before you do, I wanted to give you an update on my meeting with the Governor.'

'That is right. How did that go?'

'It didn't. Turns out Mount Athos is on Byzantine time.'

'You did not know that?'

'Of course I didn't know that. How the hell was I supposed to know that?'

Toulon shrugged. 'The same way *I* knew that. By being smart.'

Dial growled, no longer in the mood for humour. 'Henri, I don't get mad very often but I'm officially pissed off. We have eight dead monks and three missing cops, and you're being sarcastic with me? That shit needs to stop *now*!'

Toulon said nothing in his defence.

'Because of your negligence,' Dial seethed, 'I missed my best opportunity to get inside Mount Athos and find an important witness. Do you understand that?'

'*Oui.* I understand.'

'Good! Now I want you to fix it.'

'How?'

'I am taking a private boat to Mount Athos. Once I'm there, I'm going to try to talk my way past the guards. It would help if they knew that I was coming.'

Toulon asked, 'What would you like me to say?'

'I want you to call the Governor's office and explain that *you* screwed up the time of my meeting. Tell them that I take full responsibility for the error, and I will be stopping by the main dock in a few hours to apologize in person.'

'No problem, Nick. Consider it done.'

* * *

Dial didn't know much about boats since he had lived most of his life far away from the water. But it didn't take an expert to realize that Clive's boat was built for speed. It was forty feet long, painted white with red racing stripes, and looked sleeker than a missile. When Andropoulos saw it for the first time, the grin on his face was remarkably similar to the one he had before his helicopter ride from Kalampáka.

And it got even wider when they hit the open sea.

Every once in a while, Clive would crank the throttle just to prove what he was packing, and when he did, Dial and Andropoulos were thrown back in their waterproof seats. But most of the time, Clive kept his speed steady, rarely venturing more than one hundred feet from shore so he could talk about all the monasteries that they passed on their way to the main dock on Athos.

'This whole region is part of the Halkidiki Peninsula,' Clive explained. 'What's strange about it is that the peninsula has three peninsulas of its own. They're called Kassandra, Sithonia, and Athos. They stick out into the Aegean like Poseidon's trident.'

He pointed towards his left as their boat headed south. 'Athos is the easternmost peninsula of the three. It's six miles wide and thirty-five miles long. Ouranoúpoli sits on the northern end of it, serving as a boundary to the rest of civilization. Just past the village, you officially enter the republic of the Holy Mountain.'

'Is there an actual wall?' Dial wondered.

'No, there isn't. But according to Byzantine law, roads that can be travelled on by wheels are *not* permitted between Mount Athos and the outside world. And the few footpaths that exist between the two are frequently patrolled by armed guards.'

Dial listened with fascination. Prior to a few days ago, he had never heard of Mount Athos. And the reason for that was quite simple: he'd never had any reason to investigate the place. Yet in his mind, that wasn't a valid excuse for his ignorance. Mount Athos was a part of Greece, so he should have known about the Holy Mountain and all its quirks.

If he had been more knowledgeable, things would have gone a lot smoother.

'So, Nick, tell me a little more about you. What's your job at Interpol?'

'I'm the Director of the Homicide Division.'

Clive whistled, impressed. 'That's a fancy title. Does that mean you're the big cheese?'

Dial nodded. 'That's what it means.'

'What are you doing way out here? Shouldn't you be at Interpol Headquarters, bossing people round?'

'You would think so. I mean, that's what the heads of the other divisions are forced to do. But I'm kind of fortunate in that regard. The Homicide Division is only a few years old, and I was the person brought in to set up its internal structure. Since my experience is in fieldwork, I made damn sure that I was allowed to leave my office or I wouldn't have taken the job. I don't get to float around as much as

I'd like. Paperwork and meetings guarantee that. But anytime an interesting case comes along, I hit the road and see where it takes me.'

Clive smiled. 'And if there aren't any roads, you take to the sea instead.'

'Exactly.'

Several minutes later, Clive slowed his boat as they approached the first monastery that was visible from the water. Starting on the northern end of the peninsula, a massive hill ran down the centre of Athos like a rocky spine. Covered in a thick blanket of trees, it gradually rose higher and higher until it reached the peak of Mount Athos, which towered over the southern tip of the peninsula nearly 6,700 feet above the Aegean Sea.

From his current location, Dial could see the outline of its snow-capped peak, yet his focus was on Zográfou, a monastery founded in 971 AD that was nestled in the vegetation. Unlike other parts of Greece, this stretch of land was rarely cleared by human hands.

'Zográfou is unlike any other monastery on Athos. All its monks are Bulgarian, and all its services are performed in their native tongue.' Clive pointed at the monastery's tower, which was in the centre of the multi-building complex. 'That's where they keep their most prized possessions, including *Codex One*.'

'Which is what?' Dial wondered.

'The first official history book of Bulgaria. It was written by a monk named Paisios and stored here for safekeeping. You'd be surprised how many manuscripts and treasures were guarded by monasteries over the centuries. In that tower alone, there are more than ten thousand codices, written in Greek and Slavic languages. Rumour says they have even more than that, but we'll never know. Outsiders are never given full access to any of the local libraries, which is a shame – I'm a huge fan of libraries.'

Dial stared at the stone tower with its red tiled roof. As he did, thoughts of the hidden tunnel at Holy Trinity floated through his head. In many ways, Metéora was better protected than the monasteries at Mount Athos, yet due to their position on the top of natural stone pillars, the monks were limited by geology. Secret vaults had to be dug into the hard rock and accessed from above. But here on Athos, it was different. The peninsula was thirty-five miles long and six miles wide, meaning there were plenty of places to hide their most valuable relics.

Dial asked, 'How many of these monasteries have you been in?'

'I wish I could say all of them, but so far I've only been in twelve of the twenty.'

'Any treasures stand out?'

Clive whistled. 'Now that's a tough question. That's like asking someone to pick out their favourite painting at the Vatican. I mean, there are way too many treasures to name.'

'The monasteries are *that* nice?'

'Yes, they are. Keep in mind that Mount Athos

has always attracted the best artists and craftsmen from the Orthodox world. The monasteries offered food, shelter, privacy, and protection, and the artists repaid them by creating religious masterpieces in many different forms: mosaics, manuscripts, carvings, jewellery, and so on. Why do you think there are so many armed guards roaming the hills? These treasures are priceless.'

'And are all the treasures religious in nature?'

'Not all of them. Why? Do you have something in mind?'

Dial nodded. 'Anything that involves Greek soldiers.'

Clive gave it some thought. 'I remember seeing swords in a few of the monasteries. Even some old guns that were taken from invading pirates.'

'Not weapons,' he clarified. 'I meant artwork. Like stone altars or carved doors.'

'To be honest, nothing jumps out at me. That's not to say that they don't exist – because I saw some altars and doors that dazzled me. I'm talking really intricate pieces that must have taken several months to complete. But all of them had religious themes.'

Dial glanced at Andropoulos, who was listening to the conversation but remained quiet. They briefly made eye contact, and when they did, Dial nodded his head towards Clive. It was Dial's way of encouraging the young cop to ask some questions.

Andropoulos cleared his throat. 'What about books on warfare?'

'Warfare?' Clive took a moment to consider the word. 'Well, as I mentioned, Zográfou has the first history book ever written about Bulgaria. I'm sure some of its sections are devoted to soldiers and war and that type of thing. As for other monasteries, I would guess that they have the same sort of books. Particularly Greek history.'

'Why's that?' Dial wondered.

'Because seventeen of the monasteries are Greek. The other three are Russian, Serbian, and Bulgarian.'

Dial smiled at this. Of the seven monks beheaded at Holy Trinity, one was Russian, one was Bulgarian, and one was Greek. The fourth monk was from Turkey, which was where the Ecumenical Patriarchate was located. That meant all the major nationalities on Mount Athos had been represented at that late-night meeting.

He wasn't sure if that was a coincidence or not.

But he would keep it in mind as his journey continued.

63

If Payne and Jones had been travelling by themselves,
they would have called Randy Raskin for two seats
on a military flight to Izmir Air Base. Located on the
western coast of Turkey, it wasn't far from Limnos,
the Greek island where Jarkko kept his yacht.

Unfortunately for them, the US military frowned
upon hard-drinking Finns and blondes with fake
passports sneaking into a foreign country in the back
of one of its planes. Therefore, the four of them were
forced to find a different mode of transportation to
the Aegean.

Surprisingly, it was Jarkko who came up with the
solution. He was friends with a pilot in Helsinki –
the same pilot who always took him south for the
winter – who was more than happy to fly them to
Greece for a reasonable price. And since Limnos had
its own airport, they would actually get there faster
than flying to Athens on a jet and shuttling north to
the island.

Plus, a small airport with private hangars made
sneaking past customs a lot easier.

Before leaving Finland, Payne bought plenty of
supplies at the Kauppatori Market, everything from
food to warm clothes. He had never been to Mount

Athos, but he was quite familiar with the effects of altitude on air temperature. Especially at night. A brutal mission in the rugged terrain of Afghanistan had taught him that. And since the cover of darkness would aid their journey up the Holy Mountain, he made damn sure they were ready for it.

Meanwhile, Jones used Allison's computer to download as much information about Athos as possible. He wanted to plot their mission during their long flight to Greece so they could hit the ground running. Normally he would have preferred a day or two to survey the topography and scout the patrol patterns on the southern tip of the peninsula. But after thinking it over, he realized that this was a race against a nameless opponent. The man who had hired Alexei Kozlov to kill Richard Byrd was seeking the same treasure they were.

One day could make all the difference between fortune and failure.

'Hey, Jon,' Jones said from the back of the small jet. Jarkko was sitting in the cockpit, trading dirty jokes with the pilot, while Allison caught a nap in the front row.

'What?' Payne asked from across the aisle.

'Let's assume that this treasure is real, that Schliemann actually found the Statue of Zeus, and it's somehow hidden inside the mountain.'

'Okay.'

'How are we going to get it out?'

'Excuse me?'

'I mean, the damn thing is forty feet tall and made out of gold. I doubt we can carry it.'

'Speak for yourself. I've been eating a lot of sausage. And sausage means protein.'

Jones smirked. 'I'm serious. There's no way we can remove it by ourselves.'

'You're assuming that it's still in one piece. Remember, it was carried from Olympia to Constantinople and back to Greece. And when it disappeared from Constantinople, no one saw it leave. Either that was one hell of a magic trick, or they cut the throne into pieces before the trip.'

'Good point.'

'Besides, even if we find it, I don't think we should move it. After all, it's one of the Seven Wonders of the Ancient World. We would be crucified if we damaged it any further.'

Jones rubbed his eyes in frustration. 'What are you saying? You want to leave it there.'

Payne nodded. 'That's exactly what I'm saying. If we find it – and that's a giant *if* – we should stake our claim and call the Ulster Archives for advice. Petr has much more experience with this type of stuff than we do. Hell, I can't even begin to imagine the border dispute that would erupt over this. Does the treasure belong to Greece? Turkey? Or the monks of Mount Athos?'

'I vote for none of the above. I vote for us.'

'Obviously we can make our case, quoting the

ancient law of finders keepers. But it will be an uphill struggle. A hell of a lot tougher than climbing a mountain in the dark.'

Jones nodded in agreement. 'Okay. I'm with you on the whole throne thing. If we find it and it's salvageable, we leave it for the experts to move. But what about the other stuff?'

'What other stuff?'

'According to legend, the Greeks removed all their treasures from Constantinople before the city was set on fire. So there's no telling what else we might find up there.'

'I forgot all about that,' Payne teased. 'Thankfully I bought several canvas bags in Helsinki. They're perfect for carrying supplies on the way up and gold on the way down.'

Clive slowed his boat and pointed to a thick stretch of forest to the east of Zográfou. 'Buried in the trees is Kastamonítou. It's one of the monasteries I've stayed at.'

Dial strained to see it on the wooded hillside. 'Is it small?'

'Not at all. There are several buildings and a large *katholikón*. They're positioned in such a way you can't see them from the sea. From the shore, it's roughly a thirty-minute hike.'

'Any treasures of note?'

'The monastery has three miracle-working icons.'

'Which means what?'

'Just as the name implies. They have three different icons that have been responsible for miracles, holy acts that have been verified by the Church.'

Dial smirked at the explanation. 'Can any of them predict lottery numbers?'

'If they could, I'm sure you would have heard of the place.'

A few minutes later, they approached Docheiaríou, a tenth-century monastery built along the rocky shoreline. Clive pulled his boat near a stone jetty that extended out into the waters of the Singitic Gulf, so his passengers could get a better view of the boat-house where the monks kept their fishing equipment. Behind it was a small fortress, a mix of ancient buildings and colourful chapels built on top of fortified stone walls.

'Notice the height of the windows,' Clive said as he pointed to their placement seventy feet above the ground. 'This monastery was susceptible to attacks because of its position near the water, so they compensated by elevating their architecture into the air.'

'Pretty cool,' Dial admitted. 'Not as high as Metéora, but still pretty cool.'

'You've been to Metéora?'

Dial nodded but said nothing, not wanting to talk about his investigation.

Clive read between the lines. 'So *that's* why you're here. The murders at Metéora. I should've figured that out sooner, especially knowing the connection between the two places.'

'What connection is that?'

'A monk from Mount Athos actually founded Great Metéoron in the fourteenth century. That was a turbulent time round these parts – with plenty of political upheaval. Several monks followed his lead and moved to central Greece because it was safer. Metéora was better protected than Mount Athos because the monks could control who entered their monasteries. If they felt threatened, they pulled up their long ladders and no one could get up to them. But here, there was the constant threat of attack.'

'When the monks left, did they take any treasures with them?'

'Definitely,' Clive assured him. 'Round here, two of the biggest concerns have always been thieves and fires. Over the years, both have taken their toll on this community, robbing the monks of some of their finest relics. Not so at Metéora. That place was like Fort Knox.'

Dial frowned at Clive's word choice. 'What do you mean, *was*?'

'You've been there. You know what it's like. Over the past several years it's gone from a working monastery to a tourist attraction. People come and go as they please with no security whatsoever. Heck, they even filmed a James Bond movie up there. Can you imagine the monks trying to protect something of value at Metéora?'

'No, I can't,' Dial admitted.

Everything Clive said made perfect sense. Centuries

ago, Metéora had been the best place to store the most valuable relics from the Church. But that notion had faded about the same time that the doors to Metéora were opened to the general public. At that point, the monks had to find a better place to hide their treasures, and in the Orthodox world, nothing was safer than Mount Athos.

It was a country within a country, a theocracy where the monks controlled the guest list and men with guns were allowed to patrol the borders.

A place that even cops couldn't visit without permission.

64

The Spartan soldiers had left their village before dawn. When they arrived in Leonidi, a town on the shores of the Aegean, they found the boat waiting for them. It had been left by the foreigner, just as he had promised when they struck their deal several days before.

Apollo would have preferred a warship, much like the vessels that Sparta had used when it was still a maritime power. Somehow that would have been fitting, considering the mission that he was on – trying to protect the legacy of his ancestors. Instead, he would have to make do with a large white yacht. It blended in with all the other pleasure crafts that dotted the sea. Plus, it was big enough to keep his men and weapons below deck, out of sight from prying eyes.

Their journey to Mount Athos took all day. First, he and his men had to navigate through some of the Cyclades Islands – Kithnos, Andros, Tinos, and Tzia. Later they passed Alonnisos and Skyros and the rest of the Sporades Islands. The further north they travelled, the less familiar they were with the blue waters of the Aegean. Still, with the aid of a compass and a simple map, they kept a correct heading and reached their destination before the sun set in the western sky.

At first glance, Mount Athos was much taller than they had expected. The rocky terrain was covered in thick layers of green trees, and footpaths were non-existent. But the topography worked in their favour. They were used to training in the Taygetos Mountains. They knew how to fight on a slope, how to hide in the brush, and how to use the hills to their advantage. If they were forced to wage battle in an open field, they wouldn't stand a chance. Guns, bullets, and modern weapons would tear through their flesh before they could even raise their swords.

But here, on the rock-strewn peninsula where Xerxes' army once marched?

Apollo loved his chances.

Dial's tour continued as Clive drove his boat past Xenofóntos, a waterfront monastery that was founded in 1010 AD. Over the centuries, it had been destroyed and rebuilt multiple times, and this was reflected in the newer architecture of some of the buildings.

'Coming up is one of my favourites,' Clive said as he pushed the throttle forward, doubling the boat's speed in a heartbeat. 'It goes by many names: Agíou Panteleímonos, St Panteleimon, and Rosikón. Round here, they simply call it the Russian one.'

Even without an introduction, Dial would have known its country of affiliation. The onion-domed churches and colourful roofs were a dead giveaway.

The complex was built like a small Russian town. Buildings of various heights and colours surrounded a courtyard that could not be seen from the water. A century ago, more than 1,400 monks had lived inside. That was no longer possible, not since 1968 when a fire ravaged the guest wing that could house 1,000 people.

Nowadays the community was much smaller than it had been in previous centuries. Less than fifty monks lived there, but since it was the only Russian monastery in Mount Athos, it was one of the most popular to visit – especially for followers of the Russian Orthodox faith.

Three of the Russian monks were working near the shore. Despite the sunny weather, they wore black stovepipe hats and long black cloaks. Their beards were dark and bushy.

Clive slowed his boat. 'Not only are their chapels gorgeous, but you haven't heard chanting until you've heard one of their services. The Slavonic liturgy is like a symphony.'

Dial smiled. 'I'll have to take your word on that.'

'Maybe, maybe not. I'm still hoping I can get you inside.'

'I hope so, too. Speaking of which, how much further to the main port?'

'I could gun it and get you to Dáfni in two minutes, but the harbour police are stationed there. It might be best if we approach with a modicum of respect.'

* * *

Dáfni is a small port town in the centre of the Athos Peninsula. From its position on the western coast, boat traffic is monitored and visitors to the Holy Mountain are screened. A maximum of 120 Orthodox Christian visitors are allowed daily. The number of non-Orthodox Christians is capped at fourteen a day. A visitor's permit, known as a *diamoneterion*, must be acquired well in advance – unless a special invitation was issued by Karyes, the capital of Mount Athos.

Dial hoped for one of those invitations. But he knew his odds were slim.

After tying his boat to one of the smaller docks, Clive led Dial and Andropoulos towards the front gate. It was made of metal and looked rather flimsy. The man standing beside it did not. Wearing the uniform of a customs officer, his muscles bulged against his sleeves. A side arm hung at his hip like a sheriff from the Old West. His face was intense; his eyes were focused.

'Let me talk to him first,' Clive said as he walked along the quay. 'Our goal is to get you past this gate. Once inside, you still have to get through customs and his supervisor.'

'Do they speak English?' Dial wondered.

'Some do, some don't. I'll introduce you in Greek, just in case.'

'Marcus is Greek. He can serve as my translator, if that will help.'

'That can't hurt,' Clive admitted. 'Neither can your badge.'

Dial glanced round the port. It was completely empty. Early in the day, when the ferry arrived from Ouranoúpoli, a line of pilgrims stretched out to the dock. By mid-afternoon, the place was devoid of activity. It would stay that way until the ferry came again.

'Hang tight,' Clive said. He patted Dial on the shoulder, and walked over to the customs officer. The two of them had a quiet conversation in Greek. Andropoulos strained to hear their words, but the gentle waves that lapped against the rocky shore prevented it.

A minute later, Clive was waving them over for an introduction. 'This is Nick Dial, the Director of Homicide at Interpol. And this is Marcus Andropoulos, his assistant.'

The officer nodded from behind the steel fence. 'May I have your identification?'

It was phrased as a question, but it came across as an order. The officer wanted to take their badges inside the terminal for further verification. Knowing this, Dial did as requested, handing both of them through a slit in the wire fence.

The officer glanced at them, and then called out in Greek. Soon a second officer emerged from the station house. He looked remarkably similar to the first one. Young, muscular, and rather unhappy. They quickly swapped places, so the original guard could head inside.

Grabbing Dial's arm, Clive pulled him away for a private conversation.

'Don't do anything stupid like offering them a bribe,' Clive warned. 'That would be viewed as disrespectful. Instead, I would stress that you are here for the monks' safety. Tell them you're investigating the murders at Metéora, and you're trying to stop a repeat performance. That might get their attention.'

'Fortunately, that's exactly why I'm here.'

'Good. Because lying will get you nowhere.'

Dial glanced over his shoulder. The guard was staring at them. 'Any other advice?'

'No advice,' Clive said as he shook his hand. 'But I wish you luck.'

'Thanks, I appreciate it.' Dial smiled and gave him his business card. 'If I can ever be of service, just give me a call.'

'Trust me, I will. I'd love to hear how this all turns out. I'm a sucker for a good story.'

Dial and Andropoulos were waved through the front gate where they were met by the first guard. Without saying a word, he returned their badges then led them across the compound. In some ways, Dial felt as if he was in purgatory. He knew where he wanted to go; he just didn't know if he'd be allowed to get there. It was all up to the holy men who were already inside.

'What now?' Dial asked as they strolled across the tiny courtyard.

Stone buildings served as barriers on the left, right, and straight ahead. Trees and flowers dotted the perimeter, making it seem more like a town square than a customs' checkpoint, but Dial knew exactly what it was. It was a buffer zone between Mount Athos and the outside world.

'Go in there,' the guard ordered as he pointed to an open door on the left.

Dial nodded and walked in first, followed by Andropoulos. An older officer stood behind a wooden counter. He had a salt-and-pepper moustache and bushy eyebrows. He wore the same uniform as the other guards, except he had several more patches on his chest and sleeve.

'Hello,' he said in English. 'Are you Director Dial?'

Dial shook the man's hand. 'Please call me Nick. This is Marcus, my assistant.'

'My name is Petros. I am supervisor of border. How can I assist you?'

'We are investigating the massacre at Metéora and would like to enter Mount Athos to continue our investigation. We believe there is a connection between the monasteries.'

Petros sighed. 'I was told of deaths at Metéora. It is a tragedy.'

'Eight monks lost their lives that night. I would like to prevent number nine.'

'Are our monks at risk?'

Dial nodded. 'Until we catch the men who did this, all monks are at risk. That is why I'm here. To avoid another tragedy.'

Petros studied Dial's eyes, trying to gauge his sincerity. After a few seconds, he found the answer he was searching for. 'If I could, I would let you through at once. But choice is not mine. Without a permit, I must get permission from Governor in Karyes.'

'Can you try?'

'Yes, I can try. But . . .'

'But what?'

Petros leaned in closer and whispered. 'I am told he is in bad mood today. He woke up early for important meeting, and his colleague never showed.'

65

Dial and Andropoulos sat in the customs office for over two hours as Petros pleaded their case. First on the phone, and then he went to Karyes, the administrative capital, to see the Governor in person. Unfortunately, the Governor wasn't in a forgiving mood. He would reconsider their request in the morning. In the meantime, no permit was granted.

Karyes was a tiny medieval town sitting on the crest of the hill, a fifteen-minute drive from Dáfni. The only public transport was a shuttle van that zigzagged up and down the unpaved road, sending a cloud of dust into the air. Yet it looked out of place in this simple world where monks preferred to walk and supplies were carried by pack mules.

When Petros returned, he broke the news to Dial. 'I am sorry, Nick. There is nothing more I can do. Not until morning.'

Dial took it in stride. 'Thank you for trying. I'm sure you did your best.'

'I did, and so did your colleague. He called the Governor twice while I was there.'

Dial was pleased by the thought of Toulon grovelling.

'If you like, you can spend night in Dáfni.'

'Where? In here?'

Petros laughed. 'Not in this office, across courtyard. We have small hotel, market, and restaurant. You are not the first traveller who has been denied entry.'

'I don't know,' Dial said as he considered his alternatives. 'What are the odds that the Governor will let me through tomorrow morning?'

'I am not sure. It depends on his mood. But if he says no, I have other options.'

'Such as?'

'Each monastery has one abbot. If he extends a personal invitation, you may enter grounds with special permit. Twenty monasteries mean twenty chances.'

'Really? I didn't know that.'

'Most people do not. It is customs secret.'

'But if I can't come in, how can I plead my case?'

'You cannot. But I can,' Petros said. 'And most abbots are nicer than the Governor.'

As the plane touched down in Limnos, Payne stared at the Venetian castle that was perched above the island's main harbour. Built in the thirteenth century, its grey stone walls contrasted sharply with the red tiled roofs that lined the sandy beaches.

Jarkko beamed with pride. 'Is beautiful, no?'

Payne nodded. 'Very. I've never been to this part of Greece before.'

'My yacht is in marina. We will be there soon.'

'How far are we from Mount Athos?'

'You shall see shortly.'

Payne wasn't sure what Jarkko meant until they stepped out of the plane. Even though they were more than fifty miles away from the mountain, Payne could see the snow-capped peak in the distance. It towered over the Aegean as Mount Fuji towered above Japan.

Jarkko patted him on the back. 'I hope you bring coat!'

The Spartans lingered a few miles off shore until the sun dipped below the horizon. Then they eased their boat into the south-west corner of the peninsula and dropped anchor.

One by one, they jumped into the waist-deep water and made their way to the shore. Ten of them in total, all of them dressed in battle gear. Breastplates and greaves protected their bodies and shins, and helmets protected their heads. They carried shields on one arm. Swords stored in scabbards were strapped to their backs, and daggers hung from their hips. One Spartan looked different – it was Apollo, the leader of the group, who had a plume of red horsehair topping his helmet, which signified his rank.

He would set the pace. He would give the orders. He would tell them when to kill.

And soon, their swords would be bathed in blood.

Dial paced back and forth like a caged tiger. When he looked out of the window of his cramped hotel room in Dáfni, he could see the grounds of Mount Athos. He was literally a foot away from being inside. But due to his job title, he couldn't risk breaking the glass or breaking the rules.

'Son of a bitch,' he cursed to himself as he replayed the day's events in his head.

Three cops were missing, and so were all the Spartans.

The Governor was being a total prick, and time was ticking away.

Dial wondered how things could get any worse. Then the phone rang.

'Nick,' Toulon said in a soft voice, 'the police in Spárti brought in some dogs, and they found a lot of blood.'

'Where?'

'Near the entrance to the Spartan village and in a fighting pit near their school.'

'They have a fighting pit?'

'*Oui.* The blood was buried under a layer of stones and dirt. That is why they did not see it. When they dug underneath, they found blood, hair, skin, and teeth.'

'Shit.'

'Whoever was in there was hacked into pieces.'

Dial's voice hardened as his anger boiled inside. 'Any bodies?'

'No.'

'What about villagers?'

'Not yet.'

'Anything else?'

'I am sorry about before,' Toulon assured him. 'I tried calling the Governor several times, but I had no luck getting through. I can try again tomorrow, if you would like.'

'No, Henri, I'll handle customs myself.'

'Then what should I do?'

'Stay in touch with Spárti. If you learn anything, I want to know at once.'

Agíou Pávlou, or St Paul's, is the southernmost monastery on Mount Athos. Inside its walls, many treasures are protected, including fragments of the True Cross and some of the gifts brought to the baby Jesus by the Magi. Outside its community, it owns two sketes – small villages of hermitic monks who prefer to live in seclusion away from the larger monastery. Both of them, Néa Skiti and Skiti Agías Annas, are located on the south-west corner of the peninsula and are connected to St Paul's by a simple path through the dense forest.

At this time of night, the two monks did not expect to see anyone on the way to their skete. Hauling supplies on the back of mule, they heard a rustling in the trees and paused to find the source of the sound. The lead monk lifted his lantern and was stunned by the sight. A man, dressed in full armour and carrying a sword, stepped through a thicket of bushes. A second later, another soldier emerged behind them, blocking any avenue of retreat.

The monks and the mule were now trapped.

'Hello,' said a voice from the trees. The two monks turned towards their right as Apollo stepped onto the dirt path. The red plume on the top of his helmet glowed in the lantern light. 'We are seeking the next ridge. Is there a road?'

Both monks shook their heads.

'I thought not.' Apollo paused as he glanced at the dark peak that hovered above him. Its silhouette could barely be seen in the pale moonlight. 'Kill them.'

In unison, the two soldiers lifted their swords and slashed the monks' throats. Both holy men made gurgling sounds as they fell to their knees, drenched in a fountain of blood. The crash of their lanterns spooked the mule, which started kicking and braying.

The commotion was stopped a moment later when the Spartans struck again.

This time silencing the defenceless animal.

66

When Payne and Jones landed on the south-eastern tip of the peninsula, they knew nothing about the Spartans. Otherwise, they would have approached their mission differently. For starters, they would have kept Allison on the yacht, far away from the violence that was about to erupt on Mount Athos. But since they weren't expecting any bloodshed, they let her join the group.

After all, she was the expert on ancient treasures.

'I feel kind of guilty,' she said as they trudged up the narrow beach towards the first hill. 'Women aren't supposed to be here.'

'Feel free to wait with Jarkko,' Payne said from the front position.

'No way. This is a chance of a lifetime. Besides, I'm just following Schliemann's lead.'

'How so?'

'He dressed up as a Bedouin tribesman and snuck into the forbidden city of Mecca. Do you know the courage it took to do that?'

Jones smirked from behind her. 'I'm not impressed.'

'You're not impressed? It's a Muslim-only city. They would have killed him if they caught him.'

'Who cares? Been there, done that.'

Allison wanted to ask Jones, who had snuck into Mecca for a mission, what he meant by his comment, but Payne ordered them to shut up. They were heading into the first line of trees, and he wanted to move in silence, especially at the lower altitudes where they were more likely to run into guards.

According to Jarkko's map, Megístis Lávras, the largest and oldest monastery on Mount Athos, sat a few miles to the north-east of their landing point. A large Romanian skete called Prodromos was even closer, maybe a mile away. The two communities were connected by a narrow footpath that continued across the southern tip of the peninsula and eventually joined a bigger trail along the western shore. Until they crossed that road, there would be no talking.

Payne led the way, shining a tiny flashlight along the hillside so he could manoeuvre between the rocks and trees. Allison and Jones had flashlights as well, but they used them sparingly.

All of them were dressed in a similar manner. Long dark pants, sturdy shoes, and dark short-sleeved shirts. Large packs hung from their backs. Eventually, once they reached the higher elevations and the temperature dropped, they would add layers of clothes. Until then, it was important not to sweat too much or they would get dehydrated during their journey.

Mount Athos was 6,670 feet high. If Schliemann's treasure map was correct, they were searching for a cave roughly halfway up the mountain. By the time they finished their trek, the weather would be much colder, and they would be exhausted.

The guard wasn't allowed to smoke on duty, yet he did so every night. He would walk along the trail, listening to the waves as they crashed against the rocks below, and think about his life. In some ways, he was like the hermitic monks who lived in the nearby skete. He loved the peace and quiet of the southern end of the peninsula where nothing ever happened.

He had walked the trail so many times he knew the route by heart. Up ahead there was a slight dip in the path followed by a gradual climb. Nothing too steep or his lungs couldn't handle it. That was one of the drawbacks of his pack a day habit. Stench was another. If he wasn't careful, he would reek of smoke when he returned at the end of his shift.

That's why he liked smoking here. He had plenty of time to air out before he got back to Dáfni.

With a cigarette pressed between his lips, he pulled his lighter from his uniform pocket and flicked it with his thumb. A quick flash followed by a steady flame lit up his immediate surroundings. He slowly brought it towards his face when he realized something was wrong. Although it hadn't rained in days, the path and the nearby trees glistened in the firelight.

'What in the world?' he mumbled in Greek.

Intrigued, he moved a few steps closer and extended his lighter in front of him.

Then, and only then, did he see the headless mule.

The lights were out in his hotel room, but Dial was wide awake.

He laid on his bed, furious, incensed over his investigation. He had wasted an entire day, and for what? To be jerked around by the community that he was trying to protect. In his line of work, he dealt with political bullshit all the time, but normally it involved two different countries fighting over evidence or the right to prosecute a case.

But this? This was something new.

Hell, it was *so* new he didn't know how to work round it.

Dial's seething continued until he heard a knock on his door. Actually, it was more than a knock. It was more like an urgent pounding.

'Open up,' said the voice in the hall. 'It's Petros.'

Dial flipped on the light and opened the door. Petros was in civilian clothes. His hair was dishevelled, and his cheeks were flushed. His eyes were filled with passion.

'What's wrong?' Dial wondered.

'Tell me about your case,' Petros demanded as he barged into the room.

'My case? You know about my case. I'm investigating the deaths at Metéora.'

'Yes, I know. But tell me how they died.'

Earlier Dial had skipped the gruesome details, preferring not to show his cards until he was admitted to Mount Athos. Now that plan no longer seemed possible.

'One monk was thrown over the cliff. The other seven were beheaded.'

'Beheaded? By who?'

Dial stared at him. 'You wouldn't believe me if I told you.'

'Try me.'

'Men dressed as Spartans.'

'Spartans?'

'Armour, shields, swords. The whole ensemble.'

'You are serious?'

Dial nodded. 'Do you think I would've stayed the night if I was *joking*?'

'No, I don't.'

'Not only that,' he growled, 'I got word today that they killed three cops. At least we think they did because we still haven't found them.'

Petros pondered this information for several seconds before he spoke. 'Get your assistant and come with me. We are going to the mountain.'

Dial paused, surprised. 'Wait. You're letting us go inside?'

'Yes. I am granting you emergency access.'

'Why? What's happened?'

'Two monks have been killed with swords. And we just found their bodies.'

* * *

Dial and Andropoulos pinned visitor badges to their shirts and followed Petros through the gate. A four-wheel-drive vehicle resembling a large golf cart was waiting for them. Dial sat up front next to Petros. Andropoulos climbed in the back seat, which faced the rear.

'What do you know?' Dial asked.

'Not much,' Petros explained as he drove. 'I was sleeping at the barracks when I got the news. Two monks and a mule were slaughtered near Néa Skiti.'

'They killed a *mule*?'

'Cut its head clean off.'

'Who found it?'

'One of our guards.'

Dial considered the information as their cart bumped up and down along the narrow path. The vehicle had one working headlight, which barely lit the way – especially at the speed they were travelling. By the time they saw something, they were already running it over.

'How far is it?'

'Far. It's near the south-west corner of the peninsula.'

'What else is down there?'

'Two small sketes and a beach.'

'Any treasures?'

Petros shook his head. 'The sketes are small communities of hermitic monks. They live away from the monasteries to get away from all the riches.'

'And the closest monastery?'

'Agíou Pávlou. It's a few miles from the sketes.'

'Have the monks been warned?'

Petros nodded. 'We are doing that right now. Unfortunately, Mount Athos is large and our numbers are small. Especially at night.'

'What do you mean?'

'Most of the guards live elsewhere. At the end of their shift, they go home. I am one of the few employees who sleep here.'

'Hold up. How many guards are we talking?'

Petros shrugged. 'I don't know. Maybe twenty.'

'*Twenty?*' Dial blurted. 'You have twenty guards for the entire peninsula? You have that many monasteries!'

'This is true, but—'

'Stop the cart!' Dial ordered. 'Stop the cart right now!'

Petros slammed on the brakes. 'What is it? What is wrong?'

'We need guns.'

'Guns?' he stammered. 'I can't give you guns. It is not allowed.'

'Fine. Then turn round and take us back to Dáfni.'

'But—'

'But what?' Dial growled. 'These guys have killed ten monks, three cops, and a fucking mule. If you want our help, you need to give us guns. Otherwise, I'm going back to bed.'

67

To announce prayer and meal times on Mount Athos, a monk strikes a *simandro*, a carved wooden plank that echoes throughout the grounds of his monastery. In the event of an emergency, it can also be used as a warning device. One monk sounds the alarm, pounding on it rhythmically until a monk at the neighbouring monastery follows his lead. In a matter of minutes, the sound sweeps round the peninsula like war drums on a battlefield.

Bringing up the rear, Jones was the first from his group to hear it. He called ahead to Payne and Allison who stopped on the wooded hillside to listen.

'Is that because of us?' Allison wondered.

Payne shook his head. 'No way. If they'd spotted us, they would have stopped us.'

'Maybe they saw Jarkko.'

'Doing what?' Jones teased. 'Peeing off the side of his yacht? Right now he's anchored a mile off shore.'

'It's not us and it's not Jarkko,' Payne assured them. 'Something else is going on.'

Jones listened as the pounding continued. 'Do we have company?'

Payne nodded as he took the pack from his shoulders. He reached inside and pulled out his gun. 'Someone hired Kozlov to kill Richard. We hoped he'd surface some time.'

'And he was spotted?' Allison asked.

'Maybe,' Payne said. 'Or maybe he hired reinforcements to find the treasure.'

Apollo heard the sound and knew exactly what it meant. He had grown up in the Taygetos Mountains where *simandros* were common. A few seconds of clanging told the workers in the fields what time it was. But a few minutes of pounding was an alarm.

Now that the element of surprise was gone, it was time for phase two.

In Ancient Sparta, hoplites fought together in a phalanx. They stood side by side, their shields locked together to protect one another, while a second row of soldiers thrust their spears over the front wall of shields. The Spartans were so adept at this technique that they could conquer vastly larger forces while suffering minimal losses.

Unfortunately, that style of warfare would not help them here.

They weren't looking for a fight. They were looking for the book.

And they wanted to find it as quickly as possible.

In Apollo's mind, the best way to accomplish that goal was to split up. Ten soldiers marching together could be spotted from the air. But ten men spread across the mountain would be hard to stop –

especially if they were strategically placed to intercept anyone in pursuit.

The monks had stopped their pounding by the time Dial arrived at the crime scene. A duty holster carried his gun and extra ammo. Andropoulos and Petros were armed as well.

The guard who found the bodies reeked of tobacco. He had smoked half a pack while waiting for his boss to arrive. A few guards worked in the background, searching the nearby woods for clues and other victims. But the smoking guard stayed on the path, still frazzled from his gruesome discovery. Petros spoke to him in Greek while Dial walked the scene.

'Marcus,' Dial said to Andropoulos, 'these guys came ashore for a reason. We need to figure out what they're looking for.'

'How can I help?'

'Go and talk to the guards. Ask them if there's anything over here besides the sketes.'

'Yes, sir,' he said as he ran off.

Meanwhile Dial took a moment to study the trail. Normally he would have focused on the blood and the bodies, trying to work out what had happened. But that wasn't necessary in this case. He knew enough about the Spartans to recognize their handiwork, so his immediate goal was capture, not conviction. He wanted to stop his opponents before they could strike again.

Shining his flashlight along the edge of the path, Dial searched for footprints and found several in the loose soil. As far as he could tell, all of them were heading north – away from the water below towards the mountain above. That meant they weren't marching along the path towards one of the monasteries. Instead, they had been crossing the path when they came across the monks.

'Did you find something?' Petros wondered.

Dial countered the question with one of his own. 'How far are we from the beach?'

'Just over half a mile. Why?'

'Did anyone check for boats?'

'Harbour patrol was called. They will tell us if they find something.'

'If they do, tell them to lock it down. We don't want these guys escaping.'

'I will tell them.' Petros pulled out his radio and walked away.

'Sir,' Andropoulos called from behind. 'The guards assured me there is nothing over here but some caves. Centuries ago, hermits lived in them for months at a time, but that practice stopped when the sketes were built.'

'Where are the caves located?'

'All over the place. The mountain is full of them.'

'And they've been here for centuries?'

'They're caves, sir. They've been around since the dinosaurs.'

* * *

Jarkko sat on his yacht more than a mile away from the shore. Even from way out there, he had heard the monks pounding on their *simandros*. The sound rolled across the water like thunder.

Curious about all the commotion, he decided to move closer.

At this time of night, he had the biggest boat in the Singitic Gulf. Sixty-five feet long, accommodation for six, and a master bath complete with a small hot tub. If he got too close to Mount Athos, the harbour patrol would notice him for sure. Normally, he wouldn't care. He would have a drink in one hand, and he would flip them off with the other.

But tonight, he couldn't afford the extra attention.

His goal was to get close enough to assist his friends in case they needed help, but far enough away that he looked like a fisherman.

To complete his disguise, he got out a rod and reel, lit a cigar, and put up his feet.

Staring at Mount Athos, Dial asked, 'Are the monks safe?'

'All the monasteries are fortified,' Petros explained. 'Sturdy gates, heavy doors, elevated architecture. They should be fine.'

'What about the guards? What are they doing?'

'Protecting the monasteries.'

Dial grimaced. 'Twenty guards are protecting twenty monasteries? No, wait. Make that sixteen guards because some of your men are over here. I don't want to tell you how to do your job, but that seems like an inefficient use of manpower.'

'That is *not* my job. I am in charge of customs. I am not in charge of the guards.'

'Who is?'

Petros explained that the leader of the guards was currently on vacation. And the acting leader of the guards was in Karyes, trying to coordinate his men from the capital city.

'Do you have any pull with him?' Dial asked.

Petros nodded. 'I hope so. I helped him get hired.'

Dial smiled. That would make things easier. 'I don't want to overstep my bounds here, but I have a lot of experience with manhunts. Since the monks are safe, our main goal is to find the assailants as quickly as possible.'

'Yes. That would be best.'

Dial pointed to several footprints near the trail. 'The Spartans killed the monks and then continued up the mountain. I don't know where they're headed, but our best chance to find them is with as many guards as possible.'

Petros nodded in agreement. 'I will make the suggestion.'

Dial shone his flashlight on the nearby trees. Many of the branches had been disturbed. Some had been cut with swords. From the physical evidence, he guessed roughly a dozen Spartans had made the journey north.

'One more thing,' Dial added. 'Make sure they're armed as well.'

68

The Spartans moved swiftly and silently in pairs. Some of them continued up the mountain, searching for the ancient book. Others sprinted across the slope, striving to kill the guards before their search gained momentum. Without modern weapons, the Spartans had to choose their battles carefully. They couldn't wage war in an open field, so they positioned themselves for a sneak attack, using the rocks and branches as camouflage.

The first confrontation was remarkably one-sided. Two young guards, who were used to patrolling the eastern side of the peninsula, trudged up the mountain, their flashlights leading their way. The Spartans saw the beams from their position in the trees a full minute before the guards were underneath them. In unison, they leapt on top of the guards, using their weight and gravity to drive their blades through the guards' shoulders all the way to their hearts. Blood sprayed in all directions, coating the Spartans' hands and faces. And both of them loved it.

In their world, the only thing that quenched their thirst was the blood of the enemy.

And since they rarely got to taste it, they planned to drink all night.

The next pair of Spartans weren't as lucky. They had been asked to defend the south-eastern slope of Mount Athos. Since their boat had landed on the south-west corner of the peninsula, they had been forced to run across the breadth of the mountain in order to get into position.

Shortly after getting there, they spotted a single beam of light. Despite the rocks and fallen tree branches that clogged the slope, it moved up the gradient at a steady rate. The Spartans grinned in anticipation. One of them took his position in the trees above. The other ducked down behind a large boulder that was partially imbedded into the turf.

Their ambush would begin a minute later.

Fifty yards away, Payne was oblivious to their presence. There was no way for him to know the Spartans were waiting for him. They hadn't scaled the hill Payne was climbing, so no footprints marred the ground. And the Spartans had moved without light, their years of training preparing them for moments like this when they were forced to hunt in darkness.

In fact, if not for a lucky break, Payne probably would have been filleted by one of the Spartans' blades before he even knew what hit him. However, the best-trained soldiers are able to take advantage of such opportunities, letting them live another day. Many heroes could recall the landmine that didn't go off when they stepped on it, or the dropped canteen that caused them to bend over just as the bullet whizzed overhead.

In this case, it was the simple crack of a branch as the Spartan shifted his weight that alerted Payne to the danger in the trees. He glanced up just as the Spartan leapt, his sword held above him ready to strike. In one fluid motion, Payne fell backwards on to his pack and extended his arms forward. With two rapid pulls of his trigger, he sent two rounds into the night. The first caught the Spartan just below his trachea. It ripped through the cartilage of his neck and tore through the centre of his spine before it imbedded itself in a nearby branch.

Bullet number two struck the man six inches higher and slightly to the left, missing the metal flap of his helmet by a fraction of an inch. His cheekbone exploded from the impact, as did the back of his skull. By the time he landed on Payne, the Spartan was already dead. His blade clanged harmlessly to the ground, followed by Allison's screams of terror.

Jones saw the attack from his position in the rear. He charged forward, more concerned about Payne than Allison's screaming, just as the second assault began. When Payne fired his gun, he had dropped his light, which gave the hidden Spartan a window of opportunity. Using the darkness as his ally, he crept out from behind the boulder and inched down the hill.

'What the hell was that?' Payne demanded as Jones

pulled the dead Spartan off him. Blood covered the front of Payne's clothes as he struggled to make sense of what had happened.

Jones flipped the body onto its back and stared at half a face. The rest was either torn asunder from Payne's bullet or covered by the metal helmet.

'Seriously,' Payne repeated. 'What the hell was that?'

Jones was about to answer when he noticed the second Spartan. 'Behind you!'

Payne, who was sitting on the ground and facing downhill, arched his body backwards as he lifted his gun over his head. At the same time, Jones pointed his gun at the creeping shadow. Bullets sprang from both weapons as the Spartan charged forward. The first shot pinged off his shield, but his luck stopped there. From his position on the ground, Payne fired low, splintering the Spartan's legs with multiple shots. Meanwhile Jones aimed high, squeezing his trigger in rapid succession until he hit brain.

Pink mist could not be seen in the darkness. But it was there.

The Spartan fell forward and rolled, the slope of the hill and his momentum carrying him forward like a human avalanche. Eventually, he skidded to a bloody stop at Allison's feet.

Her screams echoed through the night as Payne and Jones scrambled into position.

'Shut up!' Payne ordered as he slipped off his pack.

He helped her understand his orders by clamping his hand over her mouth and pulling her back into the trees. Then he forced her to crouch near the ground.

'Stay here,' he whispered. 'Do you understand me? Stay *here*!'

She nodded her head.

'I'll be back,' he said as he ran up the hillside, searching for more Spartans.

Jones had started his search a moment before, occasionally clicking on his flashlight to hunt for footprints. As far as he could tell, only two men had been lying in wait. And they were now dead. Payne came to the same conclusion a few minutes later.

They reconvened near the bodies, hoping to learn more about their enemy. They stared at the armour with amazement. The helmets, the shields, the greaves, and swords. Both Payne and Jones were experts on the history of war. At the military academies, they had studied ancient warfare and had both particularly loved reading about the Spartans. Still, in their wildest dreams, they had never imagined they would come across hoplites on the battlefield.

It didn't make any sense – even in an archaic place like Mount Athos.

'What do you think?' Payne asked as he picked up a sword.

Jones laughed. 'What do I think? I think Jarkko dropped us off in Ancient Greece. I don't know what he paid for his yacht, but it was worth every penny.'

'DJ, I'm serious.'

'I am, too. If we hurry, maybe we can help them build the Parthenon.'

Payne grinned and turned his attention to Allison. She was standing next to him, staring at the blade he held in his hands. 'Are you okay?'

She nodded but said nothing. Prior to her trip to Russia, she had never seen anyone killed before. Now everywhere she turned, she was surrounded by death.

It would take a while for things to sink in.

'Come on,' Payne said as he tossed the sword to the ground. 'We have to get moving. It's just a matter of time before the guards investigate the gunshots.'

Dial heard the gunfire from his position on the mountain. It had come in disciplined bursts. Two shots, a long pause, and then a rapid cluster. Whoever was firing was a seasoned pro.

And they were shooting at something on the south-eastern side of Mount Athos.

'Son of a bitch,' Dial growled, realizing that his search party was on the south-western side of the mountain – the same side where the dead monks had been found. 'Who's over there?'

'Let me find out,' Petros said as he turned up his radio and started asking questions in Greek. A few minutes passed before he had an answer. 'It is not the guards.'

'Shit!' Dial blurted. 'That means one of two things. Either the Spartans are carrying guns, or there's another party on the mountain. And if I had to guess, I'd go with number two.'

'Why is that?' Andropoulos asked.

'Because if the Spartans have guns, who are they firing at? I mean, we're over here.'

'That is true.'

'It also means there might be more Spartans over *there*. Because that other party is firing at someone, and it's certainly not us.'

Dial paused, rubbing his chin in thought. As he did, Petros and Andropoulos stared at him, waiting for his next set of instructions. None of the guards had as much experience in hostile situations as Dial. For the time being, everyone was willing to follow his lead.

'Petros, we're at a serious disadvantage here. Multiple groups of armed men are climbing your mountain and we don't know why. We don't know where they're headed, and we're clueless about their numbers. The only thing we know for sure is that they're willing to kill.'

'What should we do?'

'Honestly? We shouldn't do anything. We should recall the guards and wait for reinforcements.'

'We should *wait*? They killed two monks, and we should *wait*?'

Dial nodded. 'Here's the problem. In combat, elevated positions have an advantage. We're several minutes behind them in our climb. That means, there's no way we can overtake them without going through them. If we had superior firepower or twice as many men, I'd be tempted to take those odds. But as it stands, our pursuit would be suicide.'

Petros asked, 'What if I could change the odds? What if we could get in front of them?'

'How? Do you have a helicopter I don't know about?'

He shook his head. 'No, but I have an idea that just might work.'

69

Driving as fast as he could, Petros explained his plan to Dial and Andropoulos. 'There is an old goat path up the western side of the mountain. It starts near Agíou Pávlou and crosses towards the southern face. If we hurry, we might be able to beat the soldiers to that point.'

'Why didn't you tell me that before?' Dial demanded. 'We could have set up shop on the mountain and pinned the Spartans in.'

Their vehicle hit a dip in the road. Everyone bounced roughly in their seats as Petros struggled to maintain control. He temporarily eased off the accelerator until he had righted things.

'It is not that simple. The path is too narrow for this cart to fit.'

'Then how would we get up there?'

'Motorcycles.'

Dial stared at him in disbelief. 'The monks have *motorcycles*?'

'Last year,' Petros said, 'two men came to Athos on a trip across Greece. They brought their motorcycles over on the ferry and parked them outside our walls. The men were supposed to stay for three days. Once inside, they fell in love with the monastic life.

One of the abbots gave them permission to stay longer, and they haven't left since.'

'And their bikes?'

'We moved them into storage.'

'But there's two of them, right?'

'Yes, only two.'

'But there's *three* of us.'

Petros nodded. 'Someone will have to ride double.'

'I am very experienced,' Andropoulos said from the back seat. 'I have owned a motorcycle for many years, so I can ride one up the path.'

'What about you?' Petros asked Dial as their bumpy ride continued.

Dial groaned in frustration. He hadn't driven a bike in decades. And even then, he had never taken one off pavement. Throw in the darkness factor, and Dial realized he had no choice.

He would have to rely on Andropoulos.

Payne stared at a photocopy of the treasure map that they had made in Limnos, and then glanced at the rock face above him. It was fifteen feet high and angled back towards them. There was no way they could climb it without the proper equipment.

'What now?' Jones asked as he shone his light on the ridge.

'We have to go round it.'

'Which way?'

'If we go east,' Payne said, 'we're moving closer to

the largest monastery on the peninsula. There's no telling how many guards will be over there.'

'What about west?'

'There are several monasteries and sketes, but they're a lot farther away.'

'What do you think, Allison?'

She blinked, surprised that they were asking her opinion. 'Let's go west.'

Payne nodded his approval. 'You heard the lady. West it is.'

Petros accelerated on the dual-sport bike, which was street legal but had off-road capability, and rocketed up the goat trail. Andropoulos and Dial were next, only they took things much slower. Their headlight lit the way as they crept past the weeds and trees that lined the narrow path.

'Are you all right?' Andropoulos shouted over his shoulder.

Dial ignored the question. 'Can't this thing go any faster?'

'It can go *much* faster.'

'Then quit talking and start driving.'

Andropoulos grinned. 'Yes, sir!'

In a flash, their speed tripled, and Dial found himself holding on for dear life. The young cop proved his skill by accelerating and turning like an expert. Despite the extra weight, they found themselves catching up to Petros less than a minute later.

They rode like this for nearly three miles, cutting across the western face while gradually climbing higher. Dial did mental calculations in his head and tried to figure out how high they had to go in order to guarantee that they would be ahead of the Spartans. Unfortunately, it was an equation he couldn't solve without knowing all the variables.

When did the Spartans arrive on the peninsula? How fast were they moving? Were they headed straight up the mountain, or did they start to angle towards the east or west?

Actually, Dial wasn't even sure when the Spartans would stop marching. Maybe they were heading to a cave that was only 1,000 feet from the shore. If that was so, they might have overshot the Spartans by several hundred feet.

A few seconds later, Dial found out that wasn't the case.

The two Spartans heard the roar of the engines long before they saw the headlights approach. They quickly repositioned themselves along the footpath, preparing for a sneak attack. One crouched behind a boulder to the south of the trail. The other remained standing, hidden by a thick grove of trees. On the battlefield, Spartans would never relinquish their shields – it was considered the ultimate sin because it left other soldiers in the phalanx unprotected. But here, where mobility was more important than defence, it was the right thing to do.

Both Spartans clutched their swords with two hands, ready to strike.

Petros led the charge over the crest of the hill. He was fifty feet ahead of Dial and Andropoulos, barely within range of their headlight, when the Spartan in the trees launched his assault.

As Petros sped through the night, the armoured man stepped forward and swung his weapon with all his strength. Years of discipline and training went into that swing, and it showed when his blade made contact. One moment Petros' head was attached to his neck; the next it was spinning through the air as the rest of his body shot forward on the motorcycle. Somehow the bike stayed upright for several feet before it tilted off the path and crashed into a tree, tossing the headless corpse into the air like a scarecrow in a dust storm.

Dial saw none of this from his position on the back of the second bike. But Andropoulos saw it all. The sword, the head, and the Spartan who blocked their path. Not wanting to suffer the same fate as Petros, the young Greek went into a controlled slide – hitting the brake and shifting his weight in order to minimize the impact of his fall. His front wheel went sideways, and so did he. Dial fell first, tumbling off the back of the bike and skidding to a painful stop on the up-slope of the mountain. Andropoulos was dragged twenty feet farther, tumbling along the rock-strewn turf until his momentum slowly died.

When everything stopped moving, Dial and Andropoulos were left sprawling on the side of the road. Both of them were conscious, but badly bruised and scraped. Somehow their motorcycle had twisted round on the ground, so its headlight was now pointed back at them. The bright beam of light allowed them to see, but what they saw was frightening.

Two Spartans were coming in for the kill.

Dial reached down for his gun, his fingers fumbling with the strap on his holster. Seconds passed before he heard the quiet snap that allowed him to yank his weapon free. But by then it was too late; the Spartan was upon him.

He kicked the gun out of Dial's hand and laughed as he did. He was going to enjoy this. His sword was already slathered in blood, fresh from his recent kill. Now he could add some more.

Two victims in less than a minute. His ancestors would be proud.

The Spartan lifted the sword above his head, ready to drive it through Dial's chest.

And all Dial could do was watch.

70

As the blade started forward, Dial heard the two most beautiful sounds of his entire life. A gunshot rang out from the tree line, followed by a soft gasp from the Spartan's mouth.

His cocky laughter from a moment before had been replaced by his dying breath.

Blood gushed from the hole in the warrior's neck as he slumped to the ground. As he did, he tried to use his last ounce of strength to kill one more opponent. With wide eyes, Dial watched the sword on its downward flight as it headed straight for his face. But before it made contact, multiple shots burst from the night, knocking him off balance. His blade struck the ground with so much force that it remained upright a lot longer than the Spartan did.

The sword stood at attention like a flag planted on foreign soil.

Dial turned his head and stared at it. He gulped as he did.

Four inches to the left, and he would have been dead.

'Are you all right?' called a voice from the trees.

'Yes,' Dial said, his heart pounding in his chest. 'I'm fine.'

'Show me your hands.'

'What?'

'Show me your fucking hands!'

'Okay.' From his prone position, Dial lifted his arms slowly. 'I'm unarmed.'

'Are you alone?'

'No. I was riding with my partner.'

'Your partner?'

'I'm a cop . . . Is my partner all right?'

The shooter in the trees crept closer, trying to see the face of the cop he had just saved. 'Your partner is fine. What are you doing here?'

'I'm working on a case.'

'What kind of case?'

'A homicide . . . The men with swords killed several monks.'

Silence filled the air for several seconds. Dial glanced towards the tree line where the shooter had last spoken, but saw nothing. A moment later, Dial heard footsteps behind him.

Somehow the shooter had travelled twenty feet without making a sound.

'Damn,' Dial said to himself. 'What are you doing back there?'

'I'm picking up your gun.'

'Oh.'

Dial listened closely, worried that the man was going to put a bullet in the back of his head. Some criminals got a special thrill from that, using a cop's weapon against him. Then again, if he had wanted Dial to die, why had he just saved his life?

'Can you sit up?' asked the shooter.

'Yes.'

'Then lock your hands behind your head and sit up slowly.'

Dial did as he was told, sitting up despite the pain that emerged in his ribs and back. With all the excitement, he had temporarily forgotten he had just been in a bike wreck.

Meanwhile, the shooter waited until Dial was in an upright position. Now, for the first time, he would be able to see the cop's face in the beam of the headlight. Moving quietly, he walked round to the front and stared at the man whose life he had just saved.

And he was stunned by the sight.

Payne couldn't believe his eyes. 'Nick?'

Dial flinched at the mention of his name. With one hand, he shielded the bright headlight of the motorcycle and focused on the man in front of him. He was just as shocked as Payne. 'Jon?'

'What in the hell are you doing here?'

Dial slumped to the ground in utter relief. 'Holy shit, you gave me a heart attack. I thought you were going to kill me.'

'Kill you? I just saved you.'

'I know,' he said, laughing to himself. 'But it's been a strange night.'

Dial had met Payne and Jones several years ago at Stars & Stripes, a European bar that catered to

Americans who worked overseas. They were in the MANIACs at the time, and Dial was still rising through the ranks at Interpol. The three of them hit it off, and they had kept in touch ever since – occasionally bumping into each other in the strangest places. Once at an airport in Italy. Another time at a bookstore in London. But this, by far, took the prize for their most auspicious meeting ever.

Payne helped his friend to his feet and was greeted with a friendly hug.

'Nice shooting,' Dial said as he patted Payne on the back.

Payne smiled. 'Glad I could help.'

Jones watched the embrace from afar. 'Guys? This is the *Holy* Mountain, not *Brokeback* Mountain.'

Dial laughed at the comment. 'I should've known. Where there's Payne, there's Jones.'

Jones stepped forward and shook his hand. 'Nick fuckin' Dial. I knew I recognized that big-ass chin of yours . . . What in the hell are you doing here?'

Dial grinned. 'Jon asked me the same damn thing.'

'And I'm still waiting for an answer,' Payne reminded him.

'Yeah, yeah, yeah. I'll get to it in a moment. First, how are Marcus and Petros?'.

Jones grimaced. 'Which is which?'

'Marcus is the kid.'

Jones answered. 'The kid's fine. The other one, not so much.'

Dial, who hadn't seen Petros' death, needed to

have things explained. Andropoulos filled him in the best he could, including how Jones had saved his life by shooting the other attacker.

'Speaking of which,' Payne wondered, 'who are those guys?'

Jones added, 'So far, we've killed four of them.'

'Only four?' asked Dial, who was quite familiar with their Special Forces backgrounds. 'I'm guessing there are a lot more than that.'

He took a few minutes to describe the Spartans, the murdered monks, and the missing cops. He didn't have time to go into the details of the case, but he told them enough so they would understand what was going on. 'We still aren't sure what the Spartans are looking for. But whatever it is, it must be *big*. Otherwise, they wouldn't have risked this type of exposure.'

Jones glanced at Payne but said nothing.

And Dial happened to notice. 'What?'

Payne grimaced. 'Nick, let's take a walk.'

'Why?'

'Because we need to talk.'

The two moved away from Andropoulos, so the young Greek couldn't hear what was about to be said. And Jones made sure of it by keeping an eye on him. Over the years, Payne and Dial had shared confidential information to help each other with various missions and assignments. And this was one of those times when they needed to speak in private, for both of their sakes.

'What's up?' Dial asked.

'I want to tell you why we're here. But only if it's off the record.'

Dial stared at him, wondering where this was going. 'Fine.'

'I think I know what the Spartans are looking for. It's probably the same thing we're looking for.'

'Which is?'

Payne reached into his pocket and pulled out a copy of the treasure map. 'A colleague of mine recently called me from Russia and asked for my help. By the time I responded, it was too late. Someone had killed him.'

'I'm sorry to hear that.'

Payne shrugged it off. 'DJ and I poked around a little bit and figured out why he was murdered. He was looking for this.'

Dial took the map from Payne and studied it in the beam of the headlight. He instantly recognized the geography of Mount Athos. 'Is this a *treasure* map?'

Payne nodded. 'The man who killed my colleague was a hit man who used to work for the FSB. When I questioned him, he said he'd been hired by someone with a Mediterranean accent. We assumed he might be Greek, but we don't know that for sure.'

'Why Greek?'

'Because the treasure is Greek. That is, if it even exists.'

Payne gave him a quick summary of the story of

Richard Byrd, Heinrich Schliemann, and the possible existence of the lost throne. In addition, he filled him in on all the other treasures that could have been removed from Constantinople before the fire, everything from gold relics to ancient manuscripts.

'I think you're right,' Dial said. 'Our two matters are probably related.'

'I know. So what are we going to do about it?'

Dial gave the question some thought. 'As far as I'm concerned, Interpol is here for one reason only: to catch the men who killed the monks. Everything else is a non-issue to me.'

Payne nodded in appreciation. 'Glad to hear it.'

'And,' Dial said as he pointed at the map, 'since my suspects seem to be heading towards this location, it might be nice if we could tag along with you.'

'That's fine with me. Unless . . .'

'Unless, what?'

'Unless the kid is going to be a problem.'

'You mean Marcus? He won't be a problem at all. DJ just saved his life. I really doubt he's going to ask to see your visitor's pass.'

Payne smiled. 'Good. Because there's one other thing I've been keeping from you. And it's kind of hard to explain . . .'

71

Payne asked Allison to step out of the shadows where she had been ordered to wait.

Dial stared at her in disbelief. He wasn't expecting Payne's big surprise to be a female. 'You brought a *woman* to Mount Athos? The Virgin Mary is going to be pissed off.'

Payne ignored the comment. 'Nick, this is Allison. She was with Richard Byrd when he was killed in Russia. She goes wherever I go until this thing is done.'

Dial nodded in understanding. 'Nice to meet you, Allison.'

She smiled and shook his hand. 'You, too.'

'I'm sorry to hear about your friend.'

'Thanks.'

'Okay,' Payne said, cutting them off. 'Now that the introductions are out of the way, we better get moving. The longer we stand round, the more time we waste.'

Jones walked towards Dial and handed him a radio. 'I got this from Petros. You should update the guards and tell them to stay below this ridgeline. We'll leave the headlights on as a beacon.'

'Wait,' Dial said, 'isn't that counterproductive?

Obviously the Spartans have made it this far. It stands to reason that they're ahead of us.'

'Some probably are,' Jones explained. 'But so far, we've killed four soldiers who seemed pretty intent on stopping us from climbing this mountain. My guess is there are more Spartans down there, lying in wait. Let the guards worry about those guys. We can take care of the rest.'

The Spartan scout listened from the nearby trees, and then ran off to warn Apollo.

If they stopped this group of five, who were only a few minutes behind, they would have all the time they needed to locate the book. But that task would be tougher than it sounded because these soldiers seemed to be far more competent than the other guards. The two largest men had already killed four hoplites in the last hour. Normally, it was the Spartans who showed such efficiency in battle, not their opponents.

Of course, if there was one thing the Spartans enjoyed, it was a worthy adversary.

Payne led the way, followed by Dial, Allison, Andro-poulos, and Jones. They trudged single file up the steep terrain, with enough space in between them to lessen the effects of a sneak attack. If a Spartan leapt out of a tree, he would only be able to attack one person in Payne's group before someone got off a gun-shot. At least that was Payne's rationale. The truth was that in all his years of soldiering he had never faced an opponent who preferred ancient weaponry to guns.

It forced him to view things from a whole new perspective.

Twenty minutes after leaving the motorcycles, the group came across a narrow chasm in the centre of a long ridge. Payne and Jones shone their flashlights along the steep rock face, searching for an easier way round it, while the other three members of their party caught their breath. The temperature had started to drop, and the minor injuries that Dial and Andropoulos had suffered in their bike crash had started to take their toll. Their breathing had become laboured, not only because of the thinning air but because their ribs had been bruised in the fall.

None of the three spoke as they took turns gulping bottled water.

Meanwhile, Jones caught up to Payne along the ridge. 'What do you think?'

'We either go through here or walk a half mile out of the way.'

Jones nodded. 'We have to be careful. A smart soldier would use this to his advantage.'

'I was thinking the same thing.'

The two of them walked back and joined the others. Jones explained to them what needed to be done. 'This is a classic choke point. We need to pass through it as quickly as possible. Jon will go first, followed by Nick and so on. Once you climb through, be on full alert.'

While the others got ready, Payne pulled Allison aside.

'How are you feeling?'

'I'm fine,' she answered. 'Tired, but fine.'

'Well, you're doing great. Just keep it up.'

She smiled in appreciation.

'Do you understand what we need you to do here?'

'Climb through and be ready to move.'

'Simple enough, huh?'

'I think I can handle it.'

'For the next few minutes, can you do me a small favour?'

She nodded. 'Sure. What did you have in mind?'

Payne pulled out the gun they had taken from Petros. 'Can you carry this for me?'

She stared at the weapon with disdain in her eyes.

'Listen,' he said, 'I know you're not comfortable with guns. Up until now I haven't given you one because I've seen the way you've looked at mine. But here's the problem. For the next few minutes, our numbers will be cut in half. If we're going to be attacked, this is where they're going to do it. Tactically speaking, I need to do whatever I can to strengthen our odds. That means I need everyone to be armed.'

'Well,' she said, 'since you put it like that, how can a gal resist?'

Apollo knew he was outnumbered. His scout had warned him of that. But the beauty of his plan – which was similar to King Leonidas' tactic to hold off thousands of Persians in the Battle of Thermopylae – was that he wouldn't have to fight all his opponents at once. He would wait until their numbers were divided, then he would attack.

Instead of five against three, he would fight them three against three.

Then he would pick off the others when they rushed into the fray.

The gap in the stone face was about three feet wide. During rainstorms, water gushed through the chasm like a waterfall. Over the years, it had smoothed the rock and made it slick. Traction was difficult to find. The angle of the hillside wasn't particularly steep, so ropes and anchors weren't needed. Still, in order to climb the fifteen feet to the next ridge, they needed to concentrate.

For a large man, Payne was unbelievably nimble. Most Special Forces officers were small and wiry, soldiers who could run for ever and hide in the blink of an eye, yet somehow Payne was able to keep up with them. In fact, he did more than that; he surpassed his peers by matching their agility and endurance and adding a brute strength that none of them possessed.

It was one of the reasons he had been asked to lead the MANIACs.

They were a special group, and Payne was the best of the best.

Using his hands and feet to climb, he scurried up

the rock with ease. He dropped his pack on the ridge, and then scanned the nearby trees. With gun raised, he stared into the darkness, listening for the crack of a branch or anything that seemed out of place.

But the area seemed deserted.

'Let's go,' he said to his friends, who were waiting down below.

Dial was up second. He grimaced in pain as he used his arms to assist with the climb. Though his ribs were tender to the touch, they weren't broken and weren't going to stop him. Ten seconds later, he was crouching next to his friend on top of the ridge.

'Next,' he said to Allison.

She nodded and tucked the gun in her belt, nervous about the task at hand. Unlike the men, who had all been trained in one service academy or another, she had no experience of climbing – unless she counted gym class in junior high. She was in good shape from her frequent jogs round the Stanford campus, but this was something new to her.

Rock climbing in the dark simply wasn't offered at her local health club.

While Dial stood guard, Payne kept his focus on Allison. In his hands, he held a thick tree limb that he had found on the nearby ground. If she struggled during her ascent, she could grab hold of it, and he could pull her up. 'Don't stop. Just keep moving forward.'

She followed his instructions, churning one leg after the other, using her hands to steady herself against the side of the chasm, never pausing to think. Her foot slipped once on the slick surface, but she maintained her balance with her arms and made it to the top without help.

'That was fun,' she said with a smile.

'I'm glad,' Payne said. 'Now stand over there so Marcus can take his turn.'

Allison nodded and shuffled off to the side.

A moment later, the Spartans started their attack.

72

Allison saw the Spartan before anyone else. He burst from the trees, twenty feet away from her. His shield was in one hand, his sword in the other. Since her gun was still tucked in her belt, she did the only thing she could think of. She screamed as loudly as she could.

Payne whirled in her direction and spotted the Spartan who was sprinting at them. Unable to pull his gun in time, Payne stepped in front of Allison and lowered his shoulder, hoping to duck under the Spartan's shield. A moment before impact, Payne arched his back as if he was going to tackle him. But instead of wrapping his arms, he thrust his shoulders upward, slamming the tree branch that he still held into his opponent's legs. The force, coupled with the Spartan's momentum, launched the soldier high into the air and over the edge of the ridge.

Jones, who had heard Allison's scream, was on full alert when the Spartan took flight. Like a superhero out of control, he crashed into a nearby tree and landed roughly on the ground as his helmet bounced down the hill.

But Jones showed no sympathy for the Spartan.

He stood over him and ended his life with a bullet between the eyes.

Meanwhile, on the ridge above, the other two Spartans charged into battle. Both of them had learned from the hoplite's mistake, so they approached quickly yet under control. Shields in front of them, swords ready to strike, prepared to fight to the death.

Ready for a challenge, Apollo went after Payne. During the past few minutes, he had watched Payne and knew he was their leader. They were roughly the same size and build, and both of them moved with dexterity. The main difference was in their training.

Apollo had learned his skills from the greatest warrior culture of all time.

His opponent had not.

In Apollo's mind, the outcome was all but decided.

Before Payne could recover from the previous assault, Apollo was upon him. Using his shield as a battering ram, he launched himself into Payne, knocking him on to his back. Payne skidded to a halt a few feet short of the chasm. A second later, Apollo was above him, swinging his sword as hard as he could. Somehow, through it all, Payne had held on to the tree limb. It was sturdy and knotted with age. He lifted it above his chest just in time to stop the path of the blade.

A mighty thump echoed through the night as the wood splintered from the force.

The unexpected block left the Spartan off balance. His weight was leaning forward, and his stride was too wide. Payne spotted the flaw and quickly took advantage. With a sweep of his feet, he knocked

Apollo to the ground and rolled on top of him. The limb that had once been whole was now in two pieces. Payne dropped one and used the other like a crazed drummer. Time after time, he pounded on his opponent's head and face, trying to beat him to death.

But the Spartan's helmet held firm.

Though he was dazed, years of training told Apollo what to do. With all his strength, he used his hips to thrust upward, bucking Payne into the air. The manoeuvre worked better than he could have imagined. The slope of the hill coupled with the edge of the ridge cost Payne his advantage. One moment he was pummelling the Spartan, the next he was tumbling down the chasm, losing chunks of skin as he bounced between the narrow rocks.

With a loud thud, Payne hit the ground below.

Andropoulos reached down to help him, but his hand was pushed away.

Payne simply said, 'That son of a bitch!'

Then, riding a burst of rage, he scurried back up the chasm.

Ready for round two.

Dial had his own battle to worry about. He had turned towards Allison when she screamed, which had allowed the other Spartan to slip in behind him.

Sword raised high, the Spartan was set to strike when Dial heard the clanging of armour. Instinctively, he dropped to his knees as the Spartan's blade whizzed overhead. Momentum carried the warrior forward, but he remained balanced and under control. Planting his front foot and turning, he put himself into position to swing again.

Dial lifted his gun and got off a single shot that was deflected by the Spartan's shield. A moment later he used his shield as a weapon, slamming it against the side of Dial's head.

Stunned by the blow, Dial slumped to the ground.

Blood oozed from a gash on his cheek as he tried to regain his senses.

But the Spartan wouldn't allow it. Even in the darkness, he recognized the dazed look in his opponent's eyes. It was time to finish him off.

With that in mind, the Spartan lifted his sword and prepared to strike.

After knocking Payne down the chasm, Apollo grinned in triumph. His opponent had been a worthy adversary, but like all the others before him, he had been vanquished.

Rising to his feet, Apollo searched the ridge for his next victim.

Only one person was not engaged in battle.

The woman.

The thought of fighting her disgusted him. His ancestors never had to deal with women on the battlefield, since they were all forced to stay at home. In his mind, they were good for only one thing: breeding. That had always been the Spartans' stance on women. Mothers were loved. Wives were tolerated. And girls were a wasted opportunity to have had a son.

Still, in this day and age of modern weaponry, he knew women could be dangerous. They could pull a trigger just as easily as a man. Therefore, she couldn't be overlooked.

She would be treated like all the others.

She would have to be killed at once.

Dial was dazed from the blow to his head, but somehow his instincts took over.

As the Spartan raised his sword, Dial raised his gun and fired two quick shots, just over the top of the shield. The first bullet hit the Spartan in his collarbone, shattering it with a sickening snap. The next one struck him right in the mouth. Teeth cracked like crushed ice and embedded themselves in the lining of his throat as the bullet tore through the back of his neck.

Unlike the movies, the Spartan didn't fly ten feet backwards and die quietly.

Instead, he slumped forward on top of Dial, pinning him to the ground. The whole time the Spartan was spitting and gurgling and trying to breathe, and Dial was trapped underneath.

For the next twelve seconds, he listened to the man choking on his own blood until Dial was able to squirm away. Once he did, he fired his weapon again and ended the Spartan's life.

* * *

Allison watched in horror as Payne tumbled down the chasm. A moment earlier, he had stepped in front of her and saved her from the muscular Spartan.

Now he was gone, she was alone, and Apollo was closing in.

Things did not look promising.

The last time she had fired a gun was at a summer carnival. And it hadn't even been a *real* gun. It had been an air rifle in one of those stupid games where the goal was to win a prize.

Other than that, she had no experience with weapons.

She just didn't like them. In fact, she hated the damn things.

But in this situation, she realized her gun was her new best friend.

Grabbing it from her belt, she pointed it at Apollo, who crouched low in the darkness. He held his shield in front of him, giving her nothing to aim at. All she could see was the tip of his sword and the red plume of horsehair that stood above his helmet.

Still, she knew she shouldn't wait for him to get any closer.

So Allison pulled the trigger.

The gun roared, and when it did, it jerked wildly in her hand. The bullet sailed high and wide, nowhere near her target – a common mistake for an amateur.

Undaunted, she squeezed the trigger a second time, but with a similar result.

She wasn't even close.

Apollo smirked at her incompetence and raised his sword behind him.

With a mighty swing, he used the broadside of his blade to knock the weapon from her hand. Metal hit metal with a loud clang, and the gun bounced harmlessly to the ground.

'Stupid whore,' he growled in Laconian.

Then he lifted his sword again.

Payne scurried up the chasm like a wild animal. Blood dripping, muscles straining, fuelled by pure adrenaline. His friends were in danger, and that was unacceptable.

At the top of the ridge, he glanced to his right and realized Dial was safe.

Spinning quickly, he searched for Allison and saw Apollo primed to strike. The Spartan leader was positioned perfectly. His shield protected everything from his knees to his nose. His helmet covered his head, and his greaves guarded his shins. The only gaps in his armour were the slits for his eyes and the sandals on his feet.

For Payne, it was a simple decision. He took the easiest shot available.

Aiming low, he fired three times at Apollo's feet. The first round missed in the darkness, but the second and third shots hit their targets. The muscular Spartan refused to scream as he fell to the ground in agony. When he did, his shield dipped ever so slightly, and Payne took full advantage.

He steadied his weapon and squeezed the trigger with one thought in mind.

This Spartan needed to die.

73

After the battle, Payne and Jones looked at the map and determined the cave was less than thirty minutes away. That is, if the map was accurate. The truth was they weren't sure how Schliemann knew about the treasure's location. That hadn't been revealed during their research. Still, they knew that Richard Byrd and the person who'd had him killed believed in the treasure. Apparently so did the Spartans – although all of them had died before they could be interrogated.

The group continued on in silence, some of them nursing their wounds. Dial held a cloth against his right cheek, which had been gashed by a Spartan shield. His ribs and back throbbed as well, but he never complained. Neither did Payne, who had a wide assortment of cuts and bruises from his tumble off the ridge. But as things stood, he'd fared a lot better than the men he had defeated.

As they climbed higher, Payne noticed a distinct change in the scenery. Trees were far less frequent, and flowers were virtually nonexistent. The same with grass and weeds. In a matter of hours, they had gone from the lush surroundings of the Aegean to a stark landscape reminiscent of the moon. Everywhere he looked he saw rocks and craters and few signs of life.

No wonder the Greeks chose this spot to hide a treasure.

There was no reason to come up here, except to get away from the world.

'Jon,' Allison called from behind.

Payne stopped and turned round. She was pointing at a spot to the east.

'Is that a cave?' she asked.

Payne shone his flashlight in that direction. From where he was, he couldn't be sure. But it certainly looked like one. 'Wait here. I'll go check.'

'Hold on,' Jones said from the rear of the group. 'I'm coming with you.'

Payne smirked and waited for Jones. 'How'd I know you'd want to come?'

'If you think I'm going to let you discover this alone, you're crazy.'

'Wait,' Allison said. 'I'm coming, too.'

Payne lowered his head in defeat. 'Fine! Everyone can come. The more, the merrier.'

Dial smiled and patted Payne on his shoulder. 'I'm glad to hear you say that. I was beginning to feel left out.'

Andropoulos nodded his head. 'Me, too.'

Payne laughed at their enthusiasm. No one had talked in several minutes, now everyone was begging to be included. Then again, he could hardly blame them.

He was also excited about the possibilities.

'Hey, Marcus,' Payne said. 'You're Greek, right?'

'Yes, sir.'

'What type of animals might live up here?'

'Wolves.'

Payne nodded. 'That's what I thought. Everyone stay alert.'

The group moved in unison, each of them searching the surrounding rocks for any sign of trouble. Above them to their left, they could see the towering peaks of Mount Athos in the pale moonlight. To their right was the steep slope that they had just conquered. Payne tried to imagine a forty-foot statue being hauled up the mountainside by the Ancient Greeks. It seemed unlikely. Then again, modern-day historians still don't know how the Egyptians moved the massive stones that were used to build the pyramids. So anything was possible.

Well, *almost* anything.

Because the closer Payne got to the cave, the more confident he became that the lost throne was not inside. It couldn't be. At least not in one piece. Simple geometry assured him of that.

The mouth of the cave was roughly five feet wide and six feet tall. To get through the narrow opening, Payne had to duck down so he wouldn't hit his head on the jagged rock above. Before entering, he shone his light into the interior and saw nothing but darkness.

No walls. No ceiling. Nothing but empty space.

It gave him hope that the cave opened wider.

Taking a deep breath, he crossed the threshold, wondering what he might find inside. He hoped it wouldn't be similar to the last cave he had explored, which had been on Jeju, a tiny island in South Korea. The US Army had asked him and Jones to investigate the disappearance of an ex-MANIAC, and when they arrived at the scene, the entire cavern had been bathed in blood. The stench of decomposition had lingered on their skin and hair for nearly a week.

Shining his light along the ground, he noticed a thin layer of grey dust. He crouched down and touched it with his fingers. It was coarse and similar in colour to the natural stone.

'What is it?' Allison whispered.

'I don't know. It almost feels like—'

Payne stopped in mid-sentence and signalled for everyone to be quiet. Suddenly the dust's composition was less important than what he had noticed in its surface. A set of footprints.

He crouched lower and examined them. They were human and pointing forward. The person's stride had been short and was accompanied by a secondary pattern on the left. It was circular and infrequent. Something man made. Perhaps a walking stick. Or a spear. Payne couldn't tell for sure. But he was certain of one thing: there were no tracks going out.

That meant whoever made them was still inside or had found another way out.

With a gun in his right hand and a flashlight in his left, Payne continued forward, striding over the uneven ground. Deeper inside, the cave opened slightly, its ceiling climbing to eight feet and its width stretching to ten. Payne was appreciative. Not only could he walk upright, but he had room to manoeuvre in case he was attacked.

Jones was next in line, his light burning bright. Allison was third, followed by Andropoulos and Dial. The four of them crept softly, watching Payne as he braved the tunnel ahead of them.

Suddenly, he raised his hand and signalled them to stop.

The group obliged, hardly making a sound.

Up ahead, Payne could see a solitary figure sitting in the darkness. It was an old man, wrapped in a wool blanket. He was leaning against the back wall of the cave. A cane laid by his side. He looked frail and feeble, withered with age. His beard was long and unkempt. It rested on the front of his cloak like a grey scarf. His head was tilted forward, and his eyelids were closed.

Payne wondered if the guy was still breathing.

A moment later, he got his answer.

Without opening his eyes, the old monk spoke, his words barely rising to a whisper. 'I wondered when you would arrive . . . I have been waiting for you.'

Payne grimaced in confusion. He had no idea who this man was or what he was talking about. He figured he might be a crazed hermit who lived in this cave.

'What are you doing here?' Payne asked.

The monk's eyes sprung open. He stared defiantly

at the flashlight, not willing to shield the light from his eyes. 'I wasn't talking to *you*. I was talking to *Nick*.'

From the back of the pack, Dial heard his name. It took a few seconds for things to sink in, but once they did, he knew who was hiding in the cave.

'Coming through,' Dial said as he squeezed his way past the others. He made his way to Payne, who was still shining his light on the old man.

'Do you know this guy?' he whispered.

Dial stared at the man and nodded. It was Nicolas, the old monk he had met on his first night at Metéora. The same one who appeared, forty years younger, in the framed photograph at Great Metéoron. The one man he had hoped to find at Mount Athos. And now he had.

Of course, he never expected to find him like this – actually *inside* the mountain.

'Hello, Nicolas. I've been looking for you.'

The old monk smiled at the sound of Dial's voice. 'I thought as much.'

'You're a tough man to track down.'

'I apologize . . . I have been busy.'

Dial turned on his flashlight. 'Doing what?'

'My duty.'

He took a step forward. 'Your *duty*? I'm not sure what that means.'

Nicolas grinned. 'You have come this far. You must know something.'

'Maybe so, but I was hoping you could fill me in on the rest.'

'My pleasure, Nick. What would you like to know?'

Dial raised his eyebrows in surprise. He hadn't been expecting such an offer.

But he planned on taking full advantage of it.

74

Dial crept closer, wondering what he should ask first. With so many questions, he didn't know where to start. He opted for the very beginning. 'Why were the seven monks at Metéora?'

Nicolas answered. 'That was where we always met. It gave us what we needed.'

'Which was?'

'Protection from those who sought the treasure.'

Dial glanced at Payne and nodded. This was about the lost throne.

'Why weren't you killed at Metéora like the others?'

'I did not arrive until after I was told of their deaths.'

'Why not?'

'Because I was not invited to their meeting.'

'But earlier you said *we*. You said Metéora was where *we* always met.'

Nicolas nodded. 'I also said *was*.'

'You were no longer a part of the group?'

'Age has certain limitations. Travel is one of them.'

'And yet, here you are.'

Nicolas smiled meekly. 'I had no choice. I am the only one left.'

'The only one?'

'The only one who knows where we moved the treasure.'

'You moved the treasure?'

'Long ago . . . Long before these *recent* threats.'

Dial paused. 'Hold on. If you moved the treasure, why are you here?'

'Why? Because this is where the Brotherhood comes to die.'

'The Brotherhood?'

Nicolas nodded. 'That was the name we were given long ago.'

'By whom?'

Nicolas smirked and pointed to the back corner of the cave. 'By one of them.'

Dial shone his light in that direction and was shocked by the sight. Hundreds of human skulls were stacked in a massive pile against the side wall. Many of them faced forward, creating the illusion that their empty eye sockets were staring at him. Fortunately, he did not scare easily. Or else he would have bolted from the cave.

He considered the presence of the skulls. 'Were they your brothers?'

Nicolas nodded again. 'All of them died with one thing in common.'

'Which was?'

'They died nobly, without revealing our secret. For that reason alone, they were brought here to share eternity. This is where we honour them. On our holiest mountain.'

Dial nodded in understanding. 'Which explains why you're here. None of your brothers are left to move your remains, so you came here on your own. You're sitting in the dark, waiting to die, so you can rest with your brothers in peace.'

Nicolas smiled. 'From the moment we met, I knew you were smart.'

Dial ignored the flattery. 'Trust me, I'm not *that* smart. For instance, I don't know why this mountain is covered with Spartans. Or why they killed your brothers.'

'The reason is simple. Over the centuries, many forces have sought the location of our treasure. Some of them were evil men, willing to kill us for our knowledge. Eventually we opted to fight back. Blade against blade, blood against blood, all in the name of secrecy.'

'But you're a *monk*. Doesn't violence go against your religion?'

Nicolas grimaced. 'Not if done for self-preservation. And that is what it was. We pursued those who pursued us, and struck them where they stood.'

'And the Spartans?'

Nicolas paused in thought. 'Somebody struck us.'

'Any idea who?'

He shrugged as the colour slowly drained from his face. 'I was given no names, since my involvement with the Brotherhood was ... fleeting. However, from what I have gathered, our treasure ... has been the source of recent interest ... from several collectors . . .' He paused to catch his breath. 'Including some . . . from . . . your homeland.'

Dial stepped forward, concerned by the anguish on the monk's face and his sudden shortness of breath. 'Nicolas? What's wrong? Are you all right?'

The monk wheezed. 'I will be . . . soon.'

Dial rushed forward, worried that the monk was having a heart attack. He grabbed the wool blanket that was wrapped round the old man's torso, and when he touched it, he realized it was damp. He didn't know why until he ripped it off the monk.

Nicolas had a dagger in his hand and two large slashes through the femoral arteries in his thighs. For the past few minutes, he had slowly been bleeding to death while he calmly explained where he wanted to die.

By the time Dial noticed, there was nothing he could do to prevent it.

Everyone was stunned by the turn of events. All of them had been listening to Dial's conversation, yet none of them had noticed the old man slowly dying in front of them.

His death – and his final message about the treasure being moved – was a setback they hadn't expected.

'Now what?' Payne asked Jones and Allison.

Both of them shrugged, disheartened.

Payne pulled out his copy of the treasure map.

'Why don't you two take another look at the map? Maybe we missed something important.'

Jones shook his head. 'The map worked fine. We found the cave right where it was supposed to be. But there's nothing in here.'

'I know that, but—'

'Jon,' Jones argued, 'think about it. If the Brotherhood moved the treasure in the last century, it was *after* Schliemann died, so his map wouldn't show the new location.'

Payne nodded. 'I realize that, but who's to say when the monks moved it. What if they moved it *before* Schliemann died? Maybe his map led us here for a reason. Maybe there's a secret clue that will point us to another location.'

'Somehow I doubt that.'

'Hey,' Payne said. 'I know you're disappointed and all, but we just climbed a mountain to get here. We're not going back down until you've looked round some more.'

Jones groaned in frustration. 'Fine! I'll look round the stupid cave, but if a giant boulder starts rolling at me from the ceiling, I swear to God I'll—'

He stopped in mid-sentence and cocked his head to the side.

Payne stared at him, waiting for him to finish his rant. 'You'll *what?*'

Jones ignored the question. Deep in thought, he glanced round the cave, slowly considering everything about it. 'This cave is kind of small, isn't it?'

'It's no Carlsbad Caverns, if that's what you mean.'

'No,' Jones said as he shone his flashlight all round him. 'I mean, the damn thing is *really* small. If they used to keep a huge treasure in here, where in the hell did they hide it?'

Payne paused. 'That's a very good point.'

'I mean, I doubt they just left it sitting out in the open. That wouldn't make sense. Not if the Brotherhood was as careful as they seemed to be.'

Allison looked at the mouth of the cave. 'What about the entrance? Could they have concealed it with rocks and branches?'

'That's possible,' Jones conceded. 'But unless they did it just right, it wouldn't have looked natural. And if you're trying to hide something, that's a dead giveaway.'

Payne stared at his friend, who had the slightest hint of a smile. 'Hold up. Do you know where the treasure is?'

Jones shrugged. 'I don't know. Maybe.'

Payne shone his light on Jones. There was a gleam in his eye that hadn't been there a moment before – and it wasn't a reflection of the flashlight. 'You bastard! I can tell from your face that you know where it is.'

Jones laughed. 'I'm not positive, but I do have a theory. Ironically, if I'm right about it, I just gave you a clue.'

'You gave us a clue?'

He grinned. 'If you had been paying attention, you would've noticed it.'

'You gave me a clue?'

Dial, who had been listening from the rear of the cave, spoke up. 'He said *dead*.'

Payne turned and looked at him. 'Dead?'

Dial nodded. 'He said *dead* giveaway. He's talking about the skulls.'

Jones whistled, impressed. 'Score one for Nick Dial! How did you figure that out?'

'It wasn't anything that you said,' Dial assured him. 'It was something that Nicolas said before he died. He claimed the Brotherhood brought the skulls up here to honour them. But that goes against everything that Marcus and I learned at Metéora. The monks don't keep skulls to honour them. They keep the skulls to remind them how fragile life is.'

He glanced down at Nicolas, who was lying on the ground underneath the blood-soaked blanket. 'One minute you're here, and the next you're gone.'

'Okay,' Payne said. 'I get that. But what does that have to do with the treasure?'

Dial continued. 'Nicolas didn't come up here to die. He came here to protect the treasure. And the only way he could do that was by convincing us that the Brotherhood had moved it somewhere else. Then he killed himself before we could ask him any more questions.'

'You seem pretty sure of that.'

Dial shrugged. 'He's lied to me before. I started to recognize his patterns.'

Allison asked, 'So what does that mean? They *didn't* move the treasure?'

Dial shook his head. 'They didn't have time. The Spartans killed them before they could.'

75

Payne studied the large pile of skulls stacked haphazardly against the wall. There were hundreds of them, several centuries' worth of dead monks who had sworn to guard an ancient treasure. If his friends were correct, the monks still protected it – even in death.

'Explain this to me again,' he said to Jones. 'You think the treasure is under *there*?'

'Not the treasure itself. But I think the skulls are hiding something. A fissure or a passageway.'

Payne smirked at his friend. 'A minute ago you were making fun of me when I said there might be a clue somewhere in the cave. Now you're telling me there's a secret passageway?'

Jones nodded his head. 'Yep. That's what I'm saying.'

'That sounds kind of crazy.'

Andropoulos cleared his throat. 'Actually, sir, it's not *that* crazy. Director Dial and I found a secret tunnel at Metéora. It was hidden behind a large tapestry in the monks' barracks.'

Payne glanced at him. 'You found a tunnel? What was inside?'

'Stairs and an underground vault with several

carved shelves and a fancy stone altar, but whatever had been stored in there had been moved long ago.'

'The room was empty?'

'Yes, sir. It was empty.'

Dial corrected him. 'Actually, that's inaccurate. We did find something important.'

Payne asked, 'What was that?'

'The severed heads of the Brotherhood.'

'Are you serious? The heads were down there?'

Dial nodded as pieces of the puzzle slowly fell into place. 'The Spartans slaughtered the monks, and then stacked their heads on the stone altar. At the time, we assumed that they were sending a message, but we didn't know what it was. Now I have my answer.'

'Which is?' Payne wondered.

'One of the monks – one of the seven members of the Brotherhood – must've revealed the treasure's location before his death. The stacked heads were the Spartans' way of bragging about it.'

Jones added, 'Which would explain their presence on the mountain. They knew where the treasure was hidden, and they were coming to get it.'

'It appears that way, yes.'

Payne glanced at Dial. 'It *appears* that way? Do you have another theory?'

Andropoulos said, 'He *always* has a theory.'

Dial smiled. The young cop was learning. 'For some reason, something about the Spartans' role in this still doesn't seem to fit. From what I have been told, the Spartans weren't motivated by money. Their sole purpose in life was to be the best warriors they could be. They didn't care about gold or treasure. They only cared about their reputations as soldiers.'

Payne shrugged. 'Times change. People change. Money might mean more to them now.'

'I don't know about that,' Dial argued. 'They still live in the same region of Greece and continue to speak Laconian after all of these years. They still train like their ancestors, and obviously have the same armour and weapons. On the surface, it appears they still care about the same basic things. And as far as I know, money isn't one of them.'

'Then why were they here?'

'When Marcus and I spotted the tunnel, we found these incredibly detailed carvings of soldiers and war. They appeared on the door, on the shelves, and on the stone altar. To us, they seemed completely out of place in a monastery where all of the other artwork focused on religion. Now I'm beginning to wonder if the carvings had something to do with the treasure.'

'Such as?'

Dial explained his theory. 'We were informed that the monasteries have always been used as sanctuaries, a place where artists and writers were free to work without persecution. We were also told that Spartans frowned upon the written word. Actually, that's an understatement. Writing was *forbidden* inside their culture. Everything we know about them comes from outside sources and, since we're talking about twenty-five-hundred years ago, sources are limited.'

He paused to catch his breath. 'So, and this is just a wild guess here, what if there's more to this treasure than gold? What if there are ancient books or artwork that would cast the Spartans in a negative light? What if their reason for coming here wasn't to get rich? What if they came here to protect their heritage?'

Jones laughed and patted Dial on the back. 'A wild guess? That doesn't sound like a wild guess to me. It sounds like a highly detailed hypothesis. I was half-expecting you to pull out graphs and charts.'

Dial shrugged. 'What can I say? I had a lot of time to think when we were climbing the mountain.'

'Well,' Jones said as he rubbed his hands together, 'there's only one way to see if your theory is correct. Let's find us a treasure.'

While Andropoulos guarded the entrance to the cave, the other four worked as a team. Payne and Jones handed the skulls to Dial and Allison, who moved them carefully to the other side of the cave. Slowly but surely the first pile dwindled as the new pile started to rise.

Despite the seemingly gruesome nature of their task none of them were fazed by the undertaking. In fact, the large number of skulls actually de-personalized the situation for them. In their minds, they weren't picking up skulls. They were simply clearing loose impediments from a hidden tunnel.

At least they hoped they were.

They wouldn't know for sure for another few minutes.

In the end, it was Jones who spotted the first harbinger. As he pulled a skull away from the wall, he noticed a small fissure. 'Allison, hand me a light.'

Their flashlights sat on the floor, each of them shining on the ceiling above so they could work with both hands. She picked up the closest one and handed it to him.

'Do you see something?'

'I don't know yet.'

He shone the light into the crack, which started a few feet above the ground. Because of his angle and the remaining skulls that blocked his view, he couldn't see much. But the gap definitely extended into the wall. 'There's a hole back here.'

Standing next to the pile, Payne wiped his forehead with his sleeve. 'How big is it?'

'I can't tell yet.'

'Then put down the light and get back to work.'

Jones gave him a mock salute. 'Yes, sir.'

They laughed in the gloom of the cave as they continued digging.

With each passing minute, with each skull that was carried away, their level of excitement grew. And so did the small hole. First it was a fissure. Then it became a crawl space. Before long they realized it was something more significant. It was the beginning of a stone ramp that went deep inside the core of the mountain.

The monks' construction was ingenious. Instead of cutting an arch or doorway in the side of the cave, which would have been difficult to conceal in a natural setting, they had cut through the base of the wall and dug a trench through the cave's floor. They'd used dirt and small rocks to pack the empty space below and then covered everything with skulls.

In the culture of Mount Athos, it was a wonderful deterrent.

Any hermit who stumbled upon the cave would have been reluctant to take residence in the final resting place of so many monks. And they certainly wouldn't have moved the skulls or stolen them as souvenirs. That would have been the ultimate sign of disrespect. So the skulls did much more than conceal the tunnel, they actually kept interlopers away.

Until now.

76

The digging would have been finished sooner if they'd had shovels and wheelbarrows to assist them. As it was, they were forced to dig with their hands. They used Nicolas' blood-soaked blanket to haul away dirt and debris.

Payne, who was covered in grime, shone his flashlight into the hole and made the announcement that they had been waiting for. 'I think it's big enough now.'

'Can you get through?' asked Jones, who was even dirtier than Payne.

He leaned in closer. 'Yeah, I think so.'

'Then it's *definitely* big enough. I could've slipped through an hour ago.'

Payne smiled. 'Your body could've, but your ego couldn't.'

'Trust me, my ego *isn't* my biggest feature.'

Payne rolled his eyes. 'If you're done lying to us, are you ready to go inside?'

'Of course I'm ready. I've been ready ... Who goes first?'

Payne gestured towards the hole. 'After you, my friend.'

Jones patted him on the shoulder. 'Thanks, Jon. I appreciate that.'

'No problem,' he replied. 'Scream if you feel any booby traps.'

Jones laughed as he got on his hands and knees and squirmed through the gap. Allison went next, then Dial, and finally Payne. Andropoulos stayed on guard duty, protecting the mouth of the cave – just in case more Spartans happened to wander by.

After crawling on a downward slant for nearly five feet, Jones had enough room to pull his legs underneath him. Sitting in a crouch, he reached his hand back and helped Allison through the gap before he continued onward. With every step he took, the passageway became higher until he was finally able to stand upright.

Shining his light on the passageway, he realized it had been carved into solid rock. 'Will you look at this tunnel? They did all of this by hand.'

'It's amazing,' she replied as she ran her fingers over the grey stone.

Waiting for the others to arrive, Jones pointed his light forward. A wall of darkness lingered beyond the reach of his beam. The temperature was in the low-fifties, even cooler than the cave above which had been warmed by their body heat. He put his nose into the air and took a deep whiff, worried about the presence of noxious gases. But he detected nothing.

'We're clear,' Payne said from the back.

Jones nodded and started off again down the passageway. The ground was uneven and made of solid stone. The walls were wide, approximately ten feet across. He swept his beam from side to side, searching for anything that seemed out of place. Though Payne had been joking about booby traps, Jones realized there had been a grain of truth in what he said.

As a child, Jones had read stories about real-life archaeologists who had been undone by spring snares attached to trees or Burmese tiger pits lined with sharp spears. In the Special Forces, he had learned how to build both – and several other devices to trap or kill the enemy – so he knew such things existed.

He just didn't know if they existed down here.

'Clear,' Jones called over his shoulder.

'Still clear,' Payne replied.

A few seconds later, the passageway turned sharply to the left. Jones peeked round the corner, not willing to commit his team until he knew what was waiting for them. What he saw boggled his imagination. The tunnel stopped and a natural cave began. Soaring to a height of over fifty feet, the massive cavern stretched beyond the scope of his light.

He stepped forward for a better view, and when he did, his eyes were drawn to the objects on the floor in front of him. Everywhere he looked, for as far as he could see, there were wooden crates. Some as small as backpacks; others much larger than caskets. Hundreds of ancient boxes stacked in neat rows, just sitting in the darkness waiting to be opened.

'Holy shit,' he mumbled under his breath. 'I'm fucking rich.'

Allison heard the comment and hurried up to him to see what he was talking about. She pointed her flashlight in the same direction and was staggered by the sight.

'Oh my God!' she gasped.

Jones grinned at her reaction. 'Do you like *my* treasure? I saw it first.'

Dial was an expert on body language. From his position in the passageway, he knew his friends had discovered something momentous. The look of sheer joy on both of their faces was proof of that. Still, it didn't prepare him for his first glimpse of the cavern and its bounty.

He rounded the corner and stood there in shock, his massive jaw dropping to his chest.

'Good Lord!' Dial blurted.

Payne was the last one to see the treasure. Taller than the other three, he stood behind them and marvelled at the enormity of it all: the cavern, the number of crates, and the effort it must have taken to haul this stuff from Constantinople, which was hundreds of miles away.

'There's no way the monks carried this stuff by themselves,' he said to no one in particular. 'How in the world did they keep this place a secret for so long?'

'I have no freaking idea,' Jones said. 'No idea at all. Then again, that's not what concerns me right now.'

'What does?'

'How are we going to carry this stuff *down* the mountain?'

The question lingered in the darkness as they rushed forward to open some crates. But Dial decided not to join them. Instead, he turned round and crawled back through the hole.

For the time being, he was still a law-enforcement official, and he was still working on a case. Once the smoke cleared and he got back to France, he might have to reconsider his future.

As a director at Interpol, he made a good salary and had a great pension plan, but it paled in comparison to the riches that they had found in the cavern. If Payne and Jones figured out a legal way for him to keep a share, he would be tempted to walk away from his career.

But until that day, he had other things to worry about.

Like what was happening on the mountain below.

'Coming out,' Dial called to Andropoulos, who was still guarding the mouth of the cave. The last thing he wanted was to surprise the kid and get shot by mistake. 'Any trouble out here?'

'No, sir. No trouble at all. How about you?'

'Things are good down below.'

'So,' he asked excitedly, 'did they find any treasure?'

Dial smiled at him. 'Why don't you go and look for yourself?'

'Thank you, sir. I was hoping you'd say that.'

Andropoulos turned to walk away.

'Hold up,' Dial ordered. 'Before you go, there's one other thing I forgot to mention.'

'What's that, sir?'

'Just so you know, it's been a pleasure working with you.'

Andropoulos beamed with pride. 'I was hoping you'd say that, too.'

With a smile on his face, he ran off to see the treasure.

Dial reached behind him and pulled out the radio they had taken from Petros. During their climb up the mountain, Dial had turned it off, afraid the noise might give away their position. But now they had safely reached their destination, he felt he needed to update the other guards and let them know that they were all right.

Several seconds passed before someone responded.

Without mentioning anything about the treasure, Dial filled them in on some basics. 'Sorry I've been radio silent for so long. Every time we turned round, we were under attack.'

'Are you all right?'

Dial paused, thinking about Nicolas. Somehow his death needed to be explained without revealing what had really happened. Dial didn't want to lie. Yet at the same time, he knew he didn't want to tell the full truth. 'We're fine. We found a monk, though. He didn't make it.'

The guard said, 'We had some losses, too. But we

took some Spartans with us. Right now, we're still searching the grounds, looking for more of them.'

'What about harbour patrol? Did they figure out how the Spartans got here?'

'Yes, sir. They found a boat anchored on the southern shore.'

'Anyone aboard?'

'No, sir. It was empty. But the boat had a name.' The guard paused as he searched for the information. 'It was called *The Odyssey*. It's a yacht registered in California.'

'California? The Spartans used a boat from California? Did they steal it?'

'I don't know, sir. We're still trying to reach the boat's owner.'

Dial grimaced. 'Wait. You know the owner's name? Is he Greek?'

'I don't think so, sir. His name is Richard Byrd.'

Payne, Jones, and Allison walked between the large stacks of crates, still trying to grasp how many items had been rescued from Constantinople. A few of the lids were brittle with age, so they were able to peek inside without risking damage to the precious contents.

And what they saw was amazing.

Gold relics and coins. Marble statues. Silver vases. Bronze weapons. Gemstones and jewellery. Painted vessels. Greek amphorae. And thousands of ancient scrolls.

None of them could be read until they were translated by scholars, but the fountain of knowledge that they might contain was staggering.

'Hey, Allison,' Jones said as they continued to explore, 'I just realized something.'

'What's that?'

'Your thesis is going to have one hell of an ending.'

She laughed with childlike delight. 'I was thinking the same thing.'

'Not only that,' he added. 'You teamed up with Heinrich Schliemann to find this place.'

'I know! How wild is that?'

'Pretty damn wild.'

'Actually,' she admitted, 'only one thing would make this better.'

Jones smiled. 'Figuring out how to keep everything for ourselves?'

'No,' she said. 'It would have been nice if we had found the Statue of Zeus. I mean, to discover one of the seven wonders of the world. That would have been, well, *wonderful.*'

While Jones and Allison continued to talk, Payne roamed to the far side of the cavern. In situations like this, the soldier in him always seemed to surface. Before he could enjoy the treasure, he needed to check the perimeter to make sure there were no possible threats. And if there were, he would eliminate them as quickly as possible.

Only in this case, he found no danger.

But he did find something that he couldn't believe.

'Guys,' Payne called from his position near the back of the cave. 'You have to see this.'

'See what?' Jones yelled back. 'We're busy playing with my gold.'

'Trust me, you need to see this. I can't do it justice.'

Jones and Allison walked to the back of the cavern where Payne was waiting for them to arrive. He was shining his light into an antechamber that hadn't been visible from the entrance. Though not nearly as large as the main cavern, the space was big enough to store the most important treasure that the Ancient Greeks had recovered from Constantinople.

The object Heinrich Schliemann had been looking for at the time of his death.

The one thing all of them had hoped to find.

The disassembled pieces of the lost throne.

Epilogue

Friday, 6 June
Limnos, Greece

Sixteen days had passed since the treasure had been discovered inside the holy mountain. During that time, Nick Dial had uncovered the answers to several questions.

As soon as he learned that the Spartans had used Richard Byrd's yacht for their trip to Mount Athos, Dial contacted law enforcement officials in California, who acquired search warrants for Byrd's home, office, and safe deposit box. It didn't take them long to find a direct link between Byrd and Apollo, the leader of the Spartans.

Several weeks earlier, Byrd had flown to Athens, rented a car and driven to Spárti. A hotel reservation he had made with one of his fake identities, confirmed his presence in the small town. While there, he had purchased a disposable cell phone that was found at Apollo's house, along with a map to the harbour in Leonidi where Byrd's yacht would be waiting for the Spartans, if they required transport. Phone records proved that several calls were made between Byrd and Apollo's cell phones, apparently to coordinate the search for the treasure. This included the attack at Metéora. Since the Spartan village had no regular phone lines, this was the only way for Byrd to stay in touch with the men he had convinced to do his dirty work.

With this information, the Greek police were able to question the rest of the villagers, who were eventually found in the Taygetos Mountains a few miles from their village. Most of them were uncooperative and unwilling to talk, but a few of them eventually broke down and revealed the Spartans' motivation to go to Mount Athos.

Byrd had told Apollo that the Brotherhood possessed several documents that cast the Spartans in an unfavourable light. This included a document they referred to as the 'book', a comprehensive examination of Ancient Greece and all the city-states. One section supposedly contained inside information that had been written by a disillusioned Spartan. He hated the brutal culture he had been forced to endure from birth until he was in his mid-twenties, when he finally managed to slip away. Afraid that this information would leave a permanent stain on their heritage, Apollo and his men had vowed to do whatever they could to destroy it.

But their mission had been foiled.

The book – and thousands of other documents – would soon be examined by experts.

Which experts, though, was a matter of some contention.

Legally speaking, the treasure did not belong to anyone since no one knew who had taken it to the mountain. The Brotherhood may have protected it for centuries, but that did not make it theirs. Furthermore, since the artefacts had supposedly been moved from Greece (and other parts of the world) to Constantinople and then to Mount Athos, there was no way of proving ownership of any of the items. Including the Statue of Zeus.

Was it stolen from Olympia? Or was it given to the Romans as a gift? No one knew for sure – and no one would know until everything inside the crates had been studied.

For the first few days after its discovery, Dial was able to keep news of the treasure from the outside world. He sealed off the cave and did not allow anyone inside, claiming it was an Interpol crime scene. Which, in fact, it was. Nicolas had killed himself inside the cave and as a result of the information he had provided before his death – including his claim that a collector from Dial's homeland had recently caused the monks trouble – Interpol searched the phone records of the seven monks who made up the Brotherhood, looking for anything suspicious.

One call stood out among all the others.

A few days before the abbot from Metéora had been murdered alongside his brethren, he had called an unlisted number in Russia. The conversation lasted seventeen minutes. After which, a large sum of money had been wired from an account in Athens to one in Moscow. The name on the Russian account was Alexei Kozlov, the assassin who had killed Richard Byrd.

So the Brotherhood had paid to have Byrd eliminated.

What prompted them to take such an extreme step was still unclear. Had they learned about Byrd's search for Schliemann's map? Or had they been warned about his relationship with the Spartans? Unfortunately, Dial didn't know for sure. He assumed that the Brotherhood's secret meeting at Metéora had been called so they could discuss the situation.

Ironically, it was that gathering that had made them such an easy target.

They had met to protect their organization, but the meeting had led to their slaughter.

From the deck of Jarkko's yacht, Payne stared at the light blue water of the Aegean Sea. Jones was somewhere nearby, swimming or fishing or talking to one of the local ladies that Jarkko had brought aboard. No matter where they went in Limnos, everyone knew the fun-loving Finn.

Payne would be joining them shortly, but first he had to update Dial on the latest news about the treasure. 'Nick,' he said into his cell phone, 'how's life?'

'Busy. I've spent the last two weeks trying to keep your ass out of jail.'

'If it's possible, I'd like to keep all of me out of jail. Not just my ass.'

Dial laughed. He was speaking to Payne on a secure line in his office at Interpol Headquarters. 'Don't worry. I'm a pretty good liar. I convinced the Greek government that I summoned you and DJ as my personal back-up once I learned of the trouble on Mount Athos.'

'What about Allison?' Payne wondered.

'Her presence was a little tougher to explain. Thankfully, one of my colleagues, Henri, told me that the Holy Mountain sheltered many women refugees during the Greek War of Independence in the nine-teenth century. I claimed that her life had been in danger – which technically it was – and we decided the safest place for her was with us.'

'Did they buy it?'

'Eventually. Once I pointed out that her expertise led to our discovery of the treasure, they were willing to cut her some slack.'

'Good. I'm glad to hear it.'

'Speaking of which, is she there? I'd love to tell her the good news.'

'Sorry, Nick. She left last week.'

Dial growled softly. 'Dammit, Jon. I thought I told all of you to stay in Greece until this situation was rectified.'

Payne smiled. 'Relax. She's still in Greece. She flew up to Athens to meet with Petr Ulster.'

'Petr's in Greece? What's he doing there? I thought he never left the archives.'

'Normally, he doesn't. But he was willing to make an exception. It's not every day one of the Seven Wonders of the Ancient World is discovered.'

'Good point. But what's he doing in Athens?'

'While you've been busy with legal issues, I've been dealing with the treasure. Obviously, with a discovery of this magnitude, everyone wants to get their hands on it. The Greek government says it's theirs. The Turks claim it was stolen from them. The Italians claim it belonged to the Roman Empire so they should somehow be involved. Not to mention the monks of Mount Athos, who think the treasure should belong to the monasteries.'

'And Petr?'

'For the time being, all parties decided that the treasure needed to be catalogued and preserved as quickly as possible by an independent organization. And that's where Petr comes into play. The Ulster Archives has a sterling reputation round the world, so everyone was fine with his involvement. Right now he and Allison are in Athens, trying to sort out the logistics.'

Dial paused. 'While you were listing interested parties, I couldn't help but notice that you left your name off the list.'

'Don't get me wrong, I'm definitely interested. I have a team of lawyers in Athens right now, making sure our interests are protected. That being said, we certainly aren't going to be selfish about it. Our number-one goal is to make sure that this treasure is available to the public. Back when I was a kid, I stood in a long line to see King Tut's treasure at the Smithsonian Institute. The sight of all that gold just blew me away. With that in mind, I want a new generation of kids to have the same experience with this discovery.'

'And how does DJ feel about that?'

'He's completely cool with it – as long as he's allowed to keep the throne for his backyard. He thinks it will impress his neighbours.'

Dial laughed. 'I think he's right.'

'In all seriousness, we've been assured by all parties that our team – you, me, DJ, Allison, and Marcus – will be recognized for the discovery and compensated for it.'

'And Jarkko!' shouted the Finn as he walked up behind Payne. 'Don't forget, Jarkko!'

Payne glanced back at Jarkko, who was wearing a Speedo and nothing else. The image would be burned into his memory for a very long time. 'And my half-naked friend, Jarkko.'

Dial smiled. 'I appreciate my inclusion. I truly do. And I know Marcus will be thrilled.'

'Once the dust settles, we can all get together and talk about details. But for now, rest assured that some day soon you're going to have one hell of a retirement.'

'Enough business!' Jarkko ordered. 'It is time to get off phone.'

'Go on,' Dial said, 'have some fun. I'll call you as soon as you're allowed to leave Greece.'

'Thanks, Nick. Keep me posted.'

Payne disconnected and stood up from his lounge chair. He spotted his best friend walking across the deck of the yacht. Jones was wearing a bright green floral shirt, a white bathing suit and a pair of flip-flops, an outfit that looked remarkably similar to the one he had been wearing in Florida when they heard the first message from Richard Byrd.

'It's pretty sad,' Payne said to him.

'What is?' Jones asked.

'You're about to become one of the most famous people in the world, and you still don't know how to dress.'

'Me?' Jones argued. 'Look at Jarkko. It looks like he's smuggling sausage in his shorts.'

Payne shook his head. 'No wonder he does so much business with Kaiser.'

Jones laughed loudly.

Jarkko frowned even though he didn't fully understand the comment. 'You make joke at Jarkko's expense?'

'Don't worry,' Jones assured him as he held his index finger and thumb about an inch apart. 'It was just a tiny one.'

The Finn shrugged it off. 'That is fine. Jarkko does not mind tiny joke. Do you know why?'

'No,' Payne wondered. 'Why?'

Jarkko put his arms round Payne and Jones. 'Because, my friends, it is time to drink!'

Author's Note

Some people are going to read this novel and assume that Heinrich Schliemann is a fictional character. How could someone like him – with all his quirks and crazy adventures – actually be real? Well, I have a confession to make. Not only was Schliemann a real person, but I purposely excluded many of the wilder tales about his life in order to make him seem more believable. For all the bizarre details, visit a library or run an internet search. Or, if you can get your hands on a copy, read Allison Taylor's dissertation.

She definitely earned her doctorate.

Speaking of research, one of the most difficult things about writing an international thriller is all the legwork that must be done before a single word is typed. Since the majority of action in *The Lost Throne* occurs in Greece and Russia, two countries where English is a secondary language, I was forced to Americanize the spelling of many names and cities. If you're having trouble finding details about Metéora, Spárti, or any other location in this book, make sure you try alternative spellings. Because these places actually exist. And they're fascinating.

For additional information about this novel and answers to frequently asked questions, please visit my website: www.chriskuzneski.com.

CHRIS KUZNESKI

SIGN OF THE CROSS

'Kuzneski's writing has the same raw power as the early Stephen King'
James Patterson

A Vatican priest is found murdered on the shores of Denmark – nailed
to a cross in the shadow of Hamlet's castle. He is the first victim in a
vicious killing spree that spans the world. Each horrific murder exactly
mirrors the crucifixion of Christ …

Meanwhile, deep in the Roman Catacombs of Orvieto, an archaeologist
uncovers an ancient scroll dating back two thousand years. The scroll,
he knows, holds the key to a dark and treacherous secret that will rock
the very foundations of the Church. But only if he can decipher its lost
meanings – and only if he can live long enough to reveal them .

The enemies of the truth know no law of man …

NO SECRET WILL KEEP FOREVER ...

'Harrowing, but always suspenseful, *Sign of the Cross*, makes you wish
it would never end' Clive Cussler

CHRIS KUZNESKI

SWORD OF GOD

'Chris Kusneski writes as forcefully as his tough characters act'
Clive Cussler

Tunnelling deep under one of the most holy cities in the world, an ambitious young archaeologist slowly works her way towards an unthinkable goal. Somewhere ahead is a chamber containing the collected fragments of an ancient scripture, a find of unimaginable significance ...

Meanwhile, halfway around the world, a covert military bunker holds a macabre secret. An elite special-forces officer seems to have been brutally murdered – but how, and more disturbingly, why? Any hope of solving the mystery rests on the grisly clues that remain.

As the race to uncover the truth begins, a plot unfolds that could burn all of civilization in the fires of holy Armageddon ...

THOSE WHO LIVE BY THE SWORD ...

'A non-stop locomotive of a thriller. Combines labyrinthine plot twists, global terrorism and the darkest depths of psychological warfare in a thriller that had me burning the midnight oil till breakfast ...' Vince Flynn, author of *Consent to Kill*

He just wanted a decent book to read ...

Not too much to ask, is it? It was in 1935 when Allen Lane, Managing Director of Bodley Head Publishers, stood on a platform at Exeter railway station looking for something good to read on his journey back to London. His choice was limited to popular magazines and poor-quality paperbacks – the same choice faced every day by the vast majority of readers, few of whom could afford hardbacks. Lane's disappointment and subsequent anger at the range of books generally available led him to found a company – and change the world.

'We believed in the existence in this country of a vast reading public for intelligent books at a low price, and staked everything on it'
Sir Allen Lane, 1902–1970, founder of Penguin Books

The quality paperback had arrived – and not just in bookshops. Lane was adamant that his Penguins should appear in chain stores and tobacconists, and should cost no more than a packet of cigarettes.

Reading habits (and cigarette prices) have changed since 1935, but Penguin still believes in publishing the best books for everybody to enjoy. We still believe that good design costs no more than bad design, and we still believe that quality books published passionately and responsibly make the world a better place.

So wherever you see the little bird – whether it's on a piece of prize-winning literary fiction or a celebrity autobiography, political tour de force or historical masterpiece, a serial-killer thriller, reference book, world classic or a piece of pure escapism – you can bet that it represents the very best that the genre has to offer.

Whatever you like to read – trust Penguin.